P9-BBP-126

THE BITTERWINE OATH

HANNAH WEST

HOLIDAY HOUSE NEW YORK

HOLIDAY HOUSE is registered in the U.S. Patent and Trademark Office.

Printed and bound in October 2020 at Maple Press, York, PA, USA.

www.holidayhouse.com

First Edition

1 3 5 7 9 10 8 6 4 2

Library of Congress Cataloging-in-Publication Data

Names: West, Hannah, author.

Title: The bitterwine oath / by Hannah West.

Description: First edition. | New York : Holiday House, 2020. | Audience: Ages 14–up. Audience: Grades 10–12. | Summary: Can eighteen-year-old Natalie and her great-great-grandmother's magical sisterhood end the cycle of violence in Natalie's small Texas town?

Identifiers: LCCN 2019055102 | ISBN 9780823445479 (hardcover)

Subjects: CYAC: Magic—Fiction. | Witchcraft—Fiction. Supernatural—Fiction. | Texas—Fiction.

Classification: LCC PZ7.1.W4368 Bi 2020 | DDC [Fic]—dc23

LC record available at https://lccn.loc.gov/2019055102

ISBN: 978-0-8234-4547-9 (hardcover)

For everyone who feels at home in the spooky woods,
the dusty library, and all other places where magic
seems most likely to show itself

Lillian Pickard

I did not regret befriending Malachi Rivers until the night we invoked her magic to seek revenge.

Four of us sat in a circle on the floor of an abandoned cabin in the Piney Woods, twine looped around our girlish wrists, binding us together. A grimoire lay open upon tender sprigs of herbs and bones of woodland creatures. Segments of text had been violently crossed out and revisions crammed into the margins.

Malachi Rivers was indeed that powerful; her edits and improvisations increased the potency of every charm, hex, curse, and conjuration.

Until that fateful night in the summer of 1921, our foursome, led by Malachi, had performed harmless magic for entertainment and empowerment. Dorothy Hawkins, Johanna Mead, and I revered Malachi's magic and wanted to participate. While we were bound together, we could channel it. The powerless could become powerful.

We called ourselves "Pagans of the Pines" in a spirit of cheeky rebellion. The magic had been a girlhood game to me, the grimoire nothing more than a mass-produced, curious collectible pilfered from the parlor of my cosmopolitan aunt.

But everything changed that night. Childish rebellion turned to sinister retribution.

Dorothy, Johanna, and Malachi had endured trials I could not fathom.

Malachi's father was controlling and oppressive. Johanna Mead's abusive father and uncle had beaten the boy she loved nearly to death out of a twisted sense of protectiveness. A lynch mob had murdered Dorothy Hawkins's older brother over a false accusation that he had attempted to murder a white man. Her sharecropper father had lost his land, and the family relied on charity from their church to scrape by.

Now that Malachi had nearly mastered her magic of earth, bone, and blood, the three of them wanted to claim vengeance commensurate to their suffering.

We did not mean to kill. Malachi concocted a curse that would reveal the deep evil within the hearts of the men who had wronged them, so that society would no longer accept, respect, or enable their dark deeds. Malachi had spoken the curse over the Communion wine in the sanctuary of her father's church. We watched her, witnessed her slender body rocking with power, her wrists and hands trembling. She dusted the wine with herbs, dipped her fingers into the chalice, and painted her mark on the white cloth of the Communion table—the mark we had created to represent the three elements from which she drew her power.

"The Devil's supper," I recall her whispering in the candlelight.

We returned to our consecrated ground—the cabin nestled in a forgotten forest glade—to finish our work. We would use magic to lure the men to Communion at the witching hour. They would drink the cursed wine, and their darkness would be known to all.

But as soon as we split the flesh of our fingertips and dripped blood over our preparations, I felt Malachi's magic spinning out of control, like a toy top whirling fast enough to lift off the ground and bounce about unpredictably. The other girls' anger fueled it, giving it a will of its own.

I was afraid. I wanted to stop it. But our hands were already bound, and to break the bond before our work was complete would be far more dangerous than even the darkest conjuration.

I have undoubtedly lost many a reader already with my earnest talk of magic. But I have no other pen with which to write this biography.

Any tale about Malachi that excludes magic is not about Malachi at all.

Excerpt from *Pagans of the Pines: The Untold Story of Malachi Rivers*, published 1968

ONE

Natalie Colter

— PRESENT DAY —

ONE MONTH AND TEN DAYS UNTIL THE CLAIMING

The first day of my last summer in San Solano was clammier than a fever. The sun baked the mud from last night's storm like clay in a kiln as my best friend and I ran the trail we'd forged between our two houses.

"You're falling behind, regional champ!" Lindsey Valenzuela taunted over her shoulder.

Ambition gnawed at my tired muscles and I pushed myself harder. In a few short months, I'd be a college freshman distance runner with everything to prove. I couldn't afford a lethargic summer.

My toe caught on a divot in the rough terrain and I fell, earning stinging scrapes along my palms and elbows.

Lindsey doubled back to offer me a hand, her shadow stretching over me. "You okay?"

I accepted the help and unstuck my sweaty tank top from my skin. "No offense, but when did you get faster than me?"

"It's my green juice." She slapped her bicep, way too perky for having just covered three miles in the heat. "You should try it."

"No way. It smells like toxic waste."

"Your call." Lindsey swiped caramel-highlighted dark hairs from her dewy face and grinned. "I'll just keep handing you your ass."

As I brushed dirt off my legs, a lazy wind carried perfume from clusters of pale honeysuckles, and with it, a stench of rot. I wrinkled my nose and palmed sweat from my eyes, searching the overgrown grasses. Behind a barbed-wire fence marking private pastureland, I found a bovine ribcage the size of a barrel. Scavengers had ripped away most of the meat, but flaps of decaying flesh remained.

"Gross," Lindsey said, following my look of disgust.

Like every other East Texas town, San Solano was hotter than the Devil's crack by the end of May, and the carcass reeked. But I ventured a step into chigger-ridden grasses to get a closer look.

"Nat, don't get too close!" Lindsey said.

"There's no head." I was almost relieved by the lack of a bulging tongue and hollow eye sockets. "Isn't that weird?"

"It's probably mounted in a steakhouse."

"That's an Angus farm," I said, pointing. "Why would anyone mount a cow with no horns?"

I expected to see my curiosity mirrored in her molasses-brown eyes. But she shrugged and flicked a mosquito from her patterned neon running shorts. "You're the one whose dad's a vet. I don't know anything about cows." She caught up to my insinuation and flashed me a sideways look of suspicion. "You'd better not be getting superstitious on me."

Retying my dirty-blond hair in a ponytail, I crossed back through the patches of Indian paintbrush. "I'm not saying I think the Malachians are still around or anything."

"Good."

"But don't you think it's a little unsettling?"

"It's just a dead cow!" Lindsey cried. "This town is on the verge of hysteria."

An overstatement, but San Solano was undeniably on edge. The sheriff's department had sent deputies to our classes the week before finals to hook their thumbs in their belts and lecture us against getting too rowdy this summer. "Stay away from Calvary Baptist unless you're attending a service," they'd warned, "and don't stir up trouble at the cabin in the woods. No trespassing means no trespassing."

They asked us to inform them of anything "unusual." We knew what they meant: books of curses, assortments of herbs and animal bones, or the symbol that had become shorthand for cult activity in San Solano.

But they warned us not to panic if we saw something suspicious. The most likely culprits would be local teens like us pulling pranks, or tourists who were overly fascinated with the town's violent past. Plenty of their kind would descend on San Solano in the coming days.

Maybe the police would succeed in discouraging the late-night dares and the rumors threatening to whip the town into a frenzy. But nothing would stop the curious gazes that burned the back of my neck. Nothing would stop the calls from journalists that made my mom unplug our outdated landline and forced my dad to add "veterinary business only" to his contact page.

As the only living descendants of Malachi Rivers, we were the hot ticket in town this summer.

"The twins want to meet us at Sawmill," Lindsey said, checking her phone. "Can we detour? I'm hungry."

I glanced back at the headless carcass, wondering how Lindsey could summon an appetite right now. But I decided to drop it. I could picture the sheriff teasing me for calling to report dead livestock in a pasture. He'd been my dad's best friend since their middle school days.

We hit the trail again. I couldn't shake the sense that Lindsey was pacing herself to avoid leaving me in the dust. A healthy sense of competition had been the foundation of our friendship ever since we'd borrowed our teacher's stopwatch to race across the monkey bars during third-grade recess.

I wanted to snap at her for going easy on me. I was too *fast* for her to go easy on me.

She was barely panting by the time we stepped off the trail into an overgrown meadow and crossed the country highway to Sawmill, our town's famously ramshackle barbecue joint.

The Dixon twins waited for us at a picnic table outside. The hot metal bench burned my bare thighs as I plopped down next to Abbie with my sweet tea and pulled pork sandwich. She smelled like freshly applied sunscreen, but her round, ivory face seemed to only get pinker as the sun bore down on us.

"Y'all want to do a group trip to Toledo Bend after church this Sunday?" her sister Faith asked, bending the brim of her ball cap to shade her equally sensitive face. Her button nose was still peeling from the last sunburn. "Or will you be too busy training like overachieving dorks?"

"Y'all are begging to get massacred out on those trails," Abbie added before either of us could answer.

"Technically that would be murder, not a massacre," I pointed out. "And we're not boys, so we're safe. Which is pretty ironic."

"Come on, people!" Lindsey smacked her palm on the table, rattling the condiments. "No one could ever prove that Malachi and her friends killed those dudes, and even the copycat murderers would be old by now, if they're still alive. Nothing is going to happen."

She was right about the first two things, and probably right about the third. Malachi Rivers and three other girls had faced trial for fatally poisoning a dozen men—including Malachi's father—with Communion wine in a church sanctuary in July of 1921. The motive was there, but the conclusive evidence was not. Though the men had clearly partaken of the wine just before they died, the police found that it didn't contain any identifiable toxic substances. The girls were acquitted.

Malachi had been the leader of the group, and thus the unanswered questions had circled back to her. She'd tried to make a normal life for herself after the trial, but she disappeared permanently just a handful of years later, leaving a husband and young son—my great grandfather—without a word.

And then a second massacre happened exactly fifty years after the first.

The twelve victims were, once again, all male. Unlike the first time, they were mostly young, in their teens and twenties, and hadn't committed any heinous offenses, as far as anyone knew. And unlike the first time, there was evidence of a struggle in the sanctuary: bruises and lacerations on the victims' wrists suggesting they'd been held against their will, several broken bones between them, plus destruction of church property. The actual cause of the deaths was still unknown; forensic testing proved beyond a doubt the wine contained nothing but harmless herbs.

The cases were more like kissing cousins than identical twins. Due to the discrepancies, investigators labeled the second massacre a copycat crime. And even though Malachi had been legally declared innocent, it was clear the copycats had been inspired by the rumors of her magic. Thus, the investigators lumped the events together and dubbed them the "Malachian Massacres." Both remained unsolved.

And now, the semicentennial anniversary of the massacres was creeping closer.

The town's unspoken questions had been like keepsakes tucked away in the attic. *Did* Malachi and her three friends have something to do with the deaths of the men who had traumatized them in 1921? Who had mimicked the massacre in 1971?

And most importantly, were the fanatics out there today? Would the people who revered Malachi's legacy strike again?

As if reading my thoughts, Abbie spoke up in a voice that would have paired well with a flashlight and a campfire. "Maybe the Malachians have been recruiting in secret this whole time. Maybe someone we know is one of them. It's kind of interesting to imagine—"

"Interesting?" Lindsey cut her off, instantly serious. "Real people died, Abbie."

"I know that, Lindsey," Abbie retorted. She rolled her blue eyes and jabbed at her potato salad. "Our great-great uncle died in the first massacre. He was a jerk and he deserved it, but it's not a joke to me."

The glare in Lindsey's chocolate-brown eyes melted away. "Anyway, Nat would know if the Malachians were still active."

"How would I know?" I asked, devouring a bite of my messy sandwich. I'd always been interested in the massacres from a historical standpoint, but I wasn't obsessed or anything.

"Because they would try to recruit you," Lindsey explained, as though it were obvious. "They believed Malachi Rivers could do magic, and you're related to her. Has anyone ever tried to drag you out to the woods for a creepy ritual or anything?"

"No."

"Then the cult is dead," Lindsey declared. She arched her dark brows at Abbie and slurped the last of her Dr Pepper.

"All the more reason to have some fun," Abbie said. "We know we're not in any real danger."

Faith had been studying her split ends, but she flicked her ash-brown braid over her shoulder and planted her elbows on the table. "Everyone's talked this topic to death. Are y'all in for the lake trip? With the usual crew?"

"And Levi," Abbie added. "He's back in town."

I'd already spotted the weathered blue pickup in the Langford family's driveway, but hearing his name made a pang pinch between my ribs.

Lindsey eyed me sidelong as I swilled my tea and crushed ice between my teeth. Only she knew what had happened between Levi and me before he left last August.

He'd been slated to start his freshman year at college in Dallas when his father had died suddenly of an aneurysm. Levi's mom and sister had hoped he would defer for a semester. But he didn't. He'd left.

And since finding his letter in my mailbox on the morning he'd driven away, I hadn't heard from him once.

That letter had been a stoic farewell, its careful words the cool cobalt of distance and forgetting.

"Did you hear Levi got two of his poems published in, like, a prestigious poetry review?" Faith asked. "Mrs. Langford was bragging on him at the potluck last Sunday."

"Good for him," Lindsey chirped, saving me from having to reply.

"So are y'all coming?" Faith pressed.

Lindsey fiddled with the fitness watch that left subtle tan lines on her golden-brown wrist, waiting for me to say yes before she accepted the invitation. I could tell Levi's homecoming had already raised her hackles, but she didn't need to worry about me wasting any energy on him.

"Yeah, sounds fun," I said. I only had one summer to soak up time with people I'd miss—people who'd miss me back.

The twins drove me home first, past acres upon acres of pines and meadows. When we jostled over the gravel driveway toward my family's yellow farmhouse and the guesthouse my dad had converted into a veterinary office, Maverick and Ranger, our cattle dogs, scrambled from the front porch to greet me.

"See you at graduation!" Abbie sang out the window. I waved and scratched the dogs' mottled gray-and-black coats before checking the mail, finding graduation cards from relatives and a hefty packet of summer training and nutrition tips from my future coach.

But when I shut the squealing mailbox, I noticed something odd at the base of the nearest fence post: a smooth stone with a neat engraving. I bent to scoop it up.

My mouth went dry as I traced my thumb over each familiar component of the design. A triangle pointing down with a horizontal line through the bottom third. *Earth.*

Two diagonal lines crossing through the triangle. *Bone.*

A smear of dried, dark red at the center. *Blood.*

It was the Malachian mark.

TWO

Fear caressed my vertebrae, one by one.

A staggered procession of identical talismans followed the fence posts in both directions, stretching out as far as I could see.

It had to be a hoax, right? Probably the boys' track team. A few weeks ago, we'd stolen all their car tires during practice and devised a scavenger hunt that took them hours. Capitalizing on the massacre anniversary to retaliate was wicked, but admittedly clever.

I imagined the boys meticulously carving each symbol, mixing corn syrup and food coloring to add that macabre touch of fake blood. I admired their dedication. Still, I couldn't leave the stones for someone else to find. Even my levelheaded parents might get upset. They had let the local news interview us for a profile, hoping to get ahead of the publicity, but they were tired of the attention and disruption. My dad might mention the talismans to the sheriff, and then one of these idiot boys would get in trouble. I didn't want that to happen.

Jamming the envelopes back in the mailbox, I made a basket out of the hem of my tank top and started collecting the stones. Maverick and Ranger loped ahead of me to follow the scent of cow patties, their twitching noses as purposeful as divining rods. By the time I had amassed a pile, I dabbed my temples and stared down the road. How many more could there be? The boys' most elaborate prank so far had involved wearing masks to scare us during fall cross-country practice.

I studied the engraving again. The lines were careful, precise. Other than the copper-red smear at the center, each stone was identical to the last. This had taken time, skill, maybe even special tools.

The sputter of an approaching engine startled me. I looked up to see a rusty blue pickup slow to a stop on the road.

I dropped my collection of stones, watching them tumble to the grass underfoot. My heart clambered up my throat as though trying to escape the inevitable. But I tightened my wilting ponytail and put on a smile.

To my surprise, Levi Langford didn't just shout hello and drive by. He pulled over into the grass on the side of the road, got out, and rounded his truck to greet me.

It had been so long since I'd seen him that I couldn't help looking him over. He was redheaded, tall, and broad-shouldered. Fine lashes fringed his deep-set hazel eyes. Full, almost pouty lips softened the angles of his square, clean-shaven jaw, and a pale dusting of freckles across his ruddy complexion made him look utterly guileless.

"Nat Colter," he said, sliding his arm around me in a polite hug. If he minded my sweat, he didn't show it—and if he'd seen me collecting rocks, he didn't acknowledge it.

"Levi Langford. Good to have you back."

"It's good to be home."

A few feet of distance rematerialized between us. He tucked his hands in his pockets and the veins in his arms swelled beneath the sleeves of his gray tee. Whatever else I thought of him, those arms were the Lord's work.

"What are your plans this summer?" I asked, wondering if they included staying longer than a few days. He hadn't even come home for Christmas.

"Nothing exciting. Cutting lawns and helping my mom around the house. What about you?"

"Babysitting again and volunteering with the Heritage Festival."

"Interesting year to be a part of that," he said, furrows manifesting on his freckled forehead.

"Interesting year to live in San Solano at all," I replied. I nearly brought up the talismans just to have something to talk about, to squirm out of the awkward silence I could see coming from a mile away.

But he patched over it quickly. "Congrats! I heard you swept regionals and took fifth at state in two events. You're heading to Louisiana in the fall, right?"

"That's right. I heard you had a couple poems published."

"Yeah," he said, but didn't elaborate. Instead, he deflected. "What are you majoring in?"

"History. I either want to teach or be a library archivist."

"Ah, that makes sense," he said. He looked down at his shoes while I watched the sun droop like a ripe apricot.

Eventually, he cleared his throat. "I'm sorry if I gave you whiplash. Before I left. I know it must have felt . . . abrupt."

The straightforward apology threw me off. By the most generous estimate, our romance had lasted less than a minute.

One encounter. One kiss.

It happened at his going-away party. We'd been standing in Maggie Arthur's garden, swathed in the fragrance of flowers and fresh-cut grass. The secret kiss had tasted like a pinch of salt in clear water as the tiniest beads of sweat had found their way into our mouths.

A perfect storm of raw emotions and attraction. That's all it was. I hadn't allowed myself to feel anything else. That brief encounter didn't *warrant* feelings.

But his apology broke the levee I hadn't even realized I'd built. At once, I recalled every succulent detail, the sudden charge of intensity that came like a crack of white lightning, the way it felt to rake my fingers through his shock of red hair. How it had taken him leaning down *and* me standing on tiptoe for him to kiss me good and proper. Hold the proper.

My voice shook a little as I said, "I know you were going through a lot with your dad passing away. I didn't expect..." I trailed off with a dismissive wave.

"I'm still sorry," he said.

"It's okay."

He cleared his throat. "Do you want a ride home?"

Glancing back, I realized I'd walked farther down the road than I'd thought. My family owned thirty acres. The crickets had started to trill their twilight tune, and I didn't want to be out alone after dark. I hummed my indecision and finished with, "Sure, thanks."

"Sorry it's a mess," Levi said as he opened the door for me. I climbed onto his cracked leather bench seat. A pair of work boots caked in mud took up my legroom, and a travel mug in the cup holder smelled of strong, black coffee.

"Do you want to bring the dogs?" he asked, circling the truck to unlatch the tailgate.

I leaned out the window and whistled. Maverick and Ranger cocked their heads, their ears standing upright, and bolted back from our next-door neighbor's pastureland.

I almost propped my feet on the dash before I remembered that Levi and I weren't that comfortable with each other. We'd always belonged to the same big friend group. We'd both run track and cross-country. I'd tutored his younger sister, Emmy, for a history exam. Mr. Langford would have been my senior English teacher if he hadn't passed away.

But over the years, I'd noticed Levi avoiding me. He would fall quiet when I joined a conversation and wander away soon after, letting just enough time pass to prevent seeming rude.

Our mutual friends remained oblivious to this dynamic, especially the twins. They'd grown up in church with Levi, attending all the same summer camps and Bible studies. They wouldn't believe that I could live a couple miles away from Levi, know everyone he knew, and never once hold a one-on-one conversation with him. It was statistically impossible.

And yet the kiss had been our first-ever private encounter. Even then, only a garden trellis had separated us from the other party guests.

I could think of just one explanation for Levi acting so slippery, however unreasonable it seemed: the history between our families.

Levi was Lillian Pickard's great-great grandson. Lillian was one of the four San Solano girls who had been tried for the 1921 murders of twelve men in the sanctuary of Calvary Baptist. In the late sixties, she had published a tell-all book detailing her friendship with Malachi Rivers, rambling in awe about Malachi's supernatural powers. Instead of dismissing Lillian's account entirely, the public deemed her silly and gullible—and therefore innocent.

But then the copycat massacre occurred three years after the publication of Lillian's book. The same people who had laughed her off began to blame her for sparking the secret fanaticism that resulted in a dozen more murders. Despite her narrative's unreliability, the book grew popular thanks to the assumption that it inspired dark deeds.

Personally, I was more interested in the historical facts that could be gleaned from the heaps of nonsense—the details about Malachi's past that couldn't be found in public records. In my eyes, the book gave meat and marrow to the hollow bones of a mysterious legend.

It was a riveting read. Even my late grandmother—Malachi's granddaughter—had owned a first edition of Lillian's book, bound in a faded dust jacket. I'd read it cover-to-cover more times than I could count, but Grandma Kerry had never spoken much about the massacres.

And she had never associated with the descendants of Lillian Pickard.

But that resentment had ended with Grandma Kerry and went unreciprocated. My parents were friendly with everybody. Maggie Arthur, Grandma Kerry's contemporary and another descendant of Lillian Pickard, was a family friend. She was the one who had encouraged me to volunteer for the Treasures of Texas Heritage Festival. Her granddaughter, Kate, had provided me with three full summers of well-paid work babysitting her daughter.

In other words, Levi had no reason to care about old interfamily drama.

But why else would he have avoided me all this time?

After slamming the tailgate shut, Levi hunkered in the driver's seat and turned the air vents toward me. A solicitous Southern gentleman.

"I bet your mom and sister are happy to have you back for the summer." I caught a glimpse of my untamed hair in the side mirror and frowned.

"They are," he said, his voice a low rumble. "Happy to put me to work, too. Apparently ten months is plenty of time for an old house to fall apart."

As we crept down the road, Levi rested his elbow on the window frame, frowning into the distance. It had to be difficult coming home after what happened. Maybe up in Dallas, he'd found a way to ignore his grief, stuff it in a closet with his San Solano Wolves track tees, become a new person who could pretend not to feel pain.

I remembered the strained expression he'd worn at the going-away party, just shy of a month after his dad's passing. I'd thought his mom cruel for making him suffer through the whole affair, the lemonade sips and the small talk. She seemed to have already cried herself dry, but Levi looked, in the politest way possible, like he would rather be anywhere else.

I couldn't stand to watch him like that, in the throes of grief, enduring countless pats on the back and stale questions about his future. So I braved the August heat, carrying my plate of strawberry cobbler out to the garden. I took refuge behind a trellis thick with trumpet vines. And then Levi appeared. When he noticed me there, sweating like a sinner in church, I thought he'd either paste on a stiff smile or continue his quest for solitude.

But he did neither. Instead, he gave me a thoughtful look.

"Sorry," I said abruptly, like I'd intruded on him changing in his bedroom. "You're safe here. No small talk needed. I'll go back and say I never saw you. Better yet, that I've never heard of you."

That earned a laugh. "No, you don't have to go. Let's hide here for a minute."

It surprised me that he would cast his lot with mine. He stared down at his big hands with their freckled knuckles. "It feels like my mom is punishing me for going to college. She's not going to let me leave without an embarrassing parade."

"She just wants to show you off," I said, not quite sure why I was defending her. "SMU is a good school."

"She wanted me to defer until next semester. I get it. There's so much to take care of here... sorting through Dad's things...." His hazel eyes met mine, their pulsating pupils ringed with fern green and lustrous amber. "But I'm afraid if I don't leave now, I'll never go. I'll convince myself to stay."

I chewed on my bottom lip. What did this grieving boy need right now? No more idle chitchat or claps on the shoulder.

"I think the hardest part is the regret," I heard myself say. "My grandma always wanted to share her sage advice with me, and sometimes I just brushed her off. But when she could barely hold a lucid conversation, I missed her 'teachable moments.'" I laughed softly, fending off the ache of tears. "Is there anything you regret?"

His lips parted in surprise, and then a ghost of a smile tugged at their corners. "No one's asked me that," he said, turning toward me and tangling the fingers of one hand high in the trellis. The stance made one lean line of his torso.

"Sorry," I repeated, shaking my head like a fly had flown into my ear. "I shouldn't have—"

"No, I'm glad you asked," he said. "I don't regret anything. The only thing I'd regret is missing out on opportunities he'd want me to take."

I smiled a half smile. "Then you're doing the right thing."

Something intense passed between us then. Our eyes locked. The taut silence felt as charged as an electric field. I realized with equal astonishment and certainty that he wanted to kiss me, and I stepped closer with no fear of embarrassment, no fear that I'd misinterpreted. My chin tilted upward. He leaned down slowly, reading in my eyes the answer to his unspoken question.

When his lips connected with mine, soft and unfamiliar, euphoria rushed through my veins. The cobbler slid off my plate onto the grass. *Why* he was kissing me, I couldn't say. But it was sudden and sure, wild and surreal.

He pulled away to study my face, to confirm that I wanted it as much as my lips implied. I answered by dropping my paper plate, standing on my toes, and gripping the solidness of his shoulders through the sweaty cotton shirt. I could sense turmoil inside him, tight in his muscles. His hands moved earnestly, streaming through my hair.

My only thought was *wow*.

We overheard his mom ask someone where he'd gone. Instead of startling apart, we took our time letting the kiss taper off, his thumb brushing over the apple of my cheek. We stared at each other before he said, "I guess I should get back."

I nodded.

He left.

Now, as I sat in his passenger seat, that moment felt like a fever dream. If Levi hadn't just apologized, I'd think I was as delusional as poor Lillian Pickard.

His tires kicked up chalky dust as we turned onto my driveway. I couldn't decide whether I was relieved or disappointed that our time together had ended so soon.

"Are you coming to Toledo Bend on Sunday?" I asked.

"Yeah, I think I will." He got out, opened the tailgate to release the dogs, and met me on the passenger side.

"Thanks for the ride," I said.

"Any time."

Levi Langford's truck rattled over my driveway as the sun sank over the fields.

I had to wonder if that sound, like the kiss, would be a just-this-once thing.

THREE

The screen door banged shut behind me.

"Don't look!" my mom called, peeking her perfectly coiffed blond head out from the living room. Jodi Colter couldn't even pop into the nearest gas station without a quick hair tease. "I'm wrapping your presents."

"Not looking," I said, shielding my eyes as I traipsed over the creaky hardwood toward my room, but there would be no surprises. Mom insisted on wrapping the dorm supplies we'd picked out together, including the four shopping bags of school-spirit merch she'd hoarded for me. At her insistence, she and I even had matching gold-and-purple Tigers sweatshirts. My future roommate would run for the hills.

"Make sure there's space on the camera for pictures tomorrow!" Mom called after me.

"I forbid you to take more than a hundred," I called back.

She muttered something akin to "We'll see about that" as I closed my bedroom door. I grabbed the backpack I'd tossed at the foot of my bed after school, digging through graded papers—As in history and English, low Bs in science and math—to find my cap and gown, still wrapped in plastic.

Outside my window, night eclipsed the pink-and-lavender sky. Growing up in a town that was notorious for its unexplained tragedies, I couldn't help but fear the dark. The half-serious superstitions had baked frightful fantasies into my imagination. Secret terrors seemed to cluster in the shadows of particular places.

One time, during a sleepover, I'd snuck into the hollow sanctuary of Calvary Baptist at night to touch the lectern on a dare. The Dixon twins were friends with the daughter of the church handyman, and they'd stolen the keys so we could play the most thrilling game of truth-or-dare in San Solano history. The fear I'd felt as I tiptoed between the pews was so primal that I'd barely brushed the lectern with my fingertips before forsaking my dignity and sprinting back to the others, who giggled nervously from the foyer.

The same fear set upon me any time my friends and I went looking for thrills by driving down the road that dead-ended near the cabin in the woods, the place where Malachi, Lillian, Dorothy, and Johanna had gathered a hundred years ago.

Legends of the magical clearing predated even the old cabin that sat on it—but since Malachi had come along, those legends of that strangely hallowed ground had been subjected to a century of gruesome embellishment. According to town lore, in the weeks leading up to the copycat massacre, blood-drenched talismans made of bones, twigs, and twine had dangled from the trees, and remains of mutilated animals had been scattered on the ground. The cabin itself, where the girls had supposedly conjured evil, took on a fetid—one might dare say, sulfuric—smell. That was one of the campiest claims, and I couldn't help rolling my eyes every time I heard it.

But it got campier. Some professed to see a blond girl in the woods, wearing a gown stained with blood from the waist down—Malachi in her baptismal robe. We had the town's recollection of the particularly eventful Easter Sunday service in 1918 to thank for that imagery. Malachi's father, Reverend

Rivers, had resolved to baptize her in hopes that a public profession of faith would help curb her wild behavior. But when Malachi surfaced, the water in the baptistery filled with blood, and Malachi cackled. The entire congregation witnessed it. Some called it a young girl's lark that had gone too far. Others believed it to be the work of a demonic spirit that had possessed her. Now it was widely believed to be an incident of mass hysteria and collective false memory.

I flicked on my desk lamp and shut the blinds as if to put these thoughts to bed. But I found myself drawn to the bookshelf in the corner.

Amid historical novels and dense biographies, Lillian's book looked lean and unassuming. It was my grandmother's first edition. The worn paper jacket was matte black with the silhouette of a pine forest in a sickly hunter green. The outdated, all-caps title always felt like it was screaming at my eyes.

After briefly riffling through the pages, I reshelved it. As a kid, I'd scoured every word and studied the Malachian mark for hidden meanings beyond what Lillian described, fantasizing that I might be the one to find a secret clue and solve the murders. That morbid fascination—okay, maybe it *had* been an obsession at one point—could easily engulf me again.

I didn't need to dredge up fear like dragging a lake for a body that had already wasted to particles. Nothing would come of this anniversary. Nothing. And then everything could go back to normal.

Leaving my sweaty clothes in a pile on my bathroom floor, I stepped into the shower and closed my eyes. The water soothed the scrapes from my fall.

Now that I was alone, the reckoning I'd been dreading since last August finally came. I had to face the fact that the kiss with Levi wasn't just a delectable memory that would dissolve if I dwelled on it for too long. Levi wasn't ephemeral, like the last ounce of my grandma's discontinued perfume in the vial on her dresser, which I feared to open in case the memory of her essence should evaporate forever.

He was here. In town. For the summer.

And he was *sorry*.

I wouldn't read into his apology. I would *not*.

I skulked back to my room, changed into sleep boxers and a tee, and started typing a group text to Lindsey and the twins about the talismans. But actually seeing the words raised fine hairs on my forearms, so I erased the text and sat crisscross to blow-dry my hair in front of my closet mirror. I'd barely gotten started when I noticed that *Pagans of the Pines* was sticking out from the top bookshelf as if someone had pulled it to try to access a secret room.

Through a cascade of dirty-blond strands, I glared at the reflection of the book, feeling oddly powerful, half expecting it to fall off the shelf or fly and hit the wall. It didn't. It remained there until I pushed it flush with the others, turned off the lights, and fell asleep to an orchestra of crickets and katydids.

I woke with a strangled gasp.

Something was clotting my throat, choking me. It tasted like dirt. My helpless, fraught fingers encircled the column of my neck. My pulse thrummed like hummingbird wings.

Not this again.

I coughed out the obstruction. It was too dark to see what it was, but as I clutched blindly at the substance on my sheets, clumps of damp soil molded to my grasp. I smelled a cool, earthy aroma, and felt tangling roots sift through my fingers like a freshly turned grave.

I climbed out of bed and stumbled toward my lamp.

There was no dirt on my sheets. But a gritty residue remained on my tongue.

Sometimes, I dreamed that a bloodstain bloomed across my ceiling. Drops would splash onto my forehead, rhythmic and incessant. Other times, my bones strained in their sockets, like some force was trying to dislocate them.

All my life, I'd had these dreams. They'd gotten more frequent and more vivid since I'd become a teenager. Grandma Kerry had somehow always known about them, even when my parents had no idea. Usually, she was already awake, waiting for me. Sometimes, she was standing over my bed. I used to tell myself that she must have heard me gasping and thrashing in my sleep, but in hindsight, I had to admit it seemed like strange, inexplicable intuition.

After she was gone, I started trying to rationalize the dreams. *You pushed yourself too hard in the heat today,* I thought now. *You're having some kind of retroactive heat stroke that's making you hallucinate.*

But the excuse didn't work this time. I needed Grandma Kerry.

I grabbed my pillow and raced my fear down the hall.

I didn't feel safe again until I had shut myself in her old room and leaped onto the creaky bed. I bumped my head on the regal, imposing headboard as I nestled under the covers, but I didn't care. I felt safe.

Here, nothing could hurt me.

Morning came. I knew that the episode last night had been nothing more than a dream. That's all they ever were. But none of the dreams had ever felt so real.

Rubbing my eyes, I kicked my bare feet over the side of the bed and planted them on the rug. This was a guest room now, but we hadn't changed much except for the bedding, and we'd packed away the outdated lace doilies and dorky kid pictures of my dad. Everything else was familiar, including the vanity tray on the dresser that held Grandma Kerry's old jewelry and a creased picture of Grandpa Willie—items that had helped anchor her to a sense of self when she had started to drift. She came to live with us after accidentally burning down the house where she'd lived with Grandpa Willie for decades by leaving a pot unattended on the stove.

At the vanity tray, I brushed her perfume bottle and plucked her understated twisted vine wedding band from a porcelain dish.

"Nat, are you up, baby?" Mom called from down the hall. "It's graduation day!"

Startled, I dropped the ring. It bounced with a bright *ding* across the wood planks and onto the rug, settling somewhere under the bed.

"I'm up!" I called back. I glanced at the clock and realized I had to be gussied up and on the courthouse lawn in less than an hour. I dropped to all fours, saw a glint of gold, and flattened myself to retrieve it. With the ring safely in my grasp, I wriggled back out from under the bed, rucking up the border of the rug—which revealed a deep trench carved into the wood floor.

Sitting back on my heels, I traced my finger along the rough path.

A lump formed in my throat. Curiosity overpowered any sense of urgency. Frowning, I stood up, replaced the ring, and shoved the bed frame aside. When I flung away the rug, I gasped.

The symbol of the cult spanned the space under the bed, frenzied and furious. Unlike the neat lines on the stones, it seemed to have been carved in haste, maybe even in a state of mania.

Like pressing a tender bruise, I let a horrible memory play through my thoughts. Grandma Kerry's mental decline had been inconsistent, lurching, riddled with bouts of confusion and embarrassment at her confusion, which caused her to sink into silence. But there had been a few episodes of paranoia and something her doctor had called "catastrophic reactions." One in particular had given my parents no choice but to hire a live-in caregiver.

On that day, Grandma Kerry woke up wild-eyed, the gray hair that was still tinged with youthful blond mussed from sleep—or sleeplessness. She had charged into the kitchen and seized my wrists in her surprisingly strong grip while I was preparing to leave for school. Blood streamed down her arm from her elbow, dripping onto her robin's egg blue nightgown.

"I can see them," she said. "I can smell them. They're growing stronger. It will happen again."

Dad had sat her down at the table in the breakfast nook and tried to calm her, pressing a cloth to her wound. But she erupted like a madwoman, screaming that he would never understand and how lucky he was for that. My mom whipped out her phone to call an ambulance as she ushered me away from the scene.

Now I stared at a smear of dark brown on the wood planks in her bedroom, right at the heart of the mark. Blood.

Having witnessed the determination in her stormy eyes and the sinew behind her grip, I wondered if she had spent that sleepless night secretly carving this mark and covering it up.

Dad couldn't find out about this. No one could. I would protect him from the pain for as long as possible, and I would protect what was left of my grandmother's dignity.

But haunting questions needled me: Was there any chance that the paranoia, the warning, and the mark weren't just the workings of a broken mind?

Was there any chance that Grandma Kerry had known more about her own grandmother than she'd let on?

And most crucially, was there any chance that twelve more people would die?

EXCERPT:

PAGANS OF THE PINES: THE UNTOLD STORY OF MALACHI RIVERS

Lillian Pickard, 1968

In 1905 Simeon Rivers, a sawmill worker, founded Calvary Baptist Church in San Solano, Texas. His mission was to subvert the liberalism of other protestant churches in the area. As a staunch Fundamentalist Baptist, Simeon was far from popular, but he was a hardworking, resourceful man with a measure of charisma. He purchased an acre of land for twenty-five dollars and built a church.

At the time of its establishment, Simeon and his wife Ruth had a four-year-old son named Malachi. Ruth was pregnant with their second child. They lived in a small parish house beside the church. But after Simeon had preached only a handful of services, a violent storm blew through town and demolished both structures. Ruth and Malachi were struck by debris. Ruth and her unborn child survived. The boy did not.

Grieving their beloved son and their church challenged Ruth and Simeon in different ways. Simeon, determined to honor God's calling upon his life, raised funds to rebuild. Ruth clung to the promise of her unborn child, certain that God would give her another son upon whom she could bestow the name Malachi in honor of her firstborn.

To her dismay, the second child was a girl. Ruth detached from her daughter but had been calling her Malachi for months. She had no heart to change the name. Simeon attempted to convince his wife to choose any other, but the power of Ruth's maternal grief swayed him. He wanted her to heal.

But Ruth did not heal. Since Malachi's brother had been so young when he died, Ruth mounted him on a pedestal. He was an icon of unattainable innocence and perfection who had not been afforded the chance to develop his own distinguishable traits and flaws. Every time the younger Malachi misbehaved, as children do, she was called sinful. She could never measure up to her God-fearing brother.

As Malachi grew, she developed strange powers. When she was six years old, her mother mentioned her hope of conceiving another child. Malachi screamed until Ruth's ears bled. After that, Ruth was afflicted with prolonged, heavy bleeding of a womanly nature. She often read aloud the Biblical tale of the bleeding woman who touched the hem of Jesus' robe and was healed. But Ruth was not blessed with another child, nor was her hemorrhaging resolved.

Still, every day, she prayed that the Lord would heal her.

Moreover, she prayed that the Lord would forgive her for bringing to life an abomination.

FOUR

Natalie Colter

ONE MONTH AND NINE DAYS UNTIL THE CLAIMING

I did my best to forget about the Malachian mark. But I couldn't forget about Grandma Kerry on graduation day. When she'd fallen ill, I'd realized she wouldn't live long enough to attend this ceremony, or any special occasions beyond. That didn't make it easier.

While I contended with the stubborn zipper on my graduation gown, Mom sped like a stunt driver toward the limestone courthouse at the center of historic downtown. Dad braced himself, slamming nonexistent brakes from the passenger seat as Victorian and Craftsman homes streaked past.

Downtown San Solano was the kind of place outsiders would call "quaint" and "charming" if they hadn't already found other words to describe our town—namely, "creepy" and "cursed." Venerable oaks provided verdant shade, and pretty, old churches of sundry denominations postured on almost every corner. The town square had a bakery, an art gallery, a hardware store owned by the twins' family, and a beloved diner with self-serve coffee that tasted like brake fluid. As one of the oldest settlements in the state, San Solano played host to countless historical landmarks, one being the intersection of the El Camino Real de los Tejas trail with the ruins of an eighteenth-century Spanish mission.

And the most famous landmark? On a quiet, shady street, Calvary Baptist Church loomed large over the town's reputation, the cross atop its gothic tower casting a long shadow on the jade lawn. The cabin in the clearing where Malachi supposedly performed dark magic was ominous in its own right, but it was tucked away in the woods, down a dead-end road on the outskirts of town. The church where the deaths occurred presided over our daily lives and refused to be forgotten.

We were nearly late to the ceremony, and I found my place in line right as the graduates began filing into rows of white chairs. Every paper program had already been repurposed into a fan; San Solano High insisted on holding graduation outdoors come hell or high water. When my row stood and shuffled forward to wait by the stage, I searched for Levi amid the sea of oscillating programs. A few of his close friends were graduating, and I wouldn't be surprised if he'd come. Before I could spot him, I found Lindsey in the back row, gray circles hanging under her eyes. I cocked my head, wordlessly checking on her. She smiled and waved.

My name thudded over the sound system, surprising me. I crossed the stage and filed back to my seat with my diploma in hand.

After the ceremony I found Lindsey's family immediately. Abuela Sofia showered me with hugs and kisses. Lindsey's mom, Camila, tucked a strand of Lindsey's long hair behind her ear, doting on her in Spanish. Even after three years of classes, I could only catch a few phrases.

Camila glanced at me and then asked Lindsey a question. Lindsey responded sternly, "Todavía no, pero ya pronto."

Not yet, but soon.

Before I could puzzle over Lindsey's answer to the question I hadn't understood, I noticed a jagged trio of cuts slashing across her outer forearm. A nasty, purple-black bruise spilled around each mark like blotted ink.

"What is that?" I demanded.

Her eyes widened. "You can see that?"

"It's kind of hard to miss."

Lindsey scowled at the wound. "Um... I thought I covered it with makeup."

"Makeup? You'd need latex prosthetic skin. What happened?"

She shrugged back into her gown, covering the marks. "Um... my cousin Juliana's Yorkipoo scratched me."

"*That* was from a Yorkipoo?"

"I think she had a violent reaction to my nondesigner jeans." Lindsey laughed too loudly at her own joke, told at the expense of her wealthy "influencer" cousin from Los Angeles. "You should watch out. She's carrying the little demon around in her purse."

Nerves and humor? That combination only meant one thing when it came to Lindsey Maria Valenzuela: she was lying.

But I didn't have time to call her out. I saw my dad's square face and broad smile in the crowd. Mom swooped in and went full paparazzi. My cheeks were cramping by the time I managed to steal a moment alone with Lindsey and the twins to tell them about the talismans in my yard the day before.

"And Lindsey thought *I* had a morbid sense of humor," Abbie said when I finished.

Lindsey didn't retort. Her sun-kissed brown face went ashen.

"I bet it was Grayson's idea," Faith said, glowering at a mop of sun-bleached hair in the crowd.

"Did... did anything else happen?" Lindsey asked me.

I swallowed a sudden bout of nausea. I couldn't bring myself to tell them about the mark under my grandma's bed. "No," I replied.

Lindsey nodded, satisfied.

"We have to get revenge on those idiots," Abbie whispered.

"We should forge unacceptance letters from their colleges," Faith suggested, giddy. "We'll say there was a mistake with their applications and that they've been put on a waiting list."

"Or we could kidnap them and take them to a ritual," Abbie said, a dangerous spark in her eyes.

"I just want to relax this summer, so count me out," Lindsey said.

Abbie blew her a raspberry. "Ya boring, Lindsey."

"At least I don't have to stage a fake animal sacrifice to have fun. I've got to go hang out with my cousins or they'll be pissed that they came all this way. Heads up, Juliana is coming to the lake with us tomorrow."

Abbie groaned. "She's so rude!"

"She thinks *you're* rude," Faith countered. The three of them wandered off, bickering, and my eyes immediately drew to Levi. A six-foot-two, handsome redhead would be hard for anyone to miss, even in a crowd. Our eyes met from a distance and my nerves jittered like a june bug hitting a porch light.

A slim approaching figure with shoulder-length brunette hair intercepted my gaze: Kate Wilder. Her sage-green eyes met mine and she flashed a smile that emanated more Southern charm than a debutante ball.

Kate's four-year-old daughter, Avery, released her mother's hand to squeeze my waist. I staggered with her weight and grinned. She had green eyes like Kate's, magnified by flexible prescription glasses.

"We couldn't be prouder of you, Nat," Kate said, her drawl thick enough to shame maple syrup. "You're off to bigger places and better things."

"But I still have a whole summer with this little wildling." I tousled Avery's curly cowlick until she lost interest in me and crouched to inspect a ladybug.

"Speaking of that, what would you think of cutting your hours, with a raise to make up for it?" Kate asked. "It's your last summer here and you're already helping out with the Heritage Festival."

"Are you sure?"

She dismissed my protest with a wave of her slender hand. "The festival staff needs all the help they can get. We're expecting a record number of visitors this year."

"That whole dark tourism thing is really taking off," I grumbled. "But won't that leave you high and dry with Avery?" Kate's husband held a demanding corporate job, she worked full-time at the chamber of commerce, and Avery's preschool program had already let out for the summer.

"I was talking to Emmy Langford at the potluck last Sunday, and it turns out she's looking for her first summer job," Kate said. "I thought she could take two of your days each week. She doesn't have her license yet, but Levi can drive her to and from our house. Grandma Maggie would be thrilled to hear you're freed up to help with the festival."

"That works for me," I said. "It'll be nice to add more to my résumé than 'facilitated microwaving of dinosaur-shaped chicken nuggets.'"

Kate laughed. "Perfect. I'll let Emmy know that you're—Levi Langford!" she cried, turning several heads in addition to his. "I don't believe my eyes!"

Levi sidled over, endearingly bashful. Kate's grandma and Levi's late grandma were cousins, both granddaughters of Lillian Pickard. In a small town like ours, people didn't try to keep track of the math beyond third cousins and simply "claimed kin." Levi greeted Kate first and lifted Avery up in a forklift maneuver that earned a yelp of delight from her and accentuated his forearms. Then he turned to me. "Hey! Congratulations, Nat."

"Thanks," I replied. I expected something cleverer to follow that, but I drew a blank.

Bless Kate, a perfect stranger to awkward silences. "Tell me you'll stop by Grandma Maggie's soon," she said to Levi. "She's pleased as punch that you're back in town. Are you doing lawns this summer?"

"Yes ma'am," Levi answered.

"Good. She says you're the only one who keeps the cuttings out of her garden beds."

"Tell her I'll swing by this week," Levi said.

Kate winked at him and took Avery's hand. "See you at the party, Nat," she said, and left us alone.

Once again, divine intervention saved me from floundering. Grayson Scott sprinted over in a blur of golden-tan, gangly limbs and blond hair to wrap Levi in a bear hug. "What's up, Natty Light?" he asked me.

"You'd think the mastermind behind the creepy talismans in my yard would have thought of a better nickname by now."

"Talismans?" Grayson repeated the word like he was trying out a new SAT vocabulary term. Even allowing for sarcasm, *mastermind* might have been a stretch.

Bryce Hayward joined us, his thick-framed glasses fogged from the humidity. "What talismans?" he asked, removing the lenses to clean them on his tie.

I folded my arms. "Nice prank. Y'all are lucky my parents didn't find them first."

Grayson and Bryce shared a look, more confused than conspiratorial. "We haven't done anything yet," Bryce said. He replaced his glasses and regarded me with keen, serious brown eyes.

"Sure," I said.

"No, really," he insisted. "We were thinking of getting you back during the lake trip."

Grayson whacked Bryce's shoulder. "Dude! Now they know to expect it."

"Sorry," Bryce said, digging his phone out of his pocket. "But I found something creepy, too. Or my cat found it." He showed me his screen and swiped through pictures of a translucent sachet filled with herbs and tied with twine. A dainty metal charm depicting the Malachian mark dangled from the knot. "I don't know where he got it. Milo is an indoor cat."

"So that was somewhere in your house," I concluded.

Bryce frowned. "It's creepier when you say it out loud. My mom wanted to tell the police, but I convinced her not to. Now I'm wondering if you and I both should."

Levi stuffed his hands in his pockets, sighed restlessly, and mumbled something about saying hi to a former teacher before leaving us. That boy was weird about goodbyes.

"Are you still freaking out about that thing Milo found?" Vanessa Wallace appeared, hooked an arm around Bryce's waist, and flashed a teasing smile up at her boyfriend. Just clearing five feet, she had to tilt her head back at nearly a right angle to look up at him.

"I'm not freaking out," Bryce said. "We're only talking about it because Nat found talismans with the mark at her house."

Vanessa's sable-black curls bounced as she shook her head. "You're so gullible." She gestured at me. "The track girls did it."

I snorted. "I don't have this good of a poker face."

Vanessa shrugged. Like Levi and me, she was a descendant of one of the four original Pagans of the Pines—the great-great-granddaughter of Dorothy Hawkins. But it was different for her. Dorothy Hawkins had moved on with her life. She worked as a maid for the few local families willing to accept her help, married a quiet man, and distanced herself from Malachi. Johanna Mead had relocated and reportedly changed her name. Lillian had continued to live comfortably, pouring herself into her social life and community service, only jeopardizing her recovered reputation when she decided to spill everything onto the page.

Malachi, on the other hand, remained a puzzle. And for some reason, people looked to my family to solve her.

Judging by the carving on my grandmother's floor, maybe they weren't too far off the mark.

The mark. Vanessa was a talented artist, a well-known prodigy in San

Solano. With such a careful hand, she could easily have engraved those perfectly identical talismans. But for what reason? She wasn't interested in our petty prank wars. She had her own crew. She was friendly and easygoing, but we all knew she only hung out with the track team because of Bryce.

"Come on, we're supposed to eat lunch with my fam," Vanessa said, tugging Bryce along. Judging by her blasé expression, she wasn't concerned about the cult fever.

"So, it really wasn't you?" I asked Bryce and Grayson.

"I swear." Bryce said as Vanessa herded him away.

"Swear to God," Grayson added.

I didn't want to be convinced. I didn't want to see a kaleidoscope of dark possibilities or think about my family being in danger.

But I couldn't help it. I believed them.

FIVE

Most of my graduation party guests were family friends from the Methodist church we attended. Judging by the cards and gifts amassing on the coffee table, the group was feeling generous.

Lindsey wouldn't be able to escape her cousins, but the twins arrived just in time for fajitas. Abbie stealthily swapped her virgin margarita for a real one when my mom wasn't looking.

Kate also came as promised, though Avery was teetering on the verge of her regularly scheduled meltdown. She would only tolerate her glasses for a few hours at a time, but the discomfort of her astigmatism and farsightedness made it frustrating for her and everyone within earshot.

Kate pulled me aside before she had to take Avery home. "I've got something for you from Grandma Maggie." She dug around in her massive purse and produced a book-sized parcel wrapped in postal paper and tied with red ribbon. "She said to open it when you're alone."

Avery's whimpers intensified to wails of misery. Kate rushed to leave before she went volcanic.

When the guests were gone, I retreated to my room, comforted by the warm lull of an eventful Saturday winding down: plates clinking as Mom arranged them in the dishwasher and the soothing rumble of voices floating from the back porch, where Dad and Sheriff Jason shot the breeze.

I slipped off my cork heels and exchanged my ivory lace dress for jean shorts and a San Solano Wolves tee. The brown parcel from Kate reposed in sunlight on my desk. I had just untied the wine-red ribbon when I heard my dad say, "I'm sure there's an explanation."

"The explanation is that people are goddamn freaks, Kurt," the sheriff replied. "I've seen a lot in my years of service, and this doesn't surprise me one bit."

I dropped the package on my bed and hurried barefoot through the living room toward the back porch. The screen door groaned as I joined them, inhaling the sharp scent of citronella torches. "What doesn't surprise you?" I asked.

Jason resituated to look up at me, ice cubes clinking like wind chimes in his tea glass. "Hey there, Nancy Drew." He was sitting in a rocking chair in his typical civilian clothes: jeans, a tucked-in polo shirt that hugged his belly, sunglasses parked on top of his salt-and-pepper head. My dad was giving Maverick a good scratch behind the ears. The sun caught the silver in his blond hair, and his glasses had slipped down the bridge of his nose, making him look his age.

"A couple of deer were found decapitated in the woods, their meat already eaten raw," Jason explained. "No hunter would take the heads and leave good meat to scavengers. But wild animals don't decapitate others."

"So who—or what—does that leave?" I asked.

"Look, a meth epidemic is wreaking havoc in the Piney Woods," Jason said, sounding exhausted. "The Dixons called me last week because a lady with sores on her face was shuffling around the hardware store asking where she could find a meat hook. My leading theory is that meth makes people do weird and terrible things. I'm less concerned with who did it than with who people will *think* did it."

"The cult," I supplied.

Jason nodded. "You've probably heard there were animal slayings before the copycat massacre in '71. If there are dots to connect to the Malachians, people will connect them. Everyone's a little bored, if you ask me."

I pursed my lips and debated telling them about the talismans. "What if it's not just boredom?" I asked after a moment.

I described the stones and my initial suspicions. Jason looked ready to kick some teenage boy ass until I explained that the best prank the guys had ever played amounted to a jump scare. And then I told them about the sachet Bryce found in his house.

"Is there anything you and Bryce have in common?" Jason asked. "Any reason why someone would target the two of you?"

"No. But Bryce is dating Vanessa Wallace, who's related to Dorothy Hawkins. . . ." I said this like a question.

"Are you suggesting someone might be targeting the descendants of Malachi's little crew?" Jason asked.

"I don't know." I shrugged. "I mean, it was Bryce's house, not Vanessa's."

Jason pursed his lips. I could tell it was too late to retract the implication.

"I know it sounds off the wall," Dad said, "but do you think someone could be trying to draw more tourists?"

Jason made an authoritative "simmer down" gesture. "I'd bet this is just someone trying to get a rise out of people. But even pranksters can be dangerous." He looked at me. "You should be careful, and tell me if you see or hear anything else."

I nodded, hedging out thoughts of the symbol carved beneath the bed. It wasn't as if Grandma Kerry could have anything to do with what was happening now. "Dad, should we put the dogs in the run so they stay out of the woods?"

"Better safe than sorry."

I whistled and led Maverick to the enclosure. Ranger came sprinting after him. I used the garden hose to refill the water trough, latched the gate, and went back to my room to open the gift that Kate had delivered.

Inside the brown paper was a leather journal, old, soft, and webbed with creases. Miss Maggie knew I was a history buff who loved artifacts with stories to tell.

But when I carefully lifted the cover, I found a blank first page. In fact, most of the pages were blank. I flipped through and found an undated entry in flowery handwriting: a recipe to create a "Tincture for Dreamless Sleep," and on the next page, "Eyebright Collyrium to Open the Sight."

Other than drawings of plants with corresponding descriptions, I found a handful of scattered entries, each stranger than the last. One gave instructions for setting bones. Another detailed the fine points of antique revolver maintenance. Another bore the heading "Strengthening Your Spirit Shield," with no further text. Was that meant to be some sort of outdated abstinence lecture?

Maybe this journal was a San Solano women's almanac of helpful tips and recipes. Perhaps someone had forgotten to pass it on to the next person, nipping what would have been an intriguing tradition—far more intriguing than Grandma Kerry's community cookbooks featuring eight different kinds of Jell-O salad—in the bud.

Hoping for an explanatory note from Miss Maggie, I turned the wrapping upside down and shook it. Nothing. I tried calling Kate to no avail. Finally, I scratched my chin, baffled, and paged through the journal one last time.

I found a new entry, this one dated. It was entitled, "Protection Sachet (Revised for Strengthening Purposes)."

My nerves hummed as I read the strikingly familiar handwriting, the chicken scratch of a farm girl with more important tasks than learning to write pretty.

Grandma Kerry had authored this entry.

Hellebore
Larkspur
Fennel seeds
Obsidian

Use thin white cloth and tie with twine. If charm unavailable, add Solomon's seal in same proportion as protection amulet.

Bless herbs, cleanse stone. Must be charged under a waxing moon.

The word *magic* wasn't visible anywhere, but the rustling page practically whispered it aloud.

I trembled as I traced the date of the entry: *June 1970.*

Bewildered, I turned back until I reached the beginning. The first page had been utterly blank a moment ago. But new words had appeared, as though they had been written with invisible ink that revealed itself in the light:

By the powers of earth, bone, and blood, proceed we Wardens to our noble work.

I snapped the journal shut only to find the Malachian mark stamped on the front cover, the ominous design pressed deep into the leather.

Muffling a panicked squeal, I flung the gift across my bed. It landed on my pillow with a thud that sounded too heavy for its size.

Setting aside the possibility that I was *hallucinating,* what was Miss Maggie playing at? Was this a veiled threat to expose my late grandmother as an occultist, a follower of Malachi?

Or did this suggest that Miss Maggie was one, too? Lindsey had said that if the cult still existed, they would try to recruit me.

Was this an invitation?

Another, more cynical possibility dawned on me. Dad had speculated that someone might be trying to boost town tourism. Maggie was the chair of the Heritage Festival Committee, and Kate worked at the chamber of commerce. I'd be hard-pressed to find two people more interested in increasing tourism. Was it a coincidence that Maggie had given me this gift the day after someone had placed talismans in my yard?

I chomped on my lower lip. I could tell Sheriff Jason about the journal full of invisible ink. I *should* tell him. But pointing fingers at town luminary Maggie Arthur and her granddaughter would mean risking self-sabotage. As the septuagenarian queen of food drives and ladies' luncheons, Miss Maggie had earned her own historical plaque in the town square. And if not for the babysitting job with Kate, I'd be refilling bins at Country Catfish Buffet. I could kiss any glowing recommendation letters goodbye.

That was before even considering Grandma Kerry's involvement. What if an investigation of the journal led to the discovery of the mark on her floor?

I couldn't merge my memories of Grandma Kerry blessing our meals and bandaging my scraped knees with the idea of her involvement in the occult. I knew she would never have hurt anyone. That the authors behind this journal saw themselves as "wardens" and made magical protection charms didn't comfort me one bit, and it wouldn't shield Grandma Kerry from posthumous scrutiny.

My grandmother's involvement, however she was involved, made this complicated. Dragging her memory through the mud without clarifying a few things first would be disrespectful, I decided. I would wait until I had talked to Kate and Miss Maggie to make any moves.

I tucked the journal safely in my desk drawer.

EXCERPT:

PAGANS OF THE PINES: THE UNTOLD STORY OF MALACHI RIVERS

Lillian Pickard, 1968

I have done my best to corroborate my experience and Malachi's claims with public and church records, as well as interviews with others who knew the Rivers family. Yet it came as no shock that most witnesses of Malachi's strange works tended to demur or avoid me entirely. They fear loss of status, or perhaps the decades have obfuscated their memories, leading them to doubt what they once knew to be true.

I suffer from no such fear or doubt, and neither does Joseph Wooster.

Wooster was a congregant of Calvary Baptist from 1913 to 1916. In March of 1916, twenty-year-old Wooster cornered eleven-year-old Malachi in the food cellar of the parish house. When he touched her, he was immediately stricken with paralysis of the arm. She claimed that he had lifted her dress, while he claimed he had merely touched her shoulder, attempting to pray over her.

He emerged and declared to the congregation that Malachi must have the Devil inside her. Reverend Rivers, however, believed that obsession with miracles and demons led to exuberance and exhibitionism, and was skeptical of Wooster's accusation. But neither did he believe his daughter's claim of molestation. Wooster left the church in protest. Malachi had no such freedom.

The church burned down seven days later, consumed by a cooking stove fire that leaped unexpectedly out of control in the parish house while the Rivers family spent their evening together.

When I managed to contact Wooster for an interview, he had not changed his fifty-year-old story, and in fact viewed the murders that occurred in 1921 as activity of the same dark spirits he had hoped to pray out of Malachi.

He never recovered the use of his arm.

SIX

Natalie Colter

ONE MONTH AND EIGHT DAYS UNTIL THE CLAIMING

My language intensified from uncouth to ungodly as I fought my way through after-church traffic.

Kate had finally texted me that morning. She apologized for missing my calls and asked if I could drive Avery to Emmy's house on my way home from church. She needed a last-minute babysitter and knew I was already committed to the lake trip.

No problem, I responded. *But I need to ask you about the journal from Miss Maggie when you have the time.*

I don't know much about it, but she'd adore a visit. She's busy with the ladies' luncheon and hosting a festival board meeting at her house today, but you could take Avery to see her when you work tomorrow.

With a sigh, I parked in front of Calvary Baptist to pick Avery up from Sunday school. The ambiance of the stately white church only added to the morbid tales about Malachi Rivers. The pews were rigid as soldiers, the carpet river-of-blood red, and everything creaked at the touch. A local wealthy architect had designed and donated this building after the second church building had met its demise by fire—a fire some said Malachi started.

Reverend Rivers had reportedly found the Gothic Revival style of this new building gaudy, but he didn't protest much, seeing as he got a free church and a newfangled indoor baptistery out of the deal.

Inside the foyer, I passed photographs of balding, bespectacled former pastors and spared only a glance for the sanctuary where mass murder had occurred. Twice. How did people attend services here like nothing had happened?

Fighting a shiver, I turned right at the end of the foyer. Through the open door of the fellowship hall, I saw women gathered around tables and heard Miss Maggie preparing to lead them in a prayer over their lunch.

Briefly, before she bowed her winter-white head, we locked gazes. She smiled, but her eyes were sharp as evergreen needles. Before, I'd thought of her as a sort of strict but doting fairy godmother figure. Now, I sensed an appraisal. By giving me that journal, she hoped something would change. What did she want from me? Could this venerated woman possibly be capable of evil? Poisoning wine? Sacrificing animals? *Murder?*

Screeches from the nearby nurseries scrambled my thoughts. When I reached the preschool room with the Noah's Ark mural, the teacher sagged with relief. She already had Avery's polka-dot backpack ready to go. "I'm so sorry," she said, passing it over the gate.

"For what?" I asked. And then I saw Avery. Her glasses were streaked with silver paint. She wore spray-painted cardboard armor of God, complete with a sword of the Spirit. It was not a good idea to give Avery a weapon, even a flimsy one.

"We thought all the paint was dry before we gave them the armor," the teacher said. "I tried, but I can't get it off her glasses. Her parents are going to—"

"I'll take care of it," I promised.

She nodded, on the cusp of crying tears of relief. Bless her—one preschooler was more than enough responsibility for me.

"Looks like we'll be throwing Emmy in the deep end," I muttered as I helped a whining Avery buckle into the booster seat in the back of the gray truck I'd inherited from my dad, careful not to smash her breastplate of righteousness.

On the drive, I rolled down the windows to the let the sharp paint odor subside.

The Langfords lived on ample acreage along Midnight Road. Their house was idyllic, ivory with blue shutters and nestled near a rash of trees. I had visited once to tutor Emmy at Mr. Langford's invitation, and once when Mom had enlisted me to help her group of parent volunteers make homecoming mums.

Avery dragged her feet as we mounted the porch steps. When I knocked, she pressed her face into the skirt of my yellow sundress.

Emmy answered the door, wearing a pink floral dress and a kind smile prettier than a strand of pearls. Her vibrant red hair framed a clear, pale face with full lips and pronounced cheekbones. She welcomed me with a hug, dainty as a bone china teacup, then clapped her hands on her knees. "Hi, Avery! Are you ready to have fun?"

Emmy offered her hand. I expected Avery to recoil in shyness, but after briefly scrunching up her features like a wrinkled tomato, she accepted.

"Would you mind taking her to wash her hands while I clean her glasses?" I asked, working them off Avery's dark curls. "I'll need cotton balls and pure acetone, if you have it. Nail polish remover will work fine if you don't."

"Sure thing! Follow me."

The entryway split into a hallway and a staircase, with the dining room where I'd made mums to the right. A den to the left displayed a family picture over the fireplace. The coffee table held all sorts of gorgeous books: nature photography, architecture and design, illustrated poetry. I read a few titles as we passed a bookshelf running the length of the hallway wall. It seemed no topic failed to tickle the family's intellectual fancy. You could see the passion for learning in their home the way you could smell Tex-Mex cooking regularly in mine.

Sporadic clanking welcomed us into the airy, sunlit kitchen. Where our house was usually messy with laundry and junk mail, the clutter here was books and cups of drying paintbrushes.

A dirt-streaked white tee, six inches of solid midriff, and a long pair of legs in fitted jeans stuck out from the cabinet under the kitchen sink.

I felt a pinch behind my navel. How cruel of Levi to be handy with tools and look good wielding them when I already had the memory of his lips on mine to think about. This just seemed excessive.

"Levi, do we have any pure acetone?" Emmy asked. Levi paused in the middle of twisting something with a wrench to grope through the displaced cleaning products.

I was closest to him, so I took the bottle with a peppy, "Thanks!"

His face emerged from the shadows. "Oh hey, Nat. Thanks for helping Emmy get a job."

"I was about to work at Country Catfish Buffet," Emmy said.

"Refill girl?" I asked, depositing Avery's backpack on the counter. Emmy nodded. "That job's always open. I tried it for a week and nearly got clawed to death every time I rang the fresh catfish bell. Babysitting saved me from that dangerous lifestyle."

"I know! And I don't like that they only hire girls and make them wear tiny cutoff jean shorts." Emmy made a face at Avery, who giggled in response. "Come on, we'll go get the cotton balls."

Emmy led Avery down the hall, leaving Levi and me alone in the kitchen.

"Would you mind turning on the faucet so I can check for leaks?" he asked.

"Sure."

Tiptoeing through the bottles, I edged along his body. The easiest way to reach the faucet would be to plant one foot on either side of his torso, but I considered myself a lady. Instead, I reached diagonally across the counter to make an awkward grab for the gleaming new handle. "You weren't kidding about your family putting you to work," I said over the rushing water.

"Sadly, no," he said, in a tone that betrayed how much he didn't mind being needed. "But I should have been doing this stuff all year. It's my fault. You can turn it off now. Thanks."

I did as he requested and stepped away, giving him room to negotiate his way out of the cabinet. He stood, tugging the hem of his shirt back to his waistline. The "howdy" grin he gave me was a little cockeyed, as modest as it was self-assured. Turning his sweaty back to me, he scraped gray putty from around the edges of the new faucet. I studied Avery's lenses, testing the paint with a scrape of my thumbnail just to have something to do.

Avery sped into the kitchen ahead of Emmy, as giddy as if she'd found a pile of presents waiting on her birthday.

"Somebody's in a good mood today," I teased. "But Miss Emmy's about to see what it'll take to earn her keep. It's medicine time."

Avery moaned as I dug out a package of cookies and the bubble-gum-flavored allergy medicine. "Do you want to give it to her?" I asked Emmy as I measured it out. "She gets a cookie if she doesn't try to knock the cup out of your hands, two if she doesn't whine at all. She rarely gets two cookies."

Emmy took the cup of pink liquid and sniffed it. "Mmm, smells good," she said exaggeratedly. Avery pursed her lips with the "you shall not pass" expression I knew well.

"I have to take medicine, too," Emmy said. "But mine doesn't taste nearly this yummy. If you don't take it, I sure will."

Like I hadn't tried that one before. But Avery tilted her head back so Emmy could pour the syrup in her mouth. The little punk swallowed and licked her lips, conveniently deciding it might not be poisonous swamp muck. I surrendered the cookies. "I stand corrected."

"Can I take her out to the tire swing?" Emmy asked.

"Tire swing!" Avery repeated, her mouth coated in wet cookie crumbles.

"Sure, I'll bring her glasses out when I'm done. Just remember that she can't see much."

The back door banged shut behind Emmy and Avery as they crossed the green lawn. Levi leaned against the counter and wiped his hands on a rag, his pensive features directed at the floor.

The spray paint came off easily, and soon Avery's glasses were so clean the lenses sparkled. Levi stood there, absentmindedly brushing the calluses on his hands.

"Guess I should bring these out," I said. "I need to go get ready for the lake trip."

"Do you want water or coffee before you go?" he asked, remembering his manners. "I just made a fresh pot."

"Water would be great," I said. Or a cold shower.

Levi filled a glass from the cabinet and handed it to me. I tried not to notice the tips of his warm fingers brushing mine.

"You know, your mom doesn't seem like the type to display human sexuality books on the shelves in her entryway," I said.

A laugh shook his chest. Something about the sound warmed me, like hearing the first Christmas song of the winter season on the radio. "Those were my dad's. It would probably embarrass her that you noticed. You want to see something even more surprising?"

I couldn't help but grin at the mischievous lift of his brow. "Of course."

He jerked his head. I followed him back to the front of the house. As we passed the den with the family portrait, I stared at the image of Mr. Langford. The red hair had skipped a generation—Levi's dad had had hickory brown hair and a beard of the same color—but his hazel eyes and height matched Levi's exactly. The seniors at San Solano High had all adored Mr. Langford's gregarious personality, poetic spirit, and participation-based grading system. Last year, I'd looked forward to being in his class.

Levi led me upstairs to a study with an oak desk and hundreds of books on the built-in shelves. The attic door on the far side of the room stood open, boxes scattered in front of it.

"I started cleaning out the attic and found some of my parents' old stuff." Weaving through the boxes, he reached behind the desk to retrieve a large canvas. "Imagine Jennifer Langford, small-town realtor, volunteer Baptist event coordinator, and"—he flipped it over—"painter of nudes."

I clapped a hand over my mouth to stifle a gasp-turned-laugh. It was a respectable work of art, an impressionistic flurry of bright strokes and shapes, but still a graphic depiction of two naked bodies.

"And look at this one." He set it down and hurried to grab another. The dewy, pale smudges made up a woman in the nude.

"Wow," I said. "They're beautiful."

"I always knew she liked to paint and do crafts, but I didn't know she was this talented."

"Are these your dad's books?" I asked, gesturing around.

"Yeah." Levi lifted his eyes to the shelves. A number of emotions, dark and peaceful, coexisted effortlessly in that expression. Again, I felt as if I had seen something too intimate for words, glimpsed it through a window before getting a chance to knock on the door.

An empty feeling of loss overcame me as I thought of Grandma Kerry. I wanted answers about the mark under her bed, her writing in that book.

I walked to the window facing the backyard and looked outside. Avery was a smiling blur on the tire swing.

Noticing a book of Pablo Neruda poems sitting spine-up on the window seat, I brushed the title. "Was this one of his favorites?"

"One of many," Levi said. "When I was nine, he found me reading that and put it in the restricted section." He pointed to the top shelf. I wouldn't be able to it reach it, but grown-up Levi wouldn't even have to stretch.

A stack of old photographs lay on a cardboard box nearby. I set down the book and picked up the top picture of familiar young women sitting on a porch. "Hey, that's my grandma!"

Levi moved close behind me. He smelled like sweat, in a good way. I flashed back to after the kiss, hoping he would call me, wondering if he would come home during fall break, scolding myself into getting over him when he didn't show up during winter break. It was easy now to remember why I'd hoped.

"I think Miss Maggie gave that to my mom when she was making a history exhibit for last year's Heritage Festival," he said, and I felt his deep voice near me. "My mom didn't end up using it because of the cigarettes."

I checked the date written on the back—1970—and studied the image more closely. The colors were bright but tinged with the faded yellow of early color photographs. Fair-haired Kerry sat on a lawn chair in a red floral dress with a collar and long sleeves, casually holding a cigarette, her bare toes dug in the grass. The other wore a green polka-dot skirt with a ruffled white blouse, and her chestnut hair was neatly smoothed back by a white headband. Her round, kindly eyes smiled as she took a drag from her cigarette. My fingers went stiff. "Is that Miss Maggie with my grandma? I didn't know they were friends."

"Really?" Levi asked, surprised.

I looked up at him, mentally stiff-arming my appreciation for his shapely lips and the dust of light freckles beneath his tan so I could focus. "Don't you think that's odd? I never even saw my grandma talk to her."

He gave me a curious look, narrowing his eyes as though I'd said something strange. "It's been more than fifty years. Maybe they drifted apart."

"Maybe," I agreed quietly, thinking of the secret journal in my desk drawer at home.

A feral screech drew us both to the window. "Better go check on them. Can I borrow this?"

"Be my guest." Levi gestured for me to exit the study first. I slipped the photo into the pocket of my sundress and jogged downstairs, his clunky footsteps right behind. The screeching grew louder as we rounded the corner into the kitchen and burst through the back door.

"Is she hurt?" I made a mad dash to the tire swing.

"No, I just told her that a rhyme she heard wasn't a nice thing to repeat," Emmy said, sounding distressed. "I'm sorry, I didn't mean to upset her."

"Don't worry about it." I wiped the tears off Avery's face so I could work the pink glasses back over her head. "Did you say something that wasn't nice to Miss Emmy?"

After palming away another tear, she clapped her hands together and recited, with hand motions, "Here's the church, here's the steeple, lock the doors, and kill all the people."

She laughed hysterically. I'd seen enough horror movies that the twisted nursery rhyme made goose bumps prickle down my legs.

"Avery, Miss Emmy is in charge of you now. If she says you're not allowed to do something, you have to obey her or there will be consequences. Do you understand?"

Circling her toes on the grass, Avery nodded.

"Are you sure it's okay if I watch her today?" Emmy asked.

"You'll be fine," I assured her. "She likes you! And you can text me if you need anything."

The back door swung open and Mrs. Langford appeared on the porch. Tall and elegant with a glossy, highlighted bob, she looked like someone who had it all together. Her summery blouse was tucked into slacks and topped by a linen blazer. "Hello, Natalie," she called. I thought I could see her features chill slowly, like lukewarm water poured over ice.

"Hi, Mrs. Langford."

An uncomfortable silence yawned. As a ritual, even unexpected visits in San Solano were met with an offer of sweet tea.

Did she disapprove of me? I glanced down at my dress. It was shorter than the school dress code had allowed, but not short enough to advertise the goods.

"Well, I guess I'd better go," I said, and looked at Levi. "See you at the lake?"

"Yeah, I'll see you there."

"We'll walk you out," Emmy offered, taking Avery's hand again.

The glass outer door had already shut behind Mrs. Langford. Emmy chatted aimlessly as we walked up the porch steps and into the kitchen. Levi traipsed behind us.

"Have a good day, Natalie," Mrs. Langford said, her statuesque cheek bones looking somehow cruel even as they participated in a soft smile. No "you're welcome any time" or "tell your mom I said hello."

"Bye, Mrs. Langford," I replied, attempting to sound unfazed. As Emmy led me to the front door, I overheard Levi and his mom whispering in the kitchen. Emmy was busy talking to Avery and didn't notice this not-so-discreet conversation.

"I told you to discourage Emmy from taking that job," I could hear Mrs. Langford say.

"What was I supposed to say? That certain people are off-limits?"

Off-limits? Who did Levi mean? Certainly not Kate—*she* had babysat Levi and Emmy when she was a teenager. The Langfords were close to Miss Maggie, too.

But that left only me. Did Mrs. Langford know about the kiss? Did she wrongfully think I would get her son into trouble, or hear a fabricated rumor about me being promiscuous? She didn't seem to fit the holier-than-thou, premarital purity–obsessed profile, but I couldn't think of another explanation. Except the ancient drama between Lillian and Malachi.

Lillian and Malachi. I remembered the photograph of Miss Maggie and my grandma in my pocket and itched to have another look.

Levi caught up to me. "See you later, Nat," he said, his demeanor suddenly frosty even as he opened the door for me.

"Later," I said, forcing a smile.

SEVEN

While I tied colorful pool floats down in my truck bed, Abbie deposited two coolers, a stack of Frisbees, an oversized badminton set, and a tug-of-war rope.

"What is this, field day?" I asked as I climbed into the driver's seat.

Slathering sunscreen on her arms, Faith offered an indifferent shrug. "I already tried to rein her in. Good luck."

"I thought games would be fun," Abbie said. "Oh, here comes Juliana."

She didn't sound enthused. Abbie was a self-labeled attention sponge and professional flirt, but Juliana was the only person I'd ever met who could handily beat Abbie at her own game. Abbie didn't like it.

Juliana's long black hair glided behind her like a smooth stream of espresso as she swept toward the truck, wearing a dramatic, ankle-length skirt over her swimsuit. She used her phone as a mirror to smooth down her perfectly shaped eyebrows, her nails manicured a blinding fluorescent orange.

When she climbed in with Lindsey and set her beach bag on the seat, I heard glass clinking around in its depths. This night might be a little more unruly than I'd anticipated.

I waited until everyone had buckled—Juliana finally gave in with a purse of her lips—before pulling out of my driveway. As we picked up speed, my hair blew around in the warm wind and stuck to Faith's sunscreened shoulders.

"Did y'all hear about the dead animals?" Faith asked, wrinkling her nose. "This, on top of the stones in your yard..."

"Did you know the Travel Channel is thinking of adding San Solano to a 'Haunted Tour of the South' feature?" Lindsey asked. "Someone is screaming for attention."

I chewed on my lip. This new intel tracked with my latest theory.

"Ew!" Juliana gasped, plugging her nose. "What is that?" A second later, the smell hit me. Unpleasant odors were common around town—skunk spray, roadkill, manure—but the smell that wafted through the cab was downright offensive.

"It's just the poultry litter some of the local farmers use as fertilizer," Lindsey explained. Weird, how she'd had that locked and loaded.

Juliana grimaced. "It smells like dead bodies."

Lindsey stiffened and fell quiet.

The stench faded as we drove from San Solano to the nearby national forest. I noticed Bryce's Jeep not far behind us, and behind him, Levi's truck. A car full of junior girls sped past us on the one-lane road. "How many people did you invite?" I asked Abbie.

"Don't you worry your pretty little head," Abbie said. "Everyone but Grayson has already pitched in their ten dollars, so we have more than enough food."

When we reached the nearest campground and parked by a pavilion at the swimming area, the growl of the engine gave way to insects singing and a breath of wind in the pines. The grass faded to sand at the shore, and the water looked clean and dark, glittering in the sunlight.

Loud crooning drowned out the peaceful sounds of nature as the others arrived. The evening's playlist, a victim of Grayson's questionable taste, would consist of songs about tight blue jeans, trucks, exes, and beer.

"Ugh, bro country," Lindsey said, echoing my thoughts.

I unlatched the tailgate and stepped into the bed to get the coolers. "Can I help?" Levi asked.

"Sure," I said, and hoisted one down to him.

Grayson bounded up to Lindsey and flipped his blond hair out of his eyes. He skipped the courtesy of offering to help and tried to extract a box from her hands.

"These *are* working arms, you know," she said without relinquishing.

"Just trying to be a gentleman." Grayson shrugged off a look of defeat and walked away. He and Lindsey had history, if attending her quinceañera together and flirt-fighting for three years could be called a history.

Lindsey hefted the box toward the pavilion with little effort even though it contained a heaping bag of charcoal and heavy rocks to weigh down the tablecloths. Abbie set up the games and Grayson mercilessly cranked up the volume on his playlist while smearing sunscreen on his face.

I shed my tank and shorts, stripping down to my aqua bikini. Out of the corner of my eye, I noticed that Levi's expression was pointedly neutral, and he seemed suddenly unsure of what to do with his hands. He ran them through his hair, crossed them over his chest, and finally let them fall to his sides.

Smug, I grabbed a lime-green tube and waded into the water with Lindsey and Faith.

"Guys, no one help Lindsey if she drowns!" Grayson said. "She can do everything herself. Hashtag feminism."

"Don't be a dick, Grayson," Lindsey said.

"You're so touchy today!" he exclaimed.

"You wish," Lindsey fired back with a killer smirk. Everyone burst into taunts and laughter at Grayson's expense. He paddled away in mock injury.

"So, what do y'all think about the creepy stuff that's happening?" Bryce asked. "You're not behind any of it, are you? Because I think the animal dismembering would be a bridge too far."

"No!" Abbie splashed him for emphasis, hitting Levi instead. Levi gave her a warning look, cupped his hands, and sent a squirt of water up her nose. She playfully retaliated by trying to push his head under the water. He laughed and slung her over his broad, bare shoulders, where she flailed and fake-screamed until he tossed her over his head.

My chest tightened. Was something happening between them? Was that why Levi had gone cold at his house earlier? Since Abbie flirted indiscriminately, it was hard to tell when something meant more. Levi had always been like a cousin to her, but that chaste affection could turn on a dime.

That was why I hadn't told the twins about the kiss, or the quiet that followed: I didn't want their defensiveness of me to sour an old friendship. Faith, especially, was doggedly loyal, even more so than Lindsey, whose sympathy could hit a brick wall when some harsh sense-talking was needed. If I'd told Faith, she would have taken up the banner of my cause and dragged Levi back to San Solano by the ear to make him explain himself.

Vanessa paddled by on a float. There were gauze bandages taped to her shoulder, clinical white against her warm-toned brown skin. Lindsey had covered her cuts with a bandage today, too, and the wounds were dressed the exact same way.

"Bryce, are you accusing people again?" Vanessa asked, tightening the floral scrunchie that bound her springy curls. A leather wrap bracelet with an ivory cameo pendant dangled from her wrist, even in the water. I'd never seen her without it. "He really wants to get to the bottom of this. He asked the old lady at the gas station if she'd ever decapitated a deer."

"She said 'about five hunnerd!' Apparently, she used to be a taxidermist, so dead end there." Bryce shrugged. "But get this: when we mentioned the smell in town, she was like, 'That ain't the farms. It's them satanic women boilin' blood.' "

Everyone laughed. Vanessa rolled her eyes, and then caught me glancing at her bandages. She froze and averted her gaze.

"I guess I should start grilling," Lindsey said abruptly. "Nat, you want to help?"

I wanted to bronze the sandy-white tan lines from my track uniforms and hear more about what people thought of the dead animals, but I stood up and waddled toward shore, the inner tube stuck around my middle like a tutu.

"Do you know what happened to Vanessa?" I asked.

Lindsey wrung out her shoulder-length hair and pulled a bag of marinated chicken out of a cooler. "I don't know." She shrugged. "Will you shuck the corn while I start the grill?"

"Smooth subject change," I said, snarky.

"What do you want me to say? I don't know. Maybe she just has psoriasis or something."

"Or she got viciously attacked by a Yorkipoo?" I plopped down at the nearest picnic table.

"What's your deal, Nat?"

"What's *your* deal?" The rough husk of a corncob made a satisfying crunch as I peeled it. "You're being weird. What's wrong?"

Lindsey sighed, her expression softening. "I don't know. Sorry. It's just... everyone has big plans to go college, and I haven't figured out what I'm doing yet. It's hard."

"Lindsey, it's okay," I said, feeling guilty for giving her a hard time. "We're young. We don't have to have everything figured out yet."

"But most people do. I just don't want to be stuck here, with my life on pause, while everyone moves away and moves on."

I reached over to squeeze her hand. "I may be moving away, but I won't move on. You can come visit me whenever you want."

She gave me a small smile. "I know."

Devious laughter drew my eye to the shore. Abbie had corralled everyone to play tug-of-war in the shallow water, and Bryce and Grayson had taken the opportunity to try to pants Levi. Levi dropped the rope and stumbled across the sand, yanking his swim trunks well above his waistline, managing not to reveal anything. He lunged at Grayson, but Grayson escaped vengeance and trotted around with his fists raised victoriously.

"New rule! No pantsing!" Abbie yelled, her strict tone broken by a giggle.

Levi shook sand out of his hair and strode toward the pavilion, dabbing water off his chest with a towel. "Can I help with anything?"

"You can help Nat," Lindsey offered.

Levi sat down next to me, his swim trunks dripping water onto my toes. I listened to the corn husks breaking, tuning out Grayson's laughter. His voice was always a decibel or two higher than was comfortable for everyone else, even out here on the lake.

Levi's bare foot brushed mine under the table and my shoulders gave a tiny jolt.

"Sorry," he said.

I tried to think of a clever joke, but too much time passed.

Juliana traipsed out of the water in a cutout swimsuit that probably cost more than my whole summer wardrobe. She gathered her silky black hair and extracted her phone from her beach bag to take a selfie.

"I've been getting tons of comments on the photos I've taken here." She perched next to Levi, scrolling through hundreds of replies on a post. "I had no idea the San Solano massacres were so famous. Everyone wants to know if I'm going to see the haunted cabin."

"We *could* go," Abbie said. Somehow, she was able to hear their conversation over Grayson, now rummaging through a family-sized chip bag like a starving raccoon next to her. "We'd have to be careful not to get caught, but I think it would be fun."

"Abbie," I said in a warning tone. "The police will be watching like hawks until after the anniversary of the murders."

"This is our last summer here, all together," Abbie said, gesturing grandly. "We're expected to get a little wild, right?"

"Yes!" Juliana said with a cheer. She draped an arm over Levi's shoulder. "Let's get the booze. I want to hear about this Malachi chick."

Juliana's enthusiasm drew everyone in like a tractor beam. Soon the whole group had gathered on the pavilion. She produced an expensive-looking bottle of tequila and passed it around while my friends clambered to tell the story for her followers. Levi turned down the liquor, while Juliana found so many creative reasons to touch him that she couldn't have made more contact if she'd suddenly sprouted eight sticky tentacles. She flipped her camera so they could take a selfie together.

I snuck away to join Lindsey at the grill. Vanessa stood nearby, arms crossed. The two were whispering. They stopped.

"You aren't drinking, Nat?" Vanessa asked.

I shook my head. "I'm driving, and my ass is grass if my parents catch me drinking. At the very least, they'd stop paying for my phone and change the Wi-Fi password until I leave."

"Same," Vanessa said.

"A lot of people thought Malachi started the fire that burned down the church," I heard Abbie explaining to the camera. She paused to take a swig of tequila before passing it on. "But her parents said they were with her when the flames of their cooking fire suddenly leaped out of control. Malachi said she was angry and did it with her mind."

"Tell her about Easter!" a junior girl said, making grabby hands at the tequila.

Abbie explained about the baptistery filling with blood when the reverend baptized his daughter.

"No way!" Juliana exclaimed. "She seriously laughed? That's so creepy."

"Everyone in the church saw the same thing!" Abbie's cheeks were turning red with exhilaration.

“It wasn’t real,” Grayson said. “She dyed the water or something. People thought she was possessed, but she was just messing with them. She was a preacher’s kid with daddy issues.”

“There’s no such thing as ‘daddy issues,’ Gray,” Vanessa snapped. As if cued by her anger, a wave of heat from the charcoals gusted out from the grill and forced me to take a step back. “It’s called trauma.”

“Malachi was abused by her father, and she acted out,” I added, and felt the camera’s gaze on me.

“People have always felt threatened by rebellious, strong women,” Vanessa went on. “It was a full-on, twentieth-century Bible Belt witch hunt.”

“How do you think the victims died, if Malachi and her followers didn’t kill them?” Abbie asked.

“Maybe a suicide pact?” Vanessa offered. “They gathered in a church and drank poisoned wine. That sounds like some sick Jonestown crap to me.”

“But they tested it, and there wasn’t any poison,” I pointed out.

“Not that the people who analyzed it could detect,” Vanessa said with a shrug. “The first one was in 1921, and forensic testing still wasn’t that great fifty years later. If they had kept enough of a sample to test now, I bet they’d find poison.”

“Do y’all ever wonder if maybe Malachi really did have magic powers, though?” the junior girl asked. “Like, what if everything in Lillian Pickard’s book is true?”

“I think there’s only one way to find out,” Juliana said, turning the camera back on herself. “And it’s to take a tour of the haunted cabin where Malachi did her demon magic. Eek!”

Lindsey cussed under her breath.

Blessedly, no one had brought up my connection to Malachi. Even Grayson knew better than to subject my family to more unwanted attention.

After dinner we migrated back to the water. The slanted light of dusk turned everyone's eyes to gemstones and the water to flames. I felt as though I were stuck in sweet sap, pretending this summer could last forever.

At twilight, when the moon emerged like a scoop of vanilla ice cream, we loaded up the supplies. I climbed into my truck, where the leather seats were still warm from the sunlight that had snuck so softly away.

Lindsey, Faith, and I waited in the idling vehicle while Abbie and Juliana rested their elbows on Levi's open windows, talking and laughing. I couldn't hear their conversation, but I sensed they were volunteering us to participate in criminal trespass.

Abbie and Juliana finally pranced back to us after Levi had driven away with Grayson in tow, followed by Vanessa and Bryce in the Jeep. "We're meeting them at Sawmill and riding together to the cabin," Abbie said as she hop-stepped onto the bench seat.

"No, we're not," Lindsey said, her tone intense.

"Juliana has to," Abbie said. "Her followers are expecting it."

"All the more reason not to," I pointed out. "What if it goes viral? We'll get caught."

"You don't have to show your face if you don't want to," Juliana said.

"Or you could just drop us off at our car, Nat," Faith said, surprisingly game for this adventure.

"No," Lindsey said, glaring out the window. "If you're going regardless, you might as well have more people with you."

I was pretty sure Lindsey meant for the sake of safety, but Abbie clapped her hands. "Yay! It's more fun with a group."

"But I'm only going if you promise not to climb the fence," Lindsey said. "We are just going to *look* at the cabin. No trespassing."

"Natalie's dad is best friends with the sheriff," Faith said. "It's not like we'll get in real trouble."

"I wouldn't underestimate his willingness to teach us a lesson," I muttered.

"Fine, no trespassing," Abbie agreed. "Just drive or they'll be waiting on us."

Grudgingly, I followed Levi's taillights down the road. The dark woods were a vast expanse of mystery outside the blinding brights that charged before us.

About fifteen minutes later, we turned into the dusty Sawmill parking lot, empty and lit by a single streetlight. We parked next to Bryce's Jeep and climbed into the bed of Levi's truck.

The wind slithered along my neck as we cruised down dark and lonesome back roads. The farther we ventured, the more dilapidated the sparse houses became, leaning into the earth, the paint stripped from their weatherworn surfaces.

Finally, we turned onto the dirt road that would stop dead within sight of the cabin in the clearing. The loud whirring of insects and the droning of frogs died down. Even the wind seemed stiller. That god-awful stench pervaded the air.

Levi slowed to a stop in front of the towering chain-link fence with the sign COUNTY PROPERTY—NO TRESPASSING. Just outside the reach of his headlights, cloaked in wild wisteria and tucked among towering hardwood trees, the shadow of the abandoned log cabin awaited us.

I found myself wishing one of Jason's deputies would drive up and tell us pesky kids to go home.

EXCERPT:

PAGANS OF THE PINES: THE UNTOLD STORY OF MALACHI RIVERS

Lillian Pickard, 1968

After Ruth Rivers lost her first child, her son, in the storm, she felt a disturbance in the pregnancy of her second. The child went still in her womb.

According to Ruth's own telling, rather than seek out a midwife to deliver what she knew would be a stillborn baby, she fled to the woods. Superstitions about a sacred power in the glade had endured for generations. Something older than humankind resided there. It had moved beneath the earth and whispered through the boughs long before San Solano had a name in any language. The place had seduced many a searching soul.

A logging family had built a cabin homestead on the hallowed spot but abandoned it only five months later. Most people found the wild glade and its mysterious force unsettling.

Ruth turned to this arcane power as a last resort. Her husband, the reverend, would have accused her of faithlessness for beseeching an entity other than their Christian God for help. But God had allowed her son to die, and she no longer trusted him to revive the child she carried.

Before setting foot in the glade, Ruth removed her shoes and clothing and released her golden hair. She sank to her knees and dug her hands into the earth. She wept and wept under a summer moon, crying out to the untamed power there.

And the power answered.

The trees rustled in a phantom wind. The earth moved beneath her fingers, warm and alive. She heard a tortured caw and turned to find a bird with a broken wing ambling near.

She understood the message: a life for a life. She reached for the bird and wrung its neck.

The child quickened again.

At the time, Ruth was too desperate to know or care that deep magic stakes a claim. One day she would realize and would feel ashamed of the bargain she had made in the sacred glade where the vacant cabin sat like a watchman. She would not speak of the shame until she was an old woman, mere hours from the grave.

But that unspoken shame drove her daughter back to the dark power that had left its mark, that had made her what she was.

EIGHT

Natalie Colter

Levi slammed his door and flicked on a flashlight. Abbie stumbled out of the truck bed, tipsy, and she and Juliana laughed.

Lindsey slung her alert gaze through the shadows of the surrounding pines. In the mellow moonlight, her long-lashed brown eyes swam with terror.

"You okay?" I asked her.

"Yeah, fine," she answered, landing softly on the dirt.

Vanessa and Bryce hopped out of the cab and fell into step with us, their arms around each other. Our crunching footsteps were too loud in the quiet.

"You can't see anything from here," Juliana said, balancing on her tiptoes for a better view.

A metallic rattle made me realize Abbie was mounting the fence. "Grayson, give me a boost!"

Quicker than a snake strike, Lindsey caught Abbie's wrist and hissed, "You promised."

"Ouch!" Abbie twisted away from her. "You're being a buzzkill."

"If you go in there—"

"It's okay," Vanessa interrupted Lindsey in a low voice. She clutched her elbow and guided her away. "We can wait in the truck and keep a lookout."

"Do whatever you want." Abbie clumsily planted her flip-flop on Grayson's laced fingers.

"Here, take the keys," Levi said, and tossed them to Vanessa.

"Should I stay with you, Ness?" Bryce asked.

Vanessa waved him off. "We're fine. I'll call you if we see someone coming."

Grayson helped Abbie and Juliana to the other side, and Faith, who was wearing sneakers, scaled the fence without assistance.

"Need a boost?" Levi asked, shining his flashlight in my direction. His freckle-dusted skin took on a silvery cast in the moonlight.

"Um..." I curled my fingers through the chain links and lodged the toe of my sandal in an opening, but it was too small to find purchase. "Yeah, sure."

Levi gave the flashlight to Bryce and presented a hand for me to step in. I obliged. He wrapped the other just above my ankle, his fingers warm and steady as he launched me upward with ease. I pushed myself the rest of the way and dropped down on the other side, staggering.

Levi climbed and assumed an impressive side plank position in the air before landing next to me with a thud. As we hiked up a gradual incline behind the others, the thick grasses tickled my exposed calves, shooting shivers up my spine. I found myself wishing that we could fast-forward to eating buttery waffles at the twenty-four-hour diner.

The immense pines stood in a crescent-moon formation around the cabin. Knit closely together, they filtered the celestial light and lent a bewildering beauty to the clearing they guarded—the place that Lillian Pickard had called the "sacred glade." A stray wind shuddered through the boughs, stirring up the musty-sweet scent of wisteria and pine needles and making my damp bathing suit feel cold and slimy beneath my clothes.

Even though we'd already climbed the fence, it was here—in the clearing—where I sensed that we were truly crossing a barrier. *One that shouldn't be crossed,* I couldn't help thinking.

Juliana, Grayson, Abbie, Faith, and Bryce forged heedlessly ahead. Maybe they were just being plucky. Or maybe they were unreceptive to the menacing energy of this place.

Everything in me wanted to turn back. And if Levi hadn't been there, restraining his long-legged pace to keep even with me, I might have.

"Is something wrong?" he asked, brushing my hand with his, probably by accident.

I shook my head.

"Do you want to go back to the truck?"

"No," I answered.

"You can't think of any reason we shouldn't be here?" he asked, oddly probing.

I stopped and looked up at him, frowning, but could only see a glint of his eyes in the dark. Shoving away thoughts of Grandma Kerry's mental break and the gift I'd received from Miss Maggie, I said, "Other than the obvious? No. Can you?"

"No," he said, his tone layered and indecipherable.

As we drew close, Bryce shined the flashlight on the crooked front porch. I felt the tingling of unease crawl up the back of my neck. And that awful, rotten smell coming in waves—what could it possibly be?

Death, my imagination supplied.

Invasive vines and debris cloaked the steeply sloping roof. The rundown cabin looked and felt so eerie that I almost expected to see a figure leering at us through the window.

Grayson took long strides so he could be the first to conquer the creaky porch steps. But he hesitated when he reached the front door, his Adam's apple bobbing. Only after the light from Juliana's phone camera dwelled on his face for a few seconds did he locate the courage to shove it open.

He screamed.

Most of the group scampered backward, tripping over one another. I yelped but couldn't move, engulfed by fear. Levi alone remained perfectly calm, at least enough to shield me, his rock-solid forearm like a wall in front of me.

"I got y'all so bad!" Grayson cackled.

Abbie screeched his name and added a few choice words. Faith stomped onto the porch and smacked the back of his messy blond head.

Dropping his arm, Levi looked sideways at me, as though wondering whether I'd noticed the protective gesture.

Bryce raked a rough hand through his tousled brown curls, straightened his glasses, and picked up the flashlight he'd dropped in the scuffle. "You scared the shit out of me, man," he said. Grayson gave a self-satisfied grin and led the way into the one-room dwelling.

Soft purple-gray puffs of wisteria and snarls of vines draped over the entrance. A lock of my hair got snagged as I ducked to pass through. I trapped a squeal at the back of my throat as I freed myself.

Once inside, I blinked until my eyes adjusted to the musty-smelling darkness. For all my interest in our town's history, I had never visited the cabin, content to study the black-and-white photographs in Lillian's book.

Now that I had come, it felt inevitable. Like it had always been waiting for me.

I was spellbound by the place that had lived in my imagination for so long. Maybe, in a corner of my mind more remote than this cabin, I had sheltered a child-like belief in the wondrous, dark, dangerous magic of Malachi Rivers.

Dust motes churned with each of our tentative footfalls. The only natural light was a ghostly moonbeam falling through the obscured window, reaching across the weatherworn wooden boards. No furnishings remained besides rickety chairs, shelves holding growlers and pots, and a tarnished mirror that warped our reflections.

At the center of the room, a deep ring had been carved into the wooden planks.

"This is where Malachi and her friends did their magic," I whispered. "Inside the circle."

"So creepy," Juliana said, brushing away dirt and dust from the carving with her sandal.

"It's colder inside the circle!" Faith gasped. Arm extended, she wiggled her fingers.

The others tested her claim, but no one stepped across the line, preferring to edge around it. I inserted my hand and felt a chill, like slipping off a warm wool glove on a crisp day.

"Probably just a draft." Grayson shrugged.

"From where?" Faith asked. "It's warm outside."

They bickered, but my mind muted their voices. Mesmerized, I crossed to the center of the circle. The sensation reminded me of submerging my head at the lake, listening to the world go silent, and letting the gentle current carry me where it willed. I felt peaceful.

But that didn't last long.

There was an unmistakable brush of phantom fingers traveling down my cheek, almost affectionately.

With a shriek, I leaped backward out of the circle, upending one of the chairs. A chorus of questions began, but all I could manage was, "Something touched me!"

"It's okay," Bryce said softly, showing me his palm as though trying to calm a wild horse. "It was probably a spider or a cobweb or something."

"No, I felt fingers." My breaths rasped as I traced the lingering sensation that tickled the curve of my jaw.

So far, Juliana had respected my request for privacy, but not anymore. This freak-out was being *live streamed*. As I considered the hundreds, maybe thousands of people watching, my cheeks flamed.

"Do you think there might be something here with us?" Juliana asked. "What if it's Malachi?"

"Trying to communicate with her descendant from beyond the grave?" Grayson mocked.

"Wait, what?" Juliana turned to me with a flash of hunger in her eyes. "Are you related to Malachi?"

"Okay, I think we're done here," Levi said from across the circle.

"Seriously?" Juliana scoffed. "I'm just trying to—"

"She didn't even want to be in it, Juliana," Faith reminded her.

Irritably, Juliana relented and gave a sugarcoated sign-off to her followers.

"We should replay the video," Bryce suggested. "Maybe we'll see something."

The comforting sensation that only a moment ago had settled over my skin like a balm had turned sinister, pricking every hair on my body. "I'm going back to the truck," I said.

"I'll go with you," Levi started to say. But he was nearest to Abbie when her foot broke through a rotted board, and she clung to him as she sank calf-deep through the floor. He twisted around to extricate her, but she was laughing too hard to be of much help.

I left, trampling down the sagging porch steps and forging alone into the wooded shadows. My breath caught in my throat, and I was reminded of coughing up dirt in my dream. That last one had felt so real, realer than ever. Was I losing my mind, imagining things? Things like magically appearing journal entries and otherworldly contact?

At least the twin glows of the headlights in the distance let me know I wasn't the only one ready to leave.

But as I drew closer, my footfalls silent on the lush grass, I realized the lights were actually coming from dripping, pale candles. Two figures sat within their flittering glow: Lindsey and Vanessa. Their hands rested on their knees, palms displayed. Lindsey's right wrist was bound by twine to Vanessa's left. They had traced a distinct circle around themselves on the dirt road.

I halted in my tracks. If I was playing with a full deck—I hadn't ruled out the possibility that a few cards were missing—that left two possible scenarios: either Lindsey and Vanessa were pulling a much more sophisticated trick than Grayson's amateur-hour jump scare, or...

Or Malachi still had worshippers, and my best friend was one of them.

The talismans on my property, the sachet that Bryce's cat found, the mysterious wounds that Lindsey had been so defensive about, the journal from Miss Maggie... maybe Lindsey's entanglement in the cult explained everything.

Gulping down the sour panic that crept up my throat, I dared to sneak closer and take refuge behind a pine tree. Lindsey and Vanessa were arguing in harsh whispers and hadn't noticed me.

"Because you know the Triad is going to be pissed," Vanessa was saying.

"What should we have done, chain them all in a basement?" Lindsey asked. "They were going to come here no matter what. We couldn't let them do it alone."

"We could have at least stopped Nat from coming," Vanessa said.

Why would they single me out? Why would they want me, specifically, to stay away from the cabin?

"Maybe it's *good* that she's here." Lindsey scattered a handful of pine needles at the base of the candles. She removed a bundle of dried herbs from her pocket and set it aflame, waving it around and filling the air with a haze of smoke. "Sidestepping that ridiculous blood oath hasn't worked yet, and we're running out of time."

Triad? Blood oath?

I could only hope this was a hokey, harmless society for bored small-town women, one that had nothing to do with Malachi. But the twine on their wrists and the circle in the dirt begged to differ.

"But they might sense her presence," Vanessa argued.

"If they do, we can handle it," Lindsey replied.

"They're getting more powerful, Linds."

Who were they talking about? The Triad? Was the Triad the leader, or leaders? Was Miss Maggie one of them? Was this Grandma Kerry's legacy?

It struck me that this could go far deeper than I ever imagined. What if my parents knew about this? What if Kate had been playing coy when I'd asked her about the journal? Now that I'd found out Lindsey and Vanessa's secret, I feared there was no one I could definitively check off the list of suspects.

"You think I don't know that?" Lindsey huffed, and then shook her head. "Can we stop? We're not supposed to fight inside the sacred circle."

"You're right." Vanessa sighed and closed her eyes.

They lifted their arms and bent them at the elbows, revealing marks drawn on the palms of their bound hands: on Lindsey, a dark blot, and on Vanessa, an X. If that dot was blood, then these were indisputably two of the three elements of the Malachian mark.

I dug my fingers into the rough pine tree bark, trying not to panic.

They began chanting in perfect unison.

"Shadowed night and silver moon, hark and heed the Warden's Rune. By powers of earth, blood, and bone, may our aim be clear and known. Spirits, thy strength in us confirm, that no one here should come to harm. As darkness flees from burning flame, pray let evil stake no claim. By this rite we thus decree: as we will, so mote it be."

Like a spider's prey, I was paralyzed, recalling the words that had suddenly appeared on the first page of the journal: *By the powers of earth, bone, and blood, proceed we Wardens to our noble work.* Runes, magic rituals, sacred circles... In San Solano, those things could never be harmless. In San Solano, they were flashing neon lights that spelled out *murderer.*

They called themselves the Wardens, and Lindsey and Vanessa's incantation implied that they didn't want their friends to get hurt. What about the other people of San Solano? What about someone—say, me, for example—who might unwittingly discover their dark secrets?

That Lindsey even had secrets *to* discover was a stinging slap in the face. How many sleepovers and cross-country runs and inside jokes had we shared since she fell under the spell of a violent cult?

"I feel a disturbance," Vanessa said when the chant was over, dropping her voice to a whisper. "It's Nat. She's nearby."

"Do you think she can see us?" Lindsey asked.

"I wouldn't be surprised. Her Sight is getting clearer." Vanessa opened her eyes and snapped her head in my direction. "Nat?" she called out.

With a fraught gasp, I ran. I heard rattling as one or both of them scaled the fence. Last year, I would have been able to outrun Lindsey, but she'd gotten so damn *fast* recently, and inhumanly tireless.

Scratchy underbrush tore at my legs as I ran back through the dense copse of trees toward the cabin. I barreled over the uneven terrain faster than my eyes could see in the moonlight, a swift pursuit at my heels. My toe struck something hard and I took a fall, landing on scattered rocks that scraped my flesh and bruised my limbs.

Through the throbbing pain, I propped up on my elbows to look around. Blinking into the darkness, I found that the rocks were not rocks after all. Decaying fur, empty-eyed skulls, and other unidentifiable bits of animal remains were strewn through the grass.

I lay sprawled across a pile of bones.

NINE

"Shhh!" Lindsey arrived to clamp a hand over my mouth, cutting off my shriek of horror. I scrambled to my feet and struggled to pry her away, but her sinewy arm was unmovable.

"Nat?" Levi yelled. Through the columns of trees, I watched him exit the cabin and jog toward the road, continuing to call my name.

Before I could react, a guttural noise, like a choked garbage disposal, came from the deep woods.

I froze in Lindsey's clutches, pure dread icing through my veins. I knew the calls of hogs and coyotes. This was unlike anything I'd ever heard, between human and animal.

"They're here," Vanessa whispered.

"Go," Lindsey said. "I'll catch up."

Vanessa darted through the darkness, nimbler than a deer and twice as fast. Lindsey released me, trusting me not to scream again.

She produced an herb sachet and a tiny vial of dark liquid from her pocket. Dumping fragrant herbs in her palm, she spilled three drops of the liquid and made a mixture. When she dabbed the sticky paste to my forehead, I jerked away.

"I'm trying to protect you!" she snapped, her eyes sharp in the shadows.

More strangled, animalistic moans traveled through the night. This time, it sounded like two creatures answering each other's call.

Terror gave me no choice but to capitulate. The paste felt gritty as Lindsey drew on my forehead, each stroke familiar. "When I'm done, run back to the road as fast as you can," she commanded. "You'll be safe on the other side of the fence."

"What about the others?" The cloying scent of herbs and the putrescent, rotting remains threatened to make me gag.

"I'll protect them. They're not the ones being hunted, at least not right now."

"Hunted?" I repeated feebly.

"Just do what I say, and don't mention any of this." She raised her hands again and turned her palms toward me. One was covered in the herb paste, but the dot on her other glared like a watchful pupil as she rushed through another incantation. "Powers of the still, dark earth, mislead all prying eyes. Cast thy veil of trickery; by Warden's Rune, disguise."

With that, she bounded away.

Another howl came, closer now. I sprinted to the fence so fast that I lost a sandal and slammed against the chain links. Desperation lent me strength and I managed to foist myself over. I landed unevenly on the dirt road, but someone caught me before I stumbled onto my backside.

"Whoa!" Levi said, propping me up.

I whirled to face him.

"What's wrong?" He absorbed my wild-eyed expression but didn't seem to notice the mark on my forehead. "I heard you yell and came back looking for you."

"That sound... there's something out there," I managed.

"It's just wild hogs," he said, his hand hovering near my elbow.

That was the logical explanation I wanted to believe, but I knew what I'd heard. I looked over my shoulder, expecting... What did I expect? The fear was amorphous in my mind: beastly, demonic, but undefined.

"Lindsey and Vanessa ran off, but the truck's unlocked," Levi said, gesturing. "You want to wait inside?"

I nodded. More than anything, I wanted to leave, but I clung to Lindsey's promise that I'd be safe here, no matter how gullible that made me.

"Do you want me to look for your sandal?" he asked.

I shook my head.

The bench seat creaked under my weight as I settled in and shut the door, encasing myself in silence and solitude. While Levi walked to the driver's side, I checked my forehead in the side mirror. It showed me a Malachian mark drawn messily across my skin, plastered with strands of blond hair. I looked like I'd just escaped a compound. With the hem of my shirt, I rubbed it away, leaving a dark smear on the fabric. Then I tucked my hands under my thighs to stop them from trembling.

I thought about what Lindsey had done. Could it be a ruse? The incantations, the sacred circle, even the talismans... She and Vanessa could have faked them. Maybe they even convinced Kate to give me the journal.

But that bit about "misleading prying eyes"? There was no explaining how the spell actually worked. It obscured the very obvious mark on my forehead—Levi hadn't spared it a glance.

Unless he was in on this, it made no sense. And frankly, that would be the most mean-spirited prank in history. I would only go to those lengths to punish my worst enemy.

As Levi got in the car, I came close to spilling everything. But I hesitated. Lindsey was my best friend. Didn't I owe her a chance to explain? Maybe she had been brainwashed. Maybe she was protecting me from the cult leaders after realizing she'd been deceived.

After all, she was the one who'd theorized that they would be keen to ensnare me. She could have been trying to warn me the other day.

She couldn't *really* be one of them. A Malachian. A cultist. Not Lindsey.

She would explain everything. We would tell the police as much as we needed to get her out, to get her safe.

For a protracted moment, Levi stared through the windshield at the woods, long fingers lightly drumming on the steering wheel.

"What's taking them so long?" I asked, eager to have those buttery waffles with a heaping side of damn good explanations.

"They were trying to summon the spirit that touched you," Levi said. "Anything for a thrill, right?"

I tossed my head in disapproval.

"So, what do you think that was in the cabin?" he asked.

"I'm hoping it was my imagination," I whispered. "But that's scary in its own way. I feel like I can't trust my own mind right now."

"Don't you . . . ?" he started, and trailed off.

"Don't I what?"

"I'm just . . . I'm surprised that you're afraid out here."

Insulted, I scoffed. "Everyone's afraid sometimes."

"That's not what I meant. I don't know." He tapped his fingers on the wheel again. "You confuse me."

Wait, you're *the one who's confused?* I wanted to ask. Of course, this was a natural consequence of accidentally falling for the artistic, semi-aloof, tortured-soul type, the type whose award-winning poems were framed proudly next to his athletic trophies in the cases at school. He had no inkling of how complicated he came across.

Rather than bristle at the implication that *I* was somehow to blame for our false start last summer, I let his words sink in. If he found me confusing, that meant he thought about me. He spent time trying to puzzle me together.

"How am I confusing?" The old leather squeaked as I folded my bare foot under me and angled my body toward him. I'd been so ready to get the heck out of here, but now, I felt as I had stepping into Malachi's sacred circle; fear and excitement braided together, indistinguishable and inseparable.

"Sometimes you seem like an open book. Like a normal person living a normal life. But..." He chewed on his bottom lip, deliberating. "I know you have secrets."

I laughed. "I don't have secrets! I'm an awful liar. I mean, I can lie by omission. I haven't told anyone but Lindsey about..."

Now it was my turn to trail off.

"Our kiss?" he asked.

I sucked in a rapturous breath. Not *the* kiss. *Our* kiss. "Yeah."

The cover of night gave me the freedom to shamelessly study Levi: the way his damp cotton shirt fitted his form like armor, the blunt line where his fiery hair met his soft, touchable nape, the strength of his hands gripping the steering wheel as though he couldn't trust them not to touch me.

I should have asked him what kind of secrets he thought I was keeping. But another question seemed far more urgent.

Feeling like I was diving off a cliff into waters of unknown depths, I asked, "Do you ever think about it? The kiss?"

His response was to drop his hands to his lap and frown at them. I girded myself for disappointment. Then his gaze locked on mine and a thrill spilled through me, warm and invigorating. "I think about it all the time," he said.

My breath lodged in my throat. Fear transformed so easily into desire. They both seared through my nerves and made me feel newly alive.

Levi shifted in his seat, facing me, and I watched his broad chest expand with breath. I unfolded my legs and inched toward him. He rested his hand on the seat, one step closer to making contact.

Fantasies of creating a brand-new moment to savor for weeks, even months, flooded through my mind. Those stolen seconds of sunshine, sweat, and surprise had lost so much of their addictive nectar, wrung dry by my greedy memory. This would open a new universe of sights and sensations in which to revel: the night, the stars, the close quarters, the cling of my cool clothes on my skin, the cadence of the words he'd just spoken.

But laughter and mingling voices announced the others' return. A flash-light beam bounced through the trees. I would have sacrificed myself to whatever lurked in the woods for just one more minute alone with Levi.

The cabin light seemed more garish than comforting when Abbie opened my door. "Ooh, are we interrupting something?" she asked, poking my side. "Nat and Levi... I've never even considered it before. I'm not sure how I feel about it."

"Abs, you are a slovenly drunk." I chuckled, nervous, and saw Levi's mouth quirk up out of the corner of my eye. "We were just waiting together."

"I'm not drunk!" Abbie insisted, her allegation already slipping from her mind.

"Where're Vanessa and Lindsey?" Faith asked from outside.

I swallowed the lump in my throat and shrugged. "They were gone when we got here."

Instead of giving me a chance to move, Juliana squeezed past Abbie and climbed over me to the empty space next to Levi.

"Why would they leave?" Bryce asked, peering back into the woods. "You don't think the cops came and arrested them, do you? Oh god. I should have stayed with Ness."

"They're fine, Bryce," Faith said. "They're just planning to scare us. Hurry up and get in, y'all. I don't want them sneaking up."

Abbie plopped on my lap while Juliana seemed pleased to have an excuse to jam up against Levi. This time, I didn't feel that traitorous pinch of jealousy. Instead, I was gratified that he'd been alone with me and not with her.

Faith perched on Grayson and rested her elbow on Bryce, who was pinned to the window. "Did y'all hear the coyotes?" Bryce asked, voice muffled.

"You mean the hogs?" Grayson asked.

I didn't know how anyone could confuse the two, but I didn't really care at the moment. Sandwiched between my friends, I felt safe again. Maybe Lindsey did go to all that effort for nothing but a good scare. Maybe it was a grand gesture of friendship, a fond farewell to our high school shenanigans.

A dark shadow moved by the passenger window, eliciting shouts from the others. Abbie mewled from my lap. I let out more of a pathetic whimper. Another palm slid across Levi's window, and then Vanessa's laughing face popped up. She dangled the car keys from one pointer finger and my lost sandal from the other.

Levi manually rolled down the window and accepted both. The engine gave a gurgle as it started up. Our fingers didn't touch as he handed me my sandal.

The truck bed dipped, and I turned to see Lindsey settling in. Bryce climbed out to join Vanessa, giving us a little space.

"All right, let's get out of here," Levi said in a low voice, shifting into reverse.

We headed back toward friendly streets, passing a police cruiser on its way to the cabin. Everyone but Levi ducked so we wouldn't get pulled over.

"Yikes," Grayson said. "Close call."

Next to me, Juliana scrolled through the responses to her live stream. I had to blink away to keep from getting a headache. I turned around to look at Lindsey.

Her toned arms were spread out across the wall of the cargo bed. The bandage on her wound had detached on one side and was flapping, blood-stained, in the wind. Her brown hair looked shadow-black and streamed around her like a villain's cape. I turned back around to rub the moist stain on my shirt from wiping the Malachian mark off my skin.

Per tradition when it came to late-night adventures in San Solano, someone suggested we hit up the diner. Levi dropped us off at our cars on the way. He offered me a deep nod as I climbed out, and I tucked it away as a promise that we would find a way to be alone again.

Next time I would ask what secrets he thought I was keeping. Did he believe the cult had survived? Did he think I was a part of it, because of my lineage?

His first guess might be right, but the second certainly wasn't. I would set the record straight soon enough.

As I walked around the back of his truck, I bumped into Vanessa. "Here, hold this," she said, and dumped white powder into my hand. I thought I smelled something aromatic and smoky, like charred lavender buds. "What tha—?"

"By ash of bone and cleansing fire, forget what's strange that hath transpired. Mystic events from mind now scour, to recall at an auspicious hour."

She blew, scattering the powder to the wind.

EXCERPT:

PAGANS OF THE PINES: THE UNTOLD STORY OF MALACHI RIVERS

Lillian Pickard, 1968

I met Malachi when we were thirteen. A compulsory attendance law forced her into public school, and she was something of a legend already when she joined my class. Rumors that she had paralyzed a man's arm, started the fire that had burned her father's old church, and flooded the baptistery of the new church with blood on Easter Sunday agitated the teachers and aroused our imaginations.

My parents did not entertain tawdry gossip. Upon hearing that Malachi would join my class, they encouraged me to befriend her.

Our teacher would not permit us to stare at the newcomer during lessons, but lunch on the schoolhouse lawn was another matter. It was September. Malachi sat alone under a tree, her meal untouched beside her. She was pale, tense, and very pretty, with gold hair and gray eyes the color of a wrathful summer squall. Much like a disgraced queen, she was the subject of every whisper, exhibiting the air of someone who found us unworthy of her company.

I approached and asked, "May I sit with you?"

She studied my face before she said yes, furthering my perception that it was she who had set herself apart from us, rather than the other way around.

"I'm Lillian," I said.

"I know. Miss Mauldin calls on you a lot."

I remember blushing, but secretly, I felt proud. "Did you enjoy this morning's lesson?" I asked. I opened my lunch pail and waved the hungry flies away from my bacon sandwich, apple, and slice of cake.

"I'm not any good at arithmetic," Malachi said, picking at her cuticle. "I like reading and writing."

"You'll like afternoon lessons, then," I assured her.

She leaned back on her palms and peered over my shoulder. "Who's she?"

I turned and found her looking at a girl with tangled, dull brown hair and an even duller brown dress. She sat alone, but for the boys who liked to hassle her. Underneath the grime, she was the prettiest girl in class. "Oh, that's Johanna Mead. Her papa doesn't like her coming to school, so she comes as seldom as possible. Sometimes she brings nothing but a boiled potato, and I give her some of my lunch. I'll save my cake for her. What did you bring?"

"Ham slices and a biscuit with blackberry jam. She can have it all."

I'd taken a bite of my sandwich, but guilt made it go down like a lump of clay. I wondered if I should save my whole lunch for Johanna, too. Ignoring the rumbling in my belly, I wrapped my sandwich back up and dropped it in the pail. "Why do people say you did all those terrible things?" I asked.

"I reckon it's 'cause I did. The fire was an accident, though."

"An accident? What happened?"

Malachi pursed her lips and dug into the grass with the toe of her shoe. Her clothing was quality and clean, but simple as simple could be. "I was right livid with my mama and papa that day, and I was staring at the cook stove in the parish house. Everything went out of control. My power over fire is more unwieldy than the others. That's why I never use it in spells, except for a small candle flame."

"Spells?" I repeated flatly. "You mean witchcraft? Magic?"

She nodded.

"Magic isn't real."

She didn't seem to care whether I believed her, closing her eyes and tipping her face to the sky. "You can ask the pendulum if I'm lying."

"The what?"

She sat up and dug into the pocket of her dress, extracting some kind of canine tooth tied to a leather cord.

"What is that?"

"It's a fox fang. Bones work best for divination."

I shuddered, but she had piqued my interest. "Do you kill animals to get their bones?"

"I take only what nature willingly provides," she answered.

I looked to make sure Miss Mauldin wasn't watching. "How do you use it?"

"You ask it whatever you want to know, but it has to be a question with a yes or no answer. First, you establish what means yes and what means no." She dangled the fox fang over the grass, holding the leather cord between her thumb and index finger. "Are my eyes brown?" she asked. I watched, holding my breath until the fang started swinging from side to side. "Is Lillian's hair auburn?" The fang swung forward and back. "Forward and back means yes," Malachi declared.

"It's a trick!" I said. "You're moving it yourself."

Malachi smiled. "Here, try. You'll feel it."

I looked again to make sure Miss Mauldin wasn't watching. If necessary, I could say I had only played the new student's game to make her feel included. No one had to know about my deeper curiosity.

I accepted the leather cord from Malachi and held it the way she had. "Does Malachi have real magic?"

The pendulum yanked forward and back. I gasped in awe.

After that Malachi and I became fast friends. She often ate dinner at my house but never accepted my parents' invitation to stay the night. Whenever she tarried past mealtime, Reverend Rivers would belt her for fraternizing with the "unsaved." My family were devout Episcopalians.

Right away I understood that Malachi had a complicated relationship with her parents. She both despised and pitied her mother. She would defend her father in the face of my parents' concern, but privately—to me, who was powerless to intervene—she would speak of him with blistering hatred.

Once I saw stripes on the backs of her thighs. My father had only ever whapped me lightly with a paddle, and only because I had been terribly insolent. I couldn't imagine the anger it took to make those marks on her young flesh, or how I would feel if my father had treated me thus.

"Why did he do that to you?" I remember asking her.

She finished dressing. My growth spurts made hand-me-downs of even my favorite new dresses, and Malachi was waifish enough to wear them. I remember her staring into my mirror, eyes darker than dark, the color of cold steel. " 'The blueness of a wound cleanseth away evil,' " she replied.

Sometimes I felt unworthy of Malachi's friendship. I was blind to half the world, and she was my guide. It was as though she could see in the dark and I could not. Her suffering made her sage; the darkness educated her in its terrifying mysteries. She spoke its language, and she was drawn to others who spoke it. At school, we brought Johanna into our ranks. Malachi made sure to be at my house on Monday afternoons, when Dorothy Hawkins—who worked as a housekeeper at the Cartwrights' place down the road—came to do our laundry. Dorothy trusted Malachi and spoke openly about the senseless murder of her brother. In their presence, I felt naïve and useless, a stranger to suffering even though my older brother, Daniel, had fought in the Great War and I had daily worried for his safety until he returned. I may as well have been a toddler playing in the corner while they spoke of the sins committed against them. I was once foolhardy enough to recommend that Dorothy approach my father, a lawyer, for help bringing her brother's murderers to justice. She laughed.

But Malachi assured me of my value as her friend and as her apprentice. Though I possessed no magic of my own, she recognized my gift for gathering natural materials and preparing teas, elixirs, herb bundles, and the like. She said my touch brought a playful energy to every one of her earth spells, from honey abundance jars to lavender beauty charms.

As for the pendulum that had started our friendship, I used it to try to divine whom I would marry or which dress I should order. But Malachi, Dorothy, and Johanna began to ask darker questions. Like whether they ought to seek revenge.

TEN

Natalie Colter

ONE MONTH AND SEVEN DAYS UNTIL THE CLAIMING

All through the night, sinister shadows scuttled through my dreams, but the sunrise banished them.

Basking in the moment that Levi and I had shared, I stretched languidly in bed and shivered. When would I see him next? Everyone would be at the Heritage Festival, but that was almost three weeks away. I hoped I wouldn't have to wait that long.

My alarm rang, reminding me that I needed to get ready to babysit Avery. That evening I had a meeting for festival volunteers. I wouldn't have the luxury of time to replay Levi's words like an addict needing my fix.

I threw off the sheets and bounced to my closet to get dressed, but something caught my eye. Atop the mountain of my dirty clothes hamper, my tank top from last night bore a reddish-brown stain that resembled dried blood and dirt mixed together. Frowning, I separated it from my swimsuit and gave the stain a sniff, finding it oddly fragrant. I'd earned a few bruises climbing the fence, and there were scratches on my legs from the underbrush, but I hadn't cut myself.

Someone knocked on our front door. I heard Mom greet Lindsey and welcome her inside. Maybe she'd forgotten I was working today.

Chucking the shirt back in the hamper, I grabbed a pair of shorts and a flowy floral blouse.

"Hey," Lindsey said. She cracked the door and peeked inside.

"Hey. I can't run today. It's my first full day with Avery."

"That's not why I'm here." She stepped in and closed the door. Her rich brunette hair was pulled into a neat ponytail, and she wore skintight, black athletic wear. She carried a duffel bag that usually held a change of clothes and toiletries for after our runs. "Where's the Book of Wisdom?"

"Book of Wisdom?" I asked, slinging a glance at my shelves.

She dropped the bag. It sounded curiously heavy. "The leather book Kate gave you."

"I have no idea what you're talking about."

"Wow, Vanessa did a number on you." She stalked over and snapped her fingers in my face. When that didn't accomplish what she wanted, she spoke at the ceiling, as though addressing a higher power. "This would be an auspicious hour, please and thank you!"

"What are you doing?" I sidestepped her to shed my sleeping shorts. "I need to leave for work."

"No, you don't. Kate asked Emmy to take over today."

"What? Why?"

"This is more important than your summer job. Kate knows that better than anyone."

"More important than saving up for a car that I can take to college? Because that's important."

"Yup." She scooped up my backpack and rummaged through it before heading straight for my desk drawer. "Here it is." Victorious, she held up a thick, ancient leather journal. "Maybe this will jog your memory."

"How did that get there?" I asked, buttoning my shorts and stalking over to rip it from her grasp.

"Nat, I need you to remember everything." She unzipped her duffel bag, removed a pouch, and waved it near my nose like smelling salts.

"What is that?" I asked, backing away.

"Bone ash and charred lavender buds."

"Bone ash?" I repeated. The smoky scent stirred something in the basement of my memory, something made of shadows and secrets, like an old trunk locked away, its horrors hidden from sight. I imagined the trunk covered in thick dust, imagined blowing that dust away just like Vanessa blew the herbs and ash from my hand last night. . . .

"Oh my god." I stumbled back and dropped onto the bed. From the stones in my yard to the animalistic howls that filled the night, everything came stampeding back. "What did you do to me?" I asked through gritted teeth. Talismans and cold-blooded animal sacrifice—these I could process, even if I couldn't process my best friend's involvement. What I could *not* wrap my head around was the chilling idea that someone could hijack my memories.

"I'm sorry, we just couldn't have you asking questions last night. We had to make you forget."

"You're one of them," I whispered. "A Malachian."

I expected Lindsey to avert her brown eyes, to fidget her hands. Deep down, she had to know it was wrong to associate with murderous fanatics, no matter how charismatic or coercive they may be. But her expression struck an unnerving contrast with the pictures of us wearing goofy smiles displayed around the room. The dark strokes of her eyebrows were hard lines, her glittering smile and uninhibited laugh distant memories preserved only in the frames on the wall. "That's not what we call ourselves," she replied.

"You're manipulating me. Twisting my preconceptions, making me think things are real that aren't. Is this how the Malachians brought you into their cult?"

"Like I said, that's not what we—"

"Fine, the *Wardens*. Whatever you want to call them, they killed the twelve boys in the sanctuary, didn't they? In 1971?"

Lindsey rolled her eyes, a flippant response to *murder*. I wondered how I hadn't noticed anything different about her until recently. Over the past six months, she had smiled, laughed, and socialized less. Her hips used to sway when she walked, but now her gait was plain, confident, square-shouldered, as if the cords of muscle framing her feminine curves had quietly become more pronounced. "I can't answer your questions."

"You're going to have to." I rose to her level, refusing to be intimidated. That competitiveness we shared was coming to the fore with a vengeance. "I'm not going to drop this."

"I don't want you to drop it. But last night wasn't supposed to happen the way it did. You weren't supposed to see what you saw yet, and Vanessa and I didn't know what else to do. Miss Maggie was busy with something important, and she's the only one who can answer your questions."

"Why her?" I brushed my thumb over the Malachian mark—or Warden's Rune—stamped into the cover of the journal. "Is she your leader? The Triad?"

"You heard that, huh?" she asked, defusing the tension by strolling around to look at the pictures of us. "She's one of three. Kind of implied in the name."

"What were you trying to protect me from last night? Was it them? Miss Maggie? The Triad?"

Lindsey turned. I saw the same fear in her eyes as last night. Whatever had been with us in the woods near the cabin elicited genuine terror. I just needed to find out if the Triad and what inspired that terror were one and the same.

Lindsey thought she was protecting me, but it was she who needed protection. She was in too deep.

"If you're in danger, we need to tell Jason," I pleaded, squeezing her arm. "Let's tell your mom. I just want you to be safe."

"You don't understand..." She trailed off, biting into her bottom lip. "I literally can't tell anyone anything, just like you literally couldn't remember anything."

"I overheard you and Vanessa talking about a blood oath," I said gently. "Is a blood oath what's stopping you? Is that why you have so many cuts?"

She didn't acknowledge my question. We stared each other down. For all my fascination with cults, I had never learned how to "deprogram" a victim. I didn't want to say the wrong thing and drive Lindsey away. But I didn't want to fall down the rabbit hole myself.

"I don't know whether your group is responsible for the last massacre or is just a weird Malachi fan club," I said eventually, "but I'm going to the police. I'm your best friend, and I have no choice."

"Will you tell them about your grandma?" Lindsey asked evenly. "You must have seen her contributions to the Book of Wisdom."

My eyes narrowed. "This is bigger than my grandma's reputation, and I'm not going to let you use her to shame me into silence."

Lindsey raised an eyebrow, looking impressed at my gumption.

"Come with me to the sheriff's office," I pleaded. Even though I would let my grandmother's name be dragged through the mud to save Lindsey, I wouldn't do it lightly. "As long as you haven't hurt anyone, they're not going to punish you. You're a victim."

She didn't move. I marched to the desk and reached around her to grab my keys and wallet, but she blocked me.

"I can't let you do this," she warned.

"Are you going to stop me? Hog-tie me and drag me to Miss Maggie's doorstep?"

She shrugged, but it came off more aggressive than ambivalent. "I could if I wanted to."

Scoffing, I tried again. She caught my wrist in a vise-like grip and muscled me back to the bed, tossing me on my stomach and pinning my arm behind my back.

"Stop!" I said, trying to keep my voice low.

She relented. I scrambled to face her and found her just as unruffled and determined as before. That maneuver had been effortless for her.

"There's a better way that doesn't involve fighting."

"Better way to what?" I asked.

"Keep you from doing something boneheaded. You can take a blood oath and promise me that you won't go to the police until after you've talked to Maggie."

I laughed, a little madly. "I'm not doing that."

"Listen, if it doesn't work, you can go straight to the station. But if it works, maybe you can admit that this isn't about murder and manipulation—it's about magic, and there's so much more for you to learn and understand before you cry wolf to people who can't help us."

I closed my eyes and massaged my temples. Her logic was sound, but I didn't like it. "Fine," I said.

She returned to her duffel and extracted a length of twine, a cloth, and a sheathed knife.

"Whoa!" I launched off the bed and dropped my voice to a harsh whisper. "What's with the knife?"

"It's a blood oath, Nat," she whispered back. "What did you expect?"

"I was thinking just a pinprick or something."

"It won't be bad. Trust me."

I cautiously surrendered a finger. She grabbed my hand and pricked the center of my palm. A blood drop bubbled up. She cut her own hand and bound our wrists deftly with twine. Blood to blood, she pressed our palms together.

I grimaced. Our pulses beat in our warm, slick hands. Their rhythms gradually aligned, synchronizing, straining together like magnets.

"Repeat after me," Lindsey instructed. " 'I swear that I will not approach the police or anyone besides the Wardens until I have spoken to Maggie and have a clearer understanding of the situation.' "

Raking in a weary sigh, I echoed her words, with a few corrections from her along the way.

When she was satisfied, she closed her eyes and recited an incantation. "Power of blood, our heart-sworn oath secure; may our spoken word be vigorous and ever to endure. This vow my sister shall not break, for only maker can unmake."

Before I knew it, she had severed the twine and was using the cloth to dab away the blood. "See? That wasn't so bad."

"It also isn't real."

She tossed the bloody cloth in my hamper, repacked her duffel bag, and reached for my keys, tossing them to me on her way out the door with a smirk. "Good luck with the police."

I started to storm out but remembered the journal and doubled back. Their "Book of Wisdom" was the most convincing physical evidence I had, and they'd dropped it right in my lap.

The sheriff's office was located on the square downtown, less than ten minutes away. Full of righteous determination, I drove well over the speed limit.

But as I left the open country behind and approached the grids of neighborhood streets, my truck's engine sputtered out. Rolling to a stop, I pulled onto the shoulder and realized I was only yards beyond the street sign for Willow Way, Maggie's street.

It could be a coincidence. I'd never expected my hand-me-down truck to last this long, which was why I put most of my summer job money into savings for a new car. As a test, I told myself I intended to drive to Maggie's house and turned the ignition. The engine rumbled healthily back to life. Playing along, I changed course and turned onto Willow Way. But as soon as I drove past the far side of Maggie's property line, the needle of my gas gauge flung itself from half-full to empty with almost comical certitude.

My breaths came in bursts, faster and shallower as I started to feel like a rat in maze. Until this moment, I could have believed the Wardens were nothing more than tricksters and manipulators. But now…I could see that there were powers at work here that I couldn't deny and didn't understand, powers that could warp my circumstances to prevent me from breaking the oath I'd so carelessly sworn.

Magic was real.

Whatever that meant on a grander scale, I couldn't even begin to process. But acceptance of something beyond my control—something strange and terrible—started to settle, cool, cement.

Good thing I hadn't pledged my eternal servitude.

"To Maggie's, then," I muttered, and shifted into reverse, parking under the shade of an old oak tree in front of her house.

As I trod up the path, I clutched the journal fiercely enough to leave a palm print of sweat on the aged leather. It felt heavy in my grasp, as though my acknowledgment of magic's existence had given more weight to its pages.

Malachi's power was real. That meant Lillian had told the truth in her book. She wasn't some nitwit—she was a witness, maybe even an accomplice, to accidental murder.

The Pagans of the Pines had only intended to curse the twelve men, but the curse went awry and they killed them. How had the girls' descendants made use of their magic? What was their mission, their purpose? Was the 1971 massacre a copycat crime? A ritual? Or an accident?

I knew I couldn't trust the Wardens. I wasn't here to swallow everything Maggie told me with a spoon. No, I was here to find out how Grandma Kerry had been involved, what the cultists wanted from me, and if I could pull Lindsey and Vanessa out.

Most importantly, I needed to know whether the eldest among the group were murderers…and whether they planned to kill again.

Maggie's house was exceptionally warm and inviting. A few years ago, *Southern Homestead* had featured it in their print magazine. Outside, it was white with a wraparound porch and green shutters. Fat bumblebees buzzed around the front garden, their hums underscored by a distant lawnmower. Flowers bloomed in pots and beds with such eagerness you might have thought Maggie was Demeter in human form.

But maybe she was something else.

I gathered my courage and knocked on the door. For seventy-odd years old, Maggie answered with alacrity. "Well, good morning, Miss Natalie," she said, fluffing her snowy hair. She looked dapper and harmless in a turquoise wrap, crisp Capri pants, and gaudy, granny-chic jewelry.

But I remembered the abhorrent crimes she may have committed as a young woman and steeled myself to look straight into her mint-green eyes. "I have questions for you."

"What sort of questions, hon?" she asked. Her bright smile was a touch too oblivious.

"I want to talk about the Wardens." I held the journal like a preacher giving a hellfire sermon. "I saw my grandmother's writing in here. And I know Lindsey, Vanessa, and your granddaughter are involved."

She didn't play coy. "Where did you get that?"

"Kate gave it to me as a graduation gift. She told me it was from you."

Even when Maggie smirked like a crook, she looked as regal as an old queen. "That rascal," she said, planting a fist on her hip. "She and I are two peas in a stubborn pod. Come on in."

I twisted to glance at the stretch of semirural street. It was a quiet Monday morning, and most people were already at work.

I hadn't expected to settle this on the front porch—that would be much too ill-mannered for Maggie Arthur—but I hadn't pictured myself venturing alone into her house like the protagonist of a low-budget horror film, either.

However, this place was familiar. I convinced myself to go as far as the living room, a bright haven of natural light and Bible verses painted on rustic wood signs. Wide windows with soft blue curtains lined the back wall, facing a sprawling garden that covered at least an acre, not including the greenhouse.

Maggie closed the door behind me.

"Lindsey said that a blood oath stopped her from telling me anything," I explained. "She said only you could help because you're part of the Triad… or something?"

"I'm happy to answer your questions." She clasped her hands, spotted from years of gardening in the sun. "But I can't let a guest go thirsty. I'll get you some fresh-squeezed juice and a chocolate chip muffin, and then we'll talk."

I protested, but Maggie had already retreated to the kitchen. I looked out the window and saw Levi mowing grass toward the back of the property. Sweat shone on his lean, broad shoulders. His tank top was tossed over his neck like a sweaty rag and stripes of untouched skin had turned tender pink under the scorching sun. Like a fish taking bait off a line, my heart snagged behind my ribs. I'd been on a warpath and hadn't registered the sight of his truck parked in the driveway.

"Here you are, darlin'," Maggie said, presenting a tray holding home-made muffins and two mason jars of pulpy orange juice. I accepted the drink without planning to take a sip and perched on the beige couch.

Maggie sat on the opposite love seat and crossed her ankles. "When you were born, your grandmother made the Triad swear a blood oath," she began. "We could never tell you *anything* about the Wardens. And she made the oath heritable, which means our offspring were bound to it as well. When Kerry passed on, Lindsey's grandmother wanted to unmake it."

"Is Abuela Sofia part of the Triad?" I asked.

"Yes. But to unmake it, we needed unanimous consent. I was the lone holdout."

"Why?"

"Kerry was my friend, and she outranked all of us." Maggie took a sip of her juice, set it on a coaster, and folded her hands primly in her lap. She sat like a cotillion instructor. "I wanted to respect her wishes, however unreasonable."

"So, Lindsey's grandmother can undo the oath, but she needs you to agree?"

"She's the ranking Blood Warden so yes, she can undo it. In fact, she already did. Just last night."

"But Lindsey said—"

"Lindsey doesn't know yet. The Triad privately decided it was time to bring you in, and we unmade the oath. If I had known Kate and the others were going rogue to accomplish the same ends, I would have saved them the trouble."

"What made you change your mind?"

She looked me square in the eyes. In hers, I saw a flash of something raw, unfiltered, powerful enough to drill through the punctilious veneer of a Southern matriarch. "With every day that passes, the situation becomes more urgent."

"What situation?" I croaked out the question, reluctant to know the answer. "Does it have something to do with the massacre anniversary?"

"Yes, but not for the reasons you think. We've never hurt an innocent soul."

Not that you would admit to right off the bat, I thought. *You'll wait until I'm in too deep to swim back to shore.*

"We're not planning to murder twelve young men on July first, Natalie. We're planning to protect them."

"Protect them from what?"

"There will be a time to explain that."

And of course, now isn't it. The outside threat isn't real and never has been. It's you—you're the threat.

Instead of speaking my mind, I decided to ask more questions, questions which hopefully wouldn't lead to another hedge of secrecy. "You said Lindsey's abuela is a Blood Warden. Does that mean there are—?"

"Earth Wardens and Bone Wardens, too," Maggie finished my thought. "It's hereditary. Each of the three girls who magically bound to Malachi that night received a gift. As a descendant of Lillian, I'm an Earth Warden." She gestured at her vibrant garden out back.

"I didn't know Lindsey was related to one of them."

Maggie took another sip and dabbed at her pink lipstick with a cloth napkin. "She's related to Johanna. After Johanna was acquitted of the murder charges, she moved to Colorado with her young daughter—fathered by her own uncle, before he died in the 1921 massacre—and changed her name to Jo Ann Newell. Her daughter moved back as an adult, married a young Mexican man, and gave birth to Sofia."

"Her uncle? That's horrible," I muttered, disgusted by the evils Johanna had been subjected to.

She must have realized she was pregnant after killing her uncle, and then hidden the pregnancy during the trial.

I forgot I'd decided not to drink the juice and took a swish to wash the bad taste from my mouth. "The first round of victims really did deserve punishment, didn't they?"

"You bet," Maggie said.

"What about Grandma Kerry?" I asked, trying to push Johanna's misfortunes from my mind. "You said she outranked you."

"She, like Malachi, was a triad on her own. And so are you, Natalie. You are the O negative of magic: a universal donor. Your magic strengthens every ward and protection spell. You could do spells by yourself that normally take three of us."

The lawn mower grew louder, turned, and fell quiet again as I pondered this. "I don't feel magical, or powerful, or whatever. I'm still convinced this is a load of bullhonky."

My declaration didn't quite have the thrust of truthfulness I'd hoped for, especially since I'd censored my language to accommodate her sensibilities.

"You haven't engaged your magic or unlocked your Sight."

I nearly laughed at her woo-woo tone. She didn't crack. Instead, she narrowed her keen eyes. "Have you had more vivid dreams lately? Dreams of being buried alive or choking on dirt? Of dripping with blood? Your bones breaking?"

My shock must have been plain to see.

"Mm," she said, satisfied. "Your three types of magic are suppressed and searching for an outlet. You'll have more and more as the Claiming draws near."

"The Claiming?"

"I'm afraid I've said too much for now. There's no need to be unceremonious about all this."

"But—"

She raised her hand to stop me, very much the typical church lady gossiping until holy conviction strikes and seals her lips like a vault.

"Fine, I won't ask about the Claiming. If it's hereditary, does that mean my dad is one? A Warden?"

"No, Kurt didn't inherit any gifts, and neither did my son. They only go to women."

That was a relief. Too many people in my life were already involved in this absurdity.

"That's why Kate stayed with me when her parents relocated for work," she went on. "She was a teenager, but we were close because I could truly understand her."

I felt a twinge of sadness remembering Grandma Kerry's prescient guardianship, her weight on the edge of my bed, her touch that could drive away nightmares.

The growl of the mower brought me back to the present and shook a realization loose. "Levi and Emmy are descendants of Lillian Pickard, just like you and Kate," I said. "Is Emmy one of you?"

Maggie shook her head. "That situation is complicated, even more so than yours. Emmy will never join the Wardens."

"What about Avery? She's your great-granddaughter. Will she have the same power?"

"Yes, she is an Earth Warden, and we'll involve her when the time comes."

The questions continued to spring up like whack-a-moles. These women weren't social outcasts lurking in the woods with tangled hair and blood under their fingernails. They were model citizens, people who could commit the worst crime, wash it off their hands, and never invite a lick of suspicion. "Who's the third Triad member?"

"Vanessa's grandmother, Cynthia," Maggie answered. "She's the ranking Bone Warden."

"Why didn't Grandma Kerry want you to tell me anything?" I was sure I already knew the answer: she had realized they were dangerous and wanted out. Moreover, she wanted me to have no part in this.

But I couldn't leave it alone. Maybe Grandma Kerry hadn't found the courage to break this thing wide open and bear the cross of public humiliation. But if it could save lives, I would stake my reputation, and hers, on telling the truth.

"She wanted to protect you," Maggie answered. "It's not an easy life we lead."

"Why not? What's the point of the Wardens? Is it a religion? Do you worship Malachi? Other than magic, what do you believe in?"

She plunked her glass on the coffee table. "We're at war for the soul of this town, Natalie. There's no time to waste. Your grandmother may have thought she was protecting you by keeping you in the dark, but she left you exposed and vulnerable."

"At war against what? Vulnerable to what?"

She stood up. "The rest will have to wait until our gathering tonight. Since Kate involved you without our permission, she and the other miscreants can swing by and pick you up."

"O-okay," I agreed, rising to leave.

"Until then . . ." She bustled over to rummage through her oversized purse hanging on a hook in the entryway. I wondered what sort of spell-related supplies she might extract and hoped it wasn't a knife or the forgetting powder. But she merely withdrew her wallet, stuffed to bursting with receipts and loose cash. "Would you mind running festival errands? I'll pay you your babysitting rate."

"Seriously?" I asked through a laugh. "You're not going to make me take another blood oath or wipe my memory? You're just sending me to... run errands?"

"Life doesn't grind to a halt when you're fighting to protect your town. It's vital to keep up appearances."

She held out a credit card and a shopping list written in neat, loopy cursive. Too overwhelmed to argue, I accepted.

"I can't make you trust me, Natalie." She squeezed my arm, her raised veins dark beneath her pale flesh. "But I hope I can help you understand that telling outsiders about us will only make it more difficult to keep the young men and boys in this town alive."

Repressing every urge to look at Levi in her backyard, I accepted the card and the list. "I won't tell anyone. But I want to know one more thing."

"What's that, hon?" she asked, opening the door for me.

I stepped onto her doormat and turned to face her. "What's out there in the woods near the cabin?"

The evergreen of her eyes seemed especially opaque as she said, "That's a conversation better suited for the dark."

EXCERPT:

PAGANS OF THE PINES: THE UNTOLD STORY OF MALACHI RIVERS

Lillian Pickard, 1968

Blood from Malachi's fingertip dribbled over the white cotton eyelet tea dress I'd given her to keep. It had gone out of fashion, and I had outgrown it. Even if Malachi had had the money for silk georgette dresses and cloche hats, she wouldn't have worn them.

She'd run away from home months ago. Her father had finally given up and let her be. She had become as wild as the woods around us, surviving on foraged food and whatever I could bring her. She rarely so much as brushed the blond hair that hung to her elbows, which had once been silky and full of luster. If the boys who had fancied her at school could see her now, they would fear her.

She was untamable and transcendent.

The candle flames danced across Dorothy's and Johanna's determined faces. Fear trapped my spirit in its hold. Everything I'd enjoyed about Malachi's magic until now had been child's play. They, on the other hand, had been patiently waiting for this.

It would be the most powerful conjuration she had set out to perform.

Malachi began. "I conjure and confirm upon you, spirits, who have instilled your power within me, to accomplish our revenge by the powers of earth, bone, and blood." A howling wind ripped through the cabin to tease our hair and ruffle our collars. "Project for me an angelic form, in which my spirit will temporarily dwell. Give her an amiable and pleasant countenance and make her gentle of speech. Create her of color white and gold, like a clear star. Give her a laurel crown adorned with flowers and long raiment. She will allure men of evil to the cursed wine and devour them as if by lions."

Malachi's blue eyes rolled back, revealing their milky whites. The blood we had shed across the herbs and bones glowed gold and bright. Light flowed beneath Malachi's fair skin. When she shuddered, I felt the same shudder pass through my bones.

Like a soul leaving its earthly vessel, a towering celestial figure stepped out from her body. The projection appeared just as Malachi described, so blinding and beautiful that we could hardly bear to look upon it, and were afraid to. Next to me, Malachi slumped over, unconscious, while the celestial projection departed to do her work. She would visit each of the twelve men like a holy vision, lead them to the sanctuary, and persuade them to partake of the cursed Communion. The evil inside their hearts would live on the outside for all to see. San Solano couldn't turn a blind eye, and the evildoers would be forced to live with their shame or succumb to it.

We held the sacred circle in her absence.

ELEVEN

Natalie Colter

Nerves set my knees bouncing as I sat at the breakfast nook that night, Lillian's book on the table before me. My parents had gone to bed. I'd changed into black clothes per Lindsey's texted instructions and decided to reread *Pagans of the Pines* to kill time. Three cups of coffee later, I'd finished the book, buzzing with anxious energy, and added more questions to my ever-lengthening list.

According to Lillian, the Pagans of the Pines had used dark magic in the cabin that night. The magic had gone off the rails and killed their victims. Lillian wrote that she believed their deaths were not the only consequence of dabbling in darkness. She could feel supernatural reverberations of the curse.

I wondered whether whatever prowled in the woods had something to do with that night, that curse—with the cost of using magic to seek revenge. Maggie had assured me that the Wardens weren't murderers, and maybe that was true. Maybe they really were protecting San Solano from something more fearsome than a sadistic cult.

My view of the overcast night through the bay windows started to creep me out. Now that I knew what was possible, I could no longer pretend the world was a logical place with unbendable rules. It felt lawless and shrouded in mystery.

Eager for another distraction, I glanced at the text from Levi again. *Was that you at Maggie's earlier?* he'd asked around noon.

Yeah! I'm helping with festival stuff today, I'd replied promptly.

This wasn't my first rodeo. I knew he was using our passing encounter as an excuse to initiate conversation. If he liked me, he wouldn't need much material to work with to keep the exchange going.

I waited for a response along the lines of *"You should have said hi"* or something similarly bold that would accelerate our . . . whatever this was . . . at a healthy pace. But nothing came. Either I'd misinterpreted the overture, or he'd changed his mind.

Disenchanted and insufficiently distracted, I slipped the folded flier from the volunteer meeting out of my back pocket. Beneath the general information, the final paragraph read:

> *The Treasures of Texas Heritage Festival is a day of FAMILY-FRIENDLY FUN. Out of respect for the deceased victims and their families, please do not encourage fascination with the massacres. There will be NO TRESPASSING ALLOWED at Calvary Baptist Church outside of allotted hours, and it is the responsibility of our volunteers to assist the sheriff's department by reporting suspicious persons.*

Maggie had written this. When I considered the hard work she put into to this event every year, I used to think *sacrificial*. But now I thought *control*. Running errands for her had been more like running a marathon. I'd picked up an order of shirts for staff and volunteers, dropped off fliers at every business in town, and finalized the rider with the headlining band before delivering a barbecue dinner to the meeting. But maybe the bustle was a small price for Maggie to pay in order to make sure the biggest crowds of the year didn't poke their noses where they didn't belong.

"Hey," Lindsey said, and I nearly fell out my chair. I turned to find her leaning against the kitchen counter in heavy-duty black combat boots, black jeans, and a leather chest guard. Twin daggers hung in sheaths from a belt around her waist, much bigger than the knife she'd used to seal my blood oath.

"What are those for?" I asked.

"Hunting the bad guys." She sauntered over to take a swig of my room-temperature coffee. "Let's go."

I started to get up but paused with my fingertips resting on Lillian's book. "By going with you, I'm not agreeing to anything, right? I just want to know what happened when Malachi cast her curse. I want to know what's out there. Beyond that, I don't know what I want."

"No one will make you do anything," she promised. Under the kitchen lights, her eyes were a warm, firewood brown that I felt I hadn't seen in ages. She seemed like Lindsey again, *my* Lindsey. There was a spring in her step as she led me outside. She didn't seem worried about my parents waking up and asking questions. I wondered if she had spoken a spell before entering the house.

Outside, I didn't see Kate's black SUV until I bumped into it—more magic, I guessed. Lindsey and I climbed into the back seat. Kate was driving and Vanessa sat shotgun.

"Welcome to your initiation," Vanessa said, gesturing grandly.

Kate turned on the overhead light and twisted in her seat to look at me, her green eyes swimming with emotion. "Nat, I'm so proud of you for how you've handled this so far."

"Um... thanks." I buckled my seatbelt. "I mean, I was freaked out last night at the cabin. I thought Lindsey and Vanessa—"

"Wait. *What?*" Kate flung a startled look back and forth between them. I felt Lindsey wince beside me. "You took her to the cabin?"

"Everyone was going," Lindsey said. "We couldn't let them go alone—"

"The Woodwalkers could have drained Nat of her magic. And killed her!" Kate interrupted, flicking off the light and jerking us down the rough driveway. "Letting her go anywhere near their territory was the most asinine thing possible."

"Woodwalkers?" I repeated. I thought we would turn east, out toward deeper woods and fewer people, but instead we drove to downtown, past quiet houses and shuttered shops. The eerie fluorescent lights of a corner convenience store flickered. Were we going back to Maggie's house?

"Maybe it was asinine, but it worked," Vanessa argued, ignoring me. "Her Sight opened up even more out there. Maggie said that Nat's magic would emerge when it sensed a threat. Last night, she saw straight through our beguilement."

"Your Book of Wisdom plan was too slow, Kate," Lindsey added. "It hasn't even shed all of its glamour for her yet. It just looks like a half-empty, old journal."

"Yeah, and we didn't know that the Triad would decide to let her in," Vanessa went on. "Otherwise we would have left it alone."

Kate sighed. "Well, in any case, Nat, I'm glad you're here, and I'm sorry we had to go about this backwards. If I could have told you everything outright, I would have."

"What are the Woodwalkers?" I asked.

"Jesus, Mary, and Joseph, did I say that word?" Kate asked. "Grandma Maggie's going to wring my neck. I'm not saying anything else." She mimed zipping her mouth shut.

"I'm excited you're here." Lindsey bounced to face me in her seat, her smile electric. "When you brought up the talismans in your yard, I was afraid my beguiling spell was getting weaker. But it was just your Sight opening up."

"I wasn't supposed to see those?"

She shook her head. "They were wards meant to protect you. They'd been there for months."

"What about the protection sachet that Milo found?" I asked. "Why was Bryce able to see that?"

"Cats are basically immune to magic," Vanessa explained. "Bryce never would have found it if Milo hadn't brought it right to him. That's not the first time I've had problems with that little regurgitated hairball."

"So how does the magic work?" I asked, hanging an elbow over the back of Vanessa's seat. "Each of yours is different?"

"We have our own magical domains, but we can reach beyond them in limited ways," Kate explained. "Since I'm an Earth Warden, I'm like a kitchen witch. Our domain is anything that grows, plus stones and crystals, and recipes are the foundation of most of our spells. We make elixirs, tonics, resins, oils, all that good stuff. Earth Warden strengths are summoning protection, secrecy, wellness of body and spirit, even romance."

"Could I do everything you can?" I asked.

"Yes, but actions have consequences," she said, wagging her finger unconvincingly. "Remember that before you go trying spells willy-nilly. You're a triple threat, so any carelessness on your part could do a lot of damage."

"Understood," I said, splaying my hands to show I meant no harm.

I still didn't know if I could trust the Wardens, but I wanted to. Despite the overwhelming unknowns, it occurred to me to feel envious of them, maybe even resentful. Grandma Kerry had deprived me of an upbringing that involved *magic*. Real magic that actually worked, just like Lillian had claimed. Her book described some of the harmless spells that the Pagans of the Pines had performed before they decided to seek revenge. Malachi had helped Lillian make an herbal honey love elixir to snag a boy's attention. She had healed a fawn with a broken leg. They had charmed the cabin to keep anyone from finding them after she fled her home. Until they took it too far, magic had been their comfort, their haven, and their salvation.

"Bone magic deals mostly with divination," Vanessa said matter-of-factly. "Seeing beyond the veil, communicating with ancestors, predicting the future, etcetera. Any spells to do with time, wisdom, revealing the unknown... They're all bone based." She unwrapped the layered leather bracelet from around her wrist and showed me the cameo pendant of a carved flower. "This is my pendulum. It's made of bone. And bone ash is the basis of the forgetting spell I hit you with."

"Worked like a charm," Lindsey said, giving Vanessa a congratulatory fist bump. "She was so clueless."

"It wasn't too shabby," Vanessa agreed with a grin.

I narrowed my eyes, a tad insulted that they would celebrate stealing my memories. What if Vanessa's tinkering around in my mind caused me to forget something permanently, or remember things that didn't happen? What if the moment with Levi in the truck had been nothing but a fiction to fill the void? I didn't want to consider that.

"What about blood magic?" I asked Lindsey, increasingly curious as to what I could do if I applied myself.

"Blood is more ceremonious than earth, but less mystical than bone," she answered. "It's good for making people stick to their word, which you've seen already. It's also good for justice and revenge, but..." She glanced at Kate, who kept her eyes on the road, silent. "We don't do revenge because of what happened when Malachi cast her curse."

Lindsey didn't give me a chance to ask for the missing pieces of the story. "It also symbolizes revival and rebirth," she went on, smoothing down her tight ponytail. "If you need a calming tea or a cold remedy, you go to an Earth Warden. But if you need to be brought back from the brink of death, you find a Blood Warden. And since blood contains metal, we also work well with that. We make the charms like the one on the protection sachet, and we maintain the weapons."

"Weapons?" I echoed. "Isn't magic enough of a weapon on its own?"

Vanessa and Lindsey both looked to Kate for guidance. "Usually," Kate replied, her voice soft. "But not always. Sometimes we need both."

"The weapons have been charmed," Lindsey explained.

Again, the shadow of the unknown loomed large over the conversation. What were the weapons *for*?

We turned onto a shady street a few blocks from downtown, where Calvary Baptist Church waited like a pale specter in the cloud-covered, moonless night. "Why are we here?" I asked, clenching the edge of my seat, wondering if I had made a mistake in coming.

"I know this is hard to believe, but CBC is the safest place in town," Kate assured me, pulling into the empty parking lot. The arched windows were dark, and the gothic tower cut into the sky.

My knees trembled, objecting to my decision to follow the three of them across the dewy churchyard. Thanks to Lindsey's and Grandma Kerry's entanglement with the group, I'd been eager to believe Maggie's claim that these women were not killers. But a cult leader *would* be convincing. She *would* lie. She would catch flies with honey.

I couldn't walk away, though. Not when I was so close to getting answers to questions that had haunted San Solano for a century.

Kate unlocked and opened the wooden double doors of the sanctuary. They gave a ghoulish screech. I shuffled a step closer and peered inside.

The stained-glass windows allowed only the faintest light to fall across the rows of empty pews. A black candle burned atop the Communion table, which was covered in a white cloth and positioned in front of the imposing onstage lectern.

"It's okay," Lindsey whispered. "I promise."

I tried not to think of the crime scene photos from 1971, the bodies of the twelve young men sprawled haplessly around this room.

I followed Lindsey and Vanessa down the aisle to the Communion table. Kate picked up the candle dish and held it out for me to take. "Black candles help banish fear."

Quivering, I accepted the light and cast it upward across the chancel area, illuminating the stage, the ascending rows of choir pews behind it, and the elevated baptistery that overlooked the church like a balcony. That was the same pool where Malachi once turned the water to blood. It was curtained off.

"This way," Kate said, and led us from the Communion table to a door beside the stage. The wood-paneled hallway beyond was cluttered with music stands and stacks of chairs. We passed choir rooms and the back passageway leading up to the baptistery before arriving at the end of the hall.

Kate splayed her hands across the dead-end wall and whispered an incantation. "From the undeserving gaze, this secret way conceal; but to Wardens' worthy eyes, the hidden path reveal."

She pushed. A secret door swung open to expose a steep staircase leading down. I could see a concrete floor, brick walls, and dim light shining from below.

"Go ahead," Lindsey encouraged, nudging me gently with her elbow.

My heart slammed against my throat, but I could feel the black candle nudge away the tight, cold feeling of fear and replace it with a warm feeling of peace. I descended on surprisingly steady legs, my free hand trailing along the rough bricks for lack of a railing.

This felt like the moment of truth. My research about the cult had planted unsavory images in my mind: bloodstained altars, animal sacrifices, masked disciples.

What awaited me was a sophisticated secret lair. There were two dozen women dressed in black, sitting in high-backed chairs surrounding three scarred wooden tables fit for a medieval banquet. Symbols had been carved into each of their surfaces like a centerpiece: the upside-down triangle with the horizontal dash for earth on the left, the *X* for bone at the center, and a circle, presumably representing blood, on the right.

Along the far wall, there were vast shelves packed with glass containers storing all sorts of oddities: herbs, oils, resins, salt, roots, dried insects, small bones, snakeskin, and honeycombs drowning in golden honey. There were stacks of candles, balls of twine, bundles of dried herbs, carafes of burgundy wine, and bottles of electric-green absinthe.

On the right side of the room, dozens of weapons hung on pegs or reposed on red velvet cushions in glass-front cabinets. On the left side, there was a sitting area with velvet chaises and shelves of dense books.

The staircase I'd descended was set against the corner of the room, and along the adjacent wall there were six neat bunk beds with curtains. On the far side of the beds was a pantry stocked with food and first aid kits, a kitchenette, and a doorway revealing a bathroom with a pedestal sink and filigree mirror.

This secret society wasn't just some hobby. It was an entire second life, lived in the shadows.

"Welcome, Natalie," Miss Maggie said, rising from her place at the head of the Earth Warden table. I half expected a monotone echo from the crowd, but they watched me in silence. Vanessa sat down in an empty chair at the Bone Warden table near her older sister, Brianna, and their mom. Their grandma, whom Maggie had said was the ranking Bone Warden, sat at the head. I also recognized the librarian from the San Solano Public Library.

Lindsey's mom and abuela smiled invitingly from the Blood Warden table, where Lindsey took her seat. I saw Gabby, one of Lindsey's cousins on her mother's side, who was just fourteen.

At the Earth Warden table, I recognized a purple-haired, full-figured woman in her twenties who sported a sleeve of gorgeous floral tattoos, colorful against her ivory skin. Her name was Heather Cobb, and she owned the downtown bakery, Butter Babe's. She'd recently visited my senior economics class to speak about starting a small business.

"Take a seat," Maggie offered, pointing to a chair off on its own, facing everyone. There was a stand beside it holding a glass vial and dropper next to a silver-plated chalice with an engraving of the Warden's Rune.

"I don't want to join," I told Maggie. "I mean . . . I'm not sure. I just want answers."

Kate rested a hand on my shoulder. "You don't have to do anything. Just sit for now . . . if you want to."

She took her own seat with the Earth Wardens.

"There's no chance anyone will come down here, right?" I asked, throwing a glance over my shoulder.

"We commandeered this space and charmed it more than fifty years ago," Maggie said, waving off my concerns. "Not even the pastor knows there's a basement."

Hesitating another moment, I swallowed my fears, set the black candle on the stand, and sat. "Start from the beginning. The night of the first massacre."

TWELVE

As though readying to pray, Miss Maggie set her hands together and propped them on the edge of the table. "Malachi was extremely powerful, but a revenge curse like the one she contrived that night cannot be cast without repercussions."

"I know she didn't mean to kill them," I interjected, anxious to arrive at to the part of the story I had never heard. "She just wanted to make the evil inside them visible, so they'd be ostracized from society."

"Yes, their deaths were an unexpected consequence," Maggie affirmed. "But the curse did more than bring evil to the surface. It ripped the evil out, leaving so little of the men's souls intact that their bodies perished on the spot, and the evil took on a life of its own."

My nape convulsed with a shudder. "Is that what the Woodwalkers are?" I asked. "The evil inside the twelve men as"—I paused, hunting for the right words—"animate beings?"

"Yes." Maggie nodded, her imperturbable gaze fastened on me. "The Woodwalkers roam the night as specters that only the Wardens can see. They're made of shadows, mostly, but they hunt animals and collect their remains to fabricate physical forms. They want to resemble living creatures as much as possible, and they gain strength from the remains. That strength allows them to cross our boundaries and defy our protection spells."

I shook my head. "I'm sorry—y'all are the only ones who can see them?" Malachi's magic, the forgetting spells and blood oaths, was undeniably real, but the Wardens could be scapegoating conveniently "invisible" creatures for their own crimes.

"You can, too," Maggie said, gesturing at the items on the table beside me. "That's what the collyrium is for. It allows you to see what's cloaked in the shadow of otherness. You will no longer be susceptible to deceptive charms, either. But you don't have to take it until you're ready."

I shot a glance to the glass vial and dainty dropper. Its label read, "Eyebright Collyrium to Open the Sight." Maybe Maggie *wasn't* banking on my willingness to accept this strange lore without proof. Maybe the proof would be in the pudding.

On the other hand, the collyrium might be a bluff to keep my butt in the chair so they could indoctrinate me.

Either way, I had to reckon with those animalistic, moaning howls out at the cabin in the woods and the terror I'd seen in Lindsey's eyes. My best friend could shut down, deflect, build a wall to hide her secrets, but she couldn't fake that kind of fear.

I still needed answers. I could neither accept nor rule out anything so far. I was an observer, a sponge, absorbing and not judging.

"Normally, our wards and protection spells keep the Woodwalkers confined to the woods," Maggie went on, "but we have to reinforce them. That's what we do: we bolster the protections, ward the Woodwalkers away, and teach magic to our daughters."

"Every once in a while, they manage to murder a human," Abuela Sofia said grimly. "Usually a wanderer or someone disconnected from society, someone we don't know to protect."

"They like humans best," Vanessa's grandmother, Cynthia, added. I noticed a necklace with a carved bone cameo against her umber skin. "Makes them *feel* more human."

"That's ultimately what they want," Maggie said. "They want human bodies again. And every fifty years, on the anniversary of Malachi's curse, they get their opportunity to claim them."

"You mean ... the boys in 1971 were murdered so they could be hosts?"

"Yes," Maggie said. "Every fifty years, on July first, during the witching hour, the Woodwalkers have a window, a chance to win restitution by claiming new bodies as their own. Each of the twelve Woodwalkers chooses a virile, healthy boy or young man. They look for what they consider the cream of the crop, people with the most strength and the longest lives ahead of them."

"Fifty years ago, we stopped the Woodwalkers from winning," Cynthia explained, gesturing to Maggie, Sofia, and a few other gray heads in the room. "They weren't able to permanently inhabit the bodies of the victims they'd chosen. But *we* lost, too. We weren't able to save the boys."

"We will this time," Maggie said, and I had never heard so much resolve packed into so few words.

I fiddled absentmindedly with the handle on the candle dish, thinking of my friends who would be in danger if this lore were true.

Thinking of Levi.

"How did the boys die, then?" I asked, continuing my clinical questioning. "If you stopped the Woodwalkers from taking over their bodies, why couldn't you save them?"

"We only stopped the last stage of the Claiming," Maggie explained. "There are—"

"I'll show her, Miss Maggie," Vanessa volunteered. Her black sneakers padded across the concrete floor. From behind one of the bookshelves, she wheeled out a chalkboard that looked like it had last been used for some kind of strategy session. She set it up where I could see and wiped it clean.

"There are three stages of the Claiming," she said, taking up a piece of chalk and recording the word in her graceful artist's handwriting. "The Shadowing, the Possession, and the Eviction. The Shadowing is when they select their victims—mark their territory. They can start Shadowing on the night of the last dark moon before the anniversary, when there's a new moon but you can't see it. We call it the Shadowing because the only way to know if someone's been chosen is to look at his shadow." With artistic strokes, she drew the outline of a man. "A boy who's been chosen by a Woodwalker will have two." She added twin shadows cast in opposite directions.

"The second stage is the Possession." She drew another outline of a man, but this one looked manic, with wild, tormented eyes. "On the night of the anniversary, we have to fight the Woodwalkers to keep them from taking control of the people they've Shadowed."

"The victim is still inside, alive, when the Possession takes place," her grandmother explained, "but the Woodwalker is calling the shots. The humans can't control their own bodies."

"Stage three is Eviction." Vanessa drew trees on a blank area of the board with twelve arrows pointing toward them. "The possessed bodies make their way to the cabin in the woods. There, the Woodwalkers try to evict the souls of the victims so they can claim their bodies for good."

"We were able to stop the Eviction," Maggie said. "Before the witching hour, we rounded up the Shadowed victims and brought them to the sanctuary to keep them safe. But the Woodwalkers were able to breech our defenses, possess the boys, and start the pilgrimage back to the sacred glade. The only reason they couldn't evict their souls is because we were able to keep a few of the boys' bodies captive. They struggled the whole time—"

"Which is why there were signs of violence on the corpses," I whispered, understanding.

"Right." Maggie nodded. "The Woodwalkers needed all twelve victims to undo the curse and complete the Claiming. Magic requires symmetry. They failed, but when they vacated the bodies, they killed the boys on their way out. It's like an arrow wound...tearing out the arrowhead causes far more damage than the initial injury. We didn't realize that the boys' lives were already forfeited until everything was said and done. This time, we desperately need to stop the Possession from taking place, or nothing will change."

I swallowed a bad taste coming up my throat and gripped the carved arms of my chair, waiting for the herds of questions trampling through my mind to form an orderly queue. The Wardens' answers only seemed to spawn more. "Why do the Woodwalkers have to bring them back to the cabin in the sacred glade?" I asked. "Isn't that Malachi's, like, special spot?"

"Malachi used it, but it didn't belong to her," Abuela Sofia explained from the Blood Warden table. "It's a place of ancient power. When Malachi abandoned it, the Woodwalkers took it for their own. We haven't been able to reclaim it since."

"Why don't you just take the Shadowed boys out of San Solano?" I asked.

"We tried last time," Miss Maggie said, staring off into the past. "Actually, Kerry tried. She drove Roger McElroy out of town."

"The high school quarterback, right?" I asked, leafing through my mental trove of newspaper clippings and conspiracy websites. Roger was one of the most famous victims of the 1971 massacre, a star student and athlete with a heart of gold. So much promise. Investigators had referred to him when differentiating the motives behind the two massacres. Clearly, the second massacre was not an act of revenge for the boys' evil deeds. How could it be, when Roger McElroy was respectful to everyone, and they couldn't unearth a single grievance against him no matter how deep they dug?

Maggie nodded gravely. "But Roger starting seizing right before they crossed the county line. He would have died if she'd kept driving. A part of him already belonged to the Woodwalker, and that part rebelled against any effort to save the rest of him."

"What about getting all the young guys out of San Solano *before* they're

Shadowed?" I asked. "Before the dark moon, tell them there's a hunting or paintball retreat and bus them out of here."

"That's hundreds of people, hon," Maggie replied. "And the Woodwalkers would just pick others. They'd settle for less prime real estate."

"Then evacuate the whole town!" I said, losing patience. "Use your beguiling spell thing to make them leave."

"Our magic doesn't work outside of San Solano," Cynthia said. "It's tied to the sacred place in the woods, its origin point. There's a chance we could get people to leave, but we couldn't stop them from coming to their wits and turning right around."

"Then tell them the truth!" I cried.

Lindsey's younger cousin snorted, which won her disapproving looks from her family. "What?" she asked innocently. "No one would believe us."

"Shut up, Gabby," Lindsey snapped.

"She's coming to terms with everything for the first time," Sofia told Gabby patiently. "You had to ask these questions, too."

"You're right, Abuela," Gabby said, hunching her shoulders. "Sorry, Nat. I guess since you have the triad of gifts, I expected you to, like, get it right away."

"This is a special situation," Maggie said. "The better we help Natalie understand this, the sooner she can hop into the saddle."

I pinched the bridge of my nose and tried to corral my whirling thoughts. "Why every fifty years?" I asked. "Why not every hundred? Or every year on the same day?"

"We can't say for sure," Maggie said. "But in the Old Testament, there's a holy year that occurs every fifty. During that year, there's a day of atonement, of settling disputes and forgiving debts. For these creatures, it's the opposite. It's a night of vengeance. That's the only significance we've been able to attach to the date."

"Hold up," I said, kneading my temples. "You're mixing magic and the Bible?"

"Magic spellbooks were used in early Christendom," Maggie replied, looking ruffled for the first time. "There are many syncretic traditions that involve both witchcraft and Christianity, which are—"

"What you need to know most, Nat, is that the anniversary has power," Kate interrupted, earning a withering look from her grandmother. "The Woodwalkers gain strength as it approaches. That's what happened last time, and it's happening now."

"Malachi was the first to recognize the signs before the anniversary," Maggie said, finally freeing her granddaughter from her ruthless "act like you've had some raising" glare. "Before she knew about the power the date held, she lived alone in a house in the woods. She drew magical boundaries to keep the Woodwalkers confined to the wilderness while she worked to break the curse she'd cast in 1921. She never could. So she charmed weapons to try to kill the Woodwalkers. But that didn't work, either. The weapons only fended them off. They can't be killed. And as the fifty-year anniversary approached, she noticed that they started getting restless and bold. They started crossing her boundaries that had held strong for decades."

"So, Malachi lived until she was sixty-something years old without being seen by anyone?" I asked, stunned. "How do you know that? Wait... did you *know* Malachi?"

"For a short time," Maggie said. "With all of her magical levees breaking, she sought us out. The Woodwalkers received power on the night of the curse, but so did my Grandmother Lillian. So did Johanna and Dorothy. Malachi knew that. She hoped we could help her."

"Sadly, Lillian was the only other surviving Pagan of the Pines," Cynthia explained. "Growing up in poverty didn't do Dorothy or Johanna any favors, especially at a time when people didn't live long to begin with. But their daughters and granddaughters inherited threads of Malachi's magic. We'd been stifling it, fearing it. We were scared that our reputations would suffer like our grandmothers' had."

"Malachi gave us the collyrium and the bitterwine," Maggie said.

"Bitterwine?" I asked.

"Wine boiled with ingredients to enhance our magic," she replied. "She also gave us her grimoire, which we renamed the Book of Wisdom."

I saw the older women nod their prim approval of the more Christian-friendly rebranding.

"The church was a safe, private place to protect the boys who had been marked by darkness, and we hoped that the power of our faith would add extra protection," Maggie continued. "On the night of the anniversary, we gathered them in the sanctuary. Malachi used the last of her power to reinforce the magical protections, but she died from the effort. We were on our own. And as you know, that didn't go well. That's why we need everyone. That's why we need *you,* Natalie."

The ensuing silence was heavy. Feeling everyone's eyes bore into me, I tried not to squirm. "What do the Woodwalkers, um, look like?"

Vanessa's chalk made shrill sounds as she started a new sketch. The creature she drew was tall and spindly. Its body looked wispy, its fingers long shadows that tapered like claws. Rather than a human head, atop its body was a deer skull with an extravagant pair of antlers and eye sockets deeper than graves.

I was doing my best to cling to reality, but I had already acknowledged the existence of something beyond my understanding. The blood oath had tested everything I knew to be true. It had undone me. And the soulless eyes in Vanessa's drawing threatened to wash away every ounce of remaining skepticism.

"We know it's a lot to take in, but there's no time to waste." Maggie stood up and rounded the Earth Warden table to approach me. "As soon as you're ready, you'll say our Oath and drink the bitterwine to unlock your magic. You'll have to swear to uphold your duty. After that, we'll administer the collyrium so you can see the Woodwalkers. Once you take the Oath, there will be no going back to life as usual."

I cast a glance around the room again, nervous now that the time for deliberating had arrived. Were these women lying? Were they delusional? Or did they really need me—and my magic—to help protect San Solano?

Maggie touched my shoulder and looked out across the group. "If we succeed this time, you young girls will spend the next fifty years reinforcing the wards. You'll keep yourselves hidden, protect people who venture into the woods, and teach magic to your daughters. You won't have to face the anniversary for a long time, and by then you'll be so practiced that you'll have no trouble stopping the Woodwalkers again. But first, we all need to rise to this occasion. We need to prove that we can protect the innocent. And who knows? Maybe saving the boys this time will somehow break the curse. Maybe it's always been the only way."

Maggie's hand felt weighty on my shoulder. I looked at the engraved chalice. I could smell the pungent strangeness of ingredients I could never guess, mingling to make magic. It was Malachi's recipe. The Triad had *known* Malachi.

My *grandmother* had known Malachi.

Kerry Colter had watched her ancestor die fighting to undo the curse she had cast on twelve evil men. Kerry had probably helped put Malachi to rest. Yet she had rarely spoken of her, had certainly never indicated that she'd known her, and had shielded me from this rich, secret legacy.

"Assuming all of this is true, why did Grandma Kerry make you swear never to tell me anything? Why did she think I would be safer not knowing?"

Maggie's shadow stretched to cover me. "She thought she was distancing you from danger, but that was deluded. She wasn't well, Natalie. She started that house fire to show how serious she was about severing ties, about leaving behind her old life as a Warden. She burned her magical garden, her occult books, even most of the spells she'd written. She also did it so she'd have an excuse to live with your family and be nearer to *you*... so she could keep you away from us."

I stared at her like she had just slapped me in the face. The room seemed to rock around me. When I blinked, the anger made me see bright bursts in the darkness. "That fire was an accident," I whispered. "She had dementia. She *died* from dementia."

"Yes, it's true that her mental faculties were going along with her physical ones," Maggie said, cradling my hand and patting it. Her wrinkled flesh felt cool. I thought of the papery folds of snakeskin stored in a glass jar on the shelves and shuddered. "She had lived a life that isn't easy on the mind or the bones. Take it from me. But hon, the dementia wasn't nearly as bad back then as she made it seem. Kerry was a good woman, God rest her soul, but loving you made her selfish."

"Selfish?" I echoed, anger beating like a bass drum behind my sternum. "My grandma was the opposite of selfish. You have no right to call her that."

"We all have family here, Natalie," Cynthia said, clasping her bone cameo necklace. "Of course, we don't want our loved ones to have to battle these cursed creatures or live secret lives. But this our duty. Your grandmother stopped honoring that. There's no dressing it up. She was a deserter."

Sensing the breadth of my seething anger, Kate spoke up, her voice gentle yet firm. "Nat, forget about Kerry for a minute. This is about you, not her. The Woodwalkers will sense you're vulnerable. They're growing bold, just like last time. If you're left unguarded, they'll drain your magic to increase their strength and kill you in the process."

"It's happened before," Maggie added, "to my cousin Nora."

"If you don't take the Warden's Oath and learn to protect yourself," Kate went on, "we have to keep using valuable resources to protect you."

I fumed, my chest rising and collapsing. My hands were rigid on the wooden arms of the chair. "If it's true that my grandmother was willing to burn down the house where she lived with my grandfather for decades and exaggerate her symptoms of dementia to keep me from this"—I gestured wildly—"you're out of your damned mind asking me to join." The chair squealed across the concrete as I stood. "Leave me the hell alone, and don't use any of your tricks on me or I *will* go to the police."

Lindsey started to argue, but Maggie cut her off. "Let her be. We can't force her to do her duty."

With a melancholy sigh, she slipped a sealed envelope out of her pocket. "From your grandmother," she said as she tendered it, noticeably reluctant. "When she made us take the blood oath, she also made me swear that if you ever found out the truth on your own, I would give you this, unopened."

I snatched the letter, addressed to me in Grandma Kerry's scratchy writing.

Kate stood up and rummaged around the shelves of casks and jars. "Kerry put up protections around your house, but take these just in case," she said, crossing the room to present three bundles of herbs. She removed a metal amulet with the Warden's Rune from her collar and slipped it over my head. "The bundles are for smoke cleansing. Burn one of these when you sense the presence of evil and say, 'As darkness flees from burning flame, pray let evil stake no claim.' Only use them at night. You'll be safe during the day without them. And the amulet is beguiled so no one will notice it."

Nothing but the memory of the shadows in the woods—and Vanessa's chilling artwork—convinced me to set aside my pride and accept her offering.

"You can take my car, too," she said, handing me her keys. "I'll pick it up before sunrise."

"Lindsey, you should walk her out," Maggie said. "Promise you'll think on it, Nat. We need you."

I didn't reply, and Lindsey didn't speak as she stomped up the stairs and led me back to the sanctuary. When I reached the warm outside air, I turned to Lindsey, but she had already slammed the sanctuary doors, leaving me alone.

A quiver snuck up my spine. The summer night was bright with stars and thick with humidity, just like any other. But the shadows seemed darker, more alive.

Savage and hungry, yet chillingly patient.

Natalie, my dearest girl,

If you're reading this, you've learned the truth. The Wardens have told you how valuable you are. They have asked you to join. They have told you that I kept you away for no other reason than to protect you. That's simply untrue.

I know you might think joining the Wardens is the right thing, the brave thing. But the farther you stay away from them, the safer the people you love will be.

Make your own path. Don't just stop the Claiming. Break the curse.

THIRTEEN

TWENTY-TWO DAYS UNTIL THE CLAIMING

The coffeemaker sputtered, making me jump even though I'd just pressed the brew button. I caught my breath and rubbed my puffy eyes.

For more than two weeks in a row, I'd barely slept during the night. The hours crawled by, a fog of nightmares. I dreamed I was buried alive, clawing at the dirt with no way out. Other times I was drowning in a pool of blood. Last night I'd dreamed of an agonizing ache in my bones, as though something were trying to rip me apart from the inside, and woke up to see a shadow moving outside my window.

After each dream I lit one of the herb bundles and spoke the chant. Soon I would have to tuck my tail between my legs and ask for more herbs, unless I could determine what they were. I'd even spent some time rummaging around the spice rack in the pantry to try to identify the unique scents, without much luck.

It was hard to imagine that twelve boys in this town were in danger of getting hijacked by the disembodied spirits of evil, sadistic men. But I couldn't dismiss it, either. I felt the darkness pressing close to me, caressing my mind, wanting something from me. I couldn't convince myself that the Wardens were lying or that the Woodwalkers didn't exist. I couldn't convince myself that Levi, Grayson, Bryce, or even my dad was safe from this unseen danger. If they couldn't Claim a young man, would they settle for a healthy middle-aged one? What if they were so desperate this time, they'd take any body they could get their claws on?

I'd thought about using my savings to buy my dad a surprise fishing trip to get him out of town, but he would never accept the gift, and he certainly wouldn't take three weeks off work. If my appeals became too desperate, I'd need to tell him the truth, which he wouldn't believe, and which would lead to a police investigation of Maggie and the others during a time when they couldn't afford to be distracted. The more I understood about the ramifications of Malachi's curse, the more I understood why the Wardens operated the way they did. What else could they do to protect potential victims of the Claiming?

The full moon waned each night, and the great shadow of cosmic darkness advanced. The old moon would be reborn in obscurity, freeing the Woodwalkers to hunt for their most critical prey.

Even the moon, infinitely distant as it was, was no longer just a lamp orbiting the earth. It was a harbinger of danger and death. The illusion of normalcy had cracked open and seemed to crumble around me, unsalvageable.

"Doesn't the last volunteer meeting start in ten minutes?" Mom asked, breezing into the kitchen in her scrubs, ready to pop over to work the front desk in my dad's office.

"Yeah," I croaked, and blinked lazily at the stream of strong coffee.

"Didn't sleep well again? What's wrong?"

In every shadow I see demonic creatures with black pits for eyes, I thought. *I'm scared for myself and everyone in this town, but I'm not allowed to join the only people protecting us.*

"Are you stressed about Coach's expectations?" she prodded. "I saw the summer training you're supposed to be following."

I shrugged.

She frowned sympathetically. "Maybe you should tell Miss Maggie you're not feeling well and go back to bed. She's not a drill sergeant. She'll understand."

Maggie would understand, but I didn't want her to know that the existence of the Woodwalkers had wormed its way so deeply under my skin. I'd also been refusing to acknowledge Maggie's existence, even at the festival meetings.

"I'm okay," I said, pointing at the brewing coffee. "Just need a little help."

Mom rubbed my back in soothing circles, and for the first time since storming out of the Warden hideout, I didn't feel like death and despair lurked in every corner.

Normal, I thought. *Normal is good.*

Unfortunately, my new normal consisted of working at Country Catfish Buffet. I'd stopped babysitting to distance myself from Kate. Two girls had recently quit the buffet, so the creepy manager had started me on the spot without even recognizing me from my brief stint there in the past. I hadn't seen my friends in over two weeks and had only glimpsed Levi once from afar while pumping gas on my way to work. But at least I went home exhausted enough to actually sleep for a few hours.

That exhaustion prevented me from parsing the meaning of Grandma Kerry's letter. What did she mean that I should make my own path? Obviously, she didn't want me to join the Wardens, but I was pretty sure serving up fried food for minimum wage wasn't going to break the curse, either.

"You've got to stop bringing the dogs in at night," my mom said, scanning the contents of the refrigerator. "Their hair gets everywhere."

"But," I started, an unbidden frantic edge in my voice, "what about the animal attacks?"

"They sleep in a run. They'll be fine. What kind of wild animal around here is going to jump an eight-foot, chain-link fence?"

I wasn't interested in furnishing an argument for that.

"They'll bark if they see anything," she added.

Out of habit, I grasped the Malachian charm at my throat. It had taken me a few days to get used to the beguilement, and I didn't trust it until my mom complimented my "pretty cross necklace," which I'd claimed was a graduation gift from Kate.

Grudgingly, I agreed to her terms and took my coffee to my room. I stopped in Grandma Kerry's room on the way. The power of the hidden rune beneath the bed brought me a sense of comfort that I resented.

I ran my hand along her dresser and examined the browning philodendron in a pot on her windowsill. I'd been watering it since she passed, but I'd been too busy lately. At her old house, she'd maintained a whole garden with fragrant herbs and vibrant flowers, which I now knew had been cultivated by magical means. I remembered expecting her to be more upset than she was about her beloved garden getting razed in the fire.

Maggie's accusation that Grandma Kerry had burned down her own house on purpose had stuck in my craw. Why would my grandma go to such horrible lengths to prove how serious she was about erasing her history with the Wardens? Had she really been *that* desperate to be near me—and to keep me from them?

"I'm staying away like you wanted," I whispered into the silence. "I know you weren't just being selfish, and Miss Maggie can sit on a tack for saying that. But"—I pinched one of the heart-shaped philodendron leaves and felt a pinch in my own heart—"why didn't you tell me more? Am I supposed to know something I don't? Am I supposed to use my magic without them? Don't I need someone to teach me? What if I'm not as powerful as everyone thinks...or as powerful as *you* thought?"

I felt a fleeting hope that I would experience some kind of touch, like the sensation on my face in the cabin. Nothing came, so instead I closed my eyes, inhaled, and tried to summon my magic, focusing on the leaf between my fingers.

A tickling sensation traveled over my skin, a rush through my bloodstream, an electric *zing* of synapses firing in my brain. The drooping leaf lifted its head, and its veins plumped beneath my touch. The brown spots turned green.

I gasped in awe, but the satisfaction was short-lived. My magic hit a brick wall, an invisible boundary. My head began to pound. The leaves suddenly bowed and turned brown again.

I watered the plant and left the room.

After the volunteer meeting, I changed into my work uniform—cutoff jean shorts and a fitted white tee that was too tight in the armpits—and reported for duty. After my first few shifts, the pervasive smell of greasy fried food had made me want to hose off out back, but I'd since resigned myself to it.

Today I was manning the cash register, which wasn't as awful as maintaining the buffet, especially since I got to pick the music—as long as it was country. I stood hunched over my phone, choosing a song by the band that would headline the festival on Saturday, when the bell above the door rang. Abbie, Faith, Grayson, Bryce, and Levi walked in.

Levi hadn't texted me since I'd replied to him. Same old song and dance.

Still, I devoured the sight of him, as ravenous as the customers who elbowed one another out of the way for fresh hush puppies. His skin was ruddy from yard work and his hair seemed an even more vivid shade of red than usual. I got a whiff of his intoxicating, woodsy-citrus cologne, and my icy irritation melted a drop.

"We thought we'd surprise you since you ignored my text about going to the lake." Faith pushed aside a cup of pens to lean on the counter. She wore a burnt-orange tee emblazoned with a University of Texas logo, her chosen college, which made me feel a pang of regret over how I'd spent the summer thus far. We would all be going our separate ways soon... as long as we survived the next few weeks.

"Oh god, I'm sorry," I said, smacking my forehead. "Between this and the festival, it's been—"

"Nat, it's okay. We just miss you," Abbie said. Since she couldn't bear to be sentimental for too long, she added, "And I'm going to need a forklift to get out of here 'cause I'm about to go to town on this buffet."

"Ten bucks per person to go hog wild," I said. "Twelve with a drink."

As I checked them out, I felt Levi watching me. I handed him his receipt and cup and gave him a friendly but distant smile.

Next to him, Bryce was frowning. I realized he'd barely said a word. "Why the long the face, Bryce?" I asked, doing my best bartender-therapist impression.

"Vanessa broke up with him," Abbie stage-whispered. "After two years, she's apparently too busy to date."

"And since I'm leaving for school and she's not, she thinks staying together will just delay the inevitable," he mumbled, his eyes misty behind his glasses.

"I'm sorry," I said softly, and turned to open the refrigerator of desserts and cokes behind me. "You're a catch. She'll regret it. Here, have a slice of key lime pie on the house."

"Thanks, Nat." Bryce took the plastic-wrapped plate and managed a smile that lingered a little too long.

Uh-oh, I thought. The Wardens prohibited revenge magic, but I could imagine Vanessa flouting the rules to curse Bryce's rebound crush.

I cleared my throat and looked away. "It's open seating."

"Come hang if you get a minute," Abbie said, and bounded toward the stack of plates on the buffet.

The boys followed in a cluster, but Faith stayed behind. "Are you okay?" she asked, propping her chin on her fist, observing me.

"Of course. Why?"

"I know you need to save up for a car and do your summer training and stuff, but we planned this amazing, fun summer, and you're barely around." She shrugged. "It's just not how I pictured it."

"Me neither, really," I said, unable to resist a glance at the group laughing and joking as they loaded up their plates. I wished I could go back to when I didn't know anything about the Wardens or the Woodwalkers.

"I'm glad y'all came by, though," I added, swallowing the fear that stuck in my throat. "The only people who like this place are tourists and old folks."

"Levi suggested it," Faith said, narrowing her keen, pale eyes. "I think he was hoping you'd be working."

I snorted as I punctured their receipts on the check minder. If Levi wanted to see or talk to me, he was never more than a simple text or a knock away. He didn't have to rally the troops and storm my workplace.

"Sometimes I think he might be into you." Faith tapped her short fingernails on the laminate countertop. Nails were one of the most foolproof ways to tell the twins apart if all else failed, since Abbie's were always manicured in festive colors. "He hardly ever talks to you."

"If you think that's what a crush looks like, you need to go back to elementary school," I scoffed.

"I mean, I think he might be nervous or something. I've caught him watching you since he's been home."

I looked over my shoulder and saw our friends settling into a corner booth. Levi was talking to Bryce and paying me no mind.

"He's different from other guys, Nat," Faith said quietly. "He's complicated. I've been friends with him my whole life and even I don't totally get him, plus he's been through a lot. Maybe you should be the first to make a move."

I scratched my nose to hide my reaction. If Faith weren't half of a Faith-and-Abbie combo, I'd have told her everything already. But their twin bond was sacrosanct, and they didn't keep secrets—which meant Abbie would be nudging and winking about Levi for the rest of the summer.

"Anyway . . . ," Faith finished, patting the counter. "Come over if you get a break."

"Okay," I said, feeling a striking disappointment when she left me alone.

A few more customers came in over the next fifteen minutes. Bored of studying the fishing trophies on the wall, I glanced to make sure the manager was nowhere to be seen and abandoned my post. If he got ticked, an apology and flattery would get you off scot-free. Standing up for yourself was a quick way to get fired.

I made my way over to their booth and perched on the crumb-covered bench next to Abbie. "What time do you get off?" she asked, resting her head on my shoulder.

"Eight thirty."

She groaned.

"I'm sorry if Emmy ran you off from babysitting," Levi said. "I thought you were okay sharing hours with her."

"I was. I didn't quit because of Emmy. Taking care of a kid requires a lot of energy."

Abbie raised an eyebrow. "And this doesn't?"

"So, she didn't encroach?" Levi asked in an authoritative, big-brother voice. "You can tell me if she did."

"No, I swear."

Levi's hazel eyes didn't leave mine. "I just don't want you to—"

"Levi, I *promise*. Okay?"

Silence ensued, and I didn't realize until then that my tone had been tense and Levi's shoulders tenser. Grayson tapped his fork absentmindedly on the table. Abbie fiddled with her earrings, a sign that she was feeling awkward.

"I'm so excited for the festival on Saturday," she said, cracking the tension wide open. I appreciated her for it. She pointed up at the speakers. "I love this song. I can't wait to see her play."

"Wait," Grayson said, bracing himself against the back of the booth. "The Riley Carson Band is playing the festival? Seriously?"

I nodded. "I have no idea how we snagged her. She's on tour playing way bigger venues."

"Maggie Arthur is a force to be reckoned with," Abbie said, lifting her cup in salute. "A true icon. I want to be her when I'm old. I'll be hip with the youths, too."

"Dude, Riley's a smoke show," Grayson said, smacking Levi's bicep. "I wonder if she'll recognize me."

"From where?" I asked.

"She's actually a friend of mine from college," Levi said, and my stomach pulled a painful somersault. That would explain how the board had managed to book such a high-profile band for our quaint festival. "Grayson met her when he visited me a few months ago," he added. "And no, dude, she won't recognize you. Y'all talked for less than a minute."

Was that a slight tinge of possessiveness I heard in his voice? I'd been listening to Riley's music in the dark, wakeful hours, feeling comforted by it when I couldn't get my mind off the Woodwalkers. Her lyrics made me think of Levi. Now that I knew they could potentially be *about* Levi, the voice floating over the speakers afflicted me with envy.

"You can reintroduce me," Grayson said. "Maybe she'll want a tour of the town like Juliana did. I could take her out to the cabin—"

"Don't," I snapped. "We're lucky we didn't get in trouble for it last time."

"She'd probably rather go to a bar than the boonies," Levi said. How well did he know this girl?

The bell above the door rang again. Lindsey stepped inside and removed her aviators. I nearly gasped at the bruise that ringed her left eye, a mosaic of blues and purples.

Weaving back through the maze of tables, I met her at the cash register. "Plate for one with a drink, please," she said brightly.

"I told you to leave me alone," I whispered.

"I'm hanging out with my friends. Gotta keep up appearances."

Other than the bruise, which I was sure no one else could see, she *was* keeping up appearances. Her chocolate waves were silky, and a light layer of mascara made her almond-shaped eyes pop. The black peasant dress that exposed her golden shoulders was about to turn Grayson back into her biggest, bootlicking fan—Riley Carson be damned, at least until Saturday.

I rang Lindsey up. After tucking away her cash and stuffing a dollar into the tip jar, she pulled three bundles of herbs from her bag and slid them across the counter.

"What are you doing?" I demanded.

"We figured you'd need more. I mean, you could learn to fight and then you wouldn't have to cower in the dark, lighting things on fire for protection, but…" She shrugged. "To each her own. I just thought you were better than this."

I set my jaw. "Kerry said in her letter that I could break the curse without joining the Wardens. I don't know how, but maybe you could help me."

"You don't get it, do you?" Lindsey asked, looking angry enough to karate chop my workstation into smithereens. "We're bound together, just like Lillian, Dorothy, and Johanna were bound to Malachi. Your magic is nothing without a connection to the rest of ours. We exist because of Malachi's curse. We exist to battle the Woodwalkers. We're the light that fights the dark, but a candle burning on its own will get snuffed out. I don't want you to get snuffed out. Don't try to go rogue."

She tucked her sunglasses in her hair and turned her back on me.

I hated knowing that she viewed my grandma's letter as the advice of a selfish coward, and me as even worse for honoring it.

I was bone tired when I got home, too exhausted to dream or worry about the Woodwalkers. The fear had faded to a duller, somehow darker feeling: isolation.

My hair smelled like frying oil, but I didn't even have the energy to shower. I tugged on an oversized shirt and boxers and slipped the letter from

Grandma Kerry out from under my mattress, which I'd neatly folded back into eighths along the original creases. She always liked to fold notes up tight, evidence that she had accustomed herself to keeping secrets.

I hoped that Kerry's resolve would uproot the seeds of doubt that Lindsey had planted. But before I could read her words again, deafening howls resounded through the quiet night.

I nearly jumped out of my skin. It was Maverick and Ranger barking. Bad possibilities hovered like ominous clouds in my imagination. Mom had said the dogs weren't allowed inside, but I couldn't leave them vulnerable out there.

Steeling my will, I pinched the amulet and made my way to the back of the house. I flicked on the porch light and opened the door.

The dogs stopped barking. They whined and wagged their tails as I slid aside the rusty bolt of the chain-link run. Maverick jogged past me toward the house just like I expected. But Ranger darted out of the gate and ran toward the woods at the back of our property.

I cursed and called his name, quietly. He never wandered off too far and was always back for mealtimes, so my parents would tell me to leave him be for the night if they heard me. They didn't know what I knew.

The moon was a sliver of waning crescent. I had to use my phone light to guide my steps as I ventured into the darkness that was dense as tar. My panting breaths filled up the humid night, and I swatted at the mosquitoes feasting on my legs. Maverick returned and trailed along reluctantly as I made my way toward the woods to look for Ranger.

We neared the opaque line of oaks, pines, and hickories, many of which were marked with the Warden's Rune. But I didn't see Ranger.

I listened for the rustling in the brush but heard nothing. Moving on through the scratchy brambles and sappy leaves, I encountered a treeless tract where the thin moonlight seeped through the whispering black canopies. Ranger was a stocky silhouette.

"Ranger," I hissed. He didn't turn. My heart thudded in the hollow of my throat. I trudged forward to find his hackles raised from his neck to the base of his docked tail. Maverick whimpered from behind me.

A rank stench hung in the warm air. The Wardens had said that the Woodwalkers scavenged for bodies, wearing the dead flesh and bones of other creatures. I didn't want Ranger to be one of them.

"Let's go, bud." My voice broke as I petted down his coarse hackles.

That was when I heard the gravelly breaths. They sounded ragged, animalistic . . . and *close*. I could feel a mighty presence tower above us and a hot, gamy gust blew over my face, stirring the sweaty hairs around my temple.

I locked my eyes shut. Maverick whined. A low growl rumbled in Ranger's throat.

Limbs quaking, I grabbed the amulet at my throat and held it up like a shield.

After a few unbearable beats of suspense, the creature huffed its dismay.

I sprinted back toward the porch, the dogs hot on my heels. I refused to look back until I'd slammed the sliding door shut and locked all three of us inside. Hopefully, Grandma Kerry had made this place a fortress.

When I found the courage to look through the window, I thought I saw a shadow slinking from the tree line back into the deep woods.

I sank down to the floor to catch my breath. "I don't know how long I can go on like this, Grandma," I whispered, pressing my eyes closed. Warm tears fell. "Doing nothing is so much harder than fighting back."

FOURTEEN

NINETEEN DAYS UNTIL THE CLAIMING

On the day of the Heritage Festival, joy hung in the air like a ripe fruit. The downtown square was flooded with color, from booths selling local vendors' goods to pretty flower arrangements draped on streetlamps. I held a new appreciation for the shiny lacquer the town tended to paint over the past—even if I could see the cracks.

The moon would be dark tonight. According to the Wardens, that meant the Woodwalkers could begin an earnest hunt for their Claiming prey.

I hurried out from under the enormous white tent covering the dance floor.

As I passed the petting zoo in progress, I reached down my boot to scratch the chiggers I'd gotten chasing Ranger the other night. The planning committee had asked the volunteers to wear Western boots to distinguish ourselves to guests. Aside from the fact that boots weren't very distinguishing in these parts, walkie-talkies in our hands and the word *volunteer* on our matching shirts would have done the trick.

Hordes of tourists had found their way to town already, and the event organizers had been shuffling us around all morning to meet the demand. I was crossing the overflow lot on my way to fill in for a parking attendant when I noticed some college-aged kids circled around the open trunk of a black van. One of them fidgeted with a piece of tech equipment.

"I'm just saying the cops or the FBI have to know *something*," a blond, bearded guy in a backward hat was saying. "I mean, twelve people died, and they couldn't even find anyone to charge? They were either bad at their jobs or super corrupt."

"Neither," a petite brunette girl in glasses said, gesturing at the heavyset guy with the equipment. "Paranormal activity is the only explanation. That's why we're here. If you're not a true believer, I don't want you on my team."

Bearded Guy rolled his eyes. "You know I am, Quinn, but a little skepticism is good for street cred. If there's a logical explanation, I want to find it."

"It would have been better to come on the actual anniversary of the massacres," the guy with the equipment said in a deep, dispassionate voice. "There will probably be more activity."

"They wouldn't even let us in the church any other weekend," the girl pointed out. "It's only open to the public for the choir concert. Getting to the cabin might be harder, though."

"Maybe we should try tomorrow," Bearded Guy said. "They'll be expecting people tonight."

Potential news headlines flashed through my mind, bold black letters spelling out that three young people were missing, last seen in San Solano. "Don't go there," I said instinctively, doubling back. The two who had been talking looked surprised, but the heavyset guy just directed a long, curious look at me over his paranormal thingamajig.

"Hi! Are you a local?" The girl dug a mini camera from her purse and pointed it at me. "Why shouldn't we go to the cabin?"

I collected myself and looked straight at the lens. Nothing turned people off faster than making them think the juice wasn't worth the squeeze. "Last time my friends and I went there, we almost got arrested and it wasn't even worth it," I lied. "We thought it would be creepy and it was just, like, an old house."

"Wait...," she said, squinting her eyes. "You were in that video from the cabin."

Dammit, Juliana, I thought. We were lucky that none of our parents had seen the footage. Juliana had added so many hashtags that anyone remotely interested in the sordid history of San Solano was sure to find it.

"You encountered something there, didn't you?" the girl asked. "Can you describe what it felt like?"

"Ever heard of acting?" I asked. I brandished my walkie-talkie like a shield. "I don't have time for this. Sorry."

Conveniently, a voice crackled through the speaker. "Still need help at parking."

"On my way," I replied, turning my back on the three visitors.

"Wait," the bearded guy said. His gangly arms swung as he jogged after me and produced a business card. "Here's my card. We could get coffee later and talk about the encounter."

The girl flashed him a reproachful glare. "Keep it professional, dude."

I glimpsed the words *Paranormal Investigator* as I politely tucked it into my pocket. "Y'all enjoy the festival."

As soon as they were out of sight, I pulled out my phone to text Kate. *Three paranormal sleuths are planning to go to the cabin tomorrow night,* I typed.

She responded promptly. *Thanks for letting me know.*

Half an hour later, an organizer sent me to help finish the town history exhibit at the courthouse. I walked back by the vendors' booths and saw someone selling "poisoned Communion wine" in plastic goblets. Scattered groups were drinking what were clearly grape slushies and snapping photos. The vendor also had twig talismans of the Malachian mark dangling from his stall.

Tasteful, I thought with a sigh. Heather, the tattooed baker and Earth Warden, was scolding him. "You are profiting off a tragedy," she insisted. "This is reprehensible. And single-use plastic is incredibly wasteful, sir."

The vendor, a sun-weathered man in a faded ball cap, crossed his arms. "There ain't a law against giving the people what they want, and there sure as heck ain't a law against using plastic."

Heather shook her head and marched back to her cheery yellow bakery booth.

When I entered the atrium of the limestone courthouse, I found Mrs. Langford double-checking the displays. There were old artifacts in glass cases alongside more contemporary exhibits, like the jersey of a San Solano football player who'd been drafted to the Cowboys. To visitors, it was hardly more than an excuse to escape the heat and nose around for lurid details about the massacre, which they wouldn't find here.

"Well, heck." Mrs. Langford's G-rated curse echoed from the far end of the atrium.

"Do you need some help?" I asked.

She whipped around with a safety pin in her mouth. "Oh hi, Natalie. It's nice of you to offer, but I'm just about done." She turned back and focused on affixing a pageant sash to a display board: San Solano's own Miss Texas runner-up from a decade ago, of whom we were inordinately proud. Clearly we were eager for a positive legacy.

I turned to leave, but the glass door swung open and Miss Maggie stepped inside, inspecting the displays. Strange, how she had once seemed like nothing but a kind matriarch with a drawl that dripped honey. Now her aura felt thick and enigmatic, a cloak of early morning fog.

"It looks perfect, Jennifer," she called out.

"Glad to receive a seal of approval from the great Maggie Arthur," Mrs. Langford grunted as she forced a staple into the sash. She stood back to assess her work, nodded, and gathered her supplies to leave.

"Wow," I said to Maggie after Mrs. Langford had departed without another word. "That was frosty. I thought you two were close."

"Not by choice," Maggie said matter-of-factly. She went straight over and adjusted the sash. By well-mannered Southern-lady rules of engagement, it was an insult on par with spitting on Mrs. Langford's shoe. "Jennifer hates the Wardens, but she needs us."

"Wait, she knows about us?" I asked, and immediately cringed at the reflex to categorize myself as a Warden.

"She knows enough," Maggie said. "My cousin Nora was Levi and Emmy's grandmother on their father's side. The Woodwalkers killed Nora when Mike Langford was just a boy. Mike always knew something was off about his mama's death, that she'd been a part of something dangerous. And he also knew Emmy was special... that she was one of us."

"Did he even know what you were?"

"He knew we were protecting the town from whatever killed Nora. He let us stick close to Emmy in order to protect her, but the terms changed after his passing." She clucked and turned back to me. "Jennifer never wanted anything do with us. She believes magic is antithetical to Christianity. Doesn't matter what we do, or what values we stand for. She doesn't like us. She thinks we're ungodly, which tends to chap my hide. But she respects that we keep her daughter safe. And that's enough."

"Does she know about my grandma?"

"Sure does," Maggie said, raising an eyebrow, relishing the reminder that I had skin in this game, too.

I thought of Mrs. Langford's ice-capped gaze when she had found me in her yard that Sunday afternoon. "Will she tell anyone?"

Maggie shook her head. "Couldn't if she tried and wouldn't dare."

Mrs. Langford had clearly been coerced into a blood oath.

Something else occurred to me. All along, part of me had sensed and even hoped that there was a deeper explanation for Levi avoiding me, something so powerful that it eclipsed any attraction. *This.* This was it. Not just small-town drama between rival families, though Lillian's book had made quite the intergenerational ripple. It was so much more than that. And if Levi had inherited his parents' prejudices, it could explain everything.

I could convince him that I wasn't involved, that I wasn't one of them.

A woman with a brunette, blunt bob peeked her head into the courthouse atrium, revealing bright eyes with startlingly long lashes and a proud chin. Upon seeing us, she smiled and stepped inside. She made a quick journey around the display, her cork heels clunking across the marble floor. As she approached us, I noticed the sweat drenching the underarms of her long-sleeved blouse. She wasn't from around here.

"Excuse me. Are you Maggie Arthur?" she asked.

"Guilty as charged," Miss Maggie replied cheerily. "What can I do you for?"

"I'm Alex Redding with Wayfarer, a culture and travel website based in San Diego." She shook Maggie's hand. "Could I trouble you for an interview?"

"You've come too far for me to turn you down," Maggie said.

Alex Redding fixed her eyes on me and repeated her name in my direction with more confidence than a giant font on a billboard.

"Natalie," I admitted in response, shaking her hand.

I watched her take note of my shirt and the walkie-talkie in my grasp. "If you don't mind, I would love an extra quote from a volunteer."

Maggie and I shared a conspiratorial look, striking a silent agreement that we would say nothing of my heritage.

"Uh, sure," I replied.

She smiled, ushered us to the nearest bench, and pressed record on her phone. I shifted uncomfortably in my seat.

"No one seems to want to confront your town's sinister past. Even at this history exhibit, there's no tribute to the victims who lost their lives in the Malachian Massacres. Do you see that as a sign that fear is still a part of everyday life in San Solano?"

Maggie tilted her head. "Well, you cut right to the chase, don't you?"

The journalist feigned a bashful laugh and pressed on. "Is there a reason why there's no tribute to the victims, especially given the upcoming anniversaries?"

"Flaunting tragedy for the entertainment of outsiders would be disrespectful," Maggie said, unfazed. "We at the Treasures of Texas Heritage Festival Committee like to show respect to the victims' families, while welcoming visitors with open arms."

"Do you worry that the cult could strike again?" Alex asked.

Not even the faintest of shadows passed over Maggie's face. She had lived with her secret for a long time. "Our history sparks curiosity and, dare I say, misplaced excitement. Some visitors may anticipate or even await another tragedy, but we here in San Solano feel confident that our local law enforcement will succeed in keeping everyone safe from harm."

The journalist pursed her lips, realizing she'd met her match and wouldn't be catching Maggie off-guard or uncensored.

"What do you think, Natalie?" Alex demanded.

"Um, I mean, it seems unlikely."

"Have you met many tourists eager to unmask the secrets of the notorious cult murders?"

I shrugged. "Most people are just here to have fun, I think."

She moved on from my unhelpful comment as though swatting away a gnat. "Tourism in San Solano has increased nearly sixty percent this year, according to your granddaughter at the chamber. Would you agree, Ms.

Arthur, that the spike in dark tourism has led your town to greater prosperity? It's boosting the economy, and more local businesses are thriving than ever before."

"Can't argue with statistics," Maggie said cheerily. "As I mentioned, we put a great deal of effort into our heritage tourism attractions, like this family-friendly festival, and we welcome all visitors."

Alex narrowed her blue eyes. "Wouldn't you say that ignoring the visitors' curiosity is biting the hand that feeds you?"

"San Solano was founded long before travel magazines and dark tourism, and we've managed not to fall apart since." She smiled, savagely. "This is a town, Ms. Redding, not a theme park."

"How can—" the woman started again, but I cut her off.

"I don't know what things are like in San Diego." My stifled Texas drawl spilled into my words as though my own mother had taken possession of my body. "But here, we respect our elders. Like she said, this isn't a theme park. Anyone with an appetite for gory details can go see a horror movie at the dollar theater."

Alex tucked away her irritation as neatly as her fresh-pressed blouse and stood up. "Well, thank you for your time," she said before slipping out.

A voice crackled from my walkie-talkie. "Can we get some more volunteers at Calvary Baptist? We've got people trying to sneak in, and the security guards haven't started their shifts yet."

"On my way," I replied, and headed for the door.

"Natalie," Maggie said, her voice echoing through the atrium. I turned. "Maybe today will remind you of what's at stake. The joy here, the innocence, the fragile barrier that separates people from the darkness in this town."

I knew she was trying to capitalize on our moment of camaraderie. But Grandma Kerry had not minced words. She had gone to terrible lengths to prevent me from taking the Oath, not just for the sake of protection, but of conviction. Even if I didn't understand it, I had to trust.

"There are more important bonds than the bonds of family," Maggie called as I stepped outside. I ignored her.

A few streets over at the church, I found Vanessa wearing a volunteer shirt that would have swallowed her whole if she hadn't tied the extra length in a big knot at her hip. She stood guard outside the foyer doors.

"What are you doing here?" I asked, trying to fan the sweat off my face with my collar. She hadn't been at the volunteer meetings.

"Trying to protect people. What I'm always doing," she said, but her tone had a little less bite to it than Lindsey's had a couple days ago. She didn't take my refusal to join personally. "Can you do a walk-through and make sure no one's inside? I can't keep up with these lunatics, and security isn't due for another ten."

I wanted to refuse simply because a Warden had asked. It felt like they were trying to bring me into the fold without my consent. But I didn't want regular people finding out about them any more than they did. That would put me in danger by virtue of association, not to mention impair their efforts to protect the town on the cusp of the Claiming—and mine, if I could figure out what Grandma Kerry wanted me to do.

So I did as Vanessa asked, encountering a trio of giggling preteen girls on their way out of the sanctuary. Before I could chide them, one girl in braces mumbled a self-conscious, "Sorry, it was unlocked," and led the others scuttling back outside.

I entered the empty sanctuary and crossed in front of the stage toward the choir hall. The performers were practicing in a closed classroom, but there were other voices, too.

"Do you feel that?" a girl asked. "I mean seriously, do you feel that?"

"I don't feel anything," a boy replied. "And I'm not getting a reading."

I found the paranormal "investigators" clustered on the stairs leading up to the baptistery.

"Only the choir is allowed to be here until the doors open for the performance," I said.

"Just a second." The girl wearing glasses, Quinn, put up a finger to shush me. She pushed herself off the stairs. "I sense something here." The guy holding the device pointed it up at the baptistery, but she redirected him, leading him down to the blank wall at the end of the hall, where Kate had opened the secret passage to the Warden hideout. Palms sweating, I pinched the button on my walkie-talkie. "There are three trespassers backstage in the church."

"You take your unpaid job seriously!" the girl exclaimed. The three of them stomped back down the hallway, and I heard her say under her breath, "That girl knows something."

FIFTEEN

I relegated my fear of imminent nightfall to the back of my mind until sunset, when an organizer forced me to sit down at a picnic table, shoved a plate of barbecue in my hands, and ordered me done for the day. But with the Wardens swarming, I knew the square was the safest place in town tonight.

As I tossed my plate in the trash, I caught sight of Dad's graying hair and Mom's blond poof bobbing in front of him. She spotted me and broke free from the crowd, weaving around picnic tables and blankets spread out on the grass. "This is so great, baby!" she said, planting a kiss on my sweaty hair.

"We're so proud of your hard work," Dad said, and gave me a hug. "Wow! Look at that tour bus! Riley Carson must be a big deal!"

I followed his gaze and found Levi talking to a gorgeous girl with hair like a stream of strong coffee. She wore a lace crop top over a high-waisted skirt that flattered her dense, volleyball-player build. If my heart hadn't just dived into the depths of my belly, I'd probably be awestruck by Riley. But seeing her and Levi perched together on the steps right outside her bus sucked the sparkle right out of the star sighting. There was no way of knowing, but they looked like they could have just emerged together. Levi said something that made her laugh and she shoved her hair behind her ear.

The two stood in close enough proximity that I could too easily imagine his sturdy arms encasing her, her fingers tangling at the nape of his neck, the space between them diminishing. The thought stung like a fresh blister. They'd met at college, where there were no parents, no curfews, no rules about who could be in whose room when.

A fellow volunteer named Tina approached, looking frenzied and windswept despite the lack of breeze. "Nat, I hate to ask one last thing of you, but could you help load in the opening band? We're falling behind schedule."

"Sure thing," I replied, wiping tangy barbecue sauce from my fingers with a wet nap and saying a quick goodbye to my parents. I hurried toward the temporary dance pavilion, where a plaid-clad foursome of guys was struggling to get ready for their sound check while obviously distracted by Riley's presence. Like the festival organizers, they understood that this event was small potatoes compared to other gigs she could be playing tonight.

Jumping into the action, I rolled an amp case from the back of a van and was about to heave it onto the stage when another hand covered mine. I recognized the rusty freckles and caught a blast of woodsy-fresh cologne.

"Can I get that for you?" Levi asked. I looked up—I always had to look farther up than I expected—and met his amber-flecked eyes under the string of lights crossing the pavilion, warm against descending dusk.

"I've got it," I said, and lifted. It took some elbow grease, but I managed.

"Will you get a break anytime soon?" Levi asked, leaning his hip against the stage. His brow was furrowed, his expression enigmatic.

"I don't know," I said.

"I'd like to talk when you get a chance," Levi said, his voice low and gentle, like you'd talk to a wounded animal. I could already guess why he wanted to chat: as a gentleman, he felt obligated to spell out that he and Riley were dating, especially now that I had seen them together.

I'd thought clearing up the misconception about my being a Warden would solve everything between us. Now, I realized the truth. My family legacy wasn't the only thing keeping us at a distance. I had been nothing but a short-lived, shiny distraction, a hometown heartbreak hit-and-run.

And I didn't need to hear him say it, even if he was just trying to do the decent thing. I didn't need to be pitied and coddled. He didn't owe me anything.

"I can't right now," I said stiffly. "I've got to help tear down the booths."

That was a lie, and besides, I was pretty tuckered out. But Levi didn't need to know that.

Someone kicked up the house music to take the pressure off the opening band. It blasted through the speakers and coaxed the waiting crowd onto the dance floor. Our friends started coupling off.

"Save me a dance, then?" Levi asked. My gaze traveled briefly over his fresh-shaven chin, and his slight, involuntary frown that made any breakthrough of joy twice as fulfilling to see.

"Okay," I agreed, despite myself.

Riley sidled up before I could escape. "Hey there!" she said, her gray eyes shimmering.

"Riley, this is Nat, my friend from high school," Levi explained. "She helped put the festival together." *Friend* was a stretch, but I slapped on a smile and rolled with it.

"Thank you so much for coming," I said brightly. I could have gushed about what an honor it was and how much I adored her music, but I left it at that.

"I'm happy to be here, and to see this guy." She nudged Levi's ribs, a playful, intimate gesture, and turned back to me. "Thank *you* for working so hard to put this together!"

Of course, she had to be magnanimous, too.

"Your hair is gorgeous," she said to me. "What shade would you call it?"

Levi cleared his throat and shoved his hands in his pockets.

"Um . . . dirty blond?" I tried, fearing this was some kind of inside joke or a quiz that I was failing.

"No, it's prettier than that," she mused, pursing her lips to one side, then the other. She shot Levi an oblique look. "It's more like honeycomb blond."

"That sounds better," I agreed. Usually, I could suss out when someone was being disingenuous, but I couldn't get a read.

"One dance before I warm up?" she asked Levi. She stood with her hands on her hips, long, dark curls cascading down her shoulders, daring him to refuse, knowing he sure as heck wouldn't.

"You know I'm not great at it, but all right," Levi said, his large hand enveloping hers. Over his shoulder he called back to me, "Don't forget!"

Right. The talk. As if this situation needed any clarification, let alone three minutes' worth of it. But Riley had already led him to the middle of the dance floor, and she was entwining her fingers at his ruddy nape, just like I'd pictured.

I exited the tent and marched through the crowd that had been summoned by the music, only to bump right into Emmy. Avery squealed my name and gave me a fierce hug. Her dress was covered in grass stains and she smelled like bug spray.

"I've missed you, you little cutie patootie," I said, squeezing her. "Are y'all having a good time?"

Avery nodded emphatically. "We fed the goats!"

"We just came from the petting zoo," Emmy said, brushing Avery's hair away from something sticky on her face. "Have you seen my brother, Nat?"

"He's in the pavilion."

She craned her neck to look. "Is he *dancing*?" She laughed. "I'm just glad he's having fun. Today's the anniversary of our dad's passing. I thought I should check on him before we go, but it seems like he's doing fine."

"Emmy, I'm so sorry," I said. I felt guilty for judging Mrs. Langford's churlish mood earlier, and for being short with Levi.

Emmy waved me off, her hazel eyes moistening. "We made a huge pancake breakfast this morning and fished in our pond out back. That was his favorite thing to do as a family."

"That's really nice," I said softly.

"Anyway." She wiped away a tear and took Avery's hand again. "I'd better get her home. See you later, Nat."

The band was finishing their rushed sound check when I turned back to the pavilion, my heart heavy. Levi and Riley gathered around a picnic table with the twins, Grayson, Bryce, and a handful of juniors. If I were to leave now, it would be with my dignity intact. It would show Levi that I didn't need an explanation from him.

But part of me wanted to stick it out and stay. My jealous imagination might be more ruthless than reality. Besides, I'd promised myself I wouldn't let any thorny feelings for Levi complicate my social life. Even though the summer had gone to hell in a hand basket for other reasons, I could at least keep that promise.

My truck was parked behind the courthouse, a quick jog away. I rummaged through the duffel in my floorboard and found a clean change of clothes, including a fresh bra and a cute black top with an overlapping slit that revealed a triangle of skin at my lower back. The console was a treasure trove; I found a stick of melted travel deodorant, stale mints, and a tube of mascara. I ducked down to change before crawling up to the mirror to make myself semi-presentable. Unfortunately, there was no alternative to the boots.

The opening band was in the middle of their set by the time I returned.

Levi was dancing with Abbie. Riley huddled with her band by the stage, preparing for their set. She was probably used to waiting in a fancy green room stocked with snacks, though her manager had only requested meals and water.

On my way to sit between Faith and Grayson, I was intercepted by Ryan Ashland, my truant chemistry partner from junior year. He swilled from a plastic cup that I suspected was full of beer, his eyes already red rimmed. "Hey, Nat," he said, swaying. "Wanna dance with me?"

"Maybe later," I said, knowing he wouldn't remember. He saluted with his cup and let me off the hook.

I circled the table and swung my leg over the bench. "There you are!" Faith said. "You cleaned up quick."

Grayson's blond hair flopped over his forehead as he turned his flirtatious energy in my direction. He often did that when Lindsey wasn't around to intercept. "You're gonna dance with me next song, right?" he asked, hanging an arm over my shoulder.

I reached for a sip of Abbie's Diet Dr Pepper across from me. "I suppose I can tolerate you for that long."

"That's what a guy likes to hear," he said, pumping his fist. Faith snorted into her soda cup.

In my peripheral, Levi brought Abbie twirling back, laughing goofily. His *actual* friends got to experience that side of him: easygoing, fun, openhearted. It was like they had a secret access code, while I haphazardly punched keys, hoping the system wouldn't lock me out.

The seating configuration changed as we rotated partners. The band started another cover song, and a grin crossed Faith's face. "I love this one!"

"Well, let's go then!" Bryce said, beckoning her out. Abbie and Grayson coupled off, leaving Levi and me alone at our table, catty-corner, both of us watching the band.

A minute of the song went by. Then the first chorus came and went. Just when I thought he was chickening out, he turned to me and jerked his head in the direction of the dance floor, a question on his face. I nodded.

As I followed behind him, his hand quietly found mine, sending a jolt of aching glee through my every nerve. He led me to the few feet of space we could find among the packed bodies and turned to face me.

I could feel him drawing in a breath as he resituated my hand in his grasp, then opened his left hand across the small of my back. Thanks to the cut of my top, his palm splayed smooth and warm against my skin as he guided me into our first steps.

He'd said he wasn't good at this, but he kept the rhythm just fine and brought me back close and snug after each twirl. I was more aware of my hand resting on his firm shoulder than I would be of my finger on the trigger of a loaded gun, and yet I hoped the song would last forever.

"You saw me leave Riley's bus, didn't you?" he asked.

"Um... yeah," I said. We had encountered the unpleasant part all too soon.

"We were just catching up."

"Okay," I said, as though this didn't concern me.

"We're just friends," he said, searching my eyes for a reaction. "We met in poetry workshop and realized on day one that writing is the only thing we have in common. She thinks I'm boring and broody because she parties a lot. I mean, no judgment. It's hard not to when you get free drink vouchers and no one cards you."

"Opposites attract," I said.

"Not always."

"Are you sure she feels the same way?"

"She's dating another musician. They're keeping it quiet so it doesn't look like a cheap publicity stunt when her album comes out in a few weeks."

I nodded, repressing a sigh of relief. "So why are you telling me? Worried about your reputation if you're known to have been inside a pretty girl's private tour bus?"

"Nat, I think you know why I'm telling you," he said, his voice gravelly and euphoria-inducing. He shuffled closer to me. My palm clammed up against his, and my knees felt a little wobbly. "I haven't meant to lead you on. But..."

He trailed off. The song ended with a drawn-out chord and the smash of a cymbal. "But what?" I demanded, ready for the truth. We lingered awkwardly on the floor while everyone else cleared away.

"I know what you are," he whispered. "At least, I know enough. I don't know who else might be involved, but I saw your grandma that night."

"What night?" I asked.

He set his jaw. "All I've ever gotten from Miss Maggie is deflection and lies. One of the reasons I stayed away from you for so long—and trust me, it wasn't easy—was because I didn't want to fall for a girl who had to keep secrets. So, if you believe that there's something here, like I do, please tell me the truth."

There was so much to process that I just stared in disbelief. The way he talked about staying away from me... It was like he'd been forcing himself to do it for a long time. I wondered if we knew each other better than I thought, if I'd been noticing him more than I liked to pretend. Maybe, looking back, that kiss wasn't as surprising as it seemed at first blush.

"Levi, I'm not one of them."

He shook his head and released my hand. "I shouldn't be surprised to hear another lie." His words on paper might have read as angry, but he sounded more disappointed. And exhausted.

"I'm not lying." A strange desperation overcame me. This was the last place on earth for us to discuss everything that lived in the shadows.

As if just realizing his hand was still resting on my back, he dropped it and stepped away. I felt him dislocate from our conversation like a bone from a socket. "I should have trusted my instincts," he said.

And then he was gone, leaving behind the pavilion lights that glowed like fireflies. The words rattled in my head as I watched him walk deliberately toward the overflow parking lot. I knew that if he gave me the chance, I could convince him of the choice I'd made. But would it be enough?

Finally, I stormed away from the dance floor and across the busy lawn toward my truck.

"Are you okay?"

The voice in the empty courthouse parking lot startled me. I whirled around to find Heather loading up her bakery van. She tucked her hands in the pockets of her yellow apron and leaned against her bumper, watching me.

There was no one else around. The concert would be the last event of the festival, and all the families with young kids had gone home. "I don't know what to do," I said, the pressure of tears burning the bridge of my nose. "There are consequences to being a Warden whether I join or not."

Heather opened a pastry box and placed a yellow cupcake with a fluffy tower of icing on a napkin. She held it out for me, a peace offering. My boots scuffed across the concrete as I accepted it.

"None of us had to absorb this so suddenly, like you did," she said. "It's okay to be in shock. Just sleep on your decision another night. Strange things happen under a dark moon." Tendrils of her purple hair caught the breeze as she tilted her chin to look up at the vast sky. We stood there for a minute until she sighed and said, "I'd better go. I'm on Warden duty in half an hour. Stay safe, Nat."

After she left, I sat on the curb and nibbled at the lemon cupcake, which made me feel instantly better. The entire town was enamored of Heather's bakery, and now I knew why: she charmed her baked goods. No wonder they made an appearance at every baby shower and birthday party in San Solano.

"Hey, Nat!" I looked over my shoulder to see Riley waving to flag me down. She bounced to a stop in front of my car and handed me a thin, rolled-up magazine. She smelled like expensive perfume and cigarette smoke. "I'm about to go on stage, but I wanted to give you this."

"*The East Texas Poetry Review?*" I asked, reading the title.

"Levi's poems are in there. I could tell you hadn't read them."

"Thanks," I said, but it sounded like a question. "How did you know?"

"A big reason I added this stop to my tour was to solve the mystery of the girl in that one poem," she said with a canny smile. "But turns out, it's not much of a mystery."

She jogged away, leaving me speechless.

I tore open the pages and read by the overhead light in my truck. The poem I found was beautiful, but I didn't think it was the one Riley meant. I moved on to the second one, written by Levi, and gasped at the first line.

THE OTHER SIDE OF SHADE

Levi Langford

Hiding with her in the checkered shade
of Miss Maggie's garden trellis, I see
only the thrumming blood-orange of life:
tomatoes clinging fat and worry-free to their sturdy towers,
her soft-seeming sundress, the strawberry cobbler
bubbling with heat on her paper plate.
This is the happy kind of going-away party.

Honeycomb hair gloating over one shoulder,
she asks me if there's anything I regret—
no mechanical "he-would-be-proud" or "it-will-get-easier."
Eyes outspoken as a summer storm,
sweat-slicked August freckles forgetting
that a cold day ever passed, she waits for my answer.

Up close, she is a mosaic of idiosyncrasies,
no mere stranger, no mere silhouette,
and her every inch and breath calls to my will to survive.
I meet her summer lips, and renounce Death
—his and mine—whether mine's yet to come
or has already. Until now, I was phantom-thin,
more lost than him, even though I'd purged the wrinkles
from my Oxford and rehearsed a smile.
His was the other kind of going-away party.

I hope it's not pity inspiring her to be
so generous with her blood-orange kiss,
our unpremeditated kiss,
my why-have-I-never-done-this kiss.
Tucked away in the quilted grid of garden light,
I remember everything alive needs darkness to thrive.
I see the other side of shade.

SIXTEEN

Natalie Colter

Fresh off devouring Levi's intoxicating words, I forced my prehistoric engine to roar to life.

When I reached the Langfords' house and hopped out, I heard crickets twittering amid the starlit acres of green. Levi's truck was already parked outside. I nearly lost my nerve when I mounted the porch steps, but made myself knock.

A tall figure loped down the stairs in a gray cross-country tee and gym shorts. The faceted glass door fragmented his face and the shock of red hair just before he opened it.

"Nat." I loved the way he spoke my name, startled and breathless. A few dainty moths fluttered past me into the foyer.

"I read this," I said, showing him the review. My heart felt ready to plummet to the floor. He would say it didn't mean anything, that I should separate the art from the artist.

Surprise navigated over his face, and then he flushed scarlet. Flustered, he scratched the back of his neck. "There's a reason I didn't come home and hand them out like candy."

"Can't anyone subscribe online?" I asked, as someone who had considered it myself.

He nodded, the red beginning to drain from his face, and let out a deep chuckle. "Yeah, but people only like to support the arts until it's time to pony up. I thought I was safe. It was Riley, wasn't it?"

"Yeah. She figured it out pretty quick." I found myself blushing, too. "Look, Levi, can I come in and talk to you? I have a lot to explain."

"Is someone here?" Mrs. Langford yelled from inside the house.

"I've got it!" Levi called over his shoulder. He stepped outside and shut the door. "Let's go sit out back."

I almost protested. Their house had probably been charmed to keep Emmy safe, but I didn't know the extent of the Wardens' protective boundaries. What if there was a Woodwalker prowling out there, waiting for someone to wander recklessly into the dark?

Levi was already leading the way to the side steps of the porch, and I knew I wasn't Mrs. Langford's ideal houseguest, so despite my misgivings, I trailed him past planters full of colorful flowers. Tonight, after our talk, I would convince him to leave town. Even if that meant hopping onto Riley's bus and going on tour for a few weeks—whatever got him out of San Solano until after July first. Unlike other guys in town, Levi knew enough to be warned away from here.

Out back, beyond the yard and tire swing, we reached a glistening pond with a dock. Four white chairs huddled around a stone fire pit near the shore.

The sight made my chest hurt. It reminded me of the empty fourth chair at my family's table in the breakfast nook.

Levi sat. I sank down beside him and took a deep breath. "My grandma never told me about the Wardens," I said. "I didn't know they existed until after the lake trip."

That earned a long, skeptical look.

"Really," I insisted. "She didn't want me to have anything to do with them. I don't know why."

"Because they're dangerous," he said matter-of-factly. "I've never been able to figure out if it's true, their claim that they're protecting us from something else. Miss Maggie cares more about keeping her secrets than convincing us she's telling the truth. But... but I know that what they can do is real, or at least some of it."

"The magic?" I asked. It sounded bizarre to say out loud, and Levi looked askance at me before nodding. "You said you saw my grandma 'that night.' What night? What happened?"

He stared at his clasped hands. I tried to solve the riddle of his expression but got distracted admiring the way his hair caught the starlight and jetted softly out around his temples. "Um, I'll just start from the top. My dad's mom, Nora, was one of you. She was a young single mother and pretty unstable. Sometimes she told my dad things that didn't make sense. She unloaded all her cares and fears on her four-year-old and figured he was too young to remember. But he wasn't."

My heart ached at the thought. The life I was meant to live wasn't easy.

"She died before he was old enough to clarify anything she'd told him, but he always wondered if there was any substance to her nonsensical ramblings. One night, though, my family went camping in the woods. I think Emmy was six and I was nine. While Emmy and I were gathering firewood, she had some kind of episode. I remember her skin feeling cold even though it was summer, and her eyes rolled back in her head. I thought she was going to die. My mom thought it was a stroke or a seizure and wanted to take her to the hospital, but my dad knew it was something else. Something unnatural."

I shivered, too suddenly to hide. Is this what I had been in danger of, out at the cabin? Is that what it looked like when a Woodwalker tried to drain a Warden of her life and magic?

"Nora had mentioned the church a lot in her rants, and my dad thought to bring Emmy there. He broke the lock and carried her inside and started shouting for help. My mom was screaming at him to take Emmy to the hospital, I was crying, and my dad was ignoring us both. I didn't think anyone would come. But Miss Maggie and your grandma did. They said a chant or something...and it worked."

He raked his teeth over his bottom lip and made a study of the ground, still grappling with the reality of magic.

"The Wardens told us that their gifts were hereditary. Emmy had inherited hers from Nora. They offered to take Emmy under their wing and protect her until she was old enough to learn. But they wouldn't say what she needed protecting *from*. My dad wanted to trust them. He would do anything to keep Emmy safe, even if it meant yielding to something he didn't understand. But my mom was convinced they were the cult murderers, and that they had somehow caused Emmy's 'episode' just to get their claws in her. She threatened to tell the police if they didn't stay away, so your grandma and Maggie took some kind of blood oath." He said this carefully, doubtfully, like I might call him ridiculous or accuse him of misremembering, but I nodded. "They swore the Wardens would protect Emmy without involving her, and they forced my parents to swear that they wouldn't tell anyone. My mom still planned to go to the authorities, but she couldn't. The blood oath stopped her."

I nodded again. Cricket chirps drowned out the gentle lapping of the water against the dock. I examined an angry mosquito bite blossoming on my forearm, replaying his narrative in my mind. I now knew why Kate had roped Emmy into babysitting: she wanted to guard Emmy as the anniversary approached.

"My parents spent a decade arguing about how close Maggie and the others should be allowed to get in order to protect her," Levi said. "My mom never dropped her theory that the Wardens were responsible for the murders, but my dad convinced her that they at least wanted Emmy to be safe, and that was what mattered most for us. After he died, my mom tightened the rules. It was only out of respect for my dad that she took Maggie up on the offer to host my going-away party, and she wasn't happy about Emmy accepting the job with you and Kate." He looked at me. "She wouldn't like it if she knew that poem was about you."

I let out a small gasp. I couldn't stop admiring his full lips, the strong, angular line of his chin, while the memory of our pen-worthy kiss hummed low and sweet in my thoughts.

Swallowing the urge to kiss him again, I asked, "What does Emmy know?"

"She knows she's different. She knows that Maggie and Kate are watching. She knows that she has to take her 'herbal supplements,' which apparently help protect her. And I think she may be figuring out that the danger increases the closer we get to the massacre anniversary. Weirdly, she never asked many questions." He scratched his chin, pensive. "I think she learned, like I did, that bringing it up made my parents fight. We never talked about it and did our best to stay away from you and your family without being rude enough to draw attention. My mom thought Maggie might use you to recruit Emmy. When she found out you tutored Emmy for an exam, she blew a gasket."

"I wondered why she didn't ask for my help again," I mused. "Emmy got a good grade on that test."

He smiled wryly at me. "I know there are other families involved, but I've tried not to think about that. It's tiring, being suspicious all the time." He closed his eyes briefly. "How much danger is Emmy in? How much danger are you in?"

"Not as much as you're in."

"You're referring to the massacre?" he asked.

"I can't tell you anything," I whispered, "except that you should leave town until after the anniversary."

A crease formed between his brows. I wanted to smooth it out, to steal away his reservations. "Of course." He jerked to his feet, striding to the edge of the dock.

“Their secrets aren’t mine to tell,” I said, and followed him. “Can you understand that? And can you please stop changing your mind about me from one minute to the next?”

He was staring out at the water, but he turned to face me, his expression wounded. Gently, he said, “The only thing I ever changed my mind about was whether I should act on the way I felt about you.”

That confirmation was all I needed. I stood on my toes and pressed my lips to his. His were already opening obligingly against mine, warm like fresh-brewed tea. His hand found its way to my waist and bowed me against him. I could taste in our kiss that he had been waiting for this, longing for this, just like I had.

The back door of the house squealed open, but we barely registered the sound as his arms encircled me, his lips moving with the kind of hunger that turned my knees to molten lava.

“Levi!” Emmy called from across the yard. “Mom said you left the office a wreck with dad’s stuff and need to come clean it up!”

I knew Emmy couldn’t see us in the dark, but I instinctively pulled back from him. Levi sighed. I realized my hands had found their way to his broad chest and that his heart was thrashing under my palm. “Be there in a minute!” he called.

“I’m getting eaten alive anyway,” I said, smacking another mosquito on my knee. “Maybe we should go inside. I’ll help you. I mean, if your mom will let me.”

“She’d have a hard time stopping us. But I have a better idea.”

“What?”

Without another word, he hoisted me up and threw me in the pond, ignoring my protests. I sank into the cool, refreshing darkness and paddled my way back up to the surface.

“I can’t believe you just did that,” I gasped, peeling my hair off my face. “What if my phone had been in my pocket?”

"It wasn't."

"How do you know?"

A gruff smile and a flash of eyebrows told me he'd given the region a glance or two. He kicked off his flip-flops and removed his shirt. Tan lines intersected with contours of muscle under his lightly freckled skin.

He dove in. The pond rippled with his weight, and I treaded water to stay above the surface. He emerged and grinned at me. Bashful, I let out a nervous, elated laugh. Once he realized my toes didn't touch the bottom, he waded toward me and scooped up my elbows. Weightless and wonderstruck, I had to resist the urge to wrap myself around him like a starfish.

"Do you want to go on a date with me?" he asked.

"You're supposed to be leaving town," I reminded him, even though he'd agreed to no such thing.

"I'm not going anywhere."

I shook my head. I'd have to make him. But right now, I wanted to revel in this moment, to pretend that danger didn't exist. "Are you going to take me out on the town and show me off at the dollar theater and Sawmill Barbecue?" I teased.

"Come on, San Solano isn't that pathetic. There are better places we could go. Or *a* better place, at least. Everyone's going to Tejas Grill tomorrow night. Maybe we could go together?"

So, he did want to show me off. Or he wanted our date to be casual.

Recognizing the second connotation, Levi quickly squashed my worries. "You could come over here before to watch a movie. Or maybe we could go on a walk? Should it be more extravagant than that? I don't know, I haven't done this in a while."

"No, that sounds perfect," I said, hooking my arms around his neck. I could tell his feet were flat on the floor of the pond, a solid pillar anchoring me in place. Just an hour ago, I would never have believed this turn of events possible. "I really like you, Levi."

"I really like you, too," he said through another incandescent grin, and kissed me again.

But a sudden, excruciating pain drilled through my skull, and I yelped against his lips. The throbbing sharpened to the point of being unendurable, and spread until every bone in my body ached, just like in my nightmares. I felt like I might break apart. Levi's voice sounded far away, but his hands were near, propelling me back toward the dock. I planted my fraught hands on the wood planks and wriggled up with his help.

"Nat, what's wrong?" he demanded, his voice going in and out as he knelt over me, dripping.

The knife-sharp agony began to ebb, and I gasped for breath as if I'd been drowning. I felt a warm wetness bubble up from within my ear and trickle over my right ear lobe. When I touched a trembling finger to it, I pulled away to see dark, sticky blood.

Levi snatched his discarded shirt and pressed the soft material to the side of my face. But now my other ear was bleeding, and my nose too, dribbling over my lips, sharp and metallic. The water and the streams of blood mingled together and smeared like paint on my forearms as I tried in vain to wipe it away. Thoughts running wild, I found myself thinking of Malachi, of her blood baptism, of the legends about her roaming the woods in her dripping white robe.

"Let's get you inside," Levi said, barely restraining his panic as he shouldered my weight and helped me stagger toward the back porch. The lights inside his kitchen seemed too bright as he swung open the door.

"Here, here," he said, exchanging his bloodstained shirt with a clean dish rag. "I'm going to get my phone so I can call an—"

"Levi!" A distressed cry echoed down the stairs, powerful enough to jangle the light fixture over the kitchen table. The call was so distraught, so fever pitched, that I couldn't tell whether it was Emmy or Mrs. Langford.

Levi gripped my elbow. "Come on, you can lie down while I—"

"Help us!" Mrs. Langford roared.

"It's okay, I'm okay," I assured him, waving him on. "It's just blood."

"I'm going to get you help. Hold tight."

My vision blurred, but I felt compelled to follow his trail of water as he charged barefoot to the foyer and up the stairs. Like stumbling through a funhouse in a trippy nightmare, I arrived at the upstairs landing without quite knowing how.

The commotion was coming from a room at the end of the hallway with a canopy bed and twinkle lights. Through the open door, I could see Emmy hunched on the hardwood floor in girlish satin pajamas. Her mom held back her thick, fire-red hair while she coughed up clumps of dirt.

"What is this?" Mrs. Langford shrieked at Levi, wide-eyed and paler than Emmy herself. "She's had nightmares like this, but it's never happened before."

I covered my mouth with quavering fingers. When I swallowed, I tasted blood. There was no denying it: our suppressed magic was hounding us like a cattle prod.

Something must have happened to provoke it. Something bad.

"I'll call an ambulance," Levi said, grabbing his sister's phone from the nightstand, but Mrs. Langford jerked up and seized his forearm.

"No! They'll think there's something off about her," she hissed. "They'll think she's a Malachian."

"Then what are we supposed to do?" he asked, and I heard the slender thread of calm holding him together threaten to snap.

"They can't do anything for her," his mom said over the horrid sounds of Emmy choking up a fresh clot of dirt. "It's them. It's *her*."

I'd been standing perfectly still and silent in the hallway, watching them. Mrs. Langford's manic gaze darted to meet mine.

"I'm calling Miss Maggie, then," Levi said, shrugging out of his mom's determined grip.

The pain slammed back into my skull, and I tasted dirt at the back of my throat. All three of my gifts were haunting me, ambushing me. I stumbled back down the stairs, my blood-slicked hands sliding along the railing.

I knew what I had to do.

And I knew my magic wouldn't let me rest until I did it.

"Where are you going?" Levi called after me, but I slammed the door. The keys were still in my pocket. I coaxed my truck to life, the pain abating again, and thrust the gearshift into reverse.

Feeling watched by the invisible moon, I pumped the gas pedal and roared down the country road. As I neared town, though, my truck sputtered and gave out. I'd pushed it too hard. It retained just enough momentum to roll off the road and onto the shoulder. My slippery fingers struggled to grab my phone from the cup holder, and the pain and bubbling blood returned, punishing me for slowing down.

Cringing, I slithered out of the truck and ran the last quarter mile, my wet sandals slapping the asphalt until they broke and fell off, one after the other.

A car passed, and as if tugging me around on a rope, the force within me compelled me to leap into a grassy ditch. The festival would be wrapping up a few streets—and yet a whole world—away.

Finally, my battered feet welcomed the relief of the soft churchyard. No cars were parked outside. The choir concert had ended hours ago, and the security officers must have done a good job scaring trespassers away.

The pain had nearly abated. I wiped my fist on my wet shirt and raised it to pound on the sanctuary door, but it opened before I got the chance. Vanessa absorbed the sight of me without the slightest hint of surprise. She must have divined that I was coming. She had traded her white volunteer shirt for a black ensemble. A bone pendant dangled from her neck, and a sheathed hatchet hung from her belt.

"Come on," she said, and ushered me into the candlelit sanctuary. Lindsey sat on a pew, decked out in black leather again, her hair in a high, tight ponytail that would have given me a tension headache. Heather was perched on the edge of the stage, an antique-looking firearm holstered at her hip. Vanessa's sister Brianna was pacing the aisle. They looked like they'd been expecting me, and in this condition, no less.

"What happened?" I asked, even though a part of me already knew.

"The first victim was Shadowed," Vanessa said.

"Ryan Ashland." Lindsey met me with a damp towel. "We were distracted by the snooping tourists and missed him sneaking out to the cabin with a girl."

I pressed my face into the towel, holding back a scream of frustration. Grandma Kerry had been so stingy with information. Why hadn't she told me that my magic would twist my arm, force my hand, send me staggering here even after she had told me to stay away?

What if I had done what the Wardens asked the night they first invited me here? Yes, I would have defied my dead grandmother's wishes, and that was nothing to take lightly, but maybe I could have protected Ryan Ashland.

"I want to help," I said, my voice hoarse. "And I don't think I have a choice."

SEVENTEEN

Vanessa was ready for me at the Communion table. From twin boxes with velvet lining, she retrieved the collyrium and the engraved chalice. Her brow was sweaty, and a streak of blood stained her neck. They'd already faced Woodwalkers tonight.

With the warm towel, I wiped the blood from my face and scrubbed vigorously at my arms.

"We just need to wait for the Triad," Lindsey said. "They're on their way here."

"We don't *need* to," Vanessa said, uncorking a cask of wine. "There's one of each Warden here. We could do it ourselves."

"I think we broke enough trust trying to involve Nat in the first place," Lindsey said.

Vanessa nodded and shoved the cork back into the cask. The Book of Wisdom lay open on the table next to a ball of twine. The left-hand page said, "Boiled Bitterwine," with instructions for preparation, and the title of the right-hand page read, "The Oath."

"You're making the right choice," Brianna said, crossing her arms and leaning against the stage. She was four years older than Vanessa, a few inches taller, and rather than voluminous curls, she wore her hair in chunky braids that were currently knotted in low pigtail buns. Brianna was one of a small number of single young adults who should have outgrown this town. Most twenty-something people from San Solano had left for college and stayed gone, or already had a spouse and kids, like Kate. If not for being a Warden, Brianna would have gotten the heck out of here.

"What will the bitterwine do exactly?" I asked her.

"Because of everything we've been taught about witches and demons and Satan worship, etcetera, many of us resist our magic without realizing it," Brianna explained. "The wine allows you to embrace it. It gives you strength, helps you heal faster, helps you see in the dark. It gives you everything you need to fulfill your purpose."

The ingredient list included countless herbs and plants, a few that I was pretty sure were baneful, like datura and belladonna, because Grandma Kerry had shooed me away from them in her garden. There were even more exotic ingredients, like ground animal bones, tree roots, and sparrow blood mixed with raw honey. Nausea made acidic saliva pool behind my tongue.

The sanctuary door groaned and Maggie appeared, looking surprisingly haggard. I had a feeling it wasn't purely from running the most highly attended event of the year.

"I figured I'd see you here," she said, giving me a once-over. Had she known all along that the first Shadowing would drive me back, that I had no choice in the matter?

Vanessa and Brianna's grandmother, Cynthia, emerged from the back hall, looking well rested and ready to take the night shift. "Hello, Natalie," she said knowingly.

Lindsey's abuela wasn't far behind Maggie. They knew what I was here for.

"Did Levi call you?" I asked Maggie. "Is Emmy okay?"

"She's fine now," Maggie said, locking the door behind Abuela. "I couldn't assure Jennifer that it won't happen again, but I think your willingness to take the Oath has appeased the magic on both of your behalves."

Vanessa filled the chalice. Lindsey unwound a generous length of twine and sliced it with her dagger, handing it to Sofia. Heather slid off the stage and stood with her head bowed. Vanessa, Lindsey, and Brianna stepped back, giving a wide berth to the Triad.

The older women surrounded the Communion table. Sofia beckoned for my hand and I stared at the blood drying under my fingernails as she looped twine around my wrist. Patient, steady, she connected me to the Triad, and Cynthia tied the final knot on Sofia's wrist, closing the loop.

"Read the Oath aloud," Maggie directed. "Say all three first lines since you have all three gifts."

My gaze fell to the open book. The expected rhymes were absent, replaced with straightforward prose. Malachi's power here was stripped back, laid bare, and I felt the potential of what she could summon with a simple, intentional word.

I swallowed any second thoughts and read, "I summon forth the power within me—that of earth, dark, mysterious, and giving; that of bone, enduring, wise, a teacher of the past and future; and that of blood, quick, potent, and binding. I vow to use it to protect the innocent, to fight the darkness, and to guard the precious secrets of the sisterhood here represented. I will now free my magic and open my Sight."

The Triad answered in unison, "By the powers of earth, bone, and blood, proceed we Wardens to our noble work."

Lindsey severed the twine, and the three older women stepped away from me, gesturing toward the engraved chalice and the collyrium.

"Drink the boiled bitterwine first," Maggie instructed. "You want your magic good and settled in before you see anything unsavory. It helps to hamper the fear."

The jeweled red depths of the wine caught the light, almost alluring. What was not alluring, not in the least, was the cloying, offensive smell of the unorthodox ingredients. It was so much worse than Lindsey's revolting green smoothies, which she must have loaded with a magical assortment of herbs to increase strength and endurance. All those incredible spells, and they couldn't manage to mask the taste of this stuff?

Grimacing, I tipped the chalice back and poured the brew down my throat. I finished off the dregs and slammed it back on the table.

Right away, I felt my blood quickening in my veins, the lingering pain of that torturous ache in my bones easing away, my muscles tensing in readiness.

"Here," Sofia said, motioning for me to sit on the front pew. "Lean your head back, and I'll administer the collyrium."

I did as she directed and heard the glass vial and dropper chime. The drops grew bulbous and splashed into my eyes. After I blinked them away, starry blots floated through my vision. My focus went in and out, like peering through someone else's prescription glasses. When it sharpened again, the shadows in the sanctuary seemed less dark than before.

"I suggest bunking in the hideout as the changes take effect," Sofia said, patting my shoulder. "You're going to feel—"

She was interrupted by a distant, deep voice yelling my name. Levi.

An urgent knock pounded on the door. "Nat!"

"That boy is a piece of work," Maggie huffed, starting down the aisle to answer. Another violent knock, and this time the door rattled on its hinges. "Hold your horses!" Maggie shouted, jogging the rest of the way. She unlocked the door and demanded, "What is this nonsense, Levi Langford?"

Even though we'd been together minutes ago, I felt like I was seeing him with fresh eyes. Maybe it was the collyrium, but I fancied I could see the full kaleidoscope of emotions on his face and the previously imperceptible canyons of colors in his hazel eyes, even from afar.

"Nat," he said, stepping around Maggie, relief in his breathless voice. "I saw your truck on the side of the road. I thought something"—he shook his head—"I thought something horrible had happened to you."

Before I knew it, he was there, his hand cradling my face. I felt Lindsey and Vanessa exchange glances. From their perspective, this must have escalated quickly.

"I'm okay," I assured him. "It just broke down."

"Why was that happening to you?" he asked, lifting a damp strand of my hair that looked like it'd been dyed a washed-out shade of red. "That was a lot of blood."

"I know," I said, encircling his sturdy wrist in my grip. "But it's not going to happen again. Miss Maggie said I may have bought Emmy some time, too."

"By doing what?" he asked, noticing the objects on the Communion table. Betrayal flashed in his eyes. "Did you do some kind of…ritual, or something? Did you join them?"

Without breaking our eye contact, I nodded gravely. "But it's not something I take lightly."

He released me and stepped back.

"Levi, you really need to leave town," I said, eager to touch him again, like pinching myself to rule out that I was dreaming. "Take Emmy and travel for a bit."

"Emmy can't go anywhere," Maggie said. "Her magic would revolt more dangerously than it did tonight."

"Then he can go, and we'll keep protecting her," I said.

He *had* to leave. I couldn't let him get Shadowed. I *wouldn't.* I would learn magic, learn to fight with their weapons, get stronger. If I had to, I would tie him up and force him onto a bus out of here. But he wasn't getting Shadowed.

"Nat," he whispered. "I'm not going anywhere."

"But I'm trying to protect you!" My voice boomed through the sanctuary. Somehow, no one seemed to have noticed people arguing and pounding on doors. It was a testament to the strength of the boundaries that Malachi herself had helped enforce.

"I don't want you to put yourself in danger to protect me. Just tell me what's going on, what's out there, and I can protect myself." He turned to Maggie.

She shook her head. They had had this conversation before.

Looking apt to uproot one of the pews, he clenched his fists and turned back to me. "Why did I let myself do this?" he asked. "I knew how hard it would be to care about you when you can't tell me what's happening. How do I know my mom is wrong about the Wardens when no one will tell me a goddamn thing?"

I rapped my knuckles on my forehead. Why did something so good have to be so complicated?

"Go home, hon," Maggie said softly. "Knowing what's out there won't do you any good."

"This isn't over," he said. With one last look at me, he stormed out of the sanctuary.

"Wait, Levi!" I called after him. Maybe he would let one of the Wardens escort him home. The first victim had been Shadowed, and he could be next. But by the time I flung open the door, his truck was already tearing noisily out of the grass. He'd parked in the churchyard, reckless in his urgency to reach me.

I watched his taillights shrink until he turned the corner. The door to the sanctuary finished its slow squeal behind me.

The hairs on my nape prickled. A foul stench crept up on my senses, like roadkill and mold and sulfur. I could feel a presence nearby, darker than an infinite hole and realer than my own heartbeat.

I didn't want to turn and look. What I wanted was to curl into a helpless ball. But since that wasn't an option, I faced my fear.

EIGHTEEN

An immense silhouette hunched in the middle of the road not thirty paces away. A tangle of antlers rose from its head. Its face was obscured by the shadowy trees, but I saw the outline of shoulders that were sinewy, gamy, nonhuman. It had long, tapering claws and an exposed ribcage that caught the faint golden glow from the high church windows.

A scream rose up in my throat, but I couldn't open my mouth to draw air. The Woodwalkers weren't just real. They were flesh and bone, rot and ruin.

"Nat," someone said in soothing voice. Vanessa materialized beside me, brandishing a hatchet. "Go inside."

The creature lurched forward. I threw myself back toward the sanctuary, smacking into Lindsey. Heather followed behind her with a pistol. Brianna dragged me inside by the wrist and traded places with me, slamming the door.

The door to the foyer stood open. The Triad must have gone out another way to get at the creature from behind. I was alone in here.

A cacophony of battle sounds exploded into the silence. I sank down to the red carpet between the pews to hide. On the verge of puking up the wine, I dropped my head into my hands and wished that I could close my ears to the gunshots, the metallic sounds of sharp blades slicing, and worst of all, the unearthly screeching.

After what felt like a long time, the sounds stopped. Lindsey tromped inside, the others on her heels. I expected to hear sirens burst the bubble of silence, but there was nothing. No outside reaction. Warden magic was really something to behold.

Kate had apparently arrived in the nick of time, and when she saw me, she rested her rifle against the wall and squatted next to me. "What'd I miss?"

"She took the Oath," Lindsey said, sheathing her daggers. She didn't seem to have any fresh wounds.

How did they do that? Charge out there so fearlessly and fight that… *thing*? That thing that reeked of death and looked like it had crawled from the pits of hell?

I shivered. Which man did it used to be? One of the mob murderers who had killed Dorothy's brother? Johanna's rapist uncle? Her abusive father who had done nothing to stop him?

Kate swept a stray lock of brunette hair from her face. Her mouth quirked to the side in sympathy as her sage-green eyes examined me. "Let's go down to the basement, and I'll draw you up a calming bath. Everything will be okay."

We traveled as a flock downstairs. Kate pulled me into the bathroom. She filled the claw-foot tub with warm water, steeping a loose-woven tea sachet of salts and fragrant flowers that dyed the water a mellow grayish-lavender. "This is my favorite bath tea," she said as I stripped down, shuddering, and stepped into the water. Polite with a hint of prude, she shielded her eyes and numbered off the ingredients. "It's heliotrope, hyssop, lavender, and star anise."

I leaned back and watched purple flowers slip loose and float on the water. It made me think of my swim with Levi in the pond. Everything had gone south so suddenly. "So...am I going to learn how to do what y'all did out there?" I asked after a while.

"We'll start you tomorrow," Kate said, perching on the lid of the commode. "Make sure to rest tonight. Maybe flip through the Book of Wisdom, see which spells and charms call out to you. Let the changes marinate a little."

Lindsey poked her head in. "Hey, Nat, do you need me to text your parents and tell them you're staying the night with me?"

"Yeah, I don't want them to worry. Tell them my phone died so I had to use yours."

"Where *is* your phone?" she asked.

"Oh my god! My truck!" I exclaimed, slipping a little as I tried to push myself out of the tub. "It's stalled on the side of the road and there's blood all over my steering wheel. What if Sheriff Jason sees it and tells my parents and they think I'm—?"

"Don't worry," Kate said. She handed me a towel. "I glamoured the color and license plate on my way here and wiped up most of the blood, I think. I took out your things, too. No one will know it's yours, but we should take care of it first thing tomorrow. Curiosity weakens beguilement spells."

"I'll take her home in the morning, and we'll get her dad to tow it," Lindsey said. "We'll go before dawn in case the charm wears off."

Kate approved. I tugged on an extra tee of Lindsey's and sweatpants of Vanessa's that were comfortable but too short. After a long day of work followed by a night of emotional confessions and a traumatic turn, the bottom bunk bed that Kate had made up for me should have been more enticing. But adrenaline coursed through my veins, and Vanessa and Lindsey were still wide awake and talking.

The two of them had stayed behind while the others went back out on patrol. I wondered if anyone else would be Shadowed by the time dawn came. The thought made me shudder.

While Lindsey rummaged in the pantry for snacks, I ran my finger over the spines of the books in the library corner with the tufted, poison-green velvet chaises. I hadn't noticed last time, but there was a book sitting open on the coffee table that contained handwritten annotations. Upon closer inspection, I realized it was the grimoire Lillian had stolen from her aunt's library, the one Malachi had used as a basis for some of her most powerful spells.

Beside it was an enormous leather-bound book with the Warden's Rune embossed on the cover. The edges were sprayed gold.

"Do you recognize that?" Lindsey asked, dumping a bag of chips, a jar of salsa, and a carton of ice cream coated in freezer frost onto the Earth Warden table.

She had mentioned that the Book of Wisdom had been glamoured. "Oh!" I exclaimed, and flung open the cover. There were hundreds more pages here than before, chock-full of spells, recipes, ritual instructions, and descriptions of herbs and crystals, all meticulously chronicled and organized.

"If you ever want to add a spell, a new page will appear in the right spot," Vanessa said, sitting on one of the chaises. She was sporting fresh bandages.

A book that magically generated pages should have warranted more of a reaction, but the rest of that statement was doubly intriguing. "You mean like... I could make one up?" I asked skeptically.

Vanessa tossed her legs over the head of the chaise and lay backward on the cushion, sifting her fingers through her curls. "Yeah," she said with a half shrug. "Every spell and elixir and ritual was made up by *someone*. You have more magic than any of us. Why couldn't you make something up?"

"I don't know how it works."

"Sure you do," Vanessa said. "You just have to let go of your inhibitions."

"Look for a spell you want to do," Lindsey said, and plopped on the rug with a ramekin of salsa and the bag of chips. "We'll start with that."

"All right." I heaved the book from the table and settled onto the chaise across from Vanessa's.

The table of contents alone was six pages long. There were so many different categories of magic: elixirs, teas, unctions, and ointments; divination, including tarot, pendulum use, finding lost things, and dream interpretation; beguilements like glamouring and the blanket deception that blocked normal people from noticing our magic; protective spells and charms like talismans and wards; blood rites; knot and binding magic; and, last but not least, curses accompanied by dire warnings. There were groupings of "exclusive spells" that only one type of Warden could cast, and "semi-exclusive," which meant any Warden could cast them with help from another. As if that weren't confusing enough, there were also "preferential nonexclusive" spells, wherein the elements of earth, bone, and blood worked like rock, paper, scissors, superseding one another depending on a complicated set of factors.

"You don't need to read that part," Lindsey said, peering at the book on my lap. "I mean, you could do any of them."

"Even a"—I flipped back to an interesting page in the elixirs section—" 'crystal rosewater pleasure elixir'?"

"Heather is such a badass!" Vanessa cackled. "The Triad told her to stop adding her sexy-time elixirs to the Book, but she does it anyway. Once something's written, it can't be erased. It can only be torn out, and that's basically sacrilege."

"Did you ever, like... try one?" I asked her. "To see if it worked?"

They both laughed this time. "Everything in there works," Vanessa said. "But, no, I um... I always wanted to with Bryce. We just weren't there yet." She picked at one of the button tufts on the chaise, looking instantly dour. If only Bryce knew how hard this was on her. If only we didn't have to keep secrets.

"Why, are you thinking of trying it with Levi?" Lindsey teased, and I gave her a soft punch.

"Ouch!" she exclaimed. "Careful. You're stronger than you think. So, what's the deal, anyway? With you and Levi?"

"Yeah, that was fast," Vanessa said, eyebrows hiked up.

"I think we might be a thing? Or we were, before I took the Oath. He doesn't want to date someone who can't tell him everything, so...I don't really know where that leaves us."

Lindsey sighed. "It's a hard life. You know how you've always thought my dad was a jerk for leaving us and moving to California?"

I nodded.

"Well, he was convinced my mom was cheating on him. Beguilements only go so far. He finally threatened to leave if she didn't tell him the truth about why she was always busy, and she figured it was easier to just let him go. He wanted to get full custody, but adultery doesn't factor into custody battles."

"Wow," I said. "I'm sorry, Lindsey. I guess it's better than him leaving you without cause, though. I feel bad about bashing him."

"You didn't know," she said kindly.

I continued flipping through the book. "Hey, there *is* one page that's ripped out," I said, running my finger along the torn edge. "Do y'all know what it was?"

Lindsey shook her head. "I never noticed."

"Me neither," Vanessa said. "Anything called out to you yet?"

"Hmm," I said, scratching my chin and flipping back to divination. I'd glimpsed something in the table of contents about communicating with ancestors. That snagged my attention. But I didn't want to get too deep too fast. I'd start with something else. "What's sortilege?" I asked.

"Throwing the bones," Vanessa said. "Reading objects to tell the future or find out the truth." She rolled off the chaise and went to the bunk beds to retrieve a small wooden box from her backpack. "I'll show you my sortilege set."

She placed the latched box on the coffee table and sat cross-legged on the rug. Inside, there was a pretty purple scarf holding nearly a dozen different little bones. My dad could have identified them, I was sure, but my knowledge of skeletal systems stopped at ninth-grade bio.

"Where do you get them?" I asked, setting aside the Book of Wisdom and sitting across from her at the coffee table. Lindsey scooted closer, too, and I nabbed another handful of her chips. "Do you hunt, or . . . ?"

"It sounds gross, but it's mostly roadkill. And sometimes we walk the woods to look for remains nature has already processed." Vanessa spread out the scarf with the bones and placed her palms flat on the table, her silver rings catching the light. "Each piece represents something. You could use my set, but it wouldn't work as well as one you cultivate on your own. You can pick what they represent." She pointed. "Mine are self, friend, family member, safety, wealth, love, suffering, yes, no, evil, and changeability. I try to respect the people I know and refrain from asking questions about their private lives. Honestly, it's for your sake as much as theirs, Nat. There are things that you just don't need to know, right? But"—she grinned and bit her lip—"for the sake of demonstration, let's have a little fun."

"Ooh," Lindsey said, getting more snugly situated.

Vanessa gave a self-satisfied smile as she slid five of the bones carefully away and kept six in play. She set one in the very middle, and then another, and then closed her eyes and hovered over a third. "I'm asking the family bone to be a friend tonight," she said quietly. After a moment, she dipped her head in gratitude and set that bone in the middle, as well. She gathered the other three that were in play, cupped them in her fists, and breathed on them, taking her time.

Then she asked the sortilege set, "Does Grayson think about doing it with each of the three of us on a regular basis?"

Lindsey snorted. I half-gasped, half-laughed. Vanessa threw the bones and rubbed her hands together in anticipation.

Two of the three landed close to the central pieces, and one of them was so far away it barely made it on the scarf. Vanessa laughed and pointed at the three central pieces. "These are us," she said. "The two that are closest represent love, and yes." She pointed to the farthest one. "That means no."

"Gross!" Lindsey said.

"Well, he still thinks about you the most," Vanessa laughed. "Don't need sortilege to see that."

"Ugh. I don't like him like that," Lindsey said. "I've exhausted the options in San Solano. I wish I were going to college."

My heart sank. I'd just taken an oath to defend the people of this town from supernatural predators lurking in the woods. How could I do that from a different state? The idea of e-mailing my college advisor to drop out put a big lump of preemptive regret in my gut. I'd lose my scholarship and my coveted place on the track team.

Don't just stop the Claiming. Break the curse.

Those words reverberated again, this time offering a glimmer of hope. If we could actually break Malachi's curse and rid San Solano of the Woodwalkers—for good—I could stay the course. Lindsey could go to college. Vanessa could reunite with Bryce. Brianna could move away, if she wanted. The grandmothers could focus their remaining years on relaxing and spending time with family.

"Can you see what's going to happen on the night of the Claiming?" I asked, and both of their smiles disappeared. I felt the need to justify the thought. "I mean, can we know who's going to be Shadowed by doing this? Wouldn't that be helpful?"

Vanessa placed her hand over mine. "Nat, there are things you don't try to see. It can mess with the balance of everything, become a self-fulfilling prophecy of the worst kind. There are rules. And even when there aren't rules, there's better judgment."

"Okay," I agreed. "I'll be careful."

Nodding, she scooped the bones back into the scarf. My query had darkened the mood, I could tell, but I wasn't sure why. Stopping the Claiming was our job, and it had been a logical question from my newbie perspective. But then I made the connection. "Did you break up with Bryce because of the bones?"

"I had a moment of weakness," she said, confirming my theory. "And I asked the bones whether Bryce would be Shadowed. But the more I tried to know, the closer evil came, and the farther safety went. Knowing leads to interfering, and the bones didn't want me to interfere. So I figured it was best for him—for everyone—if I distanced myself and focused on protecting the town, rather than just one person I care about."

"That's really selfless," I said.

"You know, sometimes I feel like the Pagans of the Pines cursed *us* that night, too," she said, placing the scarf back in the box.

I tried to chew on that, but the activating magic was coming in waves and it seemed to have receded for the moment, leaving me exhausted. "What happens to Ryan Ashland now?" I asked, yawning.

"Nothing, until the night of," Lindsey said, catching my contagious yawn. "He's safe until then."

Safe. What did that even mean anymore?

We went to bed. I curled up in the curtained-off darkness of the bunk below Lindsey's. Amid the unnerving transformations taking root inside me, I fell asleep thinking of Levi. My desire to protect him was galvanizing into iron resolve.

NINETEEN

EIGHTEEN DAYS UNTIL THE CLAIMING

"Hey! It's almost dawn. Are you alive?"

My eyes snapped open. Lindsey pulled aside the curtain and sat on the edge of my bed.

"I'm awake," I said, popping up so fast I almost hit my head on the top bunk.

"How do you feel?"

I took stock. I felt different. More alive. Strangely ravenous. For the first time in a month, I'd slept without waking up paralyzed by fear.

"Amazing," I answered. It was an understatement. The Wardens said I would be stronger. I tested this claim by giving Lindsey a gentle shove. She fell off the bed.

"Hey!"

"Wow," I gasped. "We should go for a run soon. Wait a second... did you throw all your qualifying races?"

She'd already found her feet again. "I was too busy with this to add more training and travel to my schedule. Come on. It's Sunday, so we'd better leave

before the pastor gets here to practice his sermon. The Triad doesn't like when we get cocky and use beguilements instead of discretion."

With a satchel full of magical oddities, I followed her out of the hideout a few minutes later. My "starter kit" is what Kate had called it. She'd made it for me months ago, just in case.

As we drove out of town, down the dark country road, my alert eyes darted from trees to street signs to unlit houses and barns, looking for something sinister waiting, watching, hunting.

"That was the closest they've been to the church, last night," Lindsey said. "They're getting bolder. Testing the boundaries again like they did before the last massacre."

A mangled animal carcass and a giant smear of blood appeared in the middle of the road. Lindsey swerved around it. "They were here," she whispered.

I gulped, but like the black candle on my first night in the hideout, the magic in me set to work. I didn't feel *un*afraid, exactly, but in control of the fear.

"My truck should be right up here," I said, pointing.

"Whoa," Lindsey breathed, slowing down. It was turned on its back next to the road like a helpless beetle, its mechanical underbelly on full display. I really, really hoped no one knew this was my car, or they'd think I'd wrecked and been dragged away by a wild animal.

"Looks like the scent of your blood got them worked up," Lindsey said. "That one last night may have tracked you from here."

The thought of a Woodwalker following me, hot on the scent while I ran barefoot through the dark, was the most terrifying thing I could imagine.

Lindsey realized the impact of her words. "Now you can fight them," she encouraged me. "You're not a sitting duck anymore." The seatbelt snapped as she parked and opened the door to the dewy predawn air. "Come on, let's put it back the right way and hope no one saw through the glamour."

"Put it back?" I repeated.

"Yeah. Turn it over."

I couldn't help but laugh. Lindsey hopped out with gazelle-like grace and disappeared around the truck. I followed. The sound of the wind rushing through the tall grasses behind me made my skin prickle.

Lindsey placed her hands on the truck and pushed. It moved.

"What the what?" I whispered.

"A little help?" she grunted. She was close to getting it balanced on two wheels now.

I ambled over and spread my hands beside hers. "I don't want to it fall back and crush us."

"It will crush me if you don't help," she said in a strangled voice.

Expecting it to be like trying to shove a concrete wall, I dug in my heels and pushed. I could feel my muscles throbbing with newfound power like a taut rubber band. The huge piece of machinery gave, teetering for a moment before groaning and crashing to its upright position.

Lindsey shook out her arms and loped around to open the driver's side door. Under the cabin light, she used her black shirt to wipe at a smear of blood left on the steering wheel. "Get in and put it in neutral so I can push it to the Sawmill parking lot," she said, pointing a quarter mile down the road. "Even with a beguilement, you always want to reduce suspicion as much as possible."

We took care of it and arrived at my house right as sunrise stained the rain clouds a dusty orange. A police cruiser was parked in the driveway. My dad and Jason went fishing before church every other Sunday, rain or shine. The only thing that alarmed me was the thought of lying to my parents *and* the sheriff at the same time.

My stomach grumbled as I swung open the screen door and smelled bacon. In the kitchen, my parents were tag-teaming breakfast while Jason sat at the table with a mug of black coffee.

"Y'all are back early!" my mom said cheerfully, slapping several more strips of bacon into a sizzling skillet for us.

"My truck broke down last night, and I didn't want to leave it there too long," I said.

"We'll deal with it after breakfast," my dad said as he stirred a pan of scrambled eggs.

My mom shook her head. "That truck is as old as the hills. It's time you got a new car. Whatever you've saved up working, we've agreed on matching half. I don't want you wasting your last summer at that catfish joint."

"Really?" I asked.

"We can't let you leave for Louisiana without a reliable car, sweetie," my dad said.

I hugged their necks, not caring that tiny drops of blazing hot grease splattered along my arm. But disappointment deflated my joy. What was I going to do about school? What would I tell my parents? Would they still want to buy me a new car if I they knew I might be dropping out?

"Ouch! I already saw the chiropractor this week!" my mom said, and I relinquished her from my grip with a mumbled apology.

"That's the weirdest thing," Jason mused. "I saw a truck flipped over on the side of the road on my way here. I ran the license plate and it's not registered to anyone. No papers or personal effects, either. I don't like to admit it, but something's off around here."

"I hope no one got hurt," Lindsey said, settling into the chair next to him.

"I just can't make sense of it." Jason glared at his coffee mug as though an answer might float to its surface, Magic 8 Ball–style. Nervous, I poured myself a glass of orange juice and hid my expression behind a big gulp. "Anyway," he said after a minute, "did y'all enjoy the festival yesterday? Even with the tourists making trouble, Miss Maggie works some serious magic every year."

Thankfully, Lindsey was ready to respond while I used my juice as cover.

My dad and Jason ate quickly so they could tow my car before heading to the lake. Mom went to do some filing at the vet office. I waited until they were gone to surrender to my ferocious appetite and eat the leftover bacon. When all was said and done, I'd gobbled down two cartons of yogurt, three fried eggs, six pieces of bacon, and toast. This new strength didn't come cheap in the fuel department.

"So, what's the permanent solution?" I asked Lindsey. "How do we break the curse? This has to stop somewhere, right?"

Lindsey bit a crunchy piece of bacon. "Not even Malachi could do that, and she tried for fifty years. But, I mean, you're related to her. You could always give it a shot after the anniversary."

"*After* the anniversary? What good will that do?"

"Prevent us from having to worry about the next one. This isn't the time to be messing around and experimenting, Nat."

"It wouldn't be messing around."

Her phone lit up on the table. She wiped her hands on a napkin and answered. "Hey, Kate. Yeah, we're ready." She looked at me and asked, "Have you ever shot a gun before?"

"Just a rifle at the shooting range."

"Did you hear that? Okay, bye." She grabbed the empty plates and put them in the dishwasher. "Kate's coming to pick us up."

Within minutes Kate arrived with Vanessa and Brianna. We headed east toward the cabin, but Kate passed the turnoff. I realized we were going somewhere else. The woods thickened up around us.

"Where are we going?"

"It's a surprise," Kate said, chipper.

"Shouldn't you be at church?" I asked. "Keeping up appearances and whatnot?"

"Routines have fallen by the wayside at this point."

"How do you keep your family from noticing anything?" I thought of the predicament Lindsey's mom had faced. There had been so much to process I hadn't even questioned Kate's balancing act.

"Beguilement spells and countless magical sleepy-time teas," she answered.

"When do you sleep?"

"From sunrise to seven thirty and on my lunch break, and any nights I'm off duty. Although this month, most of us are on duty every night."

A light rain sprinkled my window. Everything looked green and vivid during summer rains. I felt a pinch in my heart. I loved San Solano like you'd love an annoying little sister. I could tease this dinky place all I wanted, but deep down, I had a soft spot for it. What would happen if twelve more boys died? What would another unsolvable case of that magnitude do to this town?

"Do you think we can stop the deaths this time?" I asked.

"Lord willing and the creek don't rise," Kate said.

"Has anyone ever died fighting them? I mean, besides Nora."

"No, she's the only one, and she didn't exactly die fighting," Kate replied, her slender hands tightening on the steering wheel.

"What happened?" I asked.

"She cracked under pressure on the night of the massacre. After the Woodwalkers possessed the victims, Nora went to the sacred glade and relinquished her defenses. She opened her spirit to them... handed herself right over. They drained her of magic, and it made them stronger. The Triad believes they failed to stop the deaths because of her, though there's no way of knowing. There's only been one attempted Claiming. Not a fair sample size."

"Why?" I asked, bewildered. "Why in the world would she do that?"

The rearview mirror reflected her scowl. "Maybe she had misguided notions of stopping them some other way. Or maybe it was just too much for her. From what I've heard, she was a sensitive soul, like Emmy."

Some other way. How could sacrificing yourself to the enemy's benefit ever be a viable alternative to fighting?

"It was a dark time for everyone when it happened," she added. "She was a powerful Earth Warden, probably the most powerful Warden of the whole bunch besides Malachi and your grandma. It's a shame she's not around to help us. Kerry, too."

Kate turned down a gravel road that seemed to stretch on forever through the trees. Minutes ticked by as we bumped along, but finally we reached a rusted gate that was chained and locked with a padlock. Kate had a key, because of course she did, and Brianna hopped out to open the gate. We started down a driveway that was half as long as the road leading here.

At last, we came up on a secluded farmhouse with an overgrown garden. The paint was chipped, the boards weatherworn, the porch faded by sunlight, but it had otherwise stood the test of time. The place didn't look familiar, but it *seemed* familiar, like something from a dream long forgotten. I felt strangely safe. Not just safe—protected. It was an active, warm feeling.

"Are those Warden's Runes hanging from the trees?" I asked, peering at distant configurations of twigs tied with twine.

"They are," Kate said.

Instead of entering the house, the others started unloading boxes and cases from the trunk. Kate took me down a trail in the garden that led to what looked like a stone grave marker. There was no name, yet somehow I knew who rested here. "This is Malachi's grave, isn't it?" I whispered.

Kate nodded.

"I can feel her," I said, taking a knee on the soft grass. This was the only area of the property that had been neatly maintained. There was a fresh bouquet of white Easter lilies next to the marker. "I know this sounds silly," I said, noticing how the summer humidity seemed milder here, the wind soft and kind. "But I think she's glad that I'm here."

"I have no doubt about that," Kate said. She let me absorb the supernatural sense of comfort for a while before she said, "We brought you here for another reason. Come with me when you're ready."

I said a silent goodbye to Malachi and hiked with Kate through tall grasses to the back of the house. The heat brought a coating of sweat to my skin even though thick clouds obscured the sun. I fanned myself with my shirt as we approached a range of metal targets shaped like wide, boxy torsos staked into the ground. A picnic table held antique-looking weapons, ammo, and accessories.

Kate picked up two revolvers and held them out for me to take. "Your new best friends."

I inspected the old-fashioned firearms, unwilling to push anything sensitive even though I could feel that they weren't loaded. The barrels were six or seven inches long, and intricate scrollwork engravings decorated the glossy wooden handles.

"This is a flare gun," Kate said, holding up a miniature orange firearm. "Use it only in an emergency. The previous Wardens used gunshot patterns as a distress signal, but that doesn't work if you're out of bullets."

Kate buckled a leather belt with ammo pockets and holsters snugly around my waist.

"Why isn't the magic enough to fight them off?" I asked.

Kate didn't look me in the eye. "However powerful you feel, Warden magic gets slightly less potent with every generation. It wears away over time. Our grandmothers are more powerful than we are, and it doesn't have to do with age or experience. We're getting watered down, Nat. We're fading. Even Malachi wore out. We need the weapons more and more."

"So even if we manage to stop the Woodwalkers from hurting anyone—which our grandmas couldn't even do—our daughters and granddaughters will have a harder time doing the same thing?"

Kate bit her lip. "I know. It's not good news. And we've seen no signs that the Woodwalkers are weakening. It doesn't help that younger generations are waiting longer to have kids, having *fewer* kids. We could be extinct by the time the next massacre rolls around."

"Well, then we have to break the curse," I said, and saw Lindsey shake her head. "End all of this for good."

"Easier said than done, Nat." Kate sighed. "Even Malachi couldn't break it."

"Yeah, I keep hearing that," I snapped, shoving pale flyaways out of my face.

"Look, I know this is frustrating," she said, her tone mild. "I know you feel like you're cramming for a huge exam. But trust me, charmed weapons work best for keeping the Woodwalkers at bay. Magic alone works great for things like calming teas and sortilege. But we can't rely on it to engage with the evil here forever, not when it's diminishing at such an alarming rate."

I wiped misty rain from my forehead and processed this. "Okay."

"All right," Kate said, clapping her hands, sprightly again. "These are single-action revolvers from the late 1800s."

"Why do we use weapons that old?" I asked.

"They're not all this old. These two just happen to be the first weapons Malachi charmed to work on the Woodwalkers, after she came to live out here. She mixed her blood with oil and coated the guns, and they've worked ever since. She also forged the knives herself and cooled them in her blood."

"Wow . . . that must have taken a lot of blood."

"That's why we don't have a whole arsenal," she said, motioning for me to hand her one of my guns. "This is important: only load five cartridges instead of six. You don't want the hammer resting on a live round with these old beauties or it could fire off at the wrong time. Got that?"

"Got it."

"You have two guns here *not* so you can shoot both at the same time, which looks cool in movies, but it doesn't lend itself to accuracy. It's because reloading is a hassle." She pointed the gun away from us. "To shoot, you just cock the hammer and pull the trigger. Load the other gun, and then we'll practice."

I did exactly as she demonstrated, growing accustomed to the weight and feel of my new weapons. After I had loaded one with relative ease five times in a row, Kate took aim and hit a distant target with impressive accuracy.

"You try," she said. "You're going to want to go for the head or the heart. Hitting one or both of those leaves their borrowed body nothing but a bag of bones. The shadow form will flee to scavenge for a new host."

I took my stance, cocked the hammer, and pulled the trigger, trying not to flinch. My wrist snapped up smoothly as the gun fired. A loud ding answered.

"I like what we're working with," Kate said. "Try again."

Vanessa, Brianna, and Lindsey watched while my technique steadily improved. When I hit the target nine out of ten times, the Wallace sisters started hurling their hatchets at human-like wooden targets already scarred with abuse. Lindsey threw a small knife at a burl on a tree over and over as casually as if she were playing darts in a garage.

"So, we can't kill them?" I asked Kate, taking a break to wipe sweat and mist off my face and eject the shells and reload.

"They're not like us. They're not alive, so they can't be killed."

The sun emerged to beam down ruthlessly on my tanned skin. I closed my eyes and smelled wild grasses and pine trees. I could hear the faintest of winds whistling around the edges of the metal targets, my own pulse rampaging in my throat.

I extracted a revolver, took a deep breath, and shot bullet after bullet. The cocking of the hammer and the dinging of the targets created something almost like music.

A brief silence and a puff of haze followed.

"Damn, girl," Vanessa said breathlessly.

Kate's phone rang. She picked it up. "Hi, Grandma," she said. Listening for a long moment, she nodded. "Yeah, we can at least start her on patrol." She hung up and looked at us. "I'm going to help guard the cabin tonight. You four can patrol in pairs."

"Me?" I asked, my adrenaline skyrocketing.

"Do you object to that, Little Miss Sure Shot?"

I surveyed the damage I'd done to the targets.

"No," I said. "No objections."

TWENTY

As night fell, I laced up my combat boots in the dimly lit church basement. Far from a flimsy pleather fashion statement, the pair I'd inherited were hardy and battle scarred.

Camila, Lindsey's mom, sauntered up to me. "Ooh, Natalie . . . I like the new you." She slid her knives into their sheaths.

My nerves frazzled a little at the sight of everyone else saddling on their weapons over their black clothes. "You're going with Kate to the cabin?"

Camila nodded. "I wish we could petition the city to put higher fences up. But the cops would still be hanging around since it's massacre year, and we'd still have to protect them. And these tourists . . . People have no sense. If a place feels dark, stay away. Don't go asking for trouble."

"Everybody, gather round," Maggie called from the other side of the room. Lindsey and I joined the group of women forming a jagged circle.

"The first Shadowing should serve as a wake-up call," Maggie said. "The Woodwalkers' powers are multiplying. They will be more persistent. We cannot back down. I know you're tired. I know you've been rode hard and put away wet. But when I look around, I see the strongest, most fearless women I know, women who do what's right even when it's not easy. And that includes our newest Warden."

Everyone looked at me and smiled or nodded.

"Now, be blessed and safe out there," Maggie said. "By the powers of earth, bone, and blood..."

"Proceed we Wardens to our noble work," the room echoed, and we dispersed.

Heather approached me with a jar of goo that I could only guess fell under the category of "unction" in the Book of Wisdom. "Angelica root powder, wood betony oil, ground nettle, and an infusion of Solomon's seal," she explained. "It's for protection. Do you want me to apply it?"

"Yes, thank you," I said, and held out my bare arms. Heather was as thorough as a responsible mother smearing sunscreen on her child, making sure it covered every inch of skin exposed by my black tank top. By the set of her jaw, I could tell she was worried for me. That didn't bring me much comfort. I was a kid about to splash into a cold pool that was too deep. "Be safe out there," she said, screwing the lid back on the jar.

"You too," I said. My voice sounded small.

"Be careful, girls," Camila warned. "Keep in touch. Call for backup if you need it."

Kate patted me on the back as the majority of us exited the basement. I felt tenser than a guitar string wound too tight.

Lindsey and I got in her car and drove at a crawling pace, moving east through town before turning north. Houses and woods slipped by. The occasional streetlight cast an eerie glow, toying with my imagination. Never had a locked car door felt so much like a barrier between safety and danger.

"Don't worry," Lindsey said. "*Patrolling* is code for 'creating diversions to keep the cops busy.' I rode shotgun on patrol when I was fifteen, if that makes you feel better."

"A little. Why is it bad if police are checking on the cabin? It'll scare away trespassers."

"They're just more people we have to look out for."

I thought of Jason and almost laughed. He would never believe that *I* could offer *him* protection. I almost couldn't believe it myself.

"How long have you been training with knives?" I asked Lindsey as her gaze combed the darkness.

"We get our first lessons around eleven or twelve. At that age, we're old enough to understand how important keeping the secret is. When we take the Oath at fifteen, we're ready to jump in on the action."

"What if I'm not ready?"

"You'll be fine. I'm here. Besides, you're a natural with good instincts, and a Tri-Warden, or whatever you want to call it. We're not even going to be doing anything tonight. Just looking out."

Despite her reassurances, I didn't like what those instincts were telling me. As we crept down a street with a park on one side and houses on the other, I felt a sudden flutter of fear, but couldn't pinpoint why. We passed a playground with a jungle gym and a metal merry-go-round. Beyond it was a swathe of green grass that bordered an army of looming pines. We were only two miles from the town square, but it felt like twenty.

"Something's off here." Lindsey squinted at the trees, confirming my suspicion.

My phone rang. I twisted to dig it out of my back pocket and saw Kate's name.

"Hello?"

"The sheriff's prowling and we need a diversion. Lindsey will know what to do." The urgency in Kate's voice made a pang of fear flutter through me.

"Okay," I said, but she had already hung up. "They need us to distract Jason."

"Already?" Lindsey gulped. "Must be a busy night." She stretched to grab her duffel bag from the back seat and produced three empty glass bottles. "Break these on the playground. I'm going to go set off a car alarm. We need someone to call the police."

I took the bottles. "Why can't we call them ourselves, anonymously? Can you beguile a phone number?"

"We used to do that. After they showed up and found nothing wrong a few times, they started treating untraceable calls as illegitimate."

We got out. Lindsey jogged away with a promise to not leave me alone for long. I stared at the inky trees behind the park, which would have looked like a solid mass of shadows before I took the Oath. Now, I could make out individual branches reaching into the oppressive summer air.

I hoped Jason didn't show up and see through the beguilement. Explaining away the revolvers in holsters around my waist would be a challenge. He could arrest me for lacking a gun license.

I stepped onto the layer of woodchips covering the playground and threw a bottle at the merry-go-round. The burst was louder than I expected. My throw had been so fierce that minuscule glass shards showered over me. That would get the neighborhood stirring.

"What was that?" I heard someone gasp nearby.

Without stopping to think, I dove behind a garbage can. A car alarm went off in the distance.

"What's going on?" Another frenetic voice asked. "Is it working?"

I peeked out from my hiding spot. I could make out three shadows sitting on the highest platform of the jungle gym.

"No," a female voice said, not bothering to whisper. "That's not the same energy I sensed."

"Then what was that breaking sound?"

Energy. Of course, the three paranormal sleuths were in my hair again. I saw the definition of their distinct silhouettes at the top of the plastic slide: petite, gawky, and stocky. The whole gang was there. Maybe they were on their way to the cabin and stopped for a late-night séance or something. But where was their van?

The girl, Quinn, looked around, but didn't notice me in the dark. "I don't know, maybe we summoned something else, but it feels benevolent."

"Benevolent spirits don't break things," the bearded, lanky guy said. "I think we should go."

"You scared?" the other guy asked, but it didn't sound like a taunt.

"Scared that people will think we're breaking into cars," the other hissed.

I wasn't sure if the beguilement would work on them, or if I needed to cast a new one. In fact, now that I was in the field, I wasn't sure of anything. Did the Wardens really think I was ready to be here, or were they so desperate for manpower that they'd sent me out entirely unprepared?

I glanced over my shoulder, hoping to see Lindsey trotting up the road, but there was no sign of her. A lamp flicked on inside the nearest house, and eyes peeked out from the closed blinds.

"Let's get out of here," the lanky guy urged again, hanging one long leg off the jungle gym, ready to make a break for it.

"We can't," Quinn said, still sitting cross-legged on the platform. "I think the summoning worked. Something's here."

"Like what?" he asked.

The other pointed his device in a circle around him. I ducked back behind the trash can.

"Oh my god." Quinn massaged her temples, her voice taut. "There's so much anger and... and hunger."

"Hunger for what?" the one with the device asked.

A whisper of wind coiled through the air and the smell of rot invaded my senses.

I could feel the new presence. Oppressive, bleak, as unwelcome as a tap on the shoulder in a house presumed empty.

My flesh turned cold and my voice trembled, making it hard to whisper the incantation that would protect our secrets. "Powers of the still, dark earth, mislead all prying eyes. Cast thy veil of trickery; by Warden's Rune, disguise."

My human instincts, which were momentarily more compelling than my magic, urged me to run away, to dive into the car and hide until the darkness had passed. But I didn't listen to them. I came out of hiding and lunged for the jungle gym, leaping to the top of the slide. "You need to leave. Now."

TWENTY-ONE

The two guys nearly jumped out of their skins.

"You again," Quinn accused, staying put as the others shrieked and fled.

I pushed her, a gentle push by my intentions, but she fell off the platform to the layer of woodchips on the ground, her camera toppling out of her hand.

"Go!" I growled.

Her lips shaped a rude retort, but I didn't hear it over the howl that tore through the night, drowning out the sound of another car alarm.

Quinn picked up her camera and scrambled away. The others waited for her to catch up before making a break for it.

I twisted around and found three massive, ragged silhouettes drawing level with the trees behind the park.

Another surge of panic commanded me to run away.

But that wasn't an option.

I jumped off the jungle gym, covering as much ground with a simple leap than I ever had with an earnest long jump before I'd unleashed my magic. Sweat coated my palms as I grasped my revolvers, reminding myself of the targets I'd hit that morning, replaying the satisfying sound of each victory. But these thoughts soon fled from my mind, replaced with pure, primal terror.

Each of the three hideous creatures was so uniquely appalling that my eyes could only dart from one to the next to drink in each new horror.

The one on the right took a lurching stride forward. Its slumped shoulders were pure sinew, bare and red as raw meat. In place of a face was a deer skull with gaping black eye sockets and a jagged hole at the snout. Flesh clung to its exposed ribs, through which I could see a thin spine. Claws hung from the ends of its skeletal arms.

The one on the left's body was also a patchwork of bones and ragged flesh, but with the furry hide of an animal. Its legs bent at the knee and its face was a snarling coyote carcass.

The middle wore a human skull topped by reaching antlers with pointed tines.

A low grunt issued from the middle one's black vacuum of a throat, and the outside two started closing in on me, trailing rot. Their patient, uneven strides were more menacing than any swift advance.

My terrified pause was briefer than it might have been before the Oath had unlocked my magic. I shakily extracted both revolvers and cocked the right one, aiming between the eyes of the coyote-like beast.

The shot bit through the air and busted the side of the creature's skull. The one on the right had gained on me, so I cocked the hammer, shot, and missed. With only eight more bullets to my name, I resolved to aim more carefully, but only hit its jagged shoulder blade this time. The creature reeled back with a squeal, whipping around to face me again.

As I shot through the remaining rounds in one revolver, they drew ever closer. My fingers trembled as I hastened to tuck away the empty gun and draw the other.

But before I could aim, the deer-skulled monster advanced and gripped me by the throat, its claws stinging my tender skin. It threw me in an arc that defied the laws of physics. Pain exploded through my body as I hit the ground.

Fighting for breath, I stretched toward my loaded gun, which I'd dropped. But when my fingers touched the etched wood of the handle, a clawed grip latched my hair and lifted. I grunted and clasped whatever bare bones and damp, fleshy tissue I could reach to ease the excruciating pull on my scalp.

The coyote-like creature suspended me at its eye level as though I was nothing but a rag doll. My bullet had dragged away the rotting flesh along its snout, exposing a jagged range of teeth. Its eye sockets were lightless, and from the black tunnel of its throat, hot, foul breath swept over me. It reminded me of rotten food, stale dirt, decay. Its mouth stretched wider. . . .

But the middle Woodwalker, the one with the human skull that had not yet moved, emitted a harsh guttural command. The coyote lowered me and unlatched its claws from my hair, then slunk away.

I looked up to find the menacing, vacant eye sockets of the human skull leering over me.

I scrambled back on my elbows, but with one assertive motion it pinned my chest down with its claws, piercing my flesh.

A whimper left my throat. My loaded gun lay even farther out of reach, and this monster could skewer me like a piece of meat if it had the slightest inclination.

It got a wormy grip on the back of my neck and lifted my face toward it.

The blackness within the cavities of the skull—the scooped-out eyes and jagged nose and bottomless cave of a mouth—held the depths of all evil.

The creature stretched its jaw wide, straining at the hinges. *There's so much hunger,* Quinn said. Now I knew what she meant.

They hungered for my power, for the recompense they could use it to obtain. After they took it, they would kill me.

Weakness overcame me, and I began sliding into an abyss. My stomach protested the heat and smell of rot that clamped over me, holding me captive.

I heard a cry and recognized it as Lindsey's. Then I felt claws pressing into my flesh—and the weight of a revolver against my right side, with the smaller weight of one last cartridge snug against the sacred metal.

Kate had instructed me to load only five to protect from an accidental misfire. But as I'd prepared for battle with a trembling spirit, I must have loaded all six without meaning to.

My fingers slowly glided across the embossed leather of the holster to the engraved wooden grip. I extracted the gun, cocked it, opened my eyes, and pointed the barrel at the creature's marbled brown-and-white jaw.

A rain of bone shards hit my skin. The pressure of claws on my chest ripped away and a demonic squeal pierced my ears.

I sat up. Lindsey strode past me, hair loose and wild in the moonlight. She approached the staggering creature and cut her own forearm with her knife. The blade dripped with blood.

In one motion, she crisscrossed her daggers and sliced through the creature's spine. She speared its heart on the end of her knife and the Woodwalker screamed, a noise that sounded like the whole population of hell objecting to their fates. Putrefied bits of bone and flesh fell to the grass. The shadow body they had encased folded in on itself and seeped away to the trees.

"Are you okay?" Lindsey asked.

"Yeah," I grunted, and tried to stand to prove it. But as far as my legs were concerned, I'd just awakened from a coma.

"I'm so sorry," she said, rushing to help me up. "Someone tried to chase me down and I had to beguile them, and it didn't work the first time."

I waved her away and straightened, feeling the blood that pasted my shirt to my chest. With a hiss of breath, I peeled away the material and surveyed my wounds. There were two cuts on my sternum, fainter ones on the slope of each breast, and a fifth down between my ribs. One wound for each jagged claw.

Lindsey checked out the damage for herself, ignoring an oozing cut above her eyebrow that deserved attention. "Let's go," she said. She slid her knives succinctly back into their sheaths and handed me my other revolver.

I turned to follow her, realizing that we weren't alone. The paranormal chasers were still here, and Jason had arrived. The two boys appeared to be explaining something to him. Quinn stood apart from them, facing Lindsey and me, her blank expression revealed with the flash of lights on the roof of the parked cruiser. We'd meant to lure Jason away from the action, not straight to it.

Even though it was clearly already in effect, I heard Lindsey speak the beguilement under her breath for good measure. "Hey, Sheriff," she then said with a wave, as though nothing were amiss.

Jason shined his flashlight on our faces. I flinched away from the beam, but Lindsey didn't bother hiding anything.

"I should have known you two would be where the trouble is," he said, with no hint of real suspicion.

"Trouble?" Lindsey asked innocently.

"A resident in the area called about an attempted car theft."

"We didn't do anything," the heavyset guy insisted. "We heard the car alarm go off, but we weren't anywhere near it."

"My ears are still ringing," said the bearded guy. "I didn't know car alarms and coyotes could be so loud."

Because what you really heard was gunfire and Woodwalkers, I thought.

Jason flashed the light in the guy's eyes, then on the piece of equipment he had confiscated. "I believe you," he said finally. "But the park closes at sunset. Where's your vehicle?"

"We left it around the corner."

"You mean you *hid* it around the corner?" Jason clarified.

"Yeah, it's a little hard to detect anomalies in environmental data when someone crashes your investigation," the lanky guy said in a tone that wouldn't go over well with the sheriff.

Jason's eyebrows snapped down. "Cool it, kid. You're already off the hook." With a derisive grunt, he handed them back their equipment. "Drive safe and stay out of trouble. Same goes for you two," he said to us, casting a subtle glance at the woods. "What is it with everybody trespassing tonight? You know who I found out at the cabin? Levi Langford, of all people."

My heart pattered. "What was he doing there?" I asked, but Lindsey flashed me a look.

"Certainly not putting taxpayer dollars to good use," Jason said. "Y'all go home, and if you so much as think about sneaking out to the cabin, I'll throw you in the slammer."

Lindsey laughed. "We're leaving."

The two guys zipped their equipment into carrying cases and turned to look at Quinn, who was still staring at the trees.

"Quinn," snapped the bearded guy. "Are you coming?"

Her pixie-sized shadow remained motionless.

Jason got into his car. The harsh blue-and-red lights abruptly shut off. "I need to check out the situation up the street. Be gone by the time I drive back."

He left us in the dark. Lindsey asked the guys what their names were, shining her phone lights on them to check for double shadows. Now that the adrenaline was wearing off, I just wanted to go somewhere that felt safe.

Quinn remained motionless, her black dress and short dark hair flittering in the warm breeze. I approached, startling her. She turned her doe-eyed gaze on me.

"Are you okay?" I asked.

"I sense a lot that other people don't," she said, surprising me. "I saw you fighting the shadows. It was blurry, like a weird dream. But I know you protected us."

Before I could muster a reply, she hurried to catch up to the others venturing down the road.

TWENTY-TWO

"Here, drink." Heather set a dainty glass on the grainy wood counter next to the shelves of supplies in the Warden's basement, exposing a rose tattoo on her forearm and a scar that intersected it.

"What is this?" I asked as the aroma of the drink singed its way up my nostrils.

"I call it a Bootstrap, but I made it virgin for you. It's got herbs for quick healing and a comfort tea so you can—"

"Pull myself up by the bootstraps?" I asked.

She grinned. "Cheers."

From the first sip, its magic began working. I glanced to my left. Abuela Sofia was squinting at Lindsey's cut and tugging a needle through the torn skin. Neither so much as cringed.

"I feel so bad that I left you alone," Lindsey said. "I didn't expect things to go down like that."

"It turned out okay," I reminded her.

"Cálmate," Sofia demanded of Lindsey.

"Abuela, ¿ya terminaste?" Lindsey's physical reactions may not have betrayed how much pain she was in, but her tone did. Sofia snipped the suture and barely had time to bandage it before Lindsey waved her away.

"What do you think Levi was doing at the cabin?" I asked her.

"Probably trying to pressure Miss Maggie into giving him answers by causing trouble. If you ask me, she should just tell him the truth. He already knows so much. What could it hurt? But Miss Maggie, Miss Cynthia, and Abuela are stuck in their ways."

I looked around to see who was listening, even though Lindsey didn't seem to care. Only Heather and Sofia were in earshot. Sofia shook her head in disapproval, but Heather nodded emphatically while muddling herbs and scarlet flower petals with a mortar and pestle.

"What about that Quinn girl?" I asked. "Will the elders mind that she sensed something out there?"

Lindsey shrugged. "She's not the first intuitive person to cross our paths."

"My stepmom is a psychic," Heather said, pouring the muddled herbs into a jar. "She refuses to come here more than once a year. She calls San Solano a thin place, where the veil between the natural and the supernatural is more transparent. According to her, there are other thin places, but few as thin as San Solano."

Thin place. As the phrase hung in the air, I imagined San Solano on a paper-thin layer of ice and us, the Wardens, trading a life in the sunshine to bolster it from underneath.

I caught sight of my reflection in a glass jar of dried dusty miller. Strands of blond ponytail had gone rogue and streamed across my face. A few fresh bruises spattered the sides of my neck. The revolvers lay head to head on the table in front of me, the engraved grips shining in the low light. My stormy eyes—inherited from Grandma Kerry—held a gleam of determination.

I felt powerful. Tonight had awoken something in me. All the miles I'd run, all the times I'd shaken off the pain and kept going... Somehow, I'd always known that was just practice for something bigger and more important. I had always had a higher purpose: to fight in this war of shadow and soul.

The door at the top of the stairs opened. "He's giving us no choice, Grandma," Kate was saying as she tromped down to the basement. Camila and Miss Maggie followed her.

"We'll force a blood oath," Maggie said in a staunch tone. "Make him swear that he won't cause trouble again, and that he'll stay away from us if he really wants to keep Nat and Emmy safe."

My heart gave a rebellious kick. After last night in the sanctuary, I wanted Levi to come to me, not the other way around. And if our history was any indication, he wouldn't. But I still felt a thrill at hearing us grouped together, discussed like we meant something to each other. It was so new.

"You know that would only frustrate him more," Kate said. "And a blood oath unwillingly sworn is less binding."

When Camila spotted Lindsey, she clicked her tongue and hurried over to examine her wound. "¡Tu cara, mija! Te lo dije, ¡protege tu cara!"

"I know, I know," Lindsey said, pushing her away. "My face is too pretty for scars. I've heard it a million times."

"Nat, I'm so sorry," Kate said, forgetting about her argument with her grandmother and squeezing me tight. "You weren't supposed to have to fight on your first night."

"She kicked ass," Lindsey said. "Blew out one of their skulls."

"You had to finish it off," I said, embarrassed.

"Well, *we* saved lives tonight," she said. "The Woodwalkers wouldn't turn their noses up at tourists. The Shadowing would keep them local." She looked from Kate to her mom. "What happened at the cabin? The sheriff said Levi showed up."

Maggie shook her head. "That boy. He was hiding, trying to catch us in action. It's a wonder he hasn't been Shadowed up, down, and sideways."

"Did he see you?" I asked.

"No, the beguilement held," Kate answered. "But the more someone knows, the less it works. And we can't worry about him getting in the way right now. Which is why *I* think we should just tell him rather than stiff-arming him until he loses his mind."

"We can't blab the truth to anyone who suspects something," Maggie said, raising a thin white eyebrow at her granddaughter. "We took an oath to guard our secrets. If even one person knows, we could get blamed for what happens. Sofia, Cynthia, and I would get blamed for what *has* happened."

"You and Kerry were the ones who healed Emmy in front of him," Kate said, in a tiptoeing tone that suggested she wasn't accustomed to arguing with her grandmother.

"And Nora was the one who ran her mouth off when Mike Langford was a little boy."

"Yes, and what would have happened if she hadn't?" Kate crossed her arms. "Mike wouldn't have known where to bring Emmy after the Woodwalkers preyed on her. Emmy would have died just like Nora."

Maggie's cold expression was carved of stone. She wouldn't give an inch, even for her own granddaughter.

"Levi's dad is gone," Kate said. She stood to her full height, which was impressive, and there was frosty fire in her eyes. "His sister *and* the girl he likes are in danger from something he can't see or understand." She swept her hand toward me. "Our secrecy was already compromised, necessarily so, when you saved Emmy's life. Don't you think he deserves some answers?"

Sofia spoke up. "When we say the Oath, each of us agrees to protect our secrets at any cost. It is not built on coercion, but on a sense of honor. Nora broke our codes. We will not break them a second time just to fix her mistake."

"Sorry, darling," Maggie said to Kate. "I wish I could help him, too. But two wrongs don't make a right." She crossed the room to put away her pistol, ending the conversation.

Kate leaned on the counter next to me and propped her chin on her fists. "I'm worried about Levi," she said. "He's been through so much. Could you be persuaded to go check on him for me, Nat? If you need to rest, I understand, but—"

"No, I'll go," I said. Lindsey and Heather smirked at each other.

"If you want, Heather can fix you up one of her elixirs," Lindsey said. Kate's cheeks turned beetroot red.

Going along with it, Heather said, "They take a few days of steeping, but I have one already made if you want."

"I'm okay," I said, laughing. "Let's see if he'll even talk to me before we get *way* ahead of ourselves here."

SHADY SANCTUARY

Levi Langford

Baptized in sweat, we splatter-paint mosquito murals on our skin.
Sunday near noon and I'm frying like a moth on a zapper,
nape lipstick red as if blotted with church lady kisses
while Dad's forearm is dip-dyed ruddy, fading
to lily white beneath his sleeves.
Twist. Hiss. My Dr Pepper is flat as a field now,
but the nectar tastes sweeter in the Piney Woods.
The commotion of home evanesced like carbonation when
we hung a left toward Toledo Bend.

As I squash mud into boot-shaped reservoirs,
I like to pretend we're nomads, as familiar with the maze
of unharvested virgin pines as we are with the sunburst
of berries on our tongues, the muscle of a bow,
the innards of fish slated for dinner.
My skin tastes like earth as I wet the tip of my finger
to feel the breeze twisting, and in the warmth
of a still-green September, a chill nibbles up my spine.

"Keep up," says my dad, suddenly stiff as a sentry.
His eyes read the woods at my back,
and mine follow the map his have laid out. Nothin' there.

The tautness snaps out of the air and we move on to the lake,
to woo with rattle trap songs the bigmouth bass.
But that stretch of seconds chews at me,

the gaze of nature, or un-nature, upon me,
turning my arm hairs to quills.
If he's afraid of something in this shady sanctuary,
in this world,
then there's something worth fearing.

TWENTY-THREE

Natalie Colter

All the windows of Levi's house were dark except for one. A golden square of light fell on the backyard from the upstairs window of his dad's study. I leaped and grabbed the back-porch overhang, dangling for a second before maneuvering onto the asphalt shingles. It was impossibly easy.

Levi sat at the desk in sleep shorts and an old tee with holes in it, bent over piles of paper chaos.

My gentle knock startled him out of a deep reverie. An indecipherable look passed over his features and he wove through the boxes and stacks of books to open the window. I found myself once again caught off-guard by the webs of color in his hazel eyes, by the rock-hewn bone structure and the muted dust of freckles.

Without a word, he took in my appearance, which I hadn't bothered to beguile: the guns in their holsters, the dark wardrobe, the boots. His gaze lingered on the cuts across my chest. "What do you need, Nat?" he asked, turning his back on me to pick his way back to the desk. The wooden boards creaked under his bare feet.

I took the liberty of stepping inside. "I'm just checking in. Why are you up so late?"

"Going through my dad's stuff. Trying to make sense of everything he knew about the Wardens."

"What did he know?"

Levi shot me a dark look through his pale ginger eyelashes, one that said he was not obligated to indulge my curiosity.

But I refused to be cowed. I hauled a box toward the desk to sit on.

Levi sighed and shut the door to the hallway. "You look like hell," he said, but it was too soft to be an insult.

"I've had a big night."

He leaned against the desk. "Fighting demons?"

I tilted my head in surprise. "Was that your dad's guess?"

"One of them."

We locked eyes. Behind his frustration, embers of his desire for me flickered, not as bright and flashy, but somehow more intense. "You don't look like hell," he said gently. "You look beautiful. And fierce. If I were a"—he looked sideways at me and made a guess—"forest demon? I wouldn't want to cross you."

I laughed and felt heat flood into my cheeks. He kept staring at me, smiling, unabashed, and the warmth traveled down my neck. I'd managed to crack his shell again. It seemed to be getting easier.

I stood up and moseyed over to the built-in shelves, reading titles without processing them, still feeling the burn of his gaze. Soon enough I heard footsteps and felt his undeniable presence behind me.

"Did your dad know anything about how Nora died?" I asked, turning to face him.

"The coroner said the cause of death was cardiac arrest. My dad knew it wasn't true."

"I think she may have tried something new," I said. "I think she tried to stop the Wood—I mean, the 'forest demons,' using an unconventional method."

I could be wrong. Kate had softly implied that Nora might have approached the Woodwalkers with her defenses down in order to take her own life. Levi had confirmed that Nora was sensitive, maybe a little unwell. But something nagged at me. Why would Nora choose to give up in the middle of the fight? It was the first-ever Claiming. She didn't know what was going to happen, had no reason to suspect the Wardens would fail. They had surely figured out that the Woodwalkers wanted to keep the bodies, and that there was a significant reason why they were returning to the sacred glade. There should have still been an opportunity to stop the Woodwalkers from becoming human again. Why would Nora surrender before the battle was lost?

"You aren't thinking of trying 'something new,' are you?" Levi asked, propping his arm on the shelf over his head, just like he had on the garden trellis before we'd kissed the first time.

"No, I'm not," I assured him over the sound of my racing pulse, fighting the urge to pat the revolvers at my hips like I was proud of them for their work tonight. It turned out I was pretty good at the conventional tactics, and Nora's diversion hadn't worked out well for her. I would stick to the script—it was my best chance of saving Levi.

"Good," he said, and leaned down to brush his lips across mine. My touch slid from his biceps to his shoulders as I eagerly kissed him back. Riveted, he gave an answering gasp that sent a trill of delight racing through me. I felt his grip on my thigh just before he lifted me up and set me back against the bookshelf. I hooked my legs around his waist.

"Are we moving too fast?" he whispered against my lips.

"I really, really want to say no and keep doing what we're doing," I whispered back, grazing his bottom lip with my teeth. The soft noise in his throat about did me in.

"That would be the easiest thing," he said. He pulled back to look at me, his breath tickling my hair. "But I want this to feel right. Not rushed."

"We could just talk," I said with a shrug.

He grinned. "We *were* supposed to go on a date. You owe me one."

"All right, let's make a rule: no more of this until after one date with no kissing. That way we know there's more than physical attraction."

"There definitely is on my end," he said huskily.

I smiled like a helpless idiot. "Mine, too."

"But it's a pact," he agreed,

"Maybe we should kiss on it."

Levi chuckled and indulged me as I stole another greedy kiss before promptly setting me back on the floor. No matter how strong the attraction, he'd been pretty strict with himself, sticking to his pledge to stay away. I had a feeling he would hold me to our pact, and that made me want to take it back.

There was something to be said for a little restraint, though. The idea of appearing in public, somewhat official, brought a whole new set of fantasies that I'd dared not imagine before now. I pictured the next date, the one after, visiting him in Dallas, talking until the wee hours of the morning when we had to be apart. For the first time, I imagined a future in which Levi played a substantial role.

"Can you promise me something?" he asked. "I've always looked out for my sister, even before I understood what happened at the church that night. Now I know I'm not equipped to look out for her. Not the way you can."

In the low light of the study, the lines of gold in his eyes danced with concern. He could have persuaded me to promise anything.

"Are you sure you don't want to put her in a better position to protect herself?" I asked.

"And have her come out looking like that?" he asked, stroking a bruise on my arm the size of a plum. "She's not like you, Nat. She's not gutsy. She's tender. Breakable."

I didn't know how to take that. Did he think I wasn't? Did he think none of this disturbed me, just because I was capable of accepting it?

But maybe he was right. I liked fighting the Woodwalkers. I liked learning about magic. I felt more like myself now than I ever had.

"I can't lose anyone else I care about," he whispered. "Please look out for her." His gaze lifted to connect unflinchingly with mine. "Please look out for yourself."

TWENTY-FOUR

SEVEN DAYS UNTIL THE CLAIMING

Two more boys got Shadowed.

Neither happened on my watch, but I felt the reverberations. One of their names I recognized from my old church youth group, and the other I didn't know.

I'd quit my job at the catfish buffet and told my parents I was babysitting for Kate again. But I spent my time absorbing knowledge from the Book of Wisdom and off-duty Wardens. Some days I sat in Heather's cozy bakery while she worked, the Book of Wisdom glamoured next to my coffee. She would patiently answer my incessant questions, pausing only when the door over the bell dinged, signaling a customer. The academic fervor that I'd applied to my favorite classes I now turned to the task of becoming a good Warden.

After dusk I hunted the Woodwalkers. I started to hunger for the night I used to fear.

It sounded sick when I admitted it to myself. But I knew that the others had to take an ounce of pride in this to survive. I had always relished the discomfort of shin splints and the ache of tired lungs because they meant I was strong. Now I relished the burst of Woodwalker bones that followed the squeeze of my trigger, the crunch of a skull beneath my boot, my magic surging to meet my commands when I spoke the right words.

Tonight, Lindsey, Vanessa, and I had followed dark roads branching off to emptier dark roads like roots reaching deep into black soil. Our senses were attuned to the scent of death, and we had found two Woodwalkers lurking near a lone country house. We broke their bodies easily, banishing their shadow forms back to the woods, and we only had a few cuts and bruises to show for the encounter.

The wind combed through my hair, turning the sweat on my scalp cold as I stuck my head out the car window. My thumb brushed fondly over the engravings on my revolver.

Another dark car flashed its lights at us from the shoulder of the deserted country highway. We pulled to a stop as Kate rolled down her window. Brianna sat in the passenger seat, keeping an eye on the woods.

"The Triad said for y'all to take the night off," Kate said.

Lindsey cocked her head as if she hadn't heard right. "We're a week out from the Claiming."

"Exactly. We need everyone fresh. You're the only ones who haven't gotten a night off this week. At this rate you'll be useless."

I'd learned that long hours were the price we paid for being eighteen, with no spouses, kids, or protective parents. My parents had never kept me on a short leash, but this summer, they had unhooked me entirely. I had no curfew, and they didn't pry.

For the Wardens, a lack of familial oversight translated to constant overtime. I seemed to come home only to catch a nap and shower. Whenever I could, I'd drop by the Langfords' to reinforce the wards and spells and look in on Emmy. My every free minute was captive to the promise I'd made to Levi. Rest came last on the priority list.

When Kate drove away, Vanessa leaned forward and put her elbows on the console. "Everybody's out at Tejas," she said. "Do we want to go?"

"I want to sleep," Lindsey said.

"You know the first thing they'll do if they find a dozen bodies?" Vanessa numbered off on her fingers. "Ask who was acting reclusive, who recently changed their social habits, who would be secretive enough to get away with murdering twelve people and leaving no trace—"

"There won't be any bodies," Lindsey snapped.

"Of course not," Vanessa agreed. "But self-preservation is a good argument for *living a little.*"

"Is this about Bryce?" Lindsey asked, making eye contact with Vanessa in the rearview mirror. "Because the bones told you to stay away."

"I just want to make sure he's not Shadowed," she said. "That's all. Levi's there. Nat wants to go, too."

Lindsey slung a testy, tired look in my direction.

"Abbie and Faith are going to put my face on a milk carton if I don't show up somewhere." I showed her my phone and scrolled through the bank of unanswered texts. Only one of them was from Levi. It read, *Be safe out there, okay?*

We hadn't had time for the date and had somehow stuck to our guns on the pact, which was basically torture.

Lindsey griped about needing a shower as she turned toward downtown. Ignoring her, I texted Levi. *So, I know it's not an official date, but I'm coming tonight. Can it count? Please?*

Hmmm, he typed, and I could feel him smiling through the text. *Let's say it counts, but you owe me another date. Where I pick you up and say hi to your parents and wear something nicer than... what I'm wearing.*

Deal.

And then I started to type, *After this is all over...* and erased it. I didn't want to jinx anything.

Thankfully, I'd stocked up my supply bag. I cleaned off the sweat and dirt with wipes, tousled my sandy hair, and changed into pedestrian clothes.

Vanessa donned jewelry, slapdash eye makeup that turned out perfect thanks to her steady artist's hand, and a colorful headband. Lindsey wore black, barely even pretending to have a life outside of being a Warden anymore.

Tejas Grill was the only spot that stayed open late enough to slake the town's thirst for beer and socializing. Tonight, it seemed like half of our graduating class was there. I presented my driver's license to the doorman and received a giant dash on the back of my hand in permanent marker, but the power I possessed to defy him made me feel deviously smug. If I wanted to drink, I could have easily glamoured my birth date or even my face. As I developed my repertoire of spells, the possibilities felt endless.

Craning my neck, I found Levi by a pool table, wearing dark jeans and a hunter-green tee. He and Abbie were playing doubles against Grayson and Emmy. When he noticed me, he grinned from ear to ear. I couldn't help but mirror the expression.

Bryce sat at a booth with Faith, a junior girl, and one of Emmy's friends, and he turned ashen upon seeing Vanessa. As we approached the group, I could tell she was scanning him for a second shadow, but it was hard to see through the muted light and the haze of fajita smoke. Bryce glued his gaze to his menu.

"I see y'all *do* know how to read a text, since you showed up." Abbie propped against the table with a cue stick, lips pursed, but I knew she was only posturing.

"I'm sorry, Abs." I wrapped my arm around her shoulders. "It's the summer before college. We have to get used to not seeing each other every day."

"Well isn't that sweet," she muttered, tugging my hair. I knew she'd already forgiven me again.

"Nat, how did you get that bruise?" Emmy asked.

I examined the mottled mark on my forearm. She shouldn't be able to see it. I imagined the gifted blood in her veins sniffing at the beguilement, detecting something off about the ruse. "I was jogging in the woods and got whipped by a branch," I said.

"Ouch," Emmy replied. I met her hazel eyes and saw dark circles, a haunted expression beneath the cheerful varnish. I wondered if her magic had caused more episodes. Her mother hadn't done her any favors, keeping her away from us.

"Hey," Levi said into my hair, his hand briefly brushing the small of my back. "Lindsey, you want to take over for me?" He offered her his cue stick.

She shrugged. "Yeah, I'll give it a shot." Code for giving Grayson a run for his money.

The rest of us squeezed into the booth, everyone taking pains to make sure Bryce didn't have to sit next to, or directly across from, Vanessa. Levi and I ended up together next to Bryce, while Vanessa squeezed in beside Faith. Thankfully, a waitress breezed by to hand out more waters and menus before the awkwardness had a chance to rear its ugly head.

"What have y'all been up to?" Faith asked.

"I've been shut up in my room working on some digital paintings for my portfolio," Vanessa lied.

"I've been at home, mostly," I said. "I'm at Lindsey's mercy because my truck's still in the shop."

"Well, you could be at *my* mercy," Faith said. When her elastic goodwill finally reached its limit, it could snap like a stinging rubber band.

"I had homework for my summer course," I said.

Ah, the made-up summer course. It had been my saving grace. But apparently, Faith had heard enough of that one. "It's a core-credit class! How demanding could it possibly be?"

"You'd be surprised..." I trailed off when someone kicked my shin under the table. I looked up to find Vanessa's bright brown eyes sending me some kind of secret signal. I was worried I'd said something wrong until she jerked her head. Taking the hint, I found Ryan Ashland sitting at a table across the pool hall, staring at us.

He didn't *look* like Ryan Ashland. His normally shoulder-length, greasy brown hair had been groomed short and neat, but not in a "he cleans up nice" way. It was slicked to the side, old-fashioned, like he'd stepped straight out of a time machine. Instead of his usual sweat-stained tee shirt and jeans, he wore a collared button-up tucked into slacks. I might have thought he was heading off to an interview, except that it was a quarter till midnight. A glass of water sat on the table in front of him rather than his usual beer. Ryan's brother was the bartender, and whenever Ryan had bothered to show up to class, he'd always bragged about how he could get anyone a drink here.

A sickeningly rare steak stewed in its own juices on his plate. He conscientiously rolled up his shirtsleeves and cut his first bite. As he chewed, he closed his eyes and sighed like he had never tasted anything so heavenly.

Or at least, not for a hundred years, I thought.

When he opened them, he looked straight at me. Something was different about his eyes. They hadn't changed in appearance, but they seemed hooded somehow. Dark.

Shadowed.

In the middle of chewing, he smiled at me.

I quickly glanced away. Vanessa let out a quiet gasp. I felt nauseous.

Grayson squished himself onto the edge of our seat, shoving me so close to Levi that I was practically sitting on his lap. "Is this the first time you've seen Ryan since he got an Extreme Makeover: Weirdo Edition?" Grayson asked.

I couldn't find the will to reply. Faith started throwing out theories for why Ryan had decided to switch things up: he'd committed a crime and was dense enough to think nobody would recognize him with a haircut and some new clothes; he'd done it impress a girl; he was thinking of joining the military and was trying to clean up his act.

"Is everything okay?" Levi asked me, his breath minty and cool against my ear.

"Mm-hmm," I said, and took a sip of water.

Levi shifted in his seat and rested his arm on the back of the booth, almost around my shoulders. I wondered if it was just a way to reclaim some space, but then he secretly played with a strand of hair behind my back.

"Can I squeeze out?" Faith asked abruptly. Vanessa stood up. Faith shoved past her and scurried toward the bathroom.

"Is she okay?" Grayson asked.

I elbowed him and said, "Move and I'll go see."

I took the long way around to avoid passing Ryan, who watched me without blinking. Whatever was happening there, it would need to get back to the Triad as soon as possible. But I had some ruffled feathers to smooth first.

"Faith, wait!" I said, catching her arm as she passed the dart stalls. When she turned, there were tears pooling in her eyes. "What's wrong?" I asked.

She sniffled an angry sniffle, if there was such a thing. "Can we play darts so it doesn't look like I'm upset?"

"Sure," I said, with a peek over my shoulder at Ryan.

Faith snatched the cup of darts and started throwing. She was almost bad enough to be a safety hazard to the people in the stall next to us. "I thought I would be okay with it," she said.

"Okay with what?"

She dabbed at her tears with the back of her hand and gestured vaguely in the direction of our group. "Seeing you act like a couple."

I blinked at her, clueless, until the truth dawned on me. "Faith, do you like Levi?"

"Maybe." She stomped over to retrieve her darts, most of which had barely hit the board.

"I'm confused. You told me to make a move!"

"I know!" she cried, hands flailing. "I meant it, and I still do."

"Then why are you upset? Why didn't you say anything?"

The cup of darts shook under my nose. "Play with me so I don't look as upset as I am."

"You mean so you don't look like you'd rather be throwing those at a picture of my face?" I asked with a nervous laugh, picking out a couple of darts. Faith couldn't help but giggle through her tears.

"I'm upset because first of all, you didn't tell me you were dating him," she explained, serious again. "*Levi* did. It made me feel like our friendship was slipping, that leaving at the end of the summer will mean we're not in each other's lives anymore. You and Lindsey have both made me feel that way."

"I'm so sorry, Faith. I should have told you. I've just been—"

"I don't want to hear the excuses," she said. "Just let me talk. The second reason is that even though Levi told me about you two, seeing it is a lot harder than I thought it would be." She gestured from me to him. "If you had answered any of my texts and told me you were coming, then I could have... I don't know... prepared myself!"

I sighed. Having offhandedly sunk two darts in the bullseye made me feel worse, and I purposefully threw my next shot at the outside ring. "I'm so sorry. If I had known..." I trailed off. I didn't know what would happen if I had known. I would have told her about the kiss last summer. I would have tried to avoid Levi for her sake. But she still would have nudged me toward him. She was unshakably selfless.

"Don't be sorry, at least not about dating him," she said, stern and sincere. "I didn't say anything because I knew it would be weird. I mean, we treat him like our brother one minute, and then Abbie flirts with him the next...." She rolled her eyes. "But that's a whole other fish to fry. The bottom line is that if Levi had ever liked Abbie or me—which *would* be weird, don't get me wrong—he's had a million chances to make that clear. I read his poems when they were first published. It's *you*, Nat."

"What do you want me to do?" I asked, desperate.

"Nothing. I just thought I'd be able accept this before it was thrust in my face." She hiccupped out a laugh. "You know, like taking poison in small doses to immunize yourself."

"Can we talk outside?" Vanessa interrupted, tussling her way through the crowd toward us. By her fierce grip on my elbow, made even fiercer by her half dozen rings, I knew it was urgent. I looked to Faith for permission. I couldn't afford to fail her as a friend again.

She chewed on her lip. "I feel like we still need to talk. At least until things feel normal again, right?"

"Yes," I said, and turned back to Vanessa. "Can we—?"

"It's an emergency."

Faith scoffed. "Do you need a tampon or something? What else would be so urgent?"

Vanessa snapped her lips shut, at a loss for words.

"Okay, fine! Just go!" Faith said, and turned back to the dartboard, muttering under her breath.

"Faith, we'll talk soon," I insisted.

She threw her last dart and stormed off to the bathroom without another word.

"Come on," Vanessa said, tugging me away.

Thankfully, I hadn't taken off my mini shoulder purse holding my wallet and phone, so I didn't need to swing by the table and make excuses. Lindsey was already gone. Levi met my eyes through the crowd, looking concerned.

"Where are you going?" Abbie asked, intercepting us.

"Vanessa's not feeling well, so we're taking her home."

Abbie nodded, but it wasn't a supportive nod so much as an indication that she saw through my lie. "We may be going off to college soon, but that doesn't give you an excuse to be shitty friends." She turned to leave.

I gripped her wrist. "Abbie."

"What?"

I'm trying to protect this town, sat at the tip of my tongue. "There's just a lot going on. It's hard to explain."

"That's what friends are supposed to be for." She stalked away.

Defeated, I followed Vanessa through the crowd and out into the stifling summer night. Lindsey was waiting for us by the car. "What's the deal with Ryan?" she asked.

"The Shadowing has started to change him," Vanessa said.

"Do you think the Woodwalker is already in there?" I asked. "Is it too late?"

Her curls bounded as she shook her head. "No, I don't think it's too late. But I don't get it. Why didn't our grandmas warn us about this?"

"Maybe it was different last time," Lindsey said. "Maybe the Woodwalkers are getting better at this."

"That's not good," I said, the understatement of the century. They were getting stronger, while our magic diminished with every generation.

"What if he's some kind of scout?" Vanessa said.

"You think he's keeping an eye on us?" Lindsey asked.

"Not on us. He was there before we showed up."

"So, you think he might be looking for victims?"

"He could be waiting for boys to leave by themselves so he can lure them into a trap. It's easier than waiting for their prey to come to them." Vanessa whipped out her phone and typed furiously. "I'm texting Bryce to come out here. I want to drop him at his house and tell him to stay there until after the anniversary. At least it's surrounded by wards."

"Ness, you can't do that," Lindsey said, reaching for Vanessa's phone.

"Why not?" Vanessa ducked away from her. "Why do I need to obey the Triad when they're clearly keeping things from us?"

"We don't know that they are. Besides, you're the one who just said that we can't afford to raise any suspicions. If we stop the Claiming but not the murders—"

"You're the one who just said that wouldn't happen!" Vanessa argued.

"He could be stalking Emmy," I said, only half listening to their argument. "She's a sitting duck, right? Draining her of her magic would make them stronger for the Claiming."

Vanessa hushed us when she noticed Levi leave the restaurant. He was looking for us under the yellow parking lot lights. Ryan Ashland followed him and caught his attention. We ducked behind the car to watch. Their voices were indistinct rumbles. Ryan whipped out a pack of cigarettes, lit one, and took a long, satisfied drag.

"We have to tell the Triad about him," Lindsey whispered back.

"And we have to tell the boys to stay away from Ryan." Vanessa proceeded to text Bryce. Lindsey was about to try to stop her again when a distant pop sounded. We looked up to see a red flare sparkling across the sky to the east.

"The distress signal," Lindsey said. "We have to go."

As I hopped into the back seat, I grabbed for my phone and texted Levi. *STAY AWAY FROM RYAN. LOSE HIM, TAKE EMMY HOME, AND STAY THERE UNTIL I CALL YOU.*

Lindsey peeled out of the parking lot. Levi looked up and watched us go. Through the back windshield, I saw him slide his phone out of his pocket and hurry back inside. I loosed a breath of relief knowing that he had seen my warning.

"That signal looked like it could have come from the cabin," Lindsey said as we jerked the wrong direction down a one-way street.

"Brianna," Vanessa breathed. "She and Kate were on their way out there."

"It'll be okay," Lindsey assured her, slamming down the gas pedal.

Vanessa called her grandma to alert the Triad about the flare in case they hadn't seen it. Adrenaline bubbled through my veins as I strapped on my revolvers and tucked my orange flare gun in its separate holster.

The dirt road was even rougher at high speeds, and I had to grip Lindsey's seat to keep from smashing my head against the window. At long last, we found Kate's car parked in front of the gate at the end of the road.

"Oh my god," Lindsey breathed.

Pressed up against the other side of the fence like a barricade were countless mangled carcasses emanating a putrid odor. Some were dismembered, others left to decompose somewhat intact, blood matting their fur. I caught sight of a pet tag flashing on a bloody collar and had to look away.

The outline of the cabin appeared ghostly in the moonlight. There was no movement in the nearby trees, not that my enhanced night vision could catch, anyway. All was quiet. Feet light on the dirt, we climbed the gate without a sound. Lindsey lost her footing and fell back on a gaggle of bony limbs. She made a noise of disgust as I helped her to her feet.

Vanessa picked her way over the carcasses and into the trees, staying low as she circled around to the back of the cabin. We caught up and found her crouching in the undergrowth, motioning for us to stay quiet.

It was a hard command to follow once I saw what was happening for myself.

TWENTY-FIVE

Three human figures were on their knees, bound by their wrists, barely conscious: Kate, Brianna, and Heather. Their necks and faces were smeared with dark blood.

In the moonlight I counted twelve ragged outlines of bone and sinew. Antler tines and horns towered up from decaying skulls: deer, cow, coyote, goat, human. Frayed, bloody ligaments stretched over spindly shadow forms. Weapons lay scattered in the grass.

"What's happening?" I whispered.

"It was a trap," Vanessa said.

One of the Woodwalkers wore another human skull. Had the one Lindsey and I fought attacked someone else? Dug up a fresh grave? I shuddered to think that every time we proved victorious, they had to scavenge again. But we had no choice. We had to keep them at bay.

The human-skulled Woodwalker loomed over Kate, parts of it as wispy as a phantom, others as mangy as a starved woodland predator. It yanked her hair, forcing her to look up while it opened its jaws wide and sucked in a breath.

The shadow form grew, filling the bony outlines of the creature. The

Woodwalkers were bleeding our fellow Wardens so they could feast on their magic uninhibited.

My right hand traveled slowly down to my revolver. Lindsey jabbed a finger from Vanessa to herself, then made a semicircle with each hand to signal that the two of them were going to flank the scene. She mimed a whistle to tell me to wait for a signal before shooting. I nodded.

After they snuck away, I cocked my right revolver, took careful aim at the Woodwalker with the human skull, and waited.

The sound of speeding wheels on the dirt road distracted me. I hoped for Warden backup but feared it would be Jason or one of his deputies on patrol.

I didn't have time to assess the threat. A whistle pierced the air. I braced my arm and pulled the trigger.

My bullet broke off the bottom jaw of the humanoid Woodwalker. The monster snapped toward me and uttered a shriek that made my insides squirm with fear. Lindsey took the opportunity to dive at him with her knives while Vanessa launched off a fallen tree and buried her hatchet in the skull of Brianna's attacker.

She pulled the weapon out as the broken creature screamed its egress from battle. The rotten corpse it left behind dropped to the grass.

Lindsey fought the one with the human skull tooth and nail, making it hard to get another shot to take it down. Three others advanced on Vanessa, so I diverted my focus back to her. We alternated hatchet strikes and gunshots, graceful choreography in a violent play. We took two down before I ran out of ammo.

My hands were steady as I switched guns. Bullets burst a skull and pierced a heart and another and another, until six Woodwalkers remained standing and it was time to reload. I emptied the cylinder but didn't get a chance to slip in fresh cartridges before a Woodwalker with the head of a goat charged me.

One of its eyes was still intact, glaring at me with a wicked-looking stripe of pupil. I noticed the glint of Brianna's hatchet on the ground between us. Without enough time to reload, I jammed my revolvers in their holsters and scrambled to claim the weapon, brandishing it at the creature closing in, lashing at me.

Its claws were short and curved like a wildcat's, ideal for hooking into flesh and ravaging it from the inside out. I ducked and dodged, barely evading a strike that could have torn the skin off my bones. Finally, I plunged the hatchet just under its shoulder, where the sinew was thick and bare. The creature's bowed legs bent farther, bringing the skull within reach. I ripped the hatchet from the dead flesh and came down on the indent between its horns.

The bone crumbled and cracked. I planted the heel of my boot against its spine and yanked the dense, ridged horns in opposite directions. The skull split down the middle and the corpse released a screeching shadow form that fled deep into the abyss of the woods.

Lindsey had taken out another. Four against three.

But I watched, horrified, as one of them dragged Vanessa across the grass, leaving a trail of blood. Her assailant, an appalling creature so incongruously assembled that it had no distinguishable animal or human traits, yanked her arms behind her back and bound her wrists with a ragged cloth. It drew a long claw along the side of her throat, bringing forth drops of blood.

Someone sprinted around the side of the cabin and onto the battlefield, but it wasn't another Warden joining the fight. It was Levi, and he was running straight for Vanessa's attacker. He may not have been able to see the Woodwalker itself, but he could see enough to know she needed help.

I tightened my grip on Brianna's hatchet and got there first, hacking gracelessly at the creature until blood from the fresh kills it wore sprinkled over my face. The Woodwalker ejected itself from its mangled body and vanished, leaving a portentous silence in its wake.

Movement in my peripheral caught my attention. There were three Woodwalkers left. Lindsey fought one, another with a deer skull advanced on me, and the one with the human skull watched Levi. If empty black eye sockets could show hunger…

I landed a sound hit to my attacker's chest and crushed several ribs, leaving the heart vulnerable. But another seized me from behind—the one Lindsey was supposed to be fighting—and forced me to kneel on the grass, the pricks of its claws sharp on my shoulders as I struggled to no avail.

It sliced along the side of my neck. I gasped and felt warm blood trickling out.

I pressed on the wound, my knees wavering. My vision blotted black and gray. The Woodwalker would do to me what it had done to Nora Langford: plunder the magic and life from me and leave me nothing but an empty husk.

I found Lindsey to my left. Her hair had fallen loose from its tie and stuck to the scarlet blood that streaked her cheek like war paint. Her staunch gaze locked on mine and her nostrils flared with rage. We couldn't let them win.

Bolstered, I rolled onto my back, grabbed the hatchet, and took to my feet. I swung my weapon up at the one that had cut me, knocking its skull clean off. It landed near Lindsey, who toed it toward a nearby rock and smashed it to bits with the heel of her boot. The other one I decimated in a furious blur.

When I looked up, I saw Levi cutting Lindsey free with one of her knives. The Woodwalker with the human skull—the last remaining—towered over Levi while he was blind and oblivious to its presence.

A roar of infernal rage tore out of me, but the Woodwalker had already stepped into Levi, its ghostly form passing through him like a knife through butter. Levi shuddered. His eyes went dark. The moon wasn't bright enough to show a second shadow, but I could see the air around him changing, blackening, darker than a hole in the universe.

I charged, ready to tear this devil apart with my bare hands if I had to. But a shot rang out through the sacred glade, exploding the creature's skull. The Woodwalker's shadow essence screeched and departed.

Levi and I stood paralyzed, chests heaving. Maggie sauntered onto the scene, her pistol smoking. The three Triad members ran to their granddaughters first. I wobbled, but Levi was there to hold me steady, slipping off his shirt to wad it to my neck. Together, we hurried to Heather, who groaned as we helped her stand.

Kate was the only one who couldn't be immediately revived. Maggie cradled her granddaughter in her lap, brushing back her hair and pressing the hem of her shirt to the wounds. "Help us!" she called out, and it was the first time I'd heard fear in her voice. I clamped a hand over my mouth. We couldn't lose Kate.

Sofia gripped Maggie's shoulder for support as she crouched beside them and closed her eyes. She plugged Kate's wounds with her fingers, forcefully enough to make me wince, and whispered a harsh incantation. Her shoulders convulsed so aggressively that I feared the magic might rattle apart her aging frame.

Kate opened her eyes and raked in a sharp breath. Maggie laughed and kissed her forehead.

I sighed with relief, suddenly bone tired.

Steering clear of the animal remains, I carefully toted the others' weapons to the other side of the road.

Even in the dark, I could see Levi's hazel eyes roving over my features, catching on the blood painted down my neck. I wanted to be furious with him for following us out here. I wanted to scream at him for being careless with his own life when I was trying so hard to protect him. But I didn't have the energy, not when I would have done the same thing in his place.

Levi unburdened me of the extra weapons and led me to Sofia and her first aid kit. I pulled aside my curtain of blond hair and let her dab away the dirt and blood with her gentle touch. Her hands were cold, and dark circles pooled beneath her eyes. The spell she had worked on Kate had clearly drained her.

"He's Shadowed," she said when Levi walked away.

"I know," I answered, glancing his way. He spoke quietly with Maggie, whose expression was pulled taut as she loaded the weapons into the back of her car. She slammed the trunk and made her way over to me.

"Go home and rest," she said stiffly. "I'll be in touch with instructions."

Levi drove me. I winced as I scooted close to him and lay my head on his shoulder, wondering what it would feel like to fall asleep wrapped in his arms.

But somewhere in the back of my mind, I admitted that the precious days remaining might not be enough to find out.

TWENTY-SIX

ONE DAY UNTIL THE CLAIMING

I wandered into the kitchen in my bathrobe to find of smorgasbord of fried green tomatoes, fried pickles, and jalapeño hush puppies. Slices of battered okra let off an angry sizzle as Mom dropped them into the deep fryer.

After hunting until the break of dawn and sleeping straight through the afternoon, I would have been content to strap a feedbag to my face. I'd told my parents I had to stay up late to write a paper for the summer class, which was getting more mileage as an excuse than I ever anticipated.

Brianna's recovery was slow, and Heather wasn't her usual spunky self yet. Neither of them had been desperate enough to require a magical revival, which was good considering Sofia wouldn't have been able to repeat the effort without needing one herself. But it meant the two were still weak. Since I had escaped the ambush relatively unscathed, the Wardens needed me more than ever.

It was exhausting to be needed.

I'd meant to only sleep until noon, which would have given me hours to spend with Levi. But I'd squandered the day away, perhaps subconsciously realizing that as long as I stayed asleep, I could pretend the imminent Claiming was nothing but a nightmare.

"What are you making this for?" I asked my mom, voice groggy.

"There's an interdenominational prayer meeting and potluck at Calvary. We're going to unify and pray away any, you know"—she fluttered her hand, her charm bracelet tinkling—"funny business. Or at the very least, let all the hooligans know the town is watching."

"Nice euphemisms."

"I know you think it's silly to worry about ritual murders in this day and age," she said, stirring the okra around with a skimmer. "And I'm sure you'll do what your dad does and say that Miss Maggie's prayer meeting is over the top—"

"I don't think that," I said. "I think it's nice, the community coming together."

"Honey, are you scared?" she asked.

Out of reflex, I almost said no. But I hesitated. Maybe it was the constellation of tender bruises and cuts on my body. Maybe it was knowing that the Wardens had faced an ambush unlike any the group had ever seen, or knowing that three more boys had been marked for death since then. Whatever it was, it broke my resolve. "A little."

"You don't need to be. Someone's just trying to cause a stir. They have to know they're not going to get away with anything." She stroked my hair, smiled, and handed me a chafer of fried food. "Now make yourself useful and help me load the car. Dad's already at the church helping set up."

"I thought he said it was over the top."

"Yeah, but he's wrapped around my little finger," she said with a wink.

When she was gone, I brought breakfast back to my room and peeled off my robe to appraise the damage I'd been too exhausted to care about after hunting with Kate and Lindsey. Clusters of chiggers and mosquito bites added insult to injury, but the bruises were already healing and the cuts scabbing over. I wondered if our slightly accelerated healing rate meant that Brianna and Heather would be back in fighting shape before tomorrow night.

I got a text from Maggie to the group. *I'll be attending the meeting and searching for any second shadows we may have missed. I encourage those of you who are interested to attend and pray fervently that tomorrow will be the day this all ends.*

Reaching for a sense of comfort about tomorrow night, I considered going. But I didn't want to go into that sanctuary yet. Only a few hours remained before I had to fix my focus on the battle yet to come, and I wanted to spend that time with Levi.

At the same time, I feared he'd already started changing the way Ryan had changed.

The Triad had assured us that there'd been no premature takeover of any Shadowed boys before the last attempted Claiming and told us to not read too deeply into a haircut and some new clothes. They told us everything would proceed as planned and to meet at the hideout tonight to receive our instructions for tomorrow night.

Now that Levi had been Shadowed and the Claiming was coming up fast, some of the doubts I had tucked away over the past few weeks sprang out of hiding. I'd scoured Grandma Kerry's letter for any hints I might have missed between the lines but had come away empty-handed. I'd tried to weave some kind of logical context for what Nora had done during the last Claiming, but that was a dead end, too. She had let down her shield and allowed darkness to penetrate her spirit without fighting back. It made no sense.

The idea of one of those horrible creatures seizing Levi as a vessel hit me in waves of terror. How powerful would the Woodwalkers be in new bodies? What terrible things would they do to the people in this town if they had a magic that mirrored ours and were able to walk among us?

There was so much we didn't know, so much Malachi had never understood about the revenge curse she had wrought and its repercussions.

While I waited for Levi to answer my text letting him know I was awake, I sat crisscross on my bed and perused the Book of Wisdom, browsing for any spells or rituals that would be useful during the witching hour tomorrow night, when the Woodwalkers were free to possess the bodies they'd chosen and take them to the sacred glade, where they could complete the Claiming. Where they could take forever what did not belong to them.

I chanced upon the page that someone had removed. I hadn't thought about it since my first time flipping through the book. "Basically sacrilege" was the phrase Vanessa had used to describe removing an entry from the Book of Wisdom. I trailed my finger along the torn edge. The more I studied it, the surer I felt that the page hadn't been ripped out in a fit of rage, but surgically removed, sliced out. The act of a disciplined person, a rule follower. Or perhaps a rule maker.

"Hmm," I said aloud before flipping back to the divination spells. There was a spell for finding lost things, but since the missing page had never belonged to me, I wasn't sure it would work. Then again, it seemed worth a try. It required a single bone, an empty glass, to represent the hollowness of loss, and a gray candle, to stimulate clairvoyance.

The contents of my starter kit clanged and sloshed as I dragged it toward me. I'd added dozens of items, and I happened to have a gray candle stub. For bone, all I had was my newly assembled sortilege set, which Vanessa had said could never be used for anything else. I tapped my chin, thinking, and then remembered the real elk antler chew toy outside in the dog run.

Trio of items in hand, I went to Grandma Kerry's room, shoved the bed and rug aside, and sat in front of the Warden's Rune. I lit the candle and arranged the objects in a way that felt proper, with the book at the center of the mark, the antler above it, and the two other items beside it.

Centering my mind and spirit, I conjured a blurry image of the missing page and read, "A precious thing has been mislaid, surrendered, stolen, or has strayed. I ask this bone to be my guide; show me where the lost thing hides."

I waited. If the page had been destroyed, nothing would happen. That seemed the most likely outcome, and I girded myself for disappointment. But the antler scraped across the wood floor as it calibrated like a compass needle, spinning back and forth and eventually pointing northeast. Now that it was enchanted, it would show me the right direction as I journeyed, pointing me along until the lost page was found.

Pleased, I blew out the candle and collected my supplies. While I dressed—a black tank top and dark jeans had become my Warden uniform—Levi texted me back and invited me over. My capricious curiosity about the missing page could wait.

My truck was back from the shop, making cantankerous noises but otherwise functioning. On my way to Levi's, I tried calling Faith for the third time, but there was no answer. I felt guilty going to his house without making amends with her first. But after we stopped the Claiming, I told myself, thinking positive, I would do everything in my power to save my friendships.

When Levi answered the door, my first thought was that he didn't look any different, not like Ryan, not like I'd feared. He was himself, his eyes dancing mosaics of warm colors, no hint of any shadow, no evidence that anything had changed.

My second thought was regret that I'd put no effort into my appearance. He wore a loose-fitting denim button-up and smelled so good that I wanted to stand there drawing in his essence like a fragrance sample at a beauty counter. I practiced some self-control and stepped inside the quiet house, glancing into the kitchen and to the top of the stairs.

"They're at the meeting," he said. "We have the place to ourselves."

"I'm sorry I slept late. I could have come over so much sooner."

"You needed rest," he said, brushing off my apology. I could hear barely restrained excitement in his voice. "And it gave me time to get ready."

"Get ready?" I asked, looking him up and down. There was no way it had taken him more than half an hour.

He took my hand and interlaced our fingers. "Come with me."

Out back, under the shade of an oak tree near the pond, he'd set up a picnic in the bed of his truck. I gasped. White paper lanterns floated in the branches overhead. Sunflowers peeked their bright faces out of a basket on a checkered blanket that held an array of sophisticated snacks for two: a baguette, fruits, cheeses, and jams. There were pillows lined up against the back of the bed, and even mini handheld fans to help us keep cool.

"Let's try to forget about tomorrow, at least for a while," he said, tugging me by the hand. "I know you have to go at sunset, but until then . . ."

Grinning until my cheeks ached, I let him lead me across the yard. "Do you like it?" he asked as I stood next to the open tailgate, absorbing every detail. I wanted to remember this forever.

"This is the most amazing thing anyone's ever done for me." I turned to stand on tiptoe and capture his mouth with mine. He gripped my hips and lifted me onto the truck bed. His arms encircled me, sifting through my hair, holding me as if the world would end soon. Maybe ours would.

But he cut off the fervid kiss. "I don't want you to think I'm trying to take advantage of the fact that today might be the last day we—"

I laughed, my cheeks flushing hot at the mere suggestion. "I didn't think that. Besides, you said you wanted to forget about potential impending doom."

"It's harder than I thought." He sighed and settled next to me. "I can feel this weird change inside. It started the moment that . . . it happened. Otherwise, I'd have trouble believing in the Claiming."

The Triad had caved and told him what he needed to know, nothing more. "What did you see during the ambush?" I asked.

"Blurs and shadows," he answered, squinting his eyes as though reliving the moment, trying to make out what he'd seen in the dark.

"How's Emmy?"

"The nightmares are worse than ever. She choked on dirt in her sleep again. I'm ready for this to be over, for all of our sakes."

It was a strange paradox, to be dreading something imminent while feeling anxious to put it behind us. It made the next few hours feel too short and too long at the same time. Soon the warm pink hues in the sky gave way to an expanse of cool indigo, and the paper lanterns looked like fairy lights.

I realized that he and I were night and day: kept apart by the cruelty of a mysteriously magical universe, converging and sharing the same exquisite sky for moments that passed too quickly.

"I should go," I said, but made no move to leave the comfort of his embrace. I was sweating, curled up in his arms and propped against the pile of pillows, but I didn't care one bit.

"I wish you didn't have to," he whispered into my hair.

I shifted to look at him. The stunning greens and ambers in his irises glimmered, hypnotizing me. But something dark slithered through his gaze, and his arms suddenly felt like a cage.

"I have to go," I said, pushing myself up. I half expected him to try to hold me back. I remembered Vanessa's theory that Ryan had been sent out to lure potential victims to the Woodwalkers, and I scanned the woods at the back of the Langfords' yard for something lurking just beyond the Wardens' protective boundaries.

"What's wrong?" Levi asked, blinking the darkness away. Guileless and confused, he reached for my hand, but I ripped it away. "Nat..."

"I just have to go."

We both climbed out of the bed. He took in my wild, fearful expression, and didn't try to touch me again. He seemed tempted to offer words of comfort, then closed his mouth in a hard line.

And we were better off leaving it at that. Every touch brought me closer to the threshold of irrevocable pain should he die tomorrow night—or worse, should he be claimed by some other soul entirely.

TWENTY-SEVEN

The prayer meeting had ended by the time I reached the church, but there were a few stragglers outside the fellowship hall. My parents were loading up their left-overs in the car. Good. They would get home before full night descended.

I circled the block and came back when they were gone.

For the first time in a while, the sanctuary gave me the creeps. I could imagine the scene after the last massacre too clearly: the bodies spread around the room, some untouched, others battered from fighting the people who were trying to save them. The Wardens had brought the bodies of the ones who had escaped back here, leaving them for the pastor to find.

When the pastor had called the police, distraught, they'd told him not to disturb the scene and to get out in case the murderer was still there. Their reports had been factual and clinical, but shock seemed to bleed through the careful words. How could twelve more boys have died in San Solano without a trace of useful evidence—and no discernible cause of death?

"Nat," Lindsey said, emerging from the choir hall and hurrying to squeeze me in a tight hug. "I'm so, so sorry. I want you to know that I'm ready to fight with everything I have tomorrow."

"What are you sorry for?"

She stiffened and backed up a step. "Did Kate not tell you?"

"I was out back trying to call her," Kate said, sweeping in, clearly stressed. Frizzy dark hairs drifted from her ponytail, and bluish veins stood out on her pale temples. This was the first time I'd seen her looking anything close to haggard. "The cell service here…" She shook her head, realizing that was immaterial. "Nat, your dad's been Shadowed."

I stared at her. "No, no way," I finally managed. "They want young men. Why would they—?"

"I know," Kate said, gripping my shoulders as though I might burst into pieces. "It's almost like they're getting more hostile toward us."

"I put up more secret wards around the house, around everything, just in case!" I shouted, a ragged desperation in my voice. "And that was on top of my grandma's protections."

"You did everything you could," Kate assured me.

"I should have been there. I could have stopped it. I should have watched over him better."

"Do *not* blame yourself. You can't follow your loved ones around every second of every day. Believe me, I resist the temptation constantly."

A burning sob built up in my throat. Kate pulled me close, pinning me against her. "The strength they stole from us must have allowed them to work quickly. They've Shadowed the rest of their victims. All twelve. After tomorrow, whatever happens, we may need to find a way to clear out San Solano forever. Have the town condemned or something. I don't know."

"But then what happens?" I asked, raising my voice. I looked at Lindsey, who cast her eyes to the floor. "Do they take it over? Grow their dominion until they can reach the people in the next town, and the next? Where does this end, Kate? I need to know where this ends."

"I don't know." Tears sprang into her green eyes. "I don't know. But there's nothing else we can do besides be ready tomorrow night. Go be with your family for now. We've done what we could."

The screen door made a racket when I stepped inside. I could hear my parents doing dishes in the kitchen. It sounded like Dad was teasing Mom for taking the prayer meeting so seriously. When I stepped around the corner, he was trying not to laugh at her pretending-to-be-offended face.

"Ah! It worked!" he said, throwing a dish towel over his shoulder and clapping his hands. "The food summoned her again."

"I'm not hungry," I said feebly.

But he was already heaping food onto a plate for me, assembling a hodge-podge meal out of everyone's pooled leftovers, mostly carbs masquerading as vegetables. And there it was, in the bright kitchen light: a second shadow on the wall. An ordinary person would have thought it was nothing but a trick of the light. But I felt the presence of unknowable darkness. Here, in the house Grandma Kerry and I had worked so hard to protect.

Bile rose in my throat. I needed my strength, though, and forced myself to eat.

"Are the jalapeño poppers too spicy?" Mom asked, and I almost laughed at the absurd triviality of the question until I realized a drop of sweat was coursing down my forehead.

I said no and she bounced to the next thought, determined to be conversational despite my mood. "You seem to be wearing a lot of dark clothes these days. It's a shame. You look so pretty in summery colors."

Leave it to her to think a pair of black boots called for motherly intervention. In truth, I wanted *more* concern. The beguilement and my watertight alibis protected me from their prying, but I almost wished they would dig deeper so I would have an excuse to crack and confess. If there were ever a time to break a solemnly sworn oath...

"The prayer meeting was interesting today," Dad said, filling the silence. "I think some people are getting real antsy about the anniversary."

"Some of them just came to complain about the crowding," Mom said, lifting an eyebrow in disapproval. "But that's nothing to complain about. Tourists bring good business."

"I see their point, though," Dad said. "I'm getting fed up with it myself. Can't get a cup of coffee without hearing all about our haunted town." He did a dorky boogeyman impression that normally would have made me laugh out of embarrassment. Now, I just managed a smile as I stabbed around at my green bean casserole.

"Let's hope the crowding is our biggest worry," Mom said.

"Nothing's going to happen, Jodes, I promise," he said, overconfident. Dad's biggest, most lovable flaw was his overconfidence. Thankfully, he approached his veterinary work with a little more humility and scientific curiosity than he did everything else. "As much as tourists and journalists would like to think otherwise."

"No one is *wishing* for murder. They're just being realistic. The missing animal problem is concerning."

I wondered if word of the carcasses piled at the cabin had spread around. It seemed like something the police might want to keep under wraps if they'd seen it, to prevent panic. Surely, I would have caught wind of that gossip if it'd gotten out.

Then again, I hadn't even noticed that my own father was Shadowed.

"Have you seen the lost-and-found board in my office?" Dad said. "Pets run away or get lost all the time. There's nothing unusual going on."

As if to refute his statement, the dogs picked up barking like hellhounds. Every muscle in my body tensed. My weapons were outside, but I didn't want to leave Ranger and Maverick vulnerable for even the time it took to retrieve them and cast a beguilement spell.

"I'm going to let them inside." I pushed back from the table.

"I think that's best." Mom's consent spoke volumes. Normally she would complain about the shedding.

After closing the back door behind me, I took cautious strides into the darkness. But the sound of a terrified whimper made me break into a sprint.

Maverick was huddled in the corner of the dog run. There was a jagged hole in the chain-link fence. I traipsed closer and found blood in the grass outside the enclosure.

Ranger was nowhere in sight.

For a moment, I wasn't a warrior. I stood helpless, weaponless, chest heaving, tears burning in my eyes. Why had I not been more careful? I should have known this massacre would happen exactly like the one before. I should have holed up in my house with my family and my dogs and tracked their every move. If the Wardens could do nothing to stop the killings, I'd do everything in my power to make sure the people I cared about didn't suffer. Would it have been selfish? Yes. Would I care? Not one bit.

Grandma Kerry's warning nagged at me, merciless. *The farther you stay away from them, the safer the people you love will be.*

I should have listened.

My fear contorted into rage. Teeth gritted, I charged back to the porch, opened the back door and barked at poor Maverick to get inside. He obeyed my command with a quiet whine. Once he was safe indoors, I slashed across the yard toward the black clumps of trees in the distance.

As I stepped into the wild tangles, my eyes adjusted, picking out the expected shapes around me. A stir of warm wind carried the tang of blood and the sound of suckling. Of feeding. My heart fluttered against my ribcage as I ducked under a branch and saw a Woodwalker stooped over the ground with its back to me.

Hearing my approach, the creature turned to hiss in my direction, revealing a devastating array of sharp teeth, a protruding ivory snout, and a body that looked like decomposed human remains. Antlers jutted out at all angles from its head, and blood dripped from the mutilated animal parts it had carelessly stuffed together.

Ranger lay limp on the ground. Blood matted the hair on his hip and back leg, but his side swelled and collapsed with shaky breaths.

A growl ripped out of my throat as I charged at the monster and attacked with my bare hands. I clung to its antlers and tore at its empty eye sockets, prodding around for something deeper inside it that I could twist and punish. I finally pushed through to its warm, dead heart and yanked, sealing my victory.

But before the shadow animating the odious body retreated, the creature raked its long claws vengefully across my back, slicing through my skin.

I crumpled face-first on the ground, a distant scream echoing wildly in my ears. I realized it was mine. Blood surged from the wounds.

I knew what would happen to me—and to Ranger—if I didn't manage to get help. But my battered body wouldn't obey my command to move, and I realized I'd left my phone sitting on the table in the kitchen.

A quiet whimper gave me the will to turn my head, barely. Ranger limped toward me with great effort and settled down against my flank, his face so close to mine that his pointed ear tickled my cheek. Tears rolled sideways down my face and into his coarse hair.

My voice cracked as I called for help. I swallowed and tried again. No response. My parents wouldn't think much of me taking my time, since Ranger could be stubborn.

I closed my eyes, slipping into the stillness of unconsciousness. But the sound of scratchy breaths soon forced me to attention with a feverish jolt.

With one cheek pressed to the earth, I couldn't make out the shape moving in my peripheral vision. I didn't have to see it to know what it was. Another Woodwalker. I envisioned myself moving to attack, but even the twitch of readiness from my muscles pushed a devastated groan from my lips. My eyelids pressed closed again, releasing more tears. *This is the end.*

Hot, stinking breaths gusted over the side of my face and into my ear.

My bare nerves shivered, bringing on a fresh wave of pain. The Woodwalker gripped my arm and goaded my limp body into rolling over. I sobbed as my open cuts pressed against the dirt and the torn fabric of my shirt.

Face-to-face with the Woodwalker now, I looked up into the dead eyes of a putrefying black bear skull. I felt the monster's hunger for the waning life inside me, darkness pressing in from all sides.

A black void consumed me. I smelled the stale earth and decay. The magic within me began to quiver as it joined with the darkness, braiding together to become one strand. I breathed a farewell, made peace with the knowledge that the ones I loved most might never know why this happened to me.

But the world didn't fade entirely. A change writhed under the Woodwalker's shadowed form, quick as a lightning strike on a murky night. Beneath the death and darkness, beneath the evil, I saw something neither human nor Woodwalker, something shapeless and taking the shape of everything at once, effulgent gold and a void of shadows, coexisting.

A high-pitched crossover of a screech and a howl pierced my ears. The Woodwalker was calling the others toward it so that they could share in the feast, gorge themselves on the power inside me.

It wasn't over yet, but it would be soon.

And then the Woodwalker's sweltering breaths retreated. A rustling of leaves marked its departure.

Within seconds, someone arrived to cradle my head. I blinked my eyes open to find Lindsey kneeling over me.

"We're going to get you safe, okay?" she said, lifting my upper body with the kind of tenderness that told me just how bad my injuries were. I whimpered as she shifted on her knees and slid me onto her back in a fireman's carry.

"Ranger," I murmured.

"Levi!" Lindsey called out as she stood up. I heard his answering footsteps. Running. Urgent.

"Oh my god," he whispered.

"Bring Ranger to her dad. Tell him…" She cursed under her breath. "Tell him she couldn't carry him, so she asked you to help while she went to tell the authorities. So no one else could get hurt. Leave before he asks questions. Meet us at the church."

Levi's soft touch trailed along my cheek. When he pulled away, I opened my eyes to see him hunkering down to lift Ranger.

Before I sank away from the jarring pain into unconsciousness, I wondered if I had imagined the glimpse into the Woodwalker's being.

More than one pair of hands gentled me onto a bunk in the basement. The taut silence in the room—the kind you hear in a hospital—made the agony in my body and the pounding in my ears that much more intense.

Sofia banished the tension of uncertainty with a steady stream of commands. She cut my shirt and sports bra with a knife and peeled the fabric away from my flayed skin. When I cried out, Lindsey gripped my hand and squeezed. They brought me to the claw-foot tub in the bathroom, where I sobbed at the burn of the water, but nothing compared to the sting of alcohol once I was back on the bed. It lit every nerve in my body ablaze and forced sobs out of my dry lips.

The agony was soothed slightly by the pressure of a cool herb poultice stretching across my back. Lindsey tipped a glass of water to my lips and then traded it out for something stringent, a tincture of some sort. I faded away, the memory of my bizarre encounter with the Woodwalker burning like an ember in my coal-black delirium.

My return to consciousness was a slow, unsteady climb. I heard soft voices. One was deeper than the other, masculine. *Here, in the hideout?* I thought, before realizing it belonged to Levi. His words slipped through the clouds of my mind before I could capture and examine them.

I heard shifting and the creak of a chair beside me. "I know you do," Maggie said in answer to Levi's mysterious statement. "That's why you're here, instead of anywhere else, on what could be the last night of your life." A deep sigh. "Your involvement is unprecedented. I didn't know what to do with you. So I shut you out entirely, and that was unfair to you."

Levi's hand closed over mine. I wanted to comfort him, but even breathing felt like scaling a mountain.

"There's something I haven't told you," Maggie said after a moment. "When we failed to save the victims of the last Claiming, Nora surrendered herself to the Woodwalkers. She let down her defenses and let them feast on her magic and life until she died. She helped them become stronger."

The silence after Maggie's words stretched on for so long that I nearly drifted back to sleep. Finally, Levi responded. "Nat said she did it because she thought she could break the curse. What made her think that?"

"To understand that, you have to understand the source of our magic. The power in the woods has always been there, neither light nor dark. It imparted Malachi with magnificent magic when it revived her in her mother's womb. On the night Malachi cast the curse, she yoked aspects of that magic to the evil souls of the murderers and abusers."

"So... the magic of the Woodwalkers and your magic come from the same source?"

"Yes, we are cut from the same magical cloth," Maggie confirmed. "But it's where Kerry and Nora went with that that boggles the mind."

"Nat's grandma, too?" Levi asked.

I was careful not to twitch. I had no idea my grandma had been part of Nora's plan.

"Yes. We didn't know exactly what was coming before the anniversary. We just knew it would be awful. Malachi dying before the confrontation made us feel hopeless. That's when Kerry and Nora got a wild hair that they could break the curse by separating the evil from the magic that had given it life and power."

"So... they believed there was something redeemable about the Woodwalkers?"

Maggie thought for a moment. "No, it wasn't about redemption. It was about liberation. Giving the Wardens' share of the power in the woods back. And maybe there's an ounce of logic there, but their methods were too risky. They wanted everyone to do it. They said it would take us banding together, holding strong. But we couldn't consider their unthinkable approach. Purposefully giving power to our enemies, can you imagine? Kerry accepted our refusal, but Nora treated *us* like the villains for doubting her and struck out on her own. I hate that it happened, that I couldn't save my own cousin," she said, grief thick in her voice. "I want to assure you, though: Nora had her issues, but she was a capable woman, and she loved fiercely. It was her head, not her heart, that was in the wrong place. She loved her son with everything she had. It overjoyed me to see Mike carry on that love to his kids. Both of them would be so proud of you."

A shaky breath revealed to me that Levi was crying. The pain inside me surpassed even the constant ache that crawled over my torn skin.

I heard Maggie stand up and pat Levi's shoulder. After a while his breaths evened out.

"I'll make you some tea," Maggie said. "Hot tea always makes a long night easier."

Muted clanking kept me straddling the line of sleep and wakefulness. Levi stroked the skin between my forefinger and thumb.

In the quiet I played back the beginning of their conversation. *I know you do,* Maggie had said.

My echoic memory recalled something I hadn't realized I'd heard Levi say: *I love her.*

When Maggie returned, he asked, "So this—this whole hidden world, the Woodwalkers and the Wardens—began with magic in the sacred glade?"

"This didn't start with magic, hon," she replied, sounding like an old seer as she settled back into her seat. "It started with darkness in men's hearts."

EXCERPT:

PAGANS OF THE PINES: THE UNTOLD STORY OF MALACHI RIVERS

Lillian Pickard, 1968

By the time the trial began in early 1922, I hadn't seen Malachi for several weeks. Rumors went around that she wouldn't show. My parents wavered on whether her absence would be good or bad for my prospects. On the one hand, it would denote her guilt and further support the perception that she was an unruly young woman who had swept up the rest of us hysterical girls in her lunacy.

On the other, the town's ire might fall on us in her stead. My father said that people liked to have someone to punish when bad things happened. It didn't always matter whom.

That winter morning I rode my bicycle to the cabin in hopes of finding her and was relieved to see her sitting inside the sacred circle. But my relief was short-lived. A strong wind could have blown her away. Her lips were chapped to the point of bleeding. She wasn't attired for the cold, and her thin dress was filthy. She smelled like a vagrant. I didn't know how long she'd been there.

"Are you coming to the trial?" I asked her, and was struck by the haunted look in her eyes.

"Trial?" she said. "Oh, I'd forgotten."

"If you don't come, you know they'll do their best to blame Dorothy for everything," I said, but truly, I feared for myself more.

"I won't let anything happen to Dorothy," she said, and I felt she meant it. "Or any of you."

This assurance brought me comfort, and suddenly I pitied her. "Have you even been eating, Malachi?"

"Not since . . ." She couldn't seem to remember.

"What have you been doing out here?" I asked.

She stood up. She was skin and bones, like a ghost that had wasted to nothing. I could already see my father formulating a sympathy argument on her behalf: the accusations and the loss of her father had so upset her that they had impacted her health, and besides, there was no evidence pointing to this pretty, grieving girl and her friends. He would want her groomed, of course, and insist that she borrow one of my dresses. We didn't have much time.

I tried another approach. "Jack Morton has been asking about you. He was disappointed when you left school. I think he'd like to see you again. A lot of girls fancy him, you know. He's grown handsome."

She didn't acknowledge my words. She seemed to have forgotten me as she stared out the window at the deep woods.

"Malachi, what have you been doing out here?" I asked again, losing patience.

I'll never forget the chilling look in her sleepless eyes, or the answer she gave me. "Trying to understand the evil we've wrought."

TWENTY-EIGHT

Natalie Colter

THE MORNING BEFORE THE CLAIMING

Everything was still when I opened my eyes hours later, too aware of the pain singeing my flesh. A light shone from somewhere, blocked by the half-closed curtain. Lindsey now slept in the chair at my bedside.

Sleep attempted to tow me back into its depths, promising an escape from the agony. But I held on to my memories from last night. I had to stay awake. I had to make sense of this.

The Woodwalker could have devoured me. But it didn't.

I pushed up on my elbows, feeling a sensation akin to thick needles pricking every inch of my back. Someone had plugged my phone in to charge in an outlet next to the bed. I reached for it and winced at the bright screen.

Seeing a text from my dad sent a stab of panicked remorse through me. Only hours remained until his fate was determined, and I was useless.

Ranger will be okay, my dad said. *I reset his leg and put him on an IV. I slept in the clinic to watch over him. When are you coming home?*

I pressed the inner corners of my eyes to banish tears before they came. Tears of relief, of paralyzing fear, of regret that I couldn't be there—that it might look like I didn't *care* enough to be there. No summer school or social event could justify my absence this time.

I checked the hour: just before dawn. The final day had come.

I eased myself to a sitting position with a broken gasp. Maggie's confession about Kerry and Nora had seized my imagination. That's what Kerry had meant by breaking the curse: freeing the ancient power that animated the Woodwalkers. Offering our magic at the risk of giving our lives, to finally liberate San Solano from the darkness.

The group's scrutiny had caused Kerry to balk, leaving Nora on her own. Kate had said Nora was a powerful Earth Warden, but apparently, that hadn't been enough.

What if... what if Kerry could have been enough? What if *I* could be enough? What if we didn't have to risk the Woodwalkers acquiring human forms and augmenting their power? Or more losses that would devastate a town already suffering from a tragic legacy?

I dimmed the light on my phone and stood in the least excruciating way possible, which was pretty damn excruciating. My heart warmed as I silently slid aside the curtain and saw Levi sleeping on the top bunk. His presence made me aware that nothing but gauze bandages covered my torso. I looked down to find one of Lindsey's dresses shoved down to my waist like a skirt. My spare clothes must have been too tight for the injuries.

No one else was here. There was a feeling like the calm before the storm. I knew the chaos would come, and it would be brutal. But for now, the air was static, the world at a standstill.

Swaying, I crossed to the shelves of supplies and downed a glass of water sitting on the countertop. The strain of remaining upright made coils of fiery pain unwind through my body.

The monster could have killed me, yet here I stood. Did that mean Nora and Kerry had been right? That there was a creature of another nature living somewhere between layers of darkness and evil, trapped where it did not belong, lending power to the depraved beings that longed to be human again?

What did I need to do to rend them apart? Did I have enough time to find out?

Beside my bed, something rustled in my starter kit. I thought I was hallucinating until I remembered the antler I'd enchanted to find the lost page. Maybe the fact that it had become active again meant the lost page was somewhere in this room.

Suppressing a groan, I managed to extract it from my bag. It immediately started tugging like a dog on a leash and surprised me by taking me straight to the stairs leading out of the basement.

I felt a prick of guilt over abandoning Levi to wonder where I'd gone, but I had to follow my curiosity. Maybe it was the lingering delirium that fueled my determination, but I felt I had no choice.

I shrugged the bodice of Lindsey's white gauzy sundress over my bandaged torso and buckled my revolvers around my waist, holding in a sob of agony.

Levi slept curled up on his side with his hands tucked under his head. I couldn't help but smile at the childishness of the pose and the peace that had fallen over his features like pure snow.

His lashes fluttered. Refusing to think about what I was risking, I grabbed his keys and ascended the stairs with my boots tucked under my arm, biting back a cry as the cuts stretched and oozed across my back. I tottered down the empty hallway, my pulse pounding in all the broken, bruised parts of me.

Bowls of heady, fragrant herbs smoked in the sanctuary, and lit candles lined the perimeter of the room, but it was empty. I could hear voices coming from the fellowship hall, a strategizing meeting I'd been excused from. My gaze rose to the gothic chapel windows. Outside, dawn's light lurked at the horizon.

I set the antler on the Communion table. Was the missing page here in the sanctuary? Hidden and glamoured in a hymnal? Stowed away under a pew?

But the enchanted object pointed straight at the front doors of the sanctuary with no hesitation. Soundlessly, I went out and sat on the dewy grass of the churchyard to lace up my boots. Climbing into Levi's truck was no easy feat, but I managed, then set the antler on the dashboard. It balanced itself and spun to point east.

Ten minutes later I'd passed my house and the turnoff to the cabin, slowing down for the antler to react to either one, though it didn't. I kept driving, wondering if I'd given the bone the wrong intention. But then it jerked sideways to point me down a secluded country road that I recognized.

It was leading me to Malachi's house.

It was quiet at the farmhouse, other than the trilling of cicadas. I trailed through the garden and up to the peeling porch. The windows had been boarded up snug and tight. I didn't even think about trying to pry them loose in my condition. I shot the door handle clean off instead.

Dust swirled in the abandoned home, and the air was almost unbearably stuffy. But it was tidy. The retro furnishings transported me back through the decades. Mostly, it was no-frills, but there were faded floral patterns here and there, an old piano, paintings of the Piney Woods and wildlife. Ignoring the antler anxiously twitching in my grip, I toured the house where the legendary Malachi had lived.

My curiosity had nearly been sated when I noticed discolored photographs on the mantle that looked vaguely familiar. Crossing the musty living room, I took a close look and gasped. One was Grandma Kerry's elementary school picture. Another was Grandma Kerry with her parents—Malachi's son and his wife. There was a newspaper clipping in a frame about Grandma Kerry winning a prize for biggest pumpkin at the county fair. I didn't realize I was crying until I couldn't read the words anymore.

The dam broke. I sank to the floor and sobbed. Something about Malachi's shrine to the life she'd left behind shook me, saddened me, but imbued me with a strange hope. The ties between us were tighter than I'd known, five generations strong and unbroken. She'd loved Kerry the way that Kerry had loved me, in a way that only people who shared our unique burden and gifts could love. And now I felt that love from both of them.

I brushed my face where I had felt the ghostly contact inside the sacred circle on the floor of the abandoned cabin, on the night that I witnessed magic for the first time. Here, I felt someone on the other side reaching out to me again. It was cold and relieving, like a soothing compress or the fragile taste of a first winter snowfall.

In a corner of my mind, I knew I had not a second to waste. But I had never felt so safe, and sleep approached like a gentle twilight tide teasing a sandy shore.

The sound of floorboards whining under footfalls woke me. These were gentle, bare feet. A dreamlike blur outlined everything in the room, smudging and softening it.

When I opened my eyes, Grandma Kerry lowered herself down beside me. She looked comfortable. She felt at home here, too.

A pale blue nightgown hung loose on her thin frame. Her eyes looked lost, the way they had the last few months before she'd died. But as she met my startled gaze, the fog behind them cleared away. Strand by strand, her white hair darkened to dirty blonde. Her wrinkles plumped out until her skin was smooth as a fresh tub of butter. She became the girl from one of the pictures Malachi had saved.

I almost spoke her name, but I didn't want to spook her away. I knew this dream was fragile, like gossamer strands and butterfly wings. It could leave as softly as it came.

I took her hand in mine.

Somewhere, at the far reaches of my mind, a voice told me to ask her about the letter. But I felt a nudge against my thigh and startled awake.

The sun was higher in the sky through the grimy farmhouse windows. I didn't know how long I'd slept. Panic came roaring through the stillness. Angry, I looked for what had woken me, and found the antler convulsing on the dusty carpet next to me like a pet I'd forgotten to feed.

Rubbing sleep from my eyes, I hauled myself up and let the antler guide me to the kitchen. There was an enormous antique breakfront that was too big for the room. Inside I found a miniature library of magical oddities just like the one at the Warden hideout. Some of the resins and oils had gone rancid. My fingers fumbled around vials, jars, and tins, and even a bottle of bitterwine, but nothing resembled a missing page from the Book of Wisdom. Maybe someone had rolled it up and stuffed it in one of these containers like a message in a bottle? No, nothing. I wobbled, woozy from pain, and sank to the floor to take a break. Sitting, I looked up and noticed a folded piece of paper taped to the bottom of the top shelf.

I gathered the strength to rip it off and unfold it, finding that there were several pages, only one of them from the Book of Wisdom. The first was a transcribed recipe for boiled bitterwine and eyebright collyrium on ruled notebook paper, written in Grandma Kerry's handwriting. There were five pages of a diary entry, also written by her.

The pages were folded together in eighths, just like the letter that Maggie had promised to deliver to me, unopened, if I ever found out about the Wardens.

The realization dawned. Grandma Kerry hadn't left me in the dark. She'd bequeathed me everything I needed to embrace my magic and open my Sight. Yes, it would have been difficult for me to make the wine and collyrium without training from the Wardens and with no idea what half of the ingredients even were. But I could have tracked them down, diligently procured whatever I needed.

Her cryptic message made sense. It wasn't meant to be cryptic at all. She had given me a road map, but she'd entrusted it to the wrong person.

Maggie had only fulfilled part of her promise. She'd given me the letter with no possible means to obey its imperative. She had given me no choice but to either join the Wardens or wallow in my uselessness and endure the torment of my magic fighting to break free.

She had lied. She had manipulated me.

Breathless, I sat at the kitchen table and spread out the pages in front of me. The diary entry was an account of what had happened leading up to the previous Claiming. Kerry wrote of meeting Malachi for the first time, realizing who she was. She wrote of embracing her power, of feeling like herself in a way she never had before. She described how she had fallen in love with Roger McElroy and planned to tell her parents they were engaged, only to discover that he was being hunted by the "demons in the woods." She described how he had changed, how his eyes darkened, how she had lost hope of saving him until she realized what she needed to do to break the curse. She understood why Malachi could never do it alone.

Fear of failing Roger was what made her fall in line with the Wardens. And he died anyway.

She described feeling targeted by the Woodwalkers more than the others. She was a Triad on her own, like me, and she was their foremost threat.

Last, she described what the siege in the church was like. The Wardens had held out for most of the night, but in the final minutes of the witching hour, the Woodwalkers managed to break through the barriers and possess the bodies. The victims, including Roger, had obeyed their new masters fully at that point, and became desperate to get back to the sacred clearing.

When I finished reading her description of the Claiming, I felt bereft. And then I remembered what I'd come looking for.

There, laid out on the missing page from the Book of Wisdom, was a ritual for breaking the Claiming Curse, in my grandma's scratchy handwriting. She had written with such confidence, even nearly poking holes in the pages with her pen when the inspiration behind the incantation she was creating from nothing seemed to strike most zealously.

On the night of my attempted initiation, Maggie had said, "Magic requires symmetry." Everything about this ritual echoed that principle.

The binding. The four girls. The sacred glade.

Even with all three powers inside me, I wasn't enough. Just as the Woodwalkers had to bring their victims back to the sacred glade to claim their bodies, I needed to go back. *We* needed to go back.

Where it began, so must it end.

I just had to convince one of each sect of Wardens to try the unthinkable.

TWENTY-NINE

The bottle of bitterwine sloshed in Levi's front seat, where I'd buckled it in to keep it from rolling around on my way back to the church. By now he would be worried about me, and was probably ticked that I'd hijacked his ride without explanation. I hadn't checked my phone in hours.

The thought of calling Lindsey and Vanessa to a private meeting had occurred to me. But I feared they would refuse and tell the others of my plan, making it sound unhinged. I needed to cast a wide net and make my case to the whole group.

By the time I made it back, my strength was sapped. Papers clenched in my fist, I stumbled across the street and landed on the gritty asphalt, scraping my knees.

Tires screeched, and a car swerved around me. I looked up to see a red sedan with out-of-state plates jerking to a stop and its driver opening the door, punching numbers into his phone as he ran to my aid. Three numbers. Nine-one-one. I must have been a sight in my bloody white dress with antique revolvers hanging from my hips.

"Oh good, you're alive," he whispered as he knelt over me. The muffled voice of a dispatcher answered on the other end of the line. I had the wherewithal to know I should stop the guy from talking, but my limbs were made of lead. "There's a young woman in the road covered in blood," the man explained. "She's alive but she needs medical help. I'm on the corner of Liberty and—"

A windlike force snatched his phone out of his hands. Lindsey. She ended the call and tossed the phone in the grass.

"What the—" the stranger started, his expression displaying equal outrage and confusion.

She glared at the man and spoke in a low voice, sounding positively sinister. "Powers of the still, dark earth, mislead all prying eyes. Cast thy veil of trickery; by Warden's Rune, disguise."

He shuffled a step back. Lindsey helped me stand and guided me toward the church entrance.

"Hey!" the guy yelled. He wasn't fooled. The beguilement had come too late, and his tourist eyes were peeled for the peculiar amid the humdrum.

Vanessa appeared as suddenly as Lindsey had and blew bone ash in the man's face, casting the forgetting spell. Baffled, he picked up his phone and drove away.

"The beguilement isn't a miracle cure for being careless, Nat!" Lindsey snapped, leading the way to the hideout. Vanessa followed. "What were you thinking?"

I gritted my teeth and ripped away from her grip on my elbow, to my own detriment. "I'm thinking that we're wasting our goddamn time."

"What?" she asked, but I opened the door to the church and tromped down the concealed stairs, finding the Wardens gathered around the tables in the basement.

"If every last one of us stays strong throughout the witching hour, the victims *will* survive the night," Maggie was saying, but she stopped and looked up at the three of us. "Bless your heart, Natalie Colter. You look a mess. Where've you been? Kate and Levi went looking for you."

"Are we doing anything different from the last Claiming?" I demanded. "I mean, last time, twelve people died. I'd consider that a failure, wouldn't you?"

"We *are* doing things different," Maggie said, clever eyes peering suspiciously at the pages trembling in my fist. "We're much more prepared now. Your daughters and granddaughters will be even more prepared than we are. I know your dad is marked, and Levi, too, but panicking at the final hour isn't going to save them. Why don't you let Sofia fix you up with some fresh bandages and try to calm down?"

"Because preparation is not going to stop this," I said. "We can't just fight. We have to break the curse. Kerry and Nora knew how, but when they couldn't make anyone else see the truth, Kerry backed out."

"And if she hadn't, you wouldn't be here," Maggie said. "Thank God she came to her senses."

"If we do it right, we won't die. But even if we did die, aren't we supposed to be willing to sacrifice for the people of this town?"

"Not in vain," Sofia said. "Nora proved our doubts were valid. We can't protect people if we're dead. We cannot give our magic to the Woodwalkers."

"We wouldn't be giving it to them. We would be giving the magic back to *itself*, rejoining both strands of it at the source. It would go back to where it belongs, in nature. Not inside the Woodwalkers, and not inside us."

I could tell I'd lost a few people, but I pressed on. "Nora didn't prove anything except that the curse can't be broken by one of us, or two, or three. It has to be four. Kerry and Nora told you that." I shot glares to each member of the Triad. "That's why even Malachi couldn't break it alone. There had to be one girl to represent each of the original Pagans of the Pines. Magical symmetry. Kerry knew that, but no one was willing to try. No one was brave enough."

"No one was fool enough," Maggie corrected, glancing at the pages in my hand, a glint of savage fear in her green eyes.

"This is a ritual for breaking the curse," I said, unfolding it. "You ripped it from the Book of Wisdom, but Kerry stopped you from destroying it, didn't she? Her last request was that you give me her unopened letter. But you knew what was in it, and you couldn't resist. Your conscience wouldn't let you destroy her messages to me, so you hid them and charmed the letter to make it look like you'd never opened it."

The room held its breath. I felt Vanessa and Lindsey shifting uncomfortably behind me.

"Did you really hide that from her, Miss Maggie?" Heather asked.

"We all did," Maggie said, gesturing at the other two members of the Triad. "Kerry wasn't well. Her words are dangerous."

"Easy for you to say," I growled. "I'm the one the Woodwalkers are targeting most. You think it's a coincidence that they went after my dad, my boyfriend, my *dog?* You think it's a coincidence that Kerry's fiancé was Shadowed and died in the last Claiming? They hate me. They fear me. They know that I'm the key to ending this."

"Think mighty highly of yourself, don't you?" Maggie said, a cruel edge to her voice.

"I'm sorry about your father," Cynthia said, her benevolent tone contrasting with Maggie's, but I wasn't fooled into thinking she was on my side. "If I were you, I'd be desperate to try everything, too. But you're not going to convince anyone here to give up her life for something that might not even work."

"What if it did work?" I demanded. "What if it's the only thing that can?"

"We don't bank on defeat in battle," Sofia said, crossing her arms. "Even thinking it gives the darkness power."

"As far as we know, the Shadowing of Kerry's fiancé was coincidence," Maggie said. "The town was even smaller back then, and everybody knew everybody. Kerry felt responsible for both Roger's and Nora's deaths, and that was hard on her. Over the years, she stewed in the guilt and began to blame everyone else. But the reason she finally left was because no matter how long and how hard she tried to convince us, we rejected her theory. And that, my girl, isn't righteous conviction or bravery. It's just pride."

My fists clenched again, sending tongues of fire over the frayed skin beneath my shoulder blades. A thin thread that was singlehandedly helping me retain my composure snapped. "She never should have trusted you."

"Is anyone here willing to try Natalie's way?" Maggie spoke over me, ready to put a swift end to this. "Go out to the cabin and wait for the Woodwalkers to feast on your magic and drain the life out of you like they almost did to three of us last week?"

No one spoke up. The finality of the response fanned a flame of indignation inside me, but I didn't know what to do. It didn't feel right to fall in line, to give up just because no one seemed to want to take a chance on this. And I knew I couldn't march out of there without support. I would fail and die in the process.

"Let's move on," Maggie said after a few painful moments, dismissing me. "We still have a lot to cover."

I stormed out, as well as anyone in my condition could.

"I'll bring her back," I heard Lindsey say behind me. She caught up to me by the baptistery stairs. I turned to face her. "Now is not the time to buck authority," she said. "You of all people should want to play it safe."

"There is no 'safe,' Lindsey!" I cried. "Don't you get that? Or do you need someone you care about to get Shadowed so you can understand? Oh wait, that's impossible, because you distanced yourself from literally every boy you ever cared about."

"Stop." Anger ignited in her dark eyes, and a muscle twitched in her jaw. "The Triad has been doing this for decades. You may be your own Triad, but you've only been a part of this for a few weeks. You should be in there listening. They haven't told you the brutal details of the Possession. It's horrible. The fight they endured, the trauma and grief it caused them. . . . They survived a lot." She gulped and smoothed down the already smooth hair pulled taut over her scalp. "Maybe you're right," she said momentarily. "Maybe Kerry's idea could work. But maybe she was wrong. Maybe if we do what she wanted, the victims would still die, and we would, too."

"Still die?" I repeated. "Do you hear yourself? *Still* die? Even *you* don't believe tonight is going to go any differently than last time."

Her lips turned white, but she didn't yield. "I thought your joining was the best thing for us. Now I can see we were better off without you."

Before I knew it, she was gone.

My knees nearly buckled. That effort had taken all I had left to give.

Maybe my grandmother and I were the same: searching for answers, ready to defy anyone who didn't see eye-to-eye with the ones we unearthed. Was it worth rebelling against the Wardens? What if I was wrong?

The hidden door in the wall opened again, and Vanessa slipped out with fresh bandages, a cloth, and a sweater. "Let me help you before you go," she said.

I almost rejected her offer, but she guided me to the baptistery steps and sat me down. She worked the bodice of Lindsey's ragged dress down over my shoulders and started peeling the soaked bandages away. I hissed. Vanessa maintained her composure when she saw my wounds and dabbed my back with the wet cloth.

"If we fail to stop the Possession, I'm in," she whispered in my ear. "You have your Bone Warden. You should hurry and get to Emmy before they bring her here to protect her. Then all we need is a Blood Warden."

"I don't think Lindsey can be convinced," I said.

"I know. Rules and promises are important to Blood Wardens. Bone Wardens trust our intuition. But I'll work on her." Vanessa finished wrapping the new bandages and helped me slip back into the dress, topping it with a sweater to cover the dried blood. "Now, time to betray your boyfriend's trust so we can end this once and for all."

THIRTY

I hadn't wanted to need the bitterwine and collyrium when I'd left Malachi's house. Needing them would mean the other Wardens had turned their backs on me. And using them would mean breaking my word.

Yet here I was.

The wind blew hot and carried the stink of death, like roadkill warmed over. One would think it would drive away the tourists, but they swarmed the downtown square, filling the quaint shops and diners to capacity. I passed two squad cars and a uniformed officer directing traffic at one of the crosswalks.

I jerked to a stop in Kate's driveway, nearly knocking over the trash bins. Unless Kate had given her the day off, Emmy would be here babysitting Avery, protected by wards and charms.

I left my weapons in the glove box and locked the truck. Kate had never asked for her house key back, so I let myself inside, the bitterwine in one hand and the collyrium bulging in the pocket of the sweater Vanessa had given me. Avery yelled my name and launched out of her chair to hug my waist. I yelped in pain but wrapped my arms around her shoulders, thinking of her future.

I want to end this, I thought. *Not just for my family or for Levi, but for you, too.*

"Nat, what are you doing here?" Emmy asked. She was stirring macaroni on the stove. "Are you okay? You look tired."

I wasn't the only one. Emmy's thick red braid was messy and wild, her ivory skin washed out, her hazel eyes dull and ringed from exhaustion. My guess was that she hadn't slept much since the Shadowings began.

"You know something's out there, don't you?" I asked.

Tired as she was, she managed to look startled. "Um . . ." She shuddered.

"Avery, can you go in your playroom?" I asked. Usually, there was a scant chance Avery would do anything she was asked on the first try, but she skipped away and rummaged through her toy chest in the adjacent room.

"You know something's hunting you."

Emmy's pale throat bobbed as she swallowed. "It has to do with the massacres, doesn't it? With Malachi?"

"Yes. I'll explain, but I need you to know that Levi is in danger. I'm doing everything I can to protect him, even though I promised him I'd do everything I could to protect *you*. Turns out, I can't do both."

I saw something register in her eyes when I said Levi's name. She knew how I felt. An innocent smirk touched the corner of her mouth. "He's going to kill us both if we risk our lives to keep him safe."

"I know." I took her hand, relieved. "My family left yours in an hour of need, Emmy. I'll tell you everything later. But we're going to save him."

"What do I need to do?"

I clunked the bottle of bitterwine on the counter and fished the collyrium out of my pocket. "You have magic. And it's been trying to claw its way out of you. This will set it free."

Emmy didn't look surprised to hear the word *magic*. Just how much had this poor girl been pretending not to know for the sake of holding her family together? "Okay," she said.

I went straight to a cabinet with drinking glasses. I uncorked the bitterwine bottle, sniffed to make sure it hadn't soured, and poured her a glass. "Drink it all," I said.

Emmy set it to her lips and gagged, but she steeled herself and managed to polish it off. She leaned her head back for me to drop the collyrium in her eyes.

"What now?" she asked as she blinked the drops away.

"We have to go."

"But what about Avery?"

"There's an extra booster seat somewhere, right?" I asked. "The one I used to use?"

The sun stole to the west as we drove to my house. I did my best to explain everything to Emmy without alarming Avery or giving her something damning to repeat to her Sunday school teacher.

Lindsey had lied well for me to my parents. She'd painted me as a basket case after Ranger's attack. My dad was under the impression that I'd been too shaken up to go into the police station myself, so Lindsey had reported the attack for me and then taken me to her house. The warrior inside me rose up in indignation over sounding like a coward, but I was too grateful to mind. My dad didn't think the worst of me for not being at poor Ranger's side. That was what mattered.

At the vet office next door, I smoothed back Ranger's velvety ears while he slept, then gave my dad a hug that I swore to myself wouldn't be the last.

"What do you want for dinner?" Mom asked Avery in the living room, flipping through channels to find a kids' show for her unexpected guest. Avery was content on the couch, petting Maverick, who had curled up beside her. Rules had gone out the window after Ranger's injury, which my parents were struggling to explain to themselves. I told them I'd found him already hurt and didn't know what animal had attacked him.

We'd left notes on Kate's front door, the back door, the door to the garage, and the counter explaining where Avery was. I didn't want to call Kate. Letting her know Emmy and I were together would tip her off to my plan. She would stop me before I convinced Emmy to do anything reckless.

The summer class excuse wouldn't cut it this time, so I was as candid with my parents as possible. A friend was in urgent but not dire trouble. Emmy and I needed to hand off Avery while we dealt with the crisis that they weren't allowed to ask questions about. If Kate called, my mom would assure her that Avery was safe at our house.

"What now?" Emmy asked as we shut the door and crossed the front porch. I'd grabbed Lillian's book from my shelf.

"We restage the casting of the curse," I said, jogging down the steps to the driveway. "And then we wait."

"Wait for what?"

"For the Wardens to inevitably fail," I said.

Even though I hoped they wouldn't.

The day drooped like a tired eyelid. Night was inescapable.

Determination became fear, and fear became doubt. The idea of four walls and solid doors created an illusion of comfort that made me want to give up and return to the church. What if the Wardens could hold out until the end of the witching hour? As dark descended, the idea of a siege, of fighting—the thing I knew how to do best—felt safer than beckoning evil and letting down my defenses.

But when I looked at Emmy in the passenger seat, I didn't see the trembling, fragile porcelain doll from earlier. She rebraided her red hair with surprisingly steady hands and offered a supportive nod. "I'm with you, Nat."

Bolstered, I bore down on the gas pedal. We passed a squad car at the turn to the dead-end road to the cabin, but the beguilement spell I'd cast spared us any more attention than an appraising glance. We rumbled to a stop in front of the fence.

There were even more animal carcasses than there had been during the ambush.

"Sorry, I should have warned you," I said when I saw Emmy halt.

“The—the Woodwalkers did this?” she whispered.

“Yes,” I said, resisting the instinct to sugarcoat for her, reminding myself that she had agency. She had chosen to be here. “We’re only safe inside Malachi’s circle. The rest of this place is theirs.”

I crooned with pain as I boosted her to the other side. “Are you hurt?” she asked, resituating herself at the top of the fence in an attempt to clear the piles of carcasses. “Did they hurt you? The Woodwalkers?”

“Don’t worry about me, just get to the circle.”

I heard a yelp of disgust as she landed on the other side. I managed to mount the gate and heave myself over without letting on how much it hurt. I caught my breath and fell into step with her, stomping through the feral grass.

“Is there a weapon for me?” Emmy eyed my revolvers.

I dug through my satchel and produced a small ceremonial knife I used for cutting herbs and pricking my skin for spells, but it would have to do.

“I feel like I should be more scared than I am,” she said softly, unsheathing it and touching her finger to the tip.

“That’s good.” The bitterwine ingredients were hard at work, interacting with her hereditary magic. I picked up a stray bone on the way. “Hurry and grab a handful of dirt,” I said. Well aware that we were in enemy territory, I jogged toward the cabin. The sunset bled molten lava orange as we crossed the threshold.

The sacred circle awaited us.

Emmy dropped the dirt at the center without having to ask. It struck me that it might not have been my argument that had brought her here, or even desperation to save her brother. It was her own instincts.

I placed the bone atop the pile of dirt. “Here, cut off a strip of my dress,” I said. “I have plenty of blood—no need to make a new cut.”

Emmy helped me remove the sweater and sliced at the fabric, coming away with a jagged strip dyed red with blood. She sucked in a breath at the sight of my wounds. To her credit, she stayed steady even after realizing a fraction of the danger we were up against.

Lastly, I unrolled the twine from my bag. "Now, all we can do is wait," I said.

The sun lapsed, leaving us in a realm of shadow. The old, ominous fears lurked in every corner of my imagination. I thought back to sneaking into Calvary Baptist as a kid, tiptoeing through the infamous sanctuary.

But I'd chosen to take the dare. I was choosing it again.

"Natalie!" I jolted at the sound of my name.

No, Levi couldn't be here. He had the power to convince Emmy not to do this. I couldn't let that happen.

"Emmy!" Levi called out.

Don't give in, Emmy, I thought. *Please. I need you. I need you or I'll end up like Nora and all of this will be pointless.*

"What should we do?" Emmy asked. "How did he even know we were here?"

"We have to get rid of him," I said, standing. "He'll be safest at the church. I don't know why the Wardens haven't brought him there yet."

I walked outside. "What are you doing here?" I demanded as he crashed onto the porch. "You should be at the church."

"So should you," he said forcefully. "And she should be nowhere near any of this." His anger crested and buckled into something softer and more difficult to withstand. "You promised me, Nat."

"I didn't have a choice." I'd known he would be furious and hurt, but seeing him furious *at* me, hurt *by* me, was harder than I'd expected.

"We can still get to safety in the sanctuary," he said. "The Wardens want to hide Emmy in the basement."

The wisteria hanging over the doorway tickled my ravaged skin, sending a shudder between my shoulders. Bracing myself, I met his eyes. I hated the anger in his voice, the way it made me burn to win his forgiveness.

"I'm not leaving without either of you," he said.

"If it's either me or you that makes the sacrifice, why does it get to be you?" Emmy demanded, drawing even with me at the threshold. "Because you can't survive without me? What about me?"

His forehead creased. "You're my little sister. I would do anything to protect you."

He reached out to her, but she pulled away. "Then protect me from grief," she said. "Protect me from knowing I could have stopped you from dying and didn't."

Levi had nothing to say to that. He turned back to me. "You're an incredible fighter, Nat. I've seen it." He took another step toward me. "I have faith that the Wardens can win with you on their side."

He wouldn't rattle me. "We can't win the way they want to."

"So there's nothing I can say?" His hand twitched, as if he wanted to reach out and touch my face. Tenderness and longing passed over his features. I had to close my eyes for a second to gain my bearings. "I can't reason with you?" he pressed.

I opened my eyes. God, he was beautiful. Every angle, every plane, every rust-speckled inch of skin. In the burnished dusk, his eyes were bottomless reservoirs of emotion. I felt thrilled to have ever touched my lips to his, to have ever made him smile, even if those moments now felt lifetimes away.

But I didn't say that. I said, "No. We know what we're doing. Go to the church."

He sighed. "I'm sorry I had to do this."

"Do wha—?" I started to ask, but something rustled along the side of the porch. Before I could reflexively extract my revolvers, a firm grip had seized my arm and twisted it behind my back, submitting me to one knee. Pain scorched across my lacerations as Lindsey tied my hands behind my back.

"We couldn't let you do this," she said, the corners of a long black cloak rippling around me as she yanked me to my feet. "I can't believe you were willing to drag Emmy down with you."

I looked up at Emmy through loose strands of my sweaty, pale hair. Heather was there, in a cloak, too, tying Emmy's wrists more gently than Lindsey had mine. Just as I expected, Kate figured out exactly what we were doing as soon as she realized Emmy wasn't where she was supposed to be.

Emmy looked baffled, lost, scared. Had I taken advantage of her naïveté to use her for my selfish purposes? I'd thought there was enough strength inside her to finish this. But I didn't see that strength now.

Heather led Emmy toward the road, but Levi said, "I got it," and put his arm around his sister's shoulder.

Lindsey nudged me forward. What choice did I have but to fall in line?

With each step, the reality of what I'd face at the church sank in. Twelve victims. Twelve Woodwalkers. Fervent incantations whispered in the candlelight. Herbed wine that was supposed to protect but would only leave a bitter taste on the tongues of the victims slated for death. Fear in the eyes of two people I loved. At best, their deaths. At worst, that *and* the Claiming of their bodies for creatures that didn't deserve them.

The more I thought about it, the more my desperation compounded. I had to do something.

I tangled my foot between Lindsey's legs to trip her. If Emmy could and would follow my lead, we could break our bonds once we reached safety.

I ran into the forest, but I didn't make it far before Lindsey tackled me. I felt the cuts bleeding afresh as I writhed in the grass.

"Stop, she's hurt!" Emmy yelled from the road, and I saw Levi wince empathetically as he forced her to duck into the car.

Lindsey hauled me to my feet. "I'm sorry, Nat." And she sounded it.

We hiked back to the road and crossed over the gate. I glared at her in the light of the open car door.

"We need to get to the church." She tapped the hood. I yanked out of her grip but succumbed, squishing in next to Emmy.

Levi took his keys back and followed us down the deserted road.

As we drove, I turned to look at the cabin in the glade. The conviction that we would at long last break the century-old curse faded into the distance.

THIRTY-ONE

Restless tourists and locals alike loitered around the church. Police officers and security guards wearing flat expressions posted up around the building. Candlelight danced against the dusk. The town was holding vigil.

There were no obvious signs of activity inside the building. The stained-glass windows of the sanctuary were dark, the doors clearly locked for the evening. Even so, it felt like my secrets were somehow laid bare for the whole world to see.

"Jesus," Heather said. "More people showed up for this than Sunday service."

"Is my dad here?" I asked. The Wardens must have ushered the victims inside before dark. Even with the beguilement spell, I doubted they would have made it through the current mayhem undetected.

"He's in the sanctuary," Lindsey said. "Maggie told him they needed volunteers to help set up for the vigil, so he came willingly."

My stomach turned. My dad didn't scare easily, but I knew he was probably feeling apprehensive by now.

"How will we get inside?" Emmy asked.

"Charmed cloaks," Heather said. "A reinforcement to the beguilement."

She handed one to each of us. Lindsey arranged mine gently over my shoulders before nudging me out. Levi met us and accepted his cloak, donning it behind Lindsey's car. We entered through the side door to the church offices.

Kate was waiting for us. Despite her best efforts, the door groaned like a banshee as she pulled it shut. A nearby security guard cocked his head and marched over to investigate.

Kate locked the deadbolt. With a sweep of her arm, Heather guided the rest of us through the open doorway to the pastor's office.

My balance was off since my hands were tied behind my back. I stumbled against Levi. Instinctively, he steadied me, but quickly let go.

The lock on the outside door jiggled. "Come on, kids," the security guard said. "This isn't a good night to be messing around."

Another guard joined him at the door. "How'd anyone get inside? All the doors are locked."

"I don't know. See if someone can lend us a key."

A set of footsteps faded, but the first guard hung around and knocked again, harder this time. The deadbolt would prevent them from passing through with a simple key, but if they grew more determined . . . I could only hope the enchantments surrounding this place would hold.

As Emmy tied the neck of her cloak, Kate said, "Don't speak to any of the victims until Maggie gives you permission. Follow me."

My heart thudded at the sound of Jason's voice from outside. "This is the sheriff, and I can promise you that this ain't worth the trouble, my friends. I'm going to need you to open the door."

We took our chances with the cloaks and hurried down the corridor toward the sanctuary, but Kate caught me by the arm and pulled me into the empty fellowship hall.

"I know everything is at stake for you and you're feeling desperate. But your plan isn't the answer. You're looking for an escape hatch, and there isn't one."

"Kate, you know me," I said. "I jumped into battle the day after I took the Oath. I'm not looking for an escape hatch. I'm facing the truth when no one else will."

"I admire that you want to pay a debt of loyalty to Nora's family," she whispered. "But your theory can't be tested without risking too much. We can't just hand ourselves over to the enemy, especially not you. You would make them so much stronger than they already are. Now, Grandma Maggie's in rare form," she said, pointing me across the foyer to the sanctuary. "Don't provoke her."

I bit my lip to keep from arguing and followed the others. At this point, I had no choice but to let the battle play out.

The room was lit only by candlelight. The Wardens were posted at intervals around the perimeter, wearing charmed cloaks and standing dreadfully still. Eleven victims sat scattered across the front two pews, their hands and feet tied together.

They looked up at the sound of our entrance. I noticed timid amusement on some of their faces, including my dad's. It was easier in this day and age to believe this was an elaborate joke.

He didn't recognize me under the charmed hood. I averted my eyes and scanned the other faces. Ryan, who had been Shadowed the longest, didn't look surprised to be here, but a few of the other boys were quaking with fear. One of them was no older than eleven or twelve.

Maggie, Cynthia, and Sofia stood around the Communion table, fervently chanting over the wine chalice and brandishing smoke-cleansing bundles. Kate flashed me a warning look before picking up a bowl of blood and painting the Malachian mark in giant strokes on the tablecloth. The energy in the room shifted, and a few of the victims squirmed in their seats.

Lindsey shut and locked the sanctuary door behind us. I heard the metallic sound of one of her knives emerging from its sheath as she prepared to cut the ropes around my wrists.

"Wait," Maggie said to her, abruptly cutting off the chant.

Lindsey paused, no longer my friend or even my ally—just a cog in the machine chugging its way toward a cliff.

Maggie approached me, drawing too close for comfort, sizing me up.

"Here she is. The one with all the bright ideas." She raised her chin. "You know, I thought you had it in you. I thought you were stronger than your grandmother. That you were a no-nonsense kind of woman. But you have about as much sense as a broken piggy bank, and you're arrogant to boot."

"Bite me."

"You do not have permission to speak. You wasted our time, risked Emmy's life, and nearly sabotaged our efforts."

I glanced around, wondering what would happen if I struck back like a cornered snake. Vanessa was glaring at the back of Maggie's head, and Kate's eyes were downcast, but no one came to my defense.

The old woman had preached her sermon well: divisiveness is akin to weakness, and we couldn't afford to be weak.

"Let her go, but keep an eye on her," Maggie said to Lindsey.

Lindsey stepped forward and cut the ropes away. I reached underneath my cloak to tenderly touch the bandages covering the deep cuts that striped my back. My fingertips came away with fresh blood.

"Welcome," Maggie said, turning a soft expression to Emmy. Someone had already untied her wrists. The Wardens could see what I had seen on her face at the cabin: she wasn't a threat to their mission anymore. Maggie held out a length of rope and nodded at Levi. "For protection from himself," she said.

Emmy shot a glance at me from under her hood as she took the ropes. Levi didn't resist as his sister tied his hands and ankles with quivering fingers.

His stoic calm, his refusal to look me in the eye, made my heart clench like an indignant fist.

"It's going to be okay," he said to Emmy, his voice a soothing murmur. Part of me yearned to be the target of that tenderness again, but the rest of me fumed with anger.

"Are you going to tell us what the hell is going on?" one of the victims demanded, a boy I didn't recognize who looked about Emmy's age. "My mom said someone at the church needed help setting up for a vigil, but this looks like some kind of corny-ass reenactment."

Maggie slipped off her hood, and every single one of the victims gasped. I supposed there was no point in hiding ourselves now that we were locked safely inside with the victims. If we saved them, they would know that we'd saved them, and we could use the forgetting spell to clean things up afterward. If not... well, there'd be no one left to accuse us.

"All you need to know is that there is an evil out there that wants to hurt you tonight, but we want to protect you," she said. "Our goal is to keep you safe here. We have a better chance of succeeding if you suspend your disbelief and cooperate."

Cool gray-blue eyes calculating, I could see my dad considering the possibility that this wasn't a joke. The minute his calm broke would be the very minute I'd stop being able to hold myself together.

The youngest boy sucked in a deep, unsteady breath. "Hey, buddy, it's all right," Dad said from nearby. "I won't let anything happen to you, okay?"

The boy nodded. Tears filled my eyes. I knew I couldn't let them drop, or I would give myself over to every emotion, from sorrow to fury to ones I didn't have names for, tightening inside me like a coiled spring.

Kate wiped the blood off her fingers with a white towel and spoke quietly to the Triad. I was just close enough to hear. "A guard noticed them come in. He didn't see who we were, but he heard the door shut behind us—"

"Have two of the girls go outside," Cynthia said. "Tell them to make it look like it's all in good fun. They can outrun the guards and circle back while everyone's distracted. They'll think the trespassers are gone." She looked at me, sizing me up for the job, her eyes full of accusation. I'd gotten us into this mess. But I'd have a hard time outrunning the guards in my state, and the Triad didn't trust me not to escape.

They chose Lindsey and her cousin Gabby, who hurried off to do their bidding.

"Help!" the frightened boy called when they opened the door, hoping someone outside could hear him. "Somebody, please help!"

Maggie, Cynthia, and Sofia ignored him and resumed their chanting. A few more of the Shadowed victims joined the boy. They realized the futility of their efforts by the time Lindsey and Gabby returned. Lindsey nodded at the Triad to let them know they'd been successful. The police would probably lose interest and focus on keeping other people out, which worked to our advantage.

When the doors were closed and locked again, Maggie said, "You can reveal your faces now."

I noticed my dad watching me. Maybe he'd already made the connection to my recent absences, to Ranger's attack, to my urgency earlier today. Maybe the cloak could only hide so much.

If he knew I'd been wounded, held captive, and lured into a secret society, he would see *me* as the victim.

After the others had done so, I slipped off my hood. Dad blinked at me. "What's going on?" he asked, strangely calm as I approached him. "Was that you that Maggie had tied up over there?"

I sat down beside him. "I—"

"She's a danger to herself, Kurt," Maggie cut in.

"You know I was just trying to end this," I said through clenched teeth.

"End what?" he asked. "I can't help you until you tell me, Natty."

"There's no point. You won't believe it."

"I always believe you."

"You have all night," Maggie said. "But if either of you tries to escape, we'll tie her up again. Her impulsiveness has put everyone at risk."

"We won't," Dad said with a gesture of surrender, like he was negotiating a hostage situation. Maybe he thought he was.

Maggie gave us some distance, but Lindsey plopped down on the pew in front of us.

"I think I could make a break for it and get help," Dad mouthed.

"No, don't. It wouldn't make anything better." I massaged my forehead. "This is the safest place right now."

My dad scooted back against the pew, settling in. After a moment, he said, "They gave us granola bars. You want one?" With a bit of a struggle, he dug one out of his pocket and offered it to me.

I couldn't help but laugh. "They gave you granola bars?"

"Sure. Miss Maggie is a *nice* captor. She even let the little guy use the bathroom."

I accepted the offering, relieved that he hadn't jumped right into interrogating me. He was waiting for me to tell him of my own volition.

"Um," I started, "so, Grandma was part of this for most of her life. It's a secret society that protects San Solano."

"From what?"

The first bite of the granola was tough to swallow. I waited until the taste had completely washed down my throat before I began, telling him about Malachi's curse, how the Woodwalkers came to be, the powers of the Wardens, the fact that everyone here had been chosen for the Claiming. Afterward, when I found the courage to look at him, he wore an opaque expression.

"Is that what your guns are for?" he asked, surprising me again. No accusation of being brainwashed? His objectivity made me nervous. His clever mind was probably hatching an escape plan.

"Yeah, but we use magic to fight them, too."

"Okay," he said, like he was at least trying to believe me.

"You're not buying any of this, are you?"

"Did I say that?" Dad asked. "Let's just say I believe you enough to do what you tell me."

"I had another plan," I murmured. "It was Grandma's plan to stop the last Claiming, but she couldn't get enough people on board."

Currents of guilt and anger eddied in my chest, churning into hopelessness. Even if Vanessa and Emmy were still willing to do what needed to be done, Lindsey was probably even less inclined to help than before, and no other Blood Warden had volunteered.

I had no choice but to fight alongside the Wardens.

I turned toward Levi. Every gorgeous detail of his profile pricked like a thorn, from the outline of his strong jaw to the crinkle above his eyebrows. I studied and stared, silently begging him to look at me. He wouldn't.

Tears threatened my composure. I blinked them away.

"You look exhausted," Dad said. "I think you need to rest."

"But..." I didn't want to say, "But I don't have much time with you." I didn't even want to think it. And despite the nap at Malachi's house, I'd pushed my battered body beyond its limits. If I was going to be of any use, I needed sleep.

I leaned my head on his shoulder. After he'd tipped the glass of water to my lips, my eyes fluttered closed.

By the time I opened them, I could tell that hours had passed. The roots on my scalp prickled. The night had grown dark, black and unknown like the deepest part of the ocean. I checked the time: a quarter till three—a quarter till the witching hour.

Some of the victims slept, while others looked more alert than they'd probably ever been in their lives.

Dad held quiet conference with Maggie on the front pew. He was most likely trying to negotiate my freedom for his captivity.

Nice try, Dad, I thought.

Levi leaned forward and said something, and Dad nodded. What were they talking about? Emmy had dozed off, curled up on her side near her brother.

The conversation ended. Maggie and my Dad stood up. Levi shook Emmy awake. Around me, other Wardens began to stir.

"I'll make sure our audience outside has dwindled," Heather offered.

"You know what to do if they haven't," Maggie said.

The younger boy started to cry, and Kate did her best to soothe him.

Emmy said goodbye to Levi before Maggie directed her to take cover in the baptistery stairwell.

"It's about that time," Maggie said.

"On your knees in the aisle, everyone." Cynthia called out. "We'll be able to protect you best that way."

Most of the victims followed instructions. A few, including Ryan, put up a fight. Vanessa yanked his head back and forced the bitterwine down his throat. He spit it out, the part of him already claimed by the Woodwalker repulsed by the magical ingredients. But she patiently tried again, and held his mouth closed until he swallowed. She passed the chalice on to Kate, who was comforting the younger boy.

"It's going to be okay," she whispered, brushing back his hair as she encouraged to him to drink it all. She refilled it and passed it to me.

"Real wine instead of grape juice? In a Baptist church?" Dad joked. "Does Jesus know about this?"

I wanted to laugh but held it back, afraid it might turn into a sob. I tipped the chalice so he could drink. "Interesting bouquet," he concluded.

A shadow passed by the row of stained-glass windows on the opposite side of the sanctuary. Every candle in the room flickered. The air changed, carrying the stench of bodies exhumed from graves.

"I need to get ready," I said.

"Love you, Natty. Look out for yourself."

"I love you, too. Don't be scared, Dad."

"Wouldn't dream of it."

I turned away before he could see the tight expression on my face.

As I passed Levi, I dropped to my knees and touched my lips to his cheek. "I want them to be right," I whispered. "I want this to work."

Without waiting for a response, I hurried to the stage, feeling the ghost of the farewell kiss I'd hoped to receive but hadn't earned.

Maggie extracted her pistol. "Get up in the choir pews," she said to me. "You can't fight like the rest of us."

Heather returned and closed the door behind her. "Most people have gotten bored and gone home," she said to Maggie. "It's just a security guard and some kids watching from their van across the street. I reinforced the beguilement."

"We've done the best we can," Maggie said. "It's time."

Heather nodded. Kate retrieved her rifle from where it leaned against the piano.

My trigger finger itched as I waited.

As the other Wardens circled around the victims, a demonic screech cleaved through the quiet night.

Darkness covered the windows. Antler tines and horns cast dancing shadows on the walls. There were haggard breaths and restless howls. I tasted panic in my mouth, swallowed it, and cocked my revolver.

THIRTY-TWO

The wooden double doors at the front of the sanctuary shook. Not as if a person was pounding from the other side—more like a mighty, malignant wind prepared to dismantle everything in its path.

Sweat dripped down my temples as the Wardens' chants and the ruckus outside grew louder. I couldn't see my dad or Levi anymore. They'd been swallowed in the sea of black cloaks.

The doors rattled harder, the shadows surrounding the church darkened, and a few of the candles snuffed out. The smell of death overwhelmed me, threatening to banish all hope.

And then the Woodwalkers broke through, busting the locks, splintering the wood, darkening the doorway like apocalyptic horsemen from hell.

I nearly balked at the sight of all twelve creatures with their spindly bones and fresh, bleeding hides, their towering heights, their filthy claws, some hanging so low that they dragged across the carpet.

But I breathed, aimed, and squeezed the trigger.

My target tilted its antlered skull, barely dodging my bullet. I took another shot, grazing its ribs, which only seemed to make the creature angry.

It charged as other shots rang out but was thwarted by Camila and Lindsey, who whipped their blades around and evaded the effortless swipes of its claws. Other Woodwalkers advanced down the outer aisles. The cloaked women at the center held together in formation, turning to face their opponents.

The long-anticipated battle was underway, for better or worse.

A Woodwalker with a canine skull uprooted a pew and hurled it toward my comrades. Most of them ducked. I noticed Emmy, who must have come out of hiding. She merely gaped at the appalling creature, the ceremonial knife I gave her useless in her grip, until Vanessa yanked her to the floor. The heavy wooden pew struck a few elbows and skimmed hoods, but Vanessa was up again within a second, hacking away at a Woodwalker until its bones dropped at her feet. The shadow form would have to flee and find a new host. One down, eleven to go.

But the shadow didn't flee. With a screech, it shot to the far corner of the room, up in the ceiling, and stayed there. Waiting.

Maggie, Kate, Heather, and a couple others with firearms backed toward me to get better shots. The rest of the group remained staunch, huddled together in formation. Lindsey fought so swiftly that I couldn't score a clean shot at her opponent. But she didn't need me, and that was a good thing, because another made me its target. This one had a large bird beak and talons.

I shot the last cartridge in my right revolver, narrowly missing its throbbing, bloody heart, and grabbed the left revolver from the holster. The creature alighted on the top of the lectern like a gargoyle and sprang toward me through the gun smoke snaking over my head. My shot hit true, right in the heart, and blood spattered on my face as the empty carcass mowed me down. Sick of pain slashing across my skin, I roared and dug myself out of the stinking pile of remains to see the shadow form fleeing to another dark corner of the room.

A few others had been taken out. From what I'd seen, the shadow forms weren't strong enough to engage in physical altercations. I wondered what we were supposed to do to them—a topic covered in the meeting I'd stormed out of, perhaps—when Maggie shouted a threatening incantation I'd never heard, baring her teeth and twisting her fingers. The Woodwalker I'd just shot thrashed in the corner, releasing an ear-piercing squeal that seemed to vibrate on several frequencies.

I began to hope that we could hold out. How many minutes had passed already? The witching hour couldn't last forever, and if we stayed strong like this, we could win.

I'd never been more desperate to be proven wrong.

One Woodwalker lifted Kate by the throat, choking off her breath. Seeing me raise my revolver to help her out, Kate stopped trying to pry the claws from her throat and shut her eyes, waiting for me to take a shot. Her reaction made the Woodwalker look my way, but not in time to dodge the bullet that bit through its bottom jaw.

I cursed under my breath. That was supposed to be a kill shot.

Thankfully, Lindsey jumped in and speared it through the heart.

A core group of Wardens remained in the center aisle, surrounding the victims, and the remaining Woodwalkers focused on them. A stab of fear pierced my chest, and my concern for my dad and Levi blinded me to the Woodwalker looming in the corner of my vision. I didn't see it lunging for me until it was too late. Pointed fangs tore into my shoulder and I screamed.

Its hairy, wet, stinking form squirmed on top of me, but I used the heel of my boot to land a kick to the exposed vertebrae jutting out from the rotten skin. The spine collapsed and the creature writhed until Lindsey leaped onto the platform, pressed her boot down on its skull, and jabbed it through the heart. Our hands were so bloody that it was hard for her to get a good grip and help me to my feet.

Shots and screeches rang out through the sanctuary. But once I was able to unpack the visual chaos, I realized the group defending the victims had dwindled. A flash of red hair behind a swaying cloak made fresh panic pound through my veins.

Emmy huddled on the ground next to her brother. She held her knife out in frantic protest, her expression like that of a cornered cat. A sinewy, tall Woodwalker that was more bones than meat used its tapered claws to lift her by the collar. She jabbed out blindly and Sofia rushed to her aid, leaving Ryan completely vulnerable. One of the shadows lingering in the corner slithered through the air toward him, stretching a wispy fingertip in his direction. As soon as it brushed his cheek, his mouth fell agape. The shadow slid down his throat and slithered behind his eyes.

I leaped off the stage and filled in a gap in the formation. My dad watched with horror as Ryan started gnawing at the ropes around his wrist. I lunged forward to seize him by the jaw. His muscles felt powerful beneath my grip. He snapped at me and almost bit my finger off.

I called for help, but only Camila was able to break free from her fight. She leaped over two pews and executed a swift maneuver, locking Ryan's neck in a sleeper hold. There was something savage in his features. He strained and twisted until he was able to clamp onto Camila's forearm with his teeth. Camila cried out but didn't loosen her grip. Ryan went one desperate step further and started scratching at his own face, dragging his nails through his flesh and drawing blood. Camila had no choice but to let go.

I knew that once possessed, the victims would hurt anyone, even themselves, to get to the sacred glade. I had to stop him.

I whacked him on the head with the handle of my gun, hoping to sedate him. But it didn't work. He hissed at me, broke his ropes like they were dental floss, and tore out of the sanctuary into the night.

Breathless, I crouched between Levi and my dad, keeping a watchful eye out as I reloaded my revolver.

"What's happening?" my dad asked. His eyes darted at the mayhem our indiscernible enemies were causing.

I closed the loading gate and looked around. Only a few of us were still guarding the victims. The rest had scattered in the fight or chased after the escapees. One Warden, the librarian, lay on the floor, alive or dead, I couldn't tell. Lindsey engaged in a fierce match of blades and claws. Kate reloaded her rifle by the Communion table.

A Woodwalker ended a skirmish with Vanessa by tossing her against the wall. Noticing the young boy undefended, it barreled toward him. Its feral hog skull was long and thin, with tusks curling out from its mouth. I blew off one of the tusks with a bullet. Kate finished the job, and then started spouting the same unfamiliar incantation Maggie had used, the words flooding out in a panic—words that evoked the powers of good to banish evil—but it was too late. The shadow defied her and claimed its host.

I could see the boy fighting for a moment before his features froze and his eyes turned into black discs.

He lunged at Emmy and grabbed her knife, blade-first, slicing his own hand. He cut the ropes around his wrists and ankles. I gripped his forearm and tried to finagle a safe grasp on the knife, but he let out a bone-chilling screech, dropped the weapon, and ran out.

I could see now why it was impossible to intervene once the Possession took place.

A few defenders regrouped around the remaining victims, but it wasn't enough. We weren't enough.

The last few minutes or seconds or fractions of seconds shot by in a pandemonium of feverish chants and deafening gunshots. I landed a few more hits, but suddenly our enemies were all shadow, and I could no longer use my physical strength or skill against them. One, two, three more victims were possessed.

Feeling helpless, I pressed back to be near my dad and Levi. But Levi wasn't there anymore.

I looked up to see his figure silhouetted against the darkness outside the sanctuary doors. Emmy screamed his name and tugged on his arm, but he shoved her onto the concrete steps. Sobbing, she chased after him until they were both gone.

Dropping to my knees beside my dad, I covered his head with my arms. But a cold, spindly hand wrapped around the back of my neck and tossed me toward the front of the sanctuary. The top of my head struck the Communion table, and I sank to the floor.

The Woodwalker who had flung me away dropped its scavenged bones and possessed my father's body.

Cold shock overcame me. The worst had happened, and I couldn't stop it.

Most of the Wardens who could still fight had pursued the victims. Only Maggie and a few wounded Wardens remained.

Maggie tried to shut the doors, but they were crooked on their hinges. She turned back to my dad as a shudder tore through him. I thanked God I couldn't see his face from here. I thought of Levi throwing Emmy to the ground. Had she given up yet? What would the Woodwalker inside him do to her to fulfill its mission?

Fiery tears slipped down my face. It was over. We had lost, just as I'd feared.

"Dad," I said, my voice cracking as I lifted myself to my elbows. The world swayed. He flinched in my direction, and I saw gleaming black eyes.

With a ferocious, choked noise, he fought the ropes around his wrists and feet. I had wondered why the Wardens hadn't used handcuffs, but the disturbing image of one of the victims gnawing off his own wrists to get free came to mind.

I pushed off the floor, ready to chase him down when he broke free. Before I could reach him, Maggie put the barrel of her pistol to his forehead.

"Stop!" I screamed. "What are you doing?"

My dad—or the Woodwalker inside him—used the distraction as an opportunity to break free. He tore out of the church with supernatural speed and strength.

Instead of chasing after him, Maggie tucked away her pistol and sprang toward me, scooping up a snapped strand of rope. Did she have a plan for stopping him?

To my shock, she seized my wrist in a powerful grip and used her momentum to push me. I fell on my back, and my excruciating wounds protested. I didn't understand. Was she trying to protect me? Forcing me to duck from some unseen danger? It didn't occur to me to fight back until she'd tied my wrists to the leg of a pew with a swift, decisive knot.

"What are you doing?" I demanded again, kicking hard. But the element of surprise was on her side. She was out of range by the time I realized she'd betrayed me. Again.

"He wanted this," she said, withdrawing her gun. "As a contingency plan."

"Wanted what—?" I started to ask, but she had already turned her back, and I already knew the answer.

The conversation that had passed between my dad and Maggie while I was sleeping. Levi had been part of it, too. They had offered themselves to stop the completion of the Claiming, to throw off the magical symmetry.

"No!" I screamed after her, fighting against the grating rope. I pulled and chewed at the knot, but it was solid. I knew Maggie's aim was unmatched. Unless my dad had already gotten away, there was no hope.

Spinning around, I planted my feet for leverage against the pew and yanked with all of my power, but this old place had sturdy bones. I gritted my teeth and roared, and the magical strength within me cracked the wood. With the splintered pew leg dangling from my bound hands, I charged down the center aisle, screeching Maggie's name.

Everything outside was black. Even the stars seemed muted. The waning moon was hidden away, and its light was fainter than a match in a mansion.

But Maggie's white hair caught my eye. She stood at the bottom of the steps. Her hood had slipped off. I followed her silhouette, tracing the outline of her cloaked arm as she raised her pistol and took aim at a figure in the distance.

A crazed sound issued from my throat. Gripping the remnant of the pew leg in both hands, I leaped down the stairs and whipped it into the curve of her neck, throwing her aim as she pulled the trigger. We rolled together onto the concrete sidewalk, her pistol clattering in front of us. I managed to wriggle my left hand out of the bonds, but Maggie found her feet before I did.

From where I lay, I swept out my free hand and caught her ankle before she could run after my dad. She went down, smacking her face and elbows on the pavement, and turned to glare at me with a bloody nose and lip.

"You want them to win?" she demanded, prying at my fingers. "Kurt and Levi asked what they could do to save the others. They volunteered."

I held fast to her ankle, but she ripped out of my grasp. I fell back on the pavement with a sob.

I hated her. I hated everything. I hated my dad for volunteering. I hated myself for failing to convince the others to avoid this violence.

With every second that passed, I told myself I could rally. I could stop her. It wasn't too late. But it was.

My dad was gone either way.

THIRTY-THREE

I wanted to curl on my side, to cover my ears and shield my mind against the resolute gunshot that would erupt at any second. But I couldn't move.

"Nat, we have to go. Come on."

I blinked up to find Emmy's bloodstained, fiery curls tumbling around my face. Vanessa stood behind her, claw marks slashed across one cheek. Maggie had disappeared.

"We're going to finish this before she can." Vanessa tugged on my elbow, pulling me up.

"I have Levi's keys," Emmy said. "We have to hurry."

I tried to run, but I was weak, and the debris weighed me down. Emmy cursed uncharacteristically and hurried me along. We ran over the churchyard, the grass like a black sea, and pounded down the sidewalk, crashing through the hedges on the corner of the street where Levi's truck waited in the dark.

All that remained of me was blood and sweat and pain and the taste of salty tears on my lips. The curb tripped me, and I slammed against the passenger door, scraping off a chunk of paint with the splintered pew leg.

"Hold up!" someone said, and a grip restrained my arm. I snapped my head around and found Lindsey.

I yanked the rusty door handle, but she didn't release me.

"Stop! I'm trying to help you! Just hold still." A blade flashed in her hand. The rope slithered over my wrist and the pew leg clacked on the curb.

"I'm coming with you."

I grinned, feeling a little manic. We were all here. This could work. But we didn't have much time.

"Get in!" Emmy said, and started the engine. Before I even shut the door, Emmy jammed the gas pedal down so hard that we screeched across the asphalt.

"They thought I was asleep back in the sanctuary, but I heard them talking," Emmy said, ripping off her cloak and glaring at the road. "Maggie said that all it would take was one of them dying before the Eviction to stop the Claiming. Your dad and Levi said they would sacrifice themselves. Hold on."

She took a sharp right turn.

"God, I had no idea," Vanessa said. "That's messed up."

"Maggie's car wasn't far from the church," I said. "She could be halfway to the cabin now, and it doesn't take long to pull a trigger."

"Nat, I'm so sorry," Lindsey said. "I'm not sure if your plan is going to work, but Maggie's is so much worse."

Emmy jammed the gas again and Levi's truck roared in response, jolting away from the lingering lights of downtown and onto the open country roads.

The headlights revealed a figure in the middle of the street. I caught a glimpse of glinting black eyes and a bent, feral posture. Emmy gasped and swerved into a yard, striking down a mailbox. As we bumped along in the grass, I realized it was the youngest boy. We jerked to a stop. He stared blankly at us for a few seconds before tearing off. I'd never seen a human move that fast.

"Oh my lord," Emmy whispered.

"Get out of here," I said, hitting the dashboard with my open palm.

Emmy pulled back onto the road. The speedometer needle throbbed around eighty-five, barely dropping when we curved with the road. We could get there before Maggie managed to weave down the dark maze of nearly deserted streets to the cabin. But the possessed people had inhuman strength and speed on their side.

Blinding blue-and-red lights illuminated Emmy's determined face. I cursed vilely.

"What do I do?" she demanded.

"Lose him!"

"I don't even have my license!"

"Even more reason," I said, forcing myself to stay calm. "There's a curve in the road up here. We can turn off and wait for him to pass."

Emmy bit her lip as the flashing lights danced through the car.

"I think there's a dirt driveway on the left side just around the corner."

She let her foot off the gas and took the curve carefully. My guess was correct, but I failed to recall the gate spanning the width of the drive. As Emmy took the turn, metal crushed against metal and the engine made an irritated noise. But we were nestled off-road, and at least we hadn't hit one of the gigantic oak trees nearby.

I reached over and turned off the ignition, whispering the beguilement spell in unison with Vanessa and Lindsey. Everything went dark. Dust stirred around us.

The deputy sped by.

"We should run," I said. "It's not far."

"Far enough!" Emmy exclaimed.

"We can't afford to get caught."

I opened the door to make a break for it, but Emmy turned the key, churning the engine. When it sputtered to a start, she jammed it into reverse.

I nearly fell out but managed to slam the door as she backed onto the road. My whole body ached with urgency. Emmy drove as fast as she could, but I still had to fight the impulse to slam my foot on hers.

Finally, I could see the chain-link fence. Emmy jerked to a stop and ripped the keys out of the ignition. I fumbled with the ties on my cloak and left it rumpled on the leather seat. I could see the silhouettes of victims in front of the cabin, gathering in a crescent moon shape that mimicked the formation of trees surrounding the sacred glade.

Emmy mounted the fence, but Lindsey started pulling the links away from the poles. Vanessa grabbed a corner, too, and they ripped off a big enough section to allow Emmy and me to duck through while they held it.

Instead of the usual insect songs, I heard a low, menacing hum. I picked out my dad's and Levi's silhouettes among the twelve figures. They stood with their hands open, ready to offer themselves to the Woodwalkers. None of them reacted to our arrival.

"I think they're in a trance or something," Emmy whispered.

We gave them a wide berth, looping around through the trees, sneaking across the porch, and slipping in through the cabin door Emmy and I had left open.

The pile of dirt, the bone, and the bloody ribbon of fabric torn from my dress waited inside the circle. Vanessa snatched the ball of twine and unwound a long portion for Lindsey to cut.

I dug out the missing Book of Wisdom page from where it was folded up snug in my boot, then smoothed it so everyone could see.

Breathing hard, we sat around the circle and tied knots around our wrists. Once we were all connected—just like Malachi, Lillian, Dorothy, and Johanna—I closed my eyes, trying to center myself, to gather my magical wits. It was nearly impossible when all I could see behind my eyelids was Levi and my dad, their red-rimmed, blank, black eyes.

Would the ancient magic yoked to the Woodwalkers answer the

summons? Would it be able to break away from the dark souls stranded between life and death?

"Nat, concentrate," Emmy urged, squeezing my hand.

I took a deep breath. The musk of wisteria and dirt mingled with the scent of sweet grasses, calming me. I sent my thoughts back to the night the curse was cast, summoning the faces of the girls that I'd only seen in black-and-white photographs. I steeped in the significance of that moment, the price the Pagans of the Pines were prepared to demand for their suffering. Suddenly, I no longer needed to strain to imagine the scene. It unraveled before me, everything soft and gauzy in the candlelight.

Mesmerized, I stared at the faces of three young girls: Johanna, stender and beautiful with haunted brown eyes; Dorothy, her round face resolute above a prim scalloped collar, her black hair molded into silky finger waves; Lillian, auburn-haired and awkward, like parts of her had grown into a woman faster than others.

A touch brushed across my cheek, loving, affirming. Coolness slid down my throat and filled my chest, flooding through my veins until it reached the tips of my toes.

Malachi.

I looked down at my lap and found a different white dress stippled with dark blood drops. Ratted hair framed my face, longer and blonder than my own.

And most importantly, the power that poured through me was immense, dynamic, dreadful, and wondrous. I felt like I could cleave the earth in two if I desired.

The sound of a car careening down the dirt road made the vision flicker and fade, but I felt Malachi's spirit inside me, helping me maintain control.

The energy between the four of us pulled taut, forming a circle of power. I shored up my magic, Malachi's magic, and led the incantation.

"Ancient magic, we call thee near," the four of us said in unison. "We seek thee out, our purpose clear. Our mothers hath wrought pain for pain, sin for sin, and shame for shame. To evil they once yoked thy power by darkness of the witching hour. Here we gather to unyoke, unspeak the words that they once spoke. This curse we break, these wrongs amend. Where it began, so it must end."

When the chant ended, we sat, waiting, hoping, holding the circle of power strong just in case.

Maybe it was too late.

The porch creaked under unhurried footsteps. The victims began filing in, led by Levi, and formed a tighter crescent around us, their eyes still empty and blacker than obsidian. Was the Claiming complete? Had we failed?

I wanted to call out to my dad, to Levi, to see if there was anything left of them. But I was afraid to find that the last traces of them had been evicted, that I would never hear either of their laughs or see their smiles. The youngest boy took his place behind me. The back of my neck prickled.

Once the victims hemmed around us, a low, unsettling hum began. It seemed to come from everywhere and nowhere. A wind full of whispers howled through the cabin, whistling through the cracks, tangling our hair.

As though testing cold water, Ryan stepped over the twine into the circle of our bound magic. The circle destabilized, in some places falling loose and in others becoming too taut to bear. I didn't know how long it would last, this feeling of being stretched, vibrating like a threadbare string about to break.

The entity inside Ryan split as it emerged from his body. One half was just a shadow, a tangled orb of darkness that emitted a scream and dissolved to nothing. The other was less easy to define. It was sparkling gold but dark, opaque yet transparent. It hovered below the ceiling, shimmering and billowing like fabric, never taking shape.

The blackness leeched from Ryan's eyes and he crumpled outside the circle, unconscious. Our bond restabilized. I didn't know whether the departure of the supernatural beings would kill the mortal bodies of the victims. I didn't know whether my dad and Levi and the others would recover. I feared the answer.

One by one the possessed victims stepped through our circle, stealing our magic measure by measure, depleting our stores. I wondered if anything would remain of us in the end or if we'd scatter like chaff in the wind. Maybe we would all die, and people would talk about another inexplicable massacre, another violent cult ritual that had brought death to this town.

I watched my dad go through the circle, his face blank, his eyes the eyes of a stranger. The Woodwalker soul inside him revolted, but something anchored him in place, something that grew stronger by the breath. When the warring entities ripped out, he swayed. I wanted to catch him, but I knew I couldn't break the circle. I cringed as he fell hard against the wood floor, and the circle wavered.

"Keep it strong," Lindsey whispered, and pulled me back in.

Levi was the last—if he was still Levi at all. By that time, the others had worn us down, and I worried there might be nothing left. But the circle held, and when one of us wearied, another would rally.

When Levi dropped to the floor among the other unconscious bodies, the wind gained power and tore away one of the ramshackle cabin walls. Around us, floorboards creaked as they were ripped from rusty nails. Chairs and pots and broken boards whirled. Most of the ceiling flew away. Emmy let the circle break and snapped the twine to shield her brother from the debris. Lindsey, Vanessa, and I cast our bodies over the helpless, unconscious victims, even though mine couldn't take much more abuse. I stretched to reach my dad's limp hand but could only touch his fingertips.

When the wind died down, I looked around. The cabin was mostly destroyed. My body felt ancient, depleted of every last trace of its magic. And the eyes of the lifeless forms around us stared into nothing.

“He’s not breathing,” Emmy shrieked, shaking Levi. The light in his hazel eyes had gone, and his lips hung open.

I echoed Emmy’s wail of grief. “No,” I said, pressing my fingers to Dad’s wrist and feeling no trace of life.

We had stopped the Claiming. We had broken the curse. But I’d lost everything.

Tears blinded me. I sobbed so hard I couldn’t breathe. Lindsey crawled over to envelop me in her embrace as gently as she could, but I didn’t care if she hurt me. The wounds I bore now would never close, never heal.

“What’s that?” Lindsey asked. I heard a soft thud, and then another. I opened my eyes and found three dead birds lying at the center of our circle. Another fell from the starlit sky, and another.

“What is this?” Emmy asked tearfully.

“I think it’s a gift,” Vanessa said, the beginnings of a disbelieving smile on her face.

“Dead birds?” Emmy asked.

When the thuds stopped, there were twelve dead birds piled in the circle, surrounded by ruin.

A timid hope swept over me. I remembered the tale of Ruth Rivers in the sacred glade. She had wrung the neck of the bird with the broken wing to save Malachi.

A life for a life.

EPILOGUE

— SIX WEEKS LATER —

The bell above the bakery door chimed. "Welcome to Butter Babe's," I said cheerily.

Instead of eyeing the cases of colorful pastries, the two girls stared at me. Looks and whispers followed me everywhere in San Solano, but I didn't mind. Not anymore.

No one had died on the night of the massacre anniversary, so the four weirdo cultists found at the scene were free to walk the streets and cause a stir.

An observant tourist had tipped off police to a skirmish at the church. Sheriff Jason, answering the call, had seen my dad tearing through the night, black-eyed and raging. That part wasn't in the police report.

The beguilement had held a little too well, apparently, because the sheriff didn't see Maggie with her gun until *after* he'd struck her with his car.

He secured her an ambulance and pursued my dad in the direction of the cabin, where he approached with his flashlight only to see twelve birds plummet straight from the sky. Inside, there were eleven boys, one man, four girls, twelve dead birds, one bloody piece of fabric, one bone, a pile of dirt, one knife, a ball of twine, and what appeared to be a crumpled page from a spell book. Unsure whether or not he'd stumbled onto a crime scene, Jason called for backup and had the evidence bagged.

We were questioned and sent home. Our stories didn't match up worth a darn, but none of us were suspected of any actual crimes, other than my possessing firearms without a license. Since they were antiques, and since this was Texas, after all, no one saw fit to charge me for that, granted I either obtained a license or got rid of them. I chose to donate them to a museum.

Scraps of information had leaked to the hungry press. The tourist had written up an account on her blog, OccultistQuinn.com, and that had received its fair share of traction. But most people wanted to hear about *murderous* cult rituals. This latest edition of the San Solano saga was a bit dull for its typical audience.

Freed from our oaths, Lindsey and I had explained everything to Abbie and Faith, who preferred to pretend like none of it—even the drama surrounding our absences—had ever happened. Faith had bestowed upon me her full blessing to date Levi, but there wasn't much I could do with that now.

He and I had been friendly enough when we happened to see each other around, but something had changed that night. I'd been willing to risk his sister's life to save him. I'd betrayed him. I wasn't sure there was any coming back from that. As if to seal our fates, we both would be leaving for school in just a few days.

My heart told me it was over, and it was time to try to heal.

The other Wardens had done a good job healing, or at least hiding their wounds. Most of them, including Kate, had gone back to their normal lives—whatever normal meant to them now that their mission had been fulfilled, a part of their identity stripped away. Bryce and Vanessa were back together. She'd told him everything, and luckily, he'd believed her.

For me, healing was harder than expected. Thankfully, Heather had given me a job to help me save for my half of a car *and* to distract me. Until she'd brought me on, her bakes had started losing that extra bit of magic that made them irresistible. But I seemed to have a special touch.

Warden or not, I was still the great-great-granddaughter of Malachi Rivers.

The two girls ordered blueberry lavender cupcakes and whispered about me as they headed for the door, which someone held open for them.

A redheaded, tall, good-looking someone who momentarily distracted them from their shameless gossip.

Nervous, I tightened my ponytail and smoothed down my yellow apron. "Um, hi." I said.

"Hey. I'm here for the three dozen vegan strawberry."

Heather popped in from the kitchen, her purple hair in a milkmaid braid around her crown. "Just a few more minutes, Levi," she said.

"What's the occasion?" I asked, raising an eyebrow at him. "Going-away party?"

He flushed and laughed. I'd thought I was doing better, but now I had no idea how I was going to survive a whole semester or two without a glimpse of him. "No, actually it's Emmy's birthday. Hence the vegan cupcakes." He lowered his voice. "Even though she only had magic for a few hours, she's taking the Earth Warden thing pretty seriously."

I laughed.

"Do you maybe want to come to her party with me?" he asked, and the fantasies I'd entertained about our interwoven futures came roaring back. "The only reason she didn't invite you was because of me. Because I'm an idiot."

I grinned. "Yes! I mean, um . . ." I turned to look at Heather.

Levi shook his head. "It starts in, like, thirty minutes and you're working, so I completely understand if—"

"Oh, you mean you didn't know about our very personal delivery service?" Heather cut him off, bustling from the back with three daffodil-yellow boxes of cupcakes. She dropped them in my surprised hands. "Hurry, before the vegan buttercream melts!" she said, shooing me out. "It's August, for Christ's sake."

Startled, I hurried outside, wishing I had known I'd end up on a semi-date with Levi. I would have changed out of my flour-smudged black shirt and jeans. But that slipped from my mind when he stopped and caught my face in his hands, bending to bestow a kiss on my lips, as soft as the one I'd given him in the sanctuary.

This one didn't end for a long time, long enough for someone to honk at us, long enough for us to crush the corners of the top pastry box.

"I'm so sorry," he breathed. "You did all the right things. I should have trusted you."

"Come on," I said, grinning at him on my way to his truck. He'd finally gotten that dent fixed. "The buttercream's going to melt."

The blistering August sun beat down on our backs as we ran the trail between our houses. I saw Lindsey catching up out of the corner of my eye and sped ahead.

"I hate you," she said, slowing down to catch her breath. I stopped and stretched, feeling smug.

"I hate you for moving four hours away," I said.

"You're going a whole state away!"

"Fair enough," I admitted.

For once, Lindsey could look forward to a future outside of San Solano. She'd applied to the same school as Faith and Abbie. Even though she wouldn't be able to start until the spring semester, she was going to move into their apartment and get used to the campus and the city.

"Hey look," I said. A tiny field mouse skull peeked out from the tall grasses. I picked it up and looked it over.

"Your roommate is going to be so freaked out by your collections,"

Lindsey said, but the joke was underscored by sadness. The magic she had possessed her entire life had fled when the curse broke. Of all the Wardens, only I had retained even a fraction of my power. I hadn't asked Maggie, who was currently recovering from two broken hips, whether I could keep the Book of Wisdom. If she wanted it, she would have to fight me for it.

"What's wrong?" Lindsey asked.

"Just thinking," I said. "Thinking about what I could do with the magic I still have."

"Use it to ace tests."

I shook my head. "Not important enough."

"Win races."

"Cheating? Really?"

"Hunt down campus predators," she suggested.

"That's more like it, but . . . I think I might defer for a semester."

"Why?" Lindsey asked.

I didn't have an answer.

By the time I made it home and gave Ranger and Maverick each a ritual belly rub, the dissatisfaction hadn't dissipated. I tried to ignore it as I cleaned the skull for my collection, avoiding my dad so he wouldn't get his hopes up about me majoring in biology like he did when he first learned of my new interest.

Afterward I sat at my desk chair, staring outside over Grandma Kerry's now-overgrown, healthy philodendron on the windowsill. It would take over my whole room if I weren't careful.

Eventually, I rested my fingers on my keyboard and typed.

Unexplained deaths.

The most haunted places of America.

Supernatural occurrences.

Rapt, I absorbed every engrossing detail, wondering what else could be out there. I filtered out every search related to *San Solano, Texas,* looking for new mysteries to solve. But one slipped past the filter: a post on OccultistQuinn.com.

After figuring out who I was, Quinn had tracked down my contact information and called me several times, trying to get an interview for her website. I'd ignored her, except the last time, when I'd told her to stop contacting me.

But Quinn had seen so much more than most people could here in San Solano. What else could she see?

The Woodwalkers were gone, but that didn't mean I had to stop hunting down whatever dark beings existed out there. An unquenchable thirst for a challenge consumed me.

I scrolled through my incoming calls and sighed at myself as I tapped her number.

ACKNOWLEDGMENTS

I started writing this book when I was twenty-three years old, but I'll be thirty by the time it makes its way into the world. It's now clear to me that this story desperately needed to mature alongside me in order to take its true shape. From the beginning, I knew the kind of book I wanted to write, but I didn't know how to write it. After much reworking and tweaking, I almost stopped trying. A few people made sure that didn't happen, and thanks to them, I'm prouder of Nat's story than I ever believed I could be.

My editor, Sally Morgridge, deserves all of my gratitude. For the past six years, you've shepherded my most cherished ideas and understood my vision for every story. You've made me a sharper writer. Even when there was much work to do, you saw potential and rolled up your sleeves.

Thank you to my husband, Vince, who gladly went camping with me in Sabine National Forest and toured around San Augustine, Texas (the town on which San Solano is loosely based), so I could get a better feel for the area. I love that you're willing to go on adventures with me for the sake of a story.

Thank you, Sarah Goodman, for admiring this book from the very first draft, and for sharing your delectable spooky Southern stories with me. I'm so lucky to have such an incredible bestie/critique partner combo, and I (Chris Traeger voice) literally do not know what I'd do without you.

Immense and heartfelt thanks to my parents and the rest of my family and friends for your perennial support and enthusiasm. I love you all.

My humbled thanks to everyone at Holiday House who diligently helped realize the vision for this book, including Terry Borzumato-Greenberg, Mary Cash, Hannah Finne, Alexa Higbee, Eryn Levine, Cheryl Lew, Emily Mannon, Kerry Martin, Miriam Miller, Michelle Montague, and Derek Stordahl.

Thank you to Jessica Lamb, Jody Persson, Christine Day, Kali Katzmann, and Logan Garrison Savits for your notes and feedback, and to Jeff Goodman, who has never *not* had an answer to my weapon- and hunting-related inquiries.

Lastly, thank you to my grandmothers and great-grandmothers for passing down real-life hereditary magic: your talents, your recipes, your stories, and your unconditional love.